THE ACOLYTE

DAVID COMPTON

SIMON & SCHUSTER

Simon & Schuster
Rockefeller Center
1230 Avenue of the Americas
New York, NY 10020

Simon & Schuster and colophon are registered trademarks
of Simon & Schuster Inc.

Designed by Jeanette Olender
Manufactured in the United States of America

1   3   5   7   9   10   8   6   4   2

Library of Congress Cataloging-in-Publication Data
Compton, David.
The acolyte : a novel/David Compton.
p. cm.   I. Title.
PS3553.048395A64   1996   813′.54—dc20
96-8933   CIP
ISBN 0-684-80430-1

Lines from poem quoted on page 365 are from
"The Garden" in *Selected Poems of Ezra Pound,* Ezra Pound,
New Directions Books, New York, 1957.

ACKNOWLEDGMENTS

Many, many thanks to my editor Laurie Bernstein and cheerful assistant editor Annie Hughes for pushing me hard to fulfill the vision of what we thought the book could be. My gratitude also to the late Jim Adams for inspiration. I will always be grateful to Irene Webb for making many nice things possible. Deserving of special thanks is Sloan Harris, who first saw the possibilities and consistently keeps his sights a little higher than my own.

FOR MARY KATHERINE

1 ❏ ❏ ❏ ❏

Greer Whitaker knew he was being stroked and he liked it.

"Did anyone ever tell you that you're a *genius?* I wish all my candidates had campaign managers like you."

Greer—twenty-eight and handsome by his own objective reckoning in a studious sort of way—said nothing and worked hard to suppress a smile. He sat with his hands clasped behind his head and tapped a light syncopated rhythm with the toes of his shoes onto the metal folding chair which leaned precariously back against a wall covered with cork board. At the top of the board was a computer printout banner with foot-high letters: FOCUS! Beneath was a map of the state of Georgia, divided along congressional district lines, covered with pushpins and yellow Post-it notes. On the opposite wall was the candidate, smiling out from a Tommy Bickford for U.S. Senate poster.

Greer's eyes were still glued to the television screen, following the action at the end of the eight-minute video tape. For the tenth time that late July afternoon in the downtown Atlanta campaign headquarters, he watched the car back out of its parking space in front of the condominium. The camera zoomed in on the license plate. There was the sound of tires turning on pavement, then there was nothing but a dog barking in the distance. The picture blurred before it locked into focus onto the special plate with the Great Seal of the state of Georgia issued to state legislators; at the bottom was the word "Speaker." The car belonged to the Speaker of the Georgia house of representatives—also now the state's liberal Democratic nominee for the U.S. Senate, the highly probable general election opposition and Greer's nemesis.

The man in the hand-tailored suit and soft leather loafers sitting on the edge of the frayed couch in Greer's office flew in and out of Atlanta Hartsfield International Airport first class every Thursday from his office in Washington, D.C. Tony Vasquez—the media guru of the political right—stroked his beard with autoerotic enthusiasm.

"Un-*fucking*-believable," Vasquez said. "How stupid can he be? You know what you have to do, don't you?"

Greer tipped forward in his chair and reached over his desk in one quick, athletic movement. He pushed a button on the speakerphone and talked to someone on the other side of the door. He spoke evenly: "Tell Howard to clear his schedule for a tape coming over this afternoon for editing. I need a thirty-second spot ready for me to look at by ten o'clock tonight. Tell him to call me in an hour for copy. Call Deb and tell her to schedule a press conference at the capitol for ten-thirty tomorrow morning so we can be on the noon news. And get in touch with Tommy and tell him to meet me here at six A.M. tomorrow so I can show him his new ad before he goes to the Economic Club breakfast." Greer put the phone down, barely able to hide the look of triumph that was spreading across his face.

"Got 'em," said Vasquez.

Greer finally allowed himself a smile. "We got 'em, Tony."

Got 'em, again, thought Greer. Just as he had gotten them every time, every campaign he had worked on for the last fifteen years. This one felt the best, though, just as every one in the past had felt better than the previous one. It was the I'm-on-top-of-the-world high, an adrenaline fix that went directly into the bloodstream. The habit that had taken him to political junkiedom at age thirteen, when he was put in charge of delivering literature door-to-door by his father, precinct captain for a school-board race. It was kid stuff, but when his parents' friend won the election and called Greer up to the dais to share in the victory, he was hooked. Not just hooked in the lip, but hooked deep down in the guts, where you couldn't pull it out without dying.

Higher offices, bigger campaigns, more exposure. A big state race like the U.S. Senate was the one he had had his eye on for years. This was what he had been priming himself for—volunteering to do anything on the smaller statehouse races, working his way up county-wide contests, then, finally, two years ago, managing the congressional election. Developing contacts at his old job as a staffer for the Georgia state senate. He was exactly where he wanted to be. Sure, the money was lousy—a thousand a month to pay the rent and buy groceries— and he slept most nights on a cot in the campaign office, but he knew of no one doing more exciting work. Greer had done his homework. Offered his pick of several campaigns to manage this election, he had selected Tommy Bickford. Greer knew that with a little help, Tommy Bickford would be a winner.

Vasquez leaned back into the couch. "Who *is* she?"

"Secretary at the capitol. Works in the lieutenant governor's office. Not especially pretty, but a good hump from what I've been told. I've had a dozen people working opposition research for over a month. They came across a reference to a Reba Smoak when they were cross-checking police records. She posted bond for him when he was arrested for drunk driving in the early eighties."

"Nonissue now."

Greer shrugged. "He's 'fessed up to the drinking. Says it's all over; my guys tell me it is. Still goes to A.A. meetings, more for show, I suppose. Polls indicate the people don't give a damn about that stuff anymore. But the girl's another thing."

Vasquez smiled. "The girl's *definitely* another thing. So what's the angle?" Vasquez asked. "What kind of spin do we put on it?" He was testing Greer.

"Recite facts, but clearly imply an affair. The Speaker has held himself out to be an honorable family man, trying to shake his image as a slimy dealmaker in the statehouse." Greer leaned in toward Vasquez and measured a half-inch of air with his forefinger and thumb. "I was this close to throwing up during his last ad flight. Talked about how he took care of his kids by himself while his wife was recovering from cancer. Pictures of the kids hanging off him in the backyard. Wife at death's door in the hospital . . ."

". . . And piece of ass in the condo to help him forget his problems. Ought to play pretty well with the female voters of the state. He's always had solid support among women."

"This'll knock him down a few percentage points for sure."

Vasquez rocked forward on the couch and filled his briefcase with his notepads. Greer asked his assistant to call a taxi to take Vasquez back to the airport.

"I'll go over the numbers this weekend and call you Monday if I see anything we ought to talk about," said Vasquez.

"Anything else?"

Vasquez shook his head. "You're doing great work here. My job is to lay out the road map and help with the strategies. Make sure you guys are using your money efficiently to get your message out. You're in the driver's seat, Greer. Tommy's going to win the primary; the polls still show that. But we shouldn't take anything for granted. A strong showing in the primary will only help us in the general election. Tommy's going to win and you're a big part of that. I know it and Tommy knows it. I told Tommy that there's no one else he needs to even consider for his top staff job in Washington. It's not too early to start thinking about putting together a transition team. We'll talk about it next week. Better get used to the idea of moving into your new office on Capitol Hill."

"Thanks, Tony. You know I'd do just about anything to make sure Tommy gets to the Senate. The best part about this whole election is that we're about to prove that it *is* possible to elect a decent, honorable man to office. It shows that the system *does* work."

Vasquez opened the door, turned, and hesitated.

"Word of caution," Vasquez said. He looked over Greer's head to the sign on the cork board. "*Stay* focused. Let's not get sloppy and fumble to the other side. Keep Tommy away from operations—keep him away from opposition research. Make sure he's in a position where he can maintain plausible deniability if anything goes wrong. Once we start blasting away at the Speaker on moral issues, Tommy's got to remain squeaky clean."

"*I* know Tommy," said Greer. "And if there's anyone who's above reproach, it's him. I wouldn't have signed on otherwise. We're not going to have any problems there."

Vasquez was thinking of something. "And don't forget about Trippy," were his last words. The Bearded One left, leaving in his wake a somber, cautionary mood.

Trippy, Greer said to himself as he watched Vasquez get into the taxi.

But as soon as he saw that Vasquez had left the headquarters, Greer closed his office door and let out a war whoop. He smelled blood. He was going in for the kill. The latest polls with a hypothetical general election race showed Tommy even with the Speaker and gaining at a solid pace. The new TV ad would kick the whole campaign into overdrive. It was less than two weeks until the primary election. Greer had never worked on a losing campaign—this one sure as hell wasn't going to be the one to ruin his record. Tommy Bickford was going to win big and he was going to bring a new conservative agenda to Washington, along with over a dozen other new Republicans expected to win seats in the Senate. And Greer would be there at the senator's side, strolling through the Capitol corridors.

But first he had to check on Trippy Bickford, Tommy's younger cousin, who at that very moment would be sitting in a dark bar on Ponce de Leon Avenue only six blocks from campaign headquarters. When he had signed on with the campaign, Greer hadn't realized that baby-sitting an alcoholic, drug-running parolee was in the job description. Greer got a hundred dollars from the headquarters' petty cash box and set out for the Blue Dot.

A few days later, in the predawn dark, Greer watched the pilots outside running their hands over the rivets in the wing of the campaign's leased King-Air turboprop. Greer paced outside the small hangar, then went back inside to the small waiting room. Tommy was running late.

Greer was beat. He had worked at campaign headquarters until eleven o'clock the previous night, then gone over to the bar to check on Trippy. As usual, Trippy had been sitting there since late afternoon, watching the news on CNN with the bartender. Trippy favored rum punch—Hi-C Tropical and Ron Rico White—a cheap, potent mix. He was pretty stony by the time Greer got there at night.

Among the duties as campaign manager that had been assigned to Greer by Tony Vasquez was to ensure that Trippy didn't become a campaign issue. Trippy—William Freemont Bickford III—was Tommy's first cousin, the namesake of their grandfather, the once governor and now dead patriarch of the Georgia line of Bickfords. Tommy had a bit of a paunch, but Trippy was lean, owing to the fact that he had recently spent three years in a county jail on the Georgia coast after being caught smuggling cocaine through the Caribbean on his sailboat. Tommy Bickford had come himself from Atlanta to bail out his cousin and arrange for local legal counsel. But the best lawyer in the county couldn't argue for anything except a relatively lenient sentence because of his clean police record. Trippy's boat was auctioned off by the DEA. Now Trippy was out, broke, without a boat or friends, and hanging out in Atlanta. His mere presence was a liability for the Bickford campaign.

Something Trippy had said had been bugging Greer all morning. Greer and Trippy had been talking about the campaign poster taped to the mirror behind the bar. Tommy Bickford's quizzical face smiled down on the drunks. Greer had never really liked that picture of Tommy. The arched eyebrow was almost comical. Tony Vasquez had made the final decision on which photo should be used for the posters and billboards. He had said it was humanizing—took a little edge off Tommy. Tony said that the look on Tommy's face was meant to say, *You wouldn't be stupid enough to vote for that other guy, now would you?*

During their whole time together at the bar, Trippy kept referring to Tommy as a fraud. Greer had ignored the outburst, writing it off to the booze. Trippy had spent too much time on boat decks and in prison yards. Too much sun and too much rum. But this morning Greer couldn't shake a bad feeling about it.

Tommy Bickford stamped his feet coming into the small building. On the first day of August, only one week away from the primary election, the candidate was looking run-down.

Greer handed him a cup of coffee still foaming from the creamer he had stirred in. White, no sugar, Greer knew after a year of sharing their life together. Greer had been there an hour early to make sure there was fresh coffee and to meet the pilots and go over the itinerary.

Greer handed Tommy the typed agenda. Flight to Savannah. Taped interview with friendlies for the local TV noon news spot. Lunch with Rotary. Meeting with newspaper editorial staff. Flight to Columbus on the other side of the state for more TV and newspaper meetings. Jump over to Macon for appearance at cocktail fund-raiser. Then back to Atlanta for a splashy black-tie fund-raising dinner and media event with the former President.

Tommy slid the paper back across the coffee table. He kept his suit coat on. "Do I know you?" Tommy asked.

They were like a couple who had been married for years but hardly saw each other because they worked different shifts. "It's been a while, hasn't it? You're about to become a U.S. senator."

"Nominee," Tommy corrected him.

"The winner," Greer asserted. Greer handed him a memo from Vasquez. "You obviously saw last night's polls."

"I saw the ad on TV, too," Tommy said. He arched his eyebrows at Greer, got a piece of gum, rolled up the paper and threw it playfully at Greer. "Who's in charge of this chickenshit outfit, anyway?" He smiled at Greer through sleepy eyes.

"You wanna hear about Trippy?" Greer asked.

"No." Tommy squirmed. "Is he out of harm's way?" he finally said.

Greer shrugged. "I imagine he's exactly where I left him at one in the morning—sitting on a stool at the Blue Dot."

Tommy just shook his head.

The copilot came in and told them they'd be ready to leave in five minutes. He looked at Greer. "Gotta boogie if we're going to make that first meeting."

The girl in the office came around the corner.

"Telephone, Tommy. They said it was urgent. You can pick up out here."

Greer watched Tommy. He was silent, then all the color drained from his face. He said, "Thank you," and hung up, looking terribly shaken. Yet he quickly put on his artificial composure face, the one he assumed when he got bad news.

"What the hell's wrong, Tommy?"

Tommy let out a deep breath and started: "That was a friend at the *Journal-Constitution*. She said the paper is about to run an investigative piece today."

"About what?" Greer asked, genuinely perplexed.

"They claim I was connected with the drug runners on the coast."

A blast of muggy air rushed into the room, as the copilot held the door open for them. They could hear the other pilot already turning over the engines.

"*What?*"

"The early edition hits the streets in just a few hours."

Greer walked a tight circle in front of the door. "No, no, no, no, no . . ." This was unbelievable. This wasn't happening. Not to Tommy Bickford. Not to Greer Whitaker. "That's not right," Greer said. Greer got right up in Tommy's face. "Well, it's bullshit, right? There's no way. You specifically told me you didn't have any problems there, that you had nothing to do with Trippy and his drug deals! We talked about it before I signed on!"

Tommy was dazed, talking to the walls. "I wasn't completely honest with you, Greer. I'm sorry."

"Dammit, Tommy!" Greer started pacing again. "Dammit! Are you telling me it's *true?*"

The copilot was still waiting for them. "Guys?"

Greer's mind was racing. "We can fix it, Tommy, right? It was an error in judgment, that's all. A momentary lapse. False accusation. Right, Tommy? Right?" Greer moved toward the phone. "I'll call Tony Vasquez right now and we'll put something together. I'll . . ."

Tommy spoke evenly, as if he had rehearsed the moment. "We'll need to draft a statement on the plane. We'll honor our commitments for today's appearances, but that's going to be it. I have to drop out. Trust me. It's the right thing to do. It's the *only* thing to do."

"No." Greer wasn't listening at this point. He refused to believe.

Tommy Bickford drained his coffee and threw the Styrofoam cup into the trash can on his way out. "We'll talk about it on the plane."

Trippy had been right—Tommy Bickford *was* a fraud. And it was Trippy who had tipped off the papers.

It would be two more weeks before he was indicted by a federal grand jury in Atlanta, but before that, there was still the election. Greer sat with Tony Vasquez at the Blue Dot on election night watching the vote tallies come in from the counties. The FBI had sealed the Bickford campaign offices and Greer had to close Trippy's tab out the previous week. Trippy hadn't been seen in the bar since.

"We've been *screwed,*" Greer hissed through clenched teeth as he slammed an empty beer bottle down hard onto the bar. It got the attention of the bartender, but it wasn't loud enough to wake the drunks leaning against the wall in the booths.

Tony shook his head, looking at Greer. "*I* was misled," said Vasquez. "*You* were screwed. I took a lot of his money. You, on the other hand, gave everything you had to Tommy Bickford."

"How the hell could he do that? Deceive all those people working for him. The volunteers. The voters. Me! How could he do this to *me?*"

"Don't," said Vasquez. "You've got to let go of it. You can't blame yourself. Tommy would have never got as far as he did without you.

This wasn't a failure of the system. It was the failure of an individual. The system won't let you down—people will. You should feel lucky that it hit the fan before the general election and not after he took office."

Someone had been pumping quarters into the jukebox, and the sound was off on the television. On the screen was footage of a St. Simon's Island marina. Greer knew the commentator was reporting the fall of Tommy Bickford. Tommy allegedly financed the shrimpers and sailboats that had run the cocaine, arranged for payment to a friendly Panamanian bank, and acquired the three dozen small businesses around Atlanta that laundered the money back into his own pocket, some of which allegedly made its way into the campaign. Allegedly didn't matter in the voting booth.

"The irony of the whole thing is that we didn't need that money," said Greer.

Vasquez nodded. "I know, I know. You were on top of the finance chairman and the new ads were bringing in the checks. What made Trippy do that?"

Greer snorted. "*He's* a *freak*in' *lib*'ral, Tony," Greer said in perfect trochaic beat. "He's an alcoholic, but he still has a conscience. He's got very strong opinions. . . ."

"As we learned."

"Once he found out that Tommy was using the drug money to finance his Senate race, he had had enough. He had taken the rap for Tommy and spent three years in a rough prison hammering boulders into pea gravel. He wasn't about to let Tommy go to the U.S. Senate as another conservative voice. He laid it all out for the newspaper."

"No hint that something like this was going to happen?"

"I talked to him the night the first article appeared in the paper. You know what he said? He said, 'You never asked.' "

Greer had been okay until today—election day—when the full force of the ramifications finally hit home. No credit for a brilliantly run campaign and election win. No job on Capitol Hill. The bridges had all been burned on the single-minded drive toward the U.S. Senate. Everything had been given over to Tommy Bickford. There was nothing left.

Greer looked up at the television. Tommy Bickford was nominally on the ballot, and more than just a few idiots had voted for him. Some no-name Republican—a loser in November before he even entered the race—had just won the Republican primary. The Speaker had just been declared the early winner in the Democratic primary. The camera cut to a scene at the Ritz-Carlton in Buckhead, site of the Speaker's election victory party. The swank interior and happy people were a sorry contrast to the seedy bar in which Greer was hiding out. The Speaker's people had decided it was time to drop the balloons. There was the Speaker, batting balloons with his wife and kids—and *his* own campaign manager—waving victoriously and throwing kisses to the crowd. Greer imagined one landing on the pouty, wet lips of Reba Smoak, the girl whom opposition research had pegged as the Speaker's mistress. None of that mattered now.

Greer saw his own reflection in the mirror behind the bar. Then he looked at the Bickford for U.S. Senate poster. Tommy was laughing at him, saying, *You're all just a bunch of idiots, especially you, Greer Whitaker!* Greer at just that instant moved from denial into rage.

"Don't!" shouted Vasquez, making a grab for Greer's arm. But it was too late.

Greer's half-full beer bottle went sailing through space end over end with the beer spewing from it like the tail on a comet. Glass hit glass loudly and the image shattered.

Vasquez had already pulled out a roll of hundred-dollar bills by the time the bartender had arrived. He peeled off another and stuffed it into the bartender's shirt pocket. "He's a little upset," said Vasquez by way of explanation. "Bring him another." The bartender wasn't going to argue. He had gotten nearly rich on tips from baby-sitting Trippy during the day.

"This is bad, Tony. My name's already mud in this town. What else am I going to do?"

"I know how bad you wanted Washington. It's a tough break."

Greer felt as if he was just about to be hung out. After Tony left town, he was on his own.

"I can't go back to my old state senate staff job. There's a permanent mark by my name. I'm tainted by guilt by association." Greer screwed up his face and looked Vasquez directly in the eyes. "All my life had been pointing to doing this. College, graduate school. The campaigns. The career sacrifices. All I've ever wanted to do was go to Washington. Make a difference. Run a congressional office on the Hill.

Maybe run for Congress myself one day. This is pretty much the end, isn't it?"

Vasquez had narrowed his eyes as Greer was speaking. A sly smile came to his lips.

"You've got good credentials. You have a special talent for making things happen at street level. There are people who'd love to have you working for them. Are you flexible?"

Greer was sitting up straighter on the bar stool. "What do you have in mind?"

"Oh, government-type work. I've got friends in Washington. Not necessarily on the Hill. But if you still want to be where the action is . . ."

"Count me in. Who is it?"

"Take it easy for a few days. You're not in as bad a position as you think. I'll have someone give you a call as soon as things settle down."

2 ❏ ❏ ❏ ❏

A crying shame: a windowless room on a gorgeous morning in late August. Two pale faces that hadn't seen the light of day since the Nixon administration. Creaking chair backs and the clearing of throats from force-fed air.

The two CIA counterintelligence officers sat side by side at a cramped table in a small interior room at CIA headquarters at Langley, sorting packets of materials on potential new recruits sent over from the Agency's Career Training Program office in Arlington, Virginia. The room had security unusual even for Langley. Once a week, the two men met to take the first crack at the files on the Agency's prospective new spy runners to vet for any potential problems. Their primary job was to stop the infiltration of the Agency through the front door, the door that the CIA had thrown open to young patriots who would enter the Company and gain access to its secret knowledge. The applications were double-vetted as a special precaution. Once by the Office of Security, and then—unknown to the regular Agency bureaucracy—by two guys who actually gave a damn. The two were members of an informal, elite counterintelligence group that didn't exist on the Agency charts. Membership strictly limited to true red, white, and blue zealots. Membership by invitation only. No political appointees allowed.

Knowles, the one with microlength, bristle-straight hair was just finishing his third reading of a file. "Greer Whitaker," he said. "A *big* problem."

Next to Knowles sat Covey, with glasses that darkened in bright light and were now dense gray from the intensity of the halogen table lamp. "Or, *perhaps*," Covey said, "the biggest break this Agency's ever had."

They made an unlikely pair. Covey and Knowles, like an old vaude-ville comedy team. Knowles, the eternal pessimist with a Miltonian view of human nature, and Covey with a head full of reasons to find a way to make things work. The one found only flaws and was ready to discard the rough stone into the rubbish heap. The other had the better cutter's eye, saw a way to tap it, envisioned planes to strike that would yield them a brilliantly faceted gem.

Covey took the file from Knowles and scanned the FBI background investigation report on Greer Whitaker again, the preliminary report that had been prepared after Whitaker had received a call from a nameless man calling from a Washington suburb almost two weeks earlier. Obviously, Whitaker had bitten. That got the ball rolling, and now they had a forty-page Personal History Statement filled out by Whitaker himself, detailing the minutiae of his life from birth to his last waking thought, along with the FBI report that cross-checked every typed word he had sworn to be true. That and answers to the CIA's own special set of questions that they never asked the candidates directly but for which the Bureau somehow always seemed to obtain the answers.

"How'd he come in?" Covey asked, flipping to the cover page. He answered his own question. He smiled. "Ah—Tony Vasquez."

"Tony's good. He's got the best contacts out there. All those eager-beaver political junkies."

Covey squinted through his glasses. He read from the FBI report. " 'Most recently campaign manager for Tommy Bickford, who was arrested this week and awaiting trial on a million dollars' bond. No evidence to suggest subject knew of or participated in illegal drug operation.' "

The other interrupted. "He was pretty damn close to that action."

Covey shrugged. "The polygraph will find him out." He read on: " 'Father is partner in large regional commercial real estate management firm, mother a homemaker. No siblings. Moved around Southeast with family—born in Atlanta, lived in Charlotte, Nashville, Tampa, Raleigh, and Louisville, then back to Atlanta during second year in high school. Family moved away again when he was just beginning college. Graduated *summa cum laude* in political science with a 3.85 G.P.A. at Emory University in Atlanta, accepted into Phi Beta Kappa. Master's degree one year later. Courses in comparative political science, American government and politics, international relations along with courses in German language and literature. First full-time employment as staff assistant to Georgia state senate for five years until signed to manage the Bickford campaign. Excellent worker. Highly motivated. Early starter, stayed late, often attended lobbyist receptions on behalf of office. No negatives from co-workers. Very highly thought of by peers and supervisors.' "

"And Tony Vasquez."

"And good old Tony." Covey flipped to the statement given by Vasquez to the FBI agents. Just the kind of recruit the Agency was looking for: smart, resourceful, a risk-taker who didn't mind getting his hands dirty. He looked at the interview transcript. *Motivated?* Tony had been asked. *Almost a fanatic, but focused. He won't let you down.* The Agency shrink would sort all that out. He went back to the summary page. " 'Normal family life growing up. Apparently no significant current relationships. Substantial amount of time outside of work spent on political functions. Wears American flag pin in suit coat lapel. Member, Georgia Young Republicans. Listens to Rush Limbaugh on radio during lunch at his desk. Falls asleep to Rush on TV at night. Subscribes to *National Review*. Tapes Bill Buckley on *Firing Line*. Signed copy of Barry Goldwater's *Conscience of a Conservative* on bookshelf at home. Writes pro-conservative letters to editors. Cried when Nixon died.' "

"Normally our kind of guy," Knowles interjected. *"But . . ."*

"But he's an answered prayer." Covey put the FBI report down and picked up the typed Personal History Statement filled out by Whitaker. He turned to the section near the end headed FOREIGN CONTACTS that every applicant to the Agency had to fill out. There was only one name typed onto the sheet. A woman's name. No address or phone number, as had been requested by the form, just the words UNKNOWN AT THIS TIME typed in the space. But that was the only name that mattered in the entire pile of papers on the table. Perhaps the only name that really mattered in the entire CIA headquarters at that moment.

Knowles looked over at the page. "He sure knows how to pick 'em."

"Or, was *he* the one who had been picked? It seems to be the central question, doesn't it?"

Knowles shook his head. "Too risky."

"Polygraph will tell if he's been wittingly compromised. We also need to find out if he's tough enough for us." He shifted in his chair to face the other directly. "Why don't we do this. Let's see what the rest of the committee thinks. Agree?"

Knowles reached over and took the Personal History Statement back. He stared at the application for a full two minutes. Finally he spoke. "This will either be the most brilliant operation we've ever run or the worst disaster in the history of the Agency." He threw the file down in front of Covey. "Fuck the committee. Let's send it straight to the chief for approval. Skip all the bullshit. We've got enough from this preliminary FBI report. We need to get this guy in here immediately."

Covey smiled. A small victory for Democracy. He put the Personal History Statement and FBI report back into the file folder, then put the entire file into a large envelope and sealed it with a security tab, flagging it PRIORITY—REDWING on the outside. He held the packet out at arm's length with both hands and looked at it like a farsighted Episcopalian trying to read a prayer book. "Would you do the honors?"

Knowles took the envelope carefully. He stood up to leave, then looked down at Covey. "Hope we're doing the right thing. This guy has no idea what he's getting into."

Covey shook his head. "He'll know the dangers when he comes on board, just like any other recruit. We'll be giving him the experience of a lifetime." An analogy came to mind. "Just look at his background. Always the dutiful acolyte. He's looking for a cause to serve, someone or something he'd follow to the end of the earth. He's *perfect* for the job."

And with that, Knowles left to hand-deliver the file on Greer Whitaker to the section chief. The door shut, self-locked.

The passport-size picture Greer Whitaker had sent of himself with his CIA application had burned an image into Covey's mind as if he had been staring into the sun. A bright face with the chin tilted slightly upward, daring the world to take him on. The face of wide-eyed, eager youth.

There goes the future, he thought. There goes our best hope of successfully implementing REDWING. And there goes some kid named Greer Whitaker, whose life will forever be changed by being set into play as the missing piece that had fallen from heaven into their up-raised arms like some errant angel, the angel who could finally set REDWING into full operation, the angel who could save the Agency and —most likely never to be known to anyone outside their elite team of CIA supersleuths—could save some of the more cherished institutions of the American people.

3

Erich Reagor lay naked on his back in bed on the second floor of a small, well-run old hotel near the Marienplatz in Munich. On top of him was an extraordinarily beautiful woman in her early twenties, also naked, almost half his age. His eyes moved randomly around her face. He marveled at her full lips that miraculously still held a crisp line of lipstick—they never kissed when they made love. He noticed how her small ears moved slightly as she talked. She was saying something, but at that particular moment a car blasted its horn twice outside the window, and his mind drifted. After that the only thing he was thinking about was how much he hated the new Germany. The chaos. The strikes. Foreigners. The crime. He missed the order demanded and received by the Communist state.

What he really missed was Berlin.

Erich Reagor was a man formed from a mold of the Aryan ideal, forged in the Valhalla years of Nazi Germany, when the *Führer* had ordered his elite, blond SS troops to mate with fertile German maidens to produce a future generation for the Third Reich. Erich Reagor was born under the sign of the swastika, baptized into the Church of the *Übermensch*. He was a perfect Aryan baby, offered up to the higher purposes of the State.

In Berlin, on the East side of the wall, he had been a colonel in "Stasi"—the Ministry of State Security. He ran important operations in Europe, sometimes under diplomatic cover as an economic attaché, but also under deep cover as a businessman outside the diplomatic community. He recruited and ran spies, having put several high level British and West German diplomats on the Stasi payroll, along with a few important Americans.

He was one of the first in Stasi to understand fully the implications of the Wall's coming down and was quick to reach into the musty State archives and destroy most of the files that might later incriminate him as a spy runner, a Cold Warrior against the West. Others—it turned out—had not been so prescient or so lucky. Because of his deep cover, which had been carefully developed and maintained for almost thirty years, only three people in Stasi knew his true identity; the rest knew him only by cryptonym. Of those three, two were found dead within days of the government's collapse. One was by a highly probable suicide, the other by a bullet fired expertly into the mouth. The gun had been an old Russian-made Nagant revolver, the trigger pulled by Reagor as he quickly left the eastern sector of Berlin, without bothering to turn out the lights.

The third person who had known Reagor's real name—a Stasi general by the name of Peter Volk who was his immediate superior—preceded him to Munich. When the government finally fell, Reagor and Volk had already put together a survival plan, ensuring a smooth —although somewhat reluctant—transition to a capitalistic life. He and Volk knew many people on the other side in business and government and without too much trouble dumped their former lives and found work in Munich, Volk with a German security firm and Reagor with Deutsche Bayrische Werke AG–DBW—one of the huge West German conglomerates planning a blitzkrieg-like expansion into the former Eastern Communist Bloc.

In many ways, Reagor's new life at DBW was not all that much different from his old one. The pay was much better, of course, in the commercial sector, although Munich was an expensive place to live, by either East or West German standards. He still lived in an apartment, but luxurious compared to the one in East Berlin. Volk's family had been well connected in industry before World War II. Volk reacquainted himself with an old friend of his father's who was now serving on the board of DBW and—upon his recommendation—secured for Reagor a position in charge of business development in the old Eastern sector of Germany. On the recommendation of the board member, Reagor was given a job working for the young president of the company, Hans Stettler, a marketing genius who had already developed many new markets for the company in Western Europe. Reagor knew East Germany and the former Communist Bloc and had experience doing whatever it took to get things done. Together they made a good team. Stettler was the respectable front man and Reagor made things happen in the new Eastern European countries. Reagor soon became Stettler's right-hand man in the endeavor. Reagor was someone he could trust.

Stettler installed Reagor as DBW's corporate spymaster, with the euphemistic title Vice President for Business Development. The prestige of his company's name on his business card and his title allowed him to circulate comfortably among Europe's other businesses, ferreting out information on competitors, potential acquisitions, and old Communist government entities slated for privatization. He crisscrossed central and eastern Europe in his company car, a new red Porsche.

Reagor was comfortable as the behind-the-scenes man. Stettler dealt with all the corporate politics and oiled the company's bureaucracy at budget time to ensure a healthy allocation for the Business Development Department. More important, Reagor and Stettler were comfortable with each other. As in the old days at Stasi, Reagor was given free rein to run his operations as he saw fit, while Stettler handled the bullshit with management.

Stettler had been generous when it came to finding resources for Reagor. Much as in the old days, Reagor had a small but highly skilled and self-motivated staff, largely recruited from other companies after the candidates had been identified as rising stars through his substantial business contacts. The entire staff—except himself—was working in the old part of the city, away from the suburban corporate offices, in a secure, ordinary-looking two-story office building that could have passed for a small accounting firm. With the substantial resources of DBW, almost anything was possible. The young men and women working for Reagor utilized investigative techniques that surpassed any police organization or government agency in their sophistication. They tapped into Interpol's data bases. Corporate blackmail was a specialty. They dug up embarrassing information on officers of competing firms from on-line credit bureaus and police records.

Most of his staff were field people, consisting of a half dozen men and women who were responsible for gathering human intelligence and carrying out covert action against competitors. They would do whatever was necessary. They were, in effect, the equivalent of Stasi field officers. Everyone was extremely well paid and understood that what he or she was doing was at best borderline legal and if any of them were caught, no records would ever be found to associate them with DBW.

Another car blasted its horn and Reagor focused again on the girl still sitting on top of him, still talking away.

"I said, where do you want to eat?" she asked again.

She was looking at the reflection of herself in the framed picture of the German Alps over the bed, fussing with her hair.

"Why don't we go for a walk up the Maximillianstrasse to that new place?"

"If you mean the one with all the contemporary art, I think that's a bit far to walk. Let's take a taxi."

He dismissed her suggestion: "I need the exercise. I feel like I'm getting soft in this new job." He pumped up the biceps in his left arm, feeling the still substantial knot with his other hand. "I've spent so much time putting the department together and traveling that I've neglected some of the other things that used to be important."

She shook her bobbed hair sassily from side to side. "Like me?"

He grinned wickedly. "Not a chance." She tilted her head down toward his. He smoothed her hair away from her face. "After all," he said, "who's had me prisoner here playing Nazi love slave all afternoon?"

"Not funny. Let's get dressed."

"What? Not before another round of Adolf and the German shepherd?"

"That's sick," she said.

"Yes, but that's why you can't resist me," he replied, and pulled her down before she could get away.

4 ❏ ❏ ❏ ❏

On the last page of his passport under the word *Entry*—where the foreign visas were usually stamped—was a perfect, lipsticky kiss of cherry black.

The kiss was dated eight years earlier in a European script. It was the day she had granted Greer permission to enter her body, her life. That night they had made love for the first time, a quick affair carried out on the throw rug on the floor of her office. At the time, he thought it was for life. As it turned out, it was only a temporary visa. The passport indicated Heidelberg as the point of entry.

Greer tossed the passport into his open briefcase and picked up the photocopy of his Personal History Statement and turned to a section in the back. In the context of the kiss, the words FOREIGN CONTACTS at the top of the page seemed the grossest of understatements.

He threw the Personal History Statement into the briefcase, then turned to the pile of folded clothes on the bed and resumed packing his suitcase for the trip to Washington. Thank God for friends of Tony Vasquez, he thought, whatever their real names might be.

Greer stuffed clothes into the suitcase and paused a moment to let the picture reel with the continuous loop in his head project the fantasy again. The promise of excitement had been held forth for him by the CIA man on the phone. It still made his palms sweat. If all went well, he'd be back in the streets again, this time, though, making things happen as a spy runner for the CIA in the Directorate of Operations. A field officer of the Clandestine Service.

The fantasy had carried him through a week and a half of alternating high anxiety and the total frustration and paranoia of hearing absolutely nothing as he waited for the CIA to evaluate his application and for the FBI to complete its preliminary background investigation. There had been plenty of time to dream. The stories he had read about from the reading list sent by the Agency fueled his imagination like gasoline thrown on a bonfire. He was in London meeting with dissidents from some Middle Eastern country. He saw himself sweating through a short-sleeve khaki shirt in a Southeast Asia jungle, wading through swamps, pulling leeches off himself, setting up a listening post directed against a dictatorial regime. He was slamming drinks with dangerous drug runners in the back room of a cantina somewhere in South America. A quick flash of Tommy Bickford in jail: maybe *not* the drug runners, he told himself. He was making a drop for one of his agents in Berlin. He carried a sleek, powerful gun and had a briefcase full of sophisticated electronic surveillance gear. He was recruiting and running foreign agents and getting medals back in Washington. He carried a passport with an alias and wore sunglasses in airports. The more he thought about it, the more excited he got. The second call on the previous day had come from Washington much more quickly than he had expected. He was packing on Saturday, flight to Washington, D.C., on Sunday. They wanted him there immediately for evaluation. By the end of the day on Monday he would know whether or not he would be beginning his descent into the netherworld of spies.

Keeping him company on the television in the bedroom of his Druid Hills garage apartment was a videotape of Günter Grass' *Tin Drum*. Greer paused again to follow the action. He ignored the subtitles at the bottom of the screen and listened to the German. He repeated the words aloud.

"*Ich liebe dich,*" she said. I love you.

When he spoke the woman's part, he thought he heard speaking through himself the voice of someone he had once known. He tried it again, this time more exacting, with a northern German accent tinted with something more exotic, the way *she* would have said it.

"*Ich liebe dich, Herr Schneebälle.*" I love you, Mr. Snowballs.

By the time his tongue had touched his palate to close the last syllable, she was—regrettably—back.

As he remembered it, Stephanie Becker had been standing just out of reach with her bare back to him next to the dresser, lighting up one of those awful Turkish cigarettes she used to smoke. Not caring much about who might see her in the late afternoon streets, she walked naked to the window, parted the curtains and opened it a little, letting some cool air into her stuffy flat. She adjusted the curtains to a slit of light.

"Come back," he remembered saying. He turned down the corner of the duvet, welcoming her back into bed. She smoked standing up, cupping her elbow with the palm of her other hand, looking out the window.

The situation sometimes amused him still. Student and teacher. Greer, the American exchange student at Heidelberg University during his junior year in college, and she, the tutor, assigned—in the European tradition—by the university to meet with him once a week in her office to discuss how his seminars were progressing. It took him four sessions to work up enough nerve to ask her out. They went to see *The Tin Drum* on their first date at the movie theater in the student union. That night they became lovers. This afternoon, however, she was making cautious movements that told him there wouldn't be love-making unless he really insisted, and then she wouldn't enjoy it.

"Can we go to Paris before you leave?" she asked.

A strange question, because it had already been resolved. All the questions had been asked and answered already about what would happen up to the point that he would return to America. Greer wondered which half of her mind—the German half or the Turkish half—was forming words. The bags from the Christmas trip to England weren't even unpacked. "That's a long time off," he said. "Let's talk about something else."

"Seven months is not a long time."

Greer thought about that. She was right, of course. In the context of the plans they had made, seven months wasn't a long time. Stephanie was always thinking farther out than he was, a habit he attributed to her being six years older, rather than to the calculating Prussian left side of her brain. She was already a doctoral candidate and lecturer in the linguistics department at the university. He was still an undergraduate, originally come to Germany as a modern-day Teutonic Knight, a swaggering romantic. He once envisioned himself a vagabond scholar, reading Heidegger in German during the day and roaming the streets of Heidelberg at night in search of nubile Fräuleins and a stein of beer. He had come for German poets and philosophers. He found Stephanie instead.

It was times like these that he felt like a junkie, a slave to the unimaginable pleasures she had unleashed for him. She had shown him new things. How to let go sometimes. Let her do it. Let her show him once, then he could be master of the motion, the curious position of limb against limb, the wonder of how but a single powerful image was enough to keep him hard and coming until she would intervene again and tell him to save it. Save it for the next time. Save it and know you had the power to stop it.

The late-afternoon sun reached across the sky into the window of her little bedroom, its spectrum fractured by roof lines and chimney pots, lighting up her taut brown skin with rays from the lower end in a ruddy flame. She turned to him, stirring the smoke swirling around her head. She wore only her Turkish earrings and a necklace of braided gold that fell gracefully into the curves of her high breasts. Her black eyes caught the glint of red from the window and shone like burning coals. She looked like a Persian queen moving through a fire.

Stephanie stubbed out the cigarette and interlocked her arms above her head, closing her eyes, raising her chin to the ceiling, letting her black hair fall down her arching back, standing on her toes, twisting, and stretching every muscle in her body as if she were being wrung dry in front of his eyes.

"I've changed my mind," she said.

She was crazy—*really* crazy—he knew, but he loved her anyway, or maybe because of it. She was everything he wasn't. Spontaneous, completely unpredictable, vulnerable. He was straight as an arrow, in control—except when it came to her.

She slipped under the covers with him and got on top, making contact at every point, confirming that not only would she make love, but that she would insist on nothing less than her complete satisfaction. She kissed him as she straddled one of his thighs. She was already wet before he touched her. . . .

Greer called up yet another memory, the sweeter, less manic side of Stephanie. A loud snap that had broken the silence in the frigid Heidelberg flat in the middle of the night. There was a quick jingle of metal on soft wood, then nothing again.

It was four in the morning and the building's heat had been off since midnight. Two wide eyes and a nose were all that was visible of Stephanie's face in the covers. She lifted up her head into the cold room.

"*Die Maus ist tot*," she pronounced. The mouse is dead.

Buried deeper in the covers, Greer hadn't heard it. He got up and walked around to Stephanie's side of the bed. On the floor next to the wall was the sprung trap.

"Yes," said Greer. "Your audience is gone."

The only time the little brown mouse ventured into the room was when Stephanie was on top. Was it that she made different sounds during their lovemaking in that position or was it that the bed squeaked differently? He liked to watch. He was there again earlier in the night, their commotion drawing him out of a still-undetermined hole on the closet wall, from which he ran along to the bed, climbing up to the top of the headboard. From that vantage he stood on his back two feet and stared as if hypnotized by Stephanie's rhythmic motions. He stayed until she cried it was done, then ran back to the floor. He normally returned to his hole at the first sound of steam hissing through the radiator as the heat came back into the building at five in the morning.

Greer took the trap with the mouse that had been bisected at midsection and walked to the window. He opened the window and flung the trap against the black sky toward the rooftop of the building across the narrow street. He heard it bounce down the tiles of the roof's steep pitch, clattering until it landed in the gutter.

A tiny, muffled voice: *"Ich liebe dich, Herr Schneebälle."*

"The things we do for love," he said, climbing back into bed.

"My hero," she said, and was lost again with him under the comforter, prickly with feathers.

Sitting on the edge of the bed in his own apartment with the FOREIGN CONTACTS page still in his hands, Greer read her name and was reminded of how it all ended eight years ago. He was back home, missing her, when he had got her early-morning transatlantic phone call from Heidelberg.

"What do you mean you won't be coming?" he had asked. "In Paris you promised me you'd be here no later than Christmas."

The line was unusually clear that night. He heard her clearly not answering him.

"What happened to all of our plans?" he said. "We spent the entire week in Paris talking about our future. You were coming here to spend a month looking for work in the States. What's changed in only a month?"

Then interference. The sound of ghosts talking on the line, crossed wires and hushed voices. French, Arabic, English—a phantom Babel.

"I won't be coming, Greer. You left me. I won't tolerate it."

What had he done to deserve this? Like a dark asteroid on an irregular, unplotted orbit, he hadn't seen it coming. Smashing into the ocean's depths, blowing away his dreams and vaporizing his future.

"I love you, Stephanie. Nothing's changed. It's been all arranged. You're coming here. There's no reason to be upset."

But something had changed. She was silent. She was probably off her medication.

"Stephanie?"

"You bastard."

Dealing with her craziness had never been easy. There had been biweekly appointments with a psychiatrist and a drawer full of antidepressants to prove it. She was so delicate for someone who played so rough.

He hated it when she got like this. Something must have set her off. Something to knock her out of her delicately balanced equilibrium. He could calm her down and talk her through it. He had done it before.

"Stephanie, is there something you're not telling me?"

"*Bastard.* You *bastard.*" Her voice was low, possessed, scary. She was spitting on the phone. "Son of a *bitch.*"

He would reason with her. "Paris, remember? Our plans for a future together. What's happened? Why are you so upset?"

"I hate you."

"*What?*"

"Damn you to hell, Greer Whitaker."

Then silence big enough to span an ocean.

Greer was totally confused. She seemed to have been okay when he had left her a few weeks earlier. Now something had set her off. If he didn't do something—say something—he was afraid he would lose her forever.

"Can't you tell me what's wrong?"

He heard her breathing hard into the phone. He could see her slipping into an altered state, her eyes wide, glassy, fixed on a point in space. He was desperate to bring her back.

"What about Mr. Snowballs?" he asked meekly. It was the most pathetic thing he had ever said in his life.

"*Fuck* Mr. Snowballs," she said in perfectly articulated English. He had corrected her on her English pronunciation of swear words so that now they were deadly accurate. "I don't need this *shit*." Then abruptly, scornfully, "Miss me," and she hung up.

Miss me, her last humiliating words, commanding him to his own lesser insanity for several months afterward. His reply was unsophisticated, one of those occasions thought through a thousand times afterwards when having a few calm moments for reflection would have given him a more perfect retort. Why did he say it? The shock of her sudden rejection? His own shattered ego? She was apparently not well and he should have handled the situation better. What she said had made him mad at the moment and he had simply reacted in the heat of the moment.

But with *Go to hell!* he had sent her on a journey away from himself, to a glacial crevasse in his mind from which she was never supposed to climb. He screwed the lid down tightly. She was dead all right. For his own sanity. Even if she had already hung up and had never heard him say it. The Euro busy signal buzzed in his ear until he fell asleep. There would be no explanations, no apologies, no regrets. She changed to an unlisted telephone number the next day.

Greer shook himself out of this reverie, amazed at how clearly he remembered it all. He looked one last time at the smooth creases of her lipstick kiss in the passport. In the fold of the page was a strand of her hair, curled up on itself like a little black puppy asleep.

5

For the extraordinary individual who wants more than a job, this is a unique career—a way of life that will challenge the deepest resources of your intelligence, self-reliance, and responsibility. It demands an adventurous spirit . . . a forceful personality . . . superior intellectual ability . . . toughness of mind . . . and a high degree of integrity. It takes special skills and professional discipline to produce results. You will need to deal with fast-moving, ambiguous, and unstructured situations that will test your resourcefulness to the utmost.

This is the Clandestine Service, the vital human element of intelli-

gence collection. These people are the cutting edge of American intelli-
gence, an elite corps gathering the vital information needed by our policy
makers to make critical foreign policy decisions.

CIA's Career Training Program is the gateway to an overseas career.
To qualify you must have first-rate qualifications: a college degree with
an excellent academic record, strong interpersonal skills, the ability to
write clearly and accurately, and a burning interest in international af-
fairs. A graduate degree, foreign travel, foreign language proficiency, pre-
vious residency abroad, and military experience are pluses.

All applicants must successfully complete a thorough medical and
psychiatric exam, a polygraph interview, and an extensive background
investigation. The CIA is an equal opportunity employer. . . .

Greer sat in the reception area on the fifth floor of the Arlington
Chamber of Commerce Building—home to the CIA's off-site Career
Training Program offices—distracting himself by reading the glossy
trifold brochure he had picked up off the end table. Greer knew it was
a job description tailormade for him: The academics, his time abroad
studying in Germany and his German language skills, his background
in politics and government. It was a dream job. The excitement of
working overseas. The opportunity to serve his country in a meaning-
ful way. His frame of reference had changed. Before, it was Capitol
Hill. Now the whole world lay at his feet.

There was a room down the hall, an unmarked door he had passed
by earlier. His palms went sweaty, not out of excitement, but out of
dread this time. He looked at his watch again. He was only ten minutes
away from the polygraph. There was no way he wouldn't pass, he
reassured himself. So why was everything he had ever heard about it
so terrible?

He had signed a sheet of paper authorizing the CIA, FBI, or any
other U.S. government agency or its designate to obtain or confirm
information about him for the purpose of determining his suitability
for employment. What exactly had they been doing with his application? Whom had they been talking to? What could they possibly find
on him, Mr. Georgia Young Republican, Mr. Squeaky Clean?

I prefer apples to oranges. I prefer light wood paneling to dark paneling.
I sometimes have trouble holding my urine. I sometimes have visions. If
the money were right, I would join a circus or carnival.

The whole CIA application process had been a perverse series of mind games. As he waited for the polygraph, the memories of everything that had happened up to that point filled his mind.

There were meetings with nameless CIA men, the first in a hotel room at the TraveLodge in Atlanta with a field officer who claimed to have just returned from a tour of duty in Africa. There was the monstrously long document, the Personal History Statement, detailing his life. On the Saturday following the meeting at the TraveLodge, a written exam administered at the testing center of the university near his house. He spent a day completing questions meant to determine his intelligence, vocational interests, current events knowledge, language aptitude, and psychological makeup. The questions on the psychological part of the exam still bugged him. Trouble holding my urine? Join the carnival? Come on, he thought. Nonetheless, he filled in the oval circles on the computer optical scanner sheets with extra care so as not to make a mistake and have the computer peg him as a psychopath.

Then there were the strange meetings earlier that morning. The Agency put him up at the Quality Inn Central in Arlington, sent him maps and a schedule of places to be for interviews. There was a more formal language aptitude test at a language lab in Rosslyn. He took the Metro to Arlington Station. On the fifth floor of the Arlington Chamber of Commerce Building, a secretary took his picture with a Polaroid, then a man carrying his file led him to an office in the back. No pictures of the family. No golf trophies. No self-affirming statements in needlepoint made by his wife. Just Greer and another nameless CIA officer. It was there where the mysteries of the CIA's Directorate of Operations—the Clandestine Service—had first been personally revealed to him. He had read about most of it before in the reading list that the Agency had sent him. But he felt it in the gut when it came from the mouth of a real live spy runner at the CIA.

The man in the suit vest had put his feet up on the desk, put his hands behind his head, and grinned as if he were about to tell Greer an old story he really liked.

"Okay, let me give you a hypothetical situation." He shifted his focus from Greer to the ceiling. "Let's suppose we had identified a woman a few years back—let's call her Angela Smith—who was working with the Cubans to plot acts of violence against the U.S. government. *And,* let's suppose she was visiting Cuba and we made arrangements through one of our agents to have her go to bed with a Cuban soldier. And, let's suppose we photographed her in bed with the soldier doing some very—*creative things.*" Greer remembered the look the CIA man had given him." Would you have any trouble with using the photographs to blackmail her into stopping her illegal activities?"

Who couldn't say no?

There had been two other interviews during the day—one with the Agency psychiatrist and the other at CIA headquarters at Langley. The shrink was a black woman in her late fifties. There were no diplomas or board certifications on the wall. She didn't take a single note while he was with her and Greer assumed that their conversation was being secretly recorded. Lots of questions about what he thought about his father, what his friends thought of him. She showed him graphs from his written tests. She told him that he had some *very* unusual scores. She asked if he had ever considered going into business or law. He left feeling very uneasy about the session.

His last meeting had been with another nameless field officer. They met off the main lobby in a small conference room at Langley. It was the shortest meeting of them all, no more than fifteen minutes. "I've read your file," he said. He nodded along as Greer answered his question about why he wanted to join the Agency. "I'm sure you know that very few make it through to the end," he said. "We have to be very selective." He was a steely bastard, Greer thought. It almost seemed his mind had already been made up. Greer just couldn't figure out which way. . . .

But here he was, on the final leg of the trip. The FBI had apparently given him the thumbs up from their background check. It had all been so bizarre. No names. No real discussion of what he might be doing, except in the most general of terms. All of the Agency people had done their best to get him excited about the job. It was something that Greer knew he wanted badly, but what exactly was this phantom he had been chasing?

"Focus on a point on the wall in front of you."

Greer felt the pressure on his upper arm build as the technician pumped up the cuff. When he breathed in he felt the constriction of the coil across his chest. The blood pounded in the third finger on each hand where he had attached two electrodes secured with small Velcro straps. He felt his palms sweating. He was strapped into a wooden, straight-backed chair with a floor lamp shining from behind his head, the only light in the windowless room.

From his seated position, Greer found a point on the wall at eye level in the gray paint of the Arlington Chamber of Commerce building. The point was like the crosshairs in a rifle scope at the intersection of two fine cracks in the paint. The vertical crack was lost in the ceiling. Greer followed the horizontal crack off to the side, straining his eyes without moving his head to see the crack turn the corner and head toward the door of the room. By now he had spent enough time at the CIA's off-site Career Training offices in the Washington suburb to know that the crack ran throughout the entire office complex. All of the offices he had been into seemed to have been freshly painted, but they all had the same fine horizontal crack running through them. Was it some kind of permanent stress fracture that the paint couldn't hide? Were the walls simply responding to what was going on with the people inside, some paranormal manifestation of the pressures that were being created in the top two floors of the Arlington Chamber of Commerce Building?

The two-and-a-half-week journey that had begun with the call from Tony Vasquez's friend from Washington had led finally to this. The only things that now stood in the way of his becoming a field officer in the CIA's Clandestine Service were the medical exam and the polygraph.

The technician sat behind Greer next to a table on which was unfolded a medium-sized piece of hard luggage. Snugly installed inside the luggage was a polygraph machine. Greer heard him turn a knob on the apparatus and the machine came alive. Greer's mind snapped back to the present. Electricity flowed and hummed, the graph paper started scrolling, and the pens began scratching lines that would determine Greer's fate with the CIA.

Congress had long ago outlawed the polygraph's use in the private sector as being unreliable, but the national intelligence agencies still relied heavily on them to vet recruits and current employees. The books he had read about the CIA always mentioned how awful the polygraph could be. It was said more than once that the polygraph was really a form of psychological torture, more a test of wills than a scientific tool.

"Is your name Greer Michael Whitaker?" the examiner asked. He was totally out of Greer's peripheral vision.

"Yes." The technician fiddled with the knobs.

"Is today Monday?"

"Yes." More adjustments to the machine.

"Is today Wednesday?"

"No." The operator made a squeaky mark on the moving paper with a felt-tipped pen.

"Are you nervous?"

"Yes." More marks on the graph.

"Okay. All calibrated. Relax." The technician turned a screw on the cuff pump with his thumb and let the air out, then turned the machine off.

Greer thought he was joking.

"Here's the procedure," he said flatly. "We'll go through all of the questions the first time without the monitors on. You are to answer only yes or no when we get to the actual examination. On the first pass, we'll go over any exceptions to your answers and modify the questions so that you can give me a straightforward yes or no. Keep in mind that the polygraph detects any deception, not just blatant untruths. Also, remember that what goes on in here is strictly confidential, so let's get it all out. Ready to start?"

"Sure."

"Are you comfortable?"

"As comfortable as I can be, considering."

Greer was already thinking about how soon he might be entering the CIA training program. According to the first field officer who had interviewed him at Atlanta, he could expect to spend about a year in Washington training on a particular country desk. Then he would be sent to a special camp where he would be taught espionage techniques, "tradecraft" in the lingo of the CIA. After that, his first overseas assignment.

The technician rested a clipboard on his lap. He flipped to a list of triple-spaced typed questions.

"We are going to cover several areas today relevant to your employment. Specifically, criminal activity, sexual deviancy, physical and emotional health, and foreign intelligence contacts. The statement you signed and returned with your Personal History Statement indicated you understand that you must successfully complete this polygraph examination as a prerequisite for employment with the Agency. Do you have any general comments or questions at this point?"

"No."

Now the CIA polygraph operator meticulously went through the forty-page Personal History Statement that Greer had filled out. He verified old addresses, medical conditions, education, places of employment, and his family's background. He then made his way through the sensitive areas, rephrasing questions to which Greer had answered "no" to find any weaknesses or exceptions that might cause Greer problems and cause the polygraph machine to indicate deception. Like the Agency psychiatrist that Greer had been interviewed by, the technician seemed perturbed that Greer had confessed to nothing and seemed to relish the end of the off-the-machine questioning so that he could move on to the real thing.

The examiner turned the machine on and pumped up the arm cuff again, and went through the same series of questions. The subject matter made Greer nervous. He had never stolen and had never had anything approaching a homosexual experience. He was in great physical shape and he had never come into contact with a foreign intelligence operation. Still, the technician went over and over each area, rephrasing each question several times, seemingly trying to get Greer to make a confession about something—anything—however small. Greer was giving him no satisfaction.

He relieved the pressure in the arm cuff again without saying anything. Greer assumed they were finished.

"You're having a problem with the foreign-contacts area," he finally said.

Greer was jolted. He felt a rush of adrenaline and heard the pens scratching out his uncontrollable heavy breathing response.

Greer tried to talk, but had to clear his throat first. "That *can't* be," he said. Greer felt his opportunity to join the CIA slipping away. The technician, still sitting behind him out of view, was silent. Greer felt forced to say something. "How could that be a problem?"

"The polygraph is indicating a problem in that area. I read it as your being deceptive. I'm going to turn off the machine and let you have a while to think about your answers." He turned a knob and the pens went silent. Greer heard him stand up and walk out of the room, closing the door. He was still strapped into the chair.

Greer was stunned. His mind raced, not being able to concentrate on any one thought. He went over the questions in his mind, trying to figure out what had happened. There was nothing—absolutely nothing —he could think about that should have caused a problem with anything they had covered on Greer's foreign contacts. He had answered all the questions as honestly as he could.

Before he could compose himself, the technician was back.

"Let's go through it again," he said as he pumped up the cuff. He was still out of Greer's vision. Greer heard the knob turn and the pens came to life.

Greer had read once somewhere that the best way to approach a polygraph examination was to think of nothing at all. That way, extraneous thoughts couldn't work their way into the conscience and blur the unwavering concentration needed to answer questions. A blank mind was a guiltless mind. The technique wasn't working.

"What were you thinking of when I asked you about your foreign contacts?"

"*Nothing.*" Greer was indignant.

"But the polygraph indicated you were being deceptive in that area. How do you explain that?" he asked coolly.

"*Really,* I don't have an explanation. There was no deception. The machine *must* be wrong."

"Isn't there something else you want to tell me? Now would be a good time. What were you thinking about?"

"Nothing, just the questions. Stephanie Becker is the only person that I maintained contact with for any period of time—but that's it. We lost touch after a few weeks of my returning to the States. I had already mentioned her in my Personal History Statement."

"The others you socialized with in Heidelberg—people you attended classes with, people you lived near. Drinking buddies."

Greer thought for a moment. "I don't recall anything unusual," he finally said.

"Names?"

Greer was trying hard to remember anything that might help. "Helmut . . . something or other. *Braun* maybe? The guy next door to where I lived. We went out a few times for beer right after I moved in, but I'm sure there's nothing there."

"There's something there, or the machine wouldn't be indicating a problem. *Think.* There's got to be more. *Names.*"

"Okay." Greer was throwing out anything that came to mind. "The porter in the residence hall. An old guy who was in the war. Scharff? Stahl?"

"They were *your* friends."

Greer was totally frustrated. "I honestly don't know."

The unseen technician scribbled some notes.

"Back to this Stephanie Becker person. I'll ask you the same questions I asked you before. Do you have any knowledge of her working for or on the behalf of any foreign intelligence service?"

"No."

"Did she ever ask you to perform any activities that might be construed as intelligence gathering or acting in any capacity for a foreign intelligence service?"

"No. I told you that before."

"Bremerhaven's a cold place," the technician said.

Greer knew where he was going. Stephanie was from Bremerhaven, a cold port city on the North Sea, about a hundred kilometers due west of Hamburg. "I've never been."

"Lots of materials shipped back and forth through there. Lots of things that shouldn't be coming in or going out. Did Stephanie ever talk to you about that?"

"I don't know anything about that. She told me it's a cold, ugly city. She left as soon as she could and never went back."

"How can you be so sure? How do you know she's never been back? What have your contacts been with Stephanie Becker since you returned from your trip to Germany?"

"My answer's the same as before. We haven't had any contact with each other since about a month after I left Germany."

"Never an occasional telephone call or exchanging Christmas cards?"

"Nothing."

"So tell me again, how was it that you came to terminate this relationship with Stephanie Becker?"

Greer felt like shrieking. Why this? he wondered. Was Stephanie Becker going to screw up his future for the second time?

The story again—short version. "I still had my last year in college to complete when I returned home from Germany. We had talked about getting married. She was supposed to have come to the States to try to find a job here. We talked twice a week on the telephone after I left, then about a month later something went wrong. I don't know what. As you can see, I don't even have her address or phone number." Greer instinctively tried to twist in the chair to point to the FOREIGN CONTACTS page that the examiner was looking at, but he was still restrained.

Greer heard more note taking behind him on the clipboard.

"Did she ever introduce you to friends of hers. Germans or other foreign nationals?"

"Of course. She was an instructor at the university and had many friends. Faculty and students, mainly other post-graduate students."

"Did you ever spend time alone with any of these people?"

Greer was puzzled by the question. He had to think a moment. "Maybe."

"Can you be more specific?"

"It's been so long. There's nothing that comes to mind right off."

"Try."

Greer thought again. "I don't know. Nothing sticks out."

"Did the subject of your future employment back in the States ever come up in conversation with any of Stephanie's friends? What kind of work you'd be doing when you got home?"

So that's it, Greer thought. "I see what you're getting at." He thought a moment more. "I can't say that I honestly remember anything like that ever coming up. I'm not saying it didn't, but I just don't remember."

"Not even with Stephanie?"

"Of course with Stephanie. We had talked about getting married. We had our entire future planned out."

"And what did you tell her you would be doing for a career?"

"I suppose I talked about some type of government service. I was a political science major. I had been working on political campaigns since I was a teenager. She knew I was interested in a government position one day."

More note taking from behind.

"You indicated that you traveled with Stephanie Becker outside of Heidelberg. Exactly what was the extent of the travel?"

"We traveled extensively around Germany together on long weekends. During the Christmas break we left Heidelberg and went to

England, spending most of the time in London, with side trips to Oxford, then later to Durham to see the cathedral. On my way back to the United States, Stephanie and I went to Paris."

"And the last time you saw her?"

"At the airport in Paris."

"Ever go into East Germany?"

"Of course not."

"Ever go into the Soviet Union or any other Communist country?"

"No."

Pages flipping.

"So from what you've said, it would be fair to characterize your relationship with Stephanie Becker as being very close."

"Yes."

"Tell me . . ." Greer could feel the point of the question being sharpened. "What was the extent of your involvement with her while you were in Germany?"

Greer squirmed in his seat. He took a deep breath. "I told you. We had a physical relationship."

"You engaged in sex acts?"

"Yes, of course."

"Did you engage in any acts that might be considered perverted?"

Greer felt himself blush. "What exactly do you mean by perverted?"

"*You* tell me," the voice from behind said flatly.

Greer was silent, thinking about all of the crazy, wonderful times he and Stephanie had spent together. Now it was being reduced to a word game, figuring out which clinical term would be the most appropriate, the most descriptive to satisfy his CIA polygraph examiner.

"We had normal sex, just like any other couple," said Greer. He was steamed.

"Did you ever use any drugs with her?"

"No."

"By yourself?"

"No. I told you. I smoked some pot in college, but nothing over there."

"Did she?"

"Did she what?"

"Was she using drugs in your presence?"

"No." Then he remembered. He didn't want the polygraph to make him out to be a liar. "She had a prescription for antidepressants, antipsychotics, I don't remember exactly." Enough said.

"She was having mental problems?"

"She was . . . sensitive. She had an artistic temperament. She was seeing a psychiatrist twice a week."

"About what?"

"I don't know exactly."

"About you?"

What kind of question was that? Where was this line of questioning going to end up anyway?

"She was already in therapy when I met her."

"You knew this before you started to see her?"

"After."

"And you kept on seeing her, even though she was mentally unbalanced?"

"Yes." He hated to say it, but it was the truth. He heard more note taking. It couldn't be good. It probably reflected poorly on his judgment. At this point, though, there was nothing to hide.

"Did she ever act irrationally?"

Greer had to think about that. "What do you mean?"

"Did she ever do anything that you thought was something a reasonable person wouldn't do?"

Greer almost laughed out loud. Where should he begin? Her personality was defined by her irrationality. She was crazy, dangerous, and unpredictable—everything he wasn't. Plus, she had been obsessed with *him* just as much as he had been obsessed with her. How could he say she was a *total* nut case?

"She was operating on a different plane. She was like no one I've ever met. She wasn't ordinary people." And that, Greer realized, was what had endeared him so to her.

"It sounds like she was a real psycho, wasn't she?"

The question seemed rhetorical, but Greer answered it anyway. Just to make him happy.

"Yes." Oh yes. But it was her psychoses that he had probably fallen in love with, he had concluded. Her compulsive attention to details when they made love, the energy that she put into making him happy, the total self-absorption with which she had rearranged her life around his and given him more—in retrospect—than he could ever give back. Perhaps that's why it had failed. Perhaps she had figured out that he would never be as crazy, as obsessive—in a literal sense—about her as she was about him. But it didn't mean he didn't love her as much as he possibly could. Even if it wasn't as much as she could possibly love him.

"Has she ever tried to contact you since"—he was flipping back through his notes—"since approximately one month after you left Germany?"

"Not as far as I know."

"Does she know where you live?"

"I don't think so."

"You're still holding out on me," the interviewer said suddenly.

"I'm not. Really." Greer was just weary.

The examiner was unruffled. He scratched some more notes. "Let's go through all the questions again on the problem areas," he finally said. "I want you to tell me again about all of your other friends in Heidelberg. And, of course, all of Stephanie Becker's friends. Start with"—he looked down at his clipboard—"Hans Braun, your drinking buddy. Just answer yes or no."

Greer was totally lost, dazed at the thought of having to go back over all the questions again, especially the ones about Stephanie. What was the point? What was he looking for? To go back through all those questions again would take at least another two and a half hours. He was drained. . . .

After being humiliated for almost four hours in the polygraph interrogation, all that Greer had been told was that someone would be in touch. Now he was scheduled to spend the balance of the afternoon having to endure the more personal prodding with needles and probing of his orifices by the doctor performing the physical examination.

"What's that?" the doctor asked, pointing to a place between his thighs as he waited for the urine to start flowing into the cup.

"A tattoo. I got it in college."

The doctor made a note on his chart.

"What's it say?"

Greer felt himself blush. "It says 'Herr Schneebälle.' "

"What's that mean?"

Greer felt the blood pounding at his temples. His jaws locked. "It means Mr. Snowballs."

The doctor wrote some more on his chart. "*You're* Mr. Snowballs?"

He had a good laugh. "You might consider having a dermatologist remove that with laser surgery," he said.

Actually, thought Greer, a good idea. He wondered why he hadn't done it already.

6

The next day, the taxi dropped Greer off in front of the Castle, the oldest part of the Smithsonian. At ten o'clock in the morning, the end-of-summer tourists had begun filing into the building to start their tours of the museum complex. Across the street a carousel started up. A Park Service patrolman dismounted from his horse and watched the children going around. Greer queued up with the tourists, looking out of place in his suit and tie.

Greer went into the main room and walked around the scale model of Washington. Along the wall, a group of Japanese students were playing with the interactive touch-screen program. A family was clustered around a map of Washington lit up with Metro stations.

He saw the sign for Theater I and walked in to where the film was already playing. He stood in the back to let his eyes adjust to the dark. He could see three or four people sitting in a group in the middle of the little theater. Greer walked down the side aisle and took a seat in the second row next to a column, just as he had been instructed by the man on the phone only an hour and a half ago.

The film ended and the lights came on. Greer checked his watch. It was ten minutes after ten. The small group of people got up and left. In a few minutes a family came in and sat down two rows behind him. The lights went down and the film began again.

At precisely ten-fifteen, Greer felt a touch on his shoulder. He started to turn around but a voice near his ear told him not to. It was a voice he had heard before.

"Keep watching the film. When the show's over, wait a minute, then go down the hall around the corner past the sign that says EM-PLOYEES ONLY and take a right. Go into the first door on your left.

The show ended and Greer watched the second hand on his watch sweep once around before he got up and left the theater. There was no one behind him. He followed the man's directions and came to the door he had been led to. He turned the brass knob and stepped into an empty anteroom. He opened another door and looked into a high-ceilinged room with old leather-bound books lining the walls. On top of the book shelves was a bust of Thomas Jefferson. A large, ornately carved conference table was in the middle of the room, ringed with high-backed leather chairs. The room was windowless, the only light coming indirectly from the skylight in the anteroom.

The man in the shadows turned on a small banker's lamp on the table. "Shut the door," he said. The light shone up from below onto his face ghoulishly like theatrical footlights. He adjusted the lampshade downward. It was the CIA officer he had met at Langley the day before. The steely bastard.

"When can you start?" he asked.

Greer was floored. "Are you kidding?"

The CIA man extended his hand. "Congratulations. You made it. Welcome to the Company."

Greer pumped his hand vigorously. He was smiling big. "Thank you."

"My name is Bob Reed. I'll be your new boss." He pulled out one of the chairs. "Have a seat."

Greer sat down and took a better look at Reed as he settled into a chair across the table. Mid-forties. Skin stretched tight over a bony skull. A military haircut that had grown out a bit. And the piercing blue, no-nonsense eyes of a Weimaraner.

"Your scores were great," said Reed. "Top of the lot. By the way, when *can* you start?"

"Just give me a week to wrap things up in Atlanta. Where am I going?"

"Slow down," Reed said. "First assignment is here in Washington," said Reed. "Special desk I head up, reporting only to the Director of Central Intelligence himself. We've already got an apartment lined up. You can take a look at it this afternoon over in Old Town. Great neighborhood. Lived there myself when I got started with the Company."

"Sounds wonderful."

Reed was looking hard at Greer. Greer sensed he was still trying to size him up.

Reed said, "Sorry it took so long to get this finalized. We were all ready to call you in late yesterday afternoon when we realized we didn't have the Director's signature for the final sign-off. The DCI's approval was needed because of the nature of the assignment. We normally don't give new recruits postings with unofficial cover."

Greer's imagination went into overdrive.

"This is a safe room, Greer. By that, I mean that it's maintained by the agency for off-site meetings. It's soundproof and secure. Counter-intelligence does a sweep every so often to make sure it's clean—no bugs. We've got them all over the city because of all the diplomats posted here. A lot of our work in Washington is meeting with agents we've recruited at the embassies. Due to the special nature of the unit you've been assigned to—my unit—I'll be your only contact with the Agency for a while. We'll be meeting here. We'll get into details when you get started." Reed slid a file folder across the table to Greer. "You, Greer Whitaker, are one lucky son of a bitch."

The folder was printed with a wide crimson stripe running diago-nally across and marked, TOP SECRET—EYES ONLY STEEPLECHASE. The letterhead and signature indicated that the document had come di-rectly from the office of the Director of Central Intelligence, Ben Gib-bons.

"Steeplechase?" said Greer.

"It's the code name of the operation we're running. Since you're going to be under deep cover, you can just use your real name for now." Reed nudged the folder. "Go ahead. Open it."

Greer hesitated for a moment, then opened the document to the first page.

"Let me summarize for you," said Reed. "It's an outline of your personal training schedule to get you ready for your first field assign-ment. You'll spend your first week here in D.C. filling your head with every known fact about your first assignment. After that, you're going to a special camp."

"Trade craft?"

"Exactly. You remember, I'm sure, from the reading list we had sent you about our training facility, our so-called spy camp. Spy running, equipment, counterintelligence techniques, and the like. You'll spend a week there. Take that with you," Reed said, motioning to the file. "Read it, memorize it."

"Yes, sir."

Reed pulled a blank legal pad from his briefcase. "I want you to hit the ground running when you get started," he said. He began drawing interconnected boxes with names in them. He turned the pad around facing Greer and tapped the top box with his pen.

"This is the organizational chart for the agency, the Director at the top, of course. Ben Gibbons is solid. A political appointee, but served as a CIA field officer, then chief of station at a very sensitive post during the Vietnam era before he left to go to law school and became a federal district court judge, then appellate level. Well connected politically. Personal friend of the President. Well liked by the President's wife. It's no secret she was responsible for the appointment." Reed's pen moved down to the row of boxes under the Director.

"These are Ben's direct reports. Couple of these guys are strictly staffers, don't really manage anyone or anything of importance, but keep the Director's office running smoothly. Here," Reed indicated with his pen, "is where you would have normally come into the agency as a new field officer. Directorate of Operations, the meat of the organization, front line of American human intelligence gathering. These guys recruit and run spies in foreign countries and run covert operations to support the policies of the U.S. government."

Reed drew another box on the paper connected to the side of the Director with a solid dark line.

"This is me. And you. And a classified number of others who work in my unit. You won't see this box on any official charts of the agency. The name of the group is even classified. Ben and I go back together to the Nam era when we had to do things that made a lot of other men in the Agency queasy. When he came back as DCI last year, he brought me in from the field as one of his staffers. Hated it. I told him I wanted to be back in operations, so he made me an offer. Stay on working for him, but set up a new unit, completely separate from the command structure of the Directorate of Operations."

Reed put the chart back into his briefcase. "Anyway, he wanted a special unit that could move quickly without being encumbered by the bureaucracy on special, sensitive projects. He'd seen how things got hung up and screwed up waiting for approvals when he was trying to make things happen in the field some twenty-odd years ago. He vowed he'd make some changes if he ever got the chance."

Reed paused.

"We've got our charter from the Director himself," he continued. "Cleared it with the President, of course."

"Of course."

"He—Ben, that is—never flinched when I told him what resources I'd need. Money has never been a problem. He's got millions in discretionary funds that no one on the Intelligence Committees in Congress has review of. It's people, though, that will make the difference. The right kind of people. People like you. People whom I can trust to follow orders and not get squeamish when things start getting interesting. Although I can't talk specifics, I can tell you that my unit is relatively small. Just a handful of men and women who can be relied on to execute some of the most important, most sensitive assignments coming straight from the White House and the Director's office. Are you starting to get the picture? I handpicked you myself, Greer, from all the other applicants. That was the only problem I ran into when I started setting this thing up. Everyone wants the best working in his department. Problem was that the head of Operations didn't even know I was putting together my own shop. Would have got really pissed off at that, I guarantee you. So Ben had the people in personnel send me the files on the top five percent of any group of applicants so I could look them over in his office and pull a few like you. *Very* few, Greer."

"You won't regret it." Greer said.

"You can see, I'm sure, why you're being handled a little differently, not quite the normal career path. The Agency just doesn't hire new people and then utilize considerable resources to establish them with deep covers—unofficial covers, I might add—except in rare instances. The usual thing is to bring them along in a training curriculum at Langley, then send them off to a post with diplomatic cover at an embassy. Obviously, since no one outside of the Director and myself can know of your employment with the Agency, you are going to be working independently from the regular support groups at Langley, so you'll have to rely on your own resourcefulness—and me, of course."

"Of course."

"If you get into trouble, I don't know you. Nobody knows you. Officially, you're not official. Understand? We're establishing your cover so well that no one could say you're anything other than what you've got to believe yourself you are—a young, low-key, highly competent academician."

"Academician?"

"Your paycheck will be cut by a computer at a phony research institute that's a front for your work."

Reed snapped shut his briefcase and set it onto the floor. "No more questions for now. I need you back here one week from today—no later. Call me after you get into town. We'll go over things in more detail."

"No problem. I'll move my things from Atlanta immediately, and tie up any loose ends."

Reed wrote on a card. "Call me at that number tomorrow and we'll make arrangements to get you back here so I can get you started. You're going to be on a crash schedule to get you ready for your first assignment. Get some rest now. You won't get much for a while once we get started. Any questions?"

"What's my cover going to be when I get back into town?"

"Research associate at the Library of Congress. You'll have your own office in the Thomas Jefferson Building near the Capitol. Fits in perfectly with the political nature of your first assignment."

Greer imagined himself going to work, taking the front steps of the library building two at a time. He was on his way to Washington after all. "Brilliant," Greer said.

"We've got a lot of important work to do."

Reed and Greer stood and shook hands, then Reed turned and walked out without another word.

7 ❑ ❑ ❑ ❑

Arriving at his office before anyone else at DBW, Erich Reagor unlocked the cabinet behind his desk and turned on his computer. He typed in his password and accessed his office monitoring system.

Unknown to any of the company officials, Reagor had bugged the senior executive offices at DBW with voice-activated microphones, more out of curiosity and habit than for any other reason. A software program converted the voice recordings from the executive offices into written conversations stored in the computer's memory.

It was Monday morning. On Monday mornings he spent a few minutes reviewing and deleting old computer files. He held files for a year, then destroyed them for security reasons if they were obsolete. So on the first-year anniversary of the recording, Reagor scanned the computer transcription of the conversation that had taken place in the office of his boss, Hans Stettler.

Reagor remembered the occasion well. He had come in and checked the status of the monitoring system to see if any conversations had been picked up after he had left the building the previous night. Just after he had gone around seven o'clock, the computer indicated that there was some activity in Stettler's office. The key word "Reagor" flashed with the number 15 beside it, indicating how many times his name was mentioned.

Reagor pulled up the old file onto the screen. The computer recognized Stettler, of course. But Reagor still couldn't precisely identify the other person in the room from the context of the discussion and the computer didn't recognize the voice print as someone from inside the company. Reagor scrolled back to the top of the verbatim text and read the year-old dialogue.

"You're looking tired, old friend," the computer recorded the visitor as saying.

"You would be, too, if you ever got a real job," replied Stettler. "You know what kind of pressure I'm under. It's not the company performance, but now this pet project of your ministry. Everyone's gone now. Shall we talk?"

"Let's do it."

The computer registered a noise and conjectured a door closing.

Stettler spoke first. "The primary thing is, of course, to insulate our own company. There's obviously a huge opportunity for us all here and there is the national issue, but we can't afford to send DBW down the toilet. If you follow the public disclosures—and I know you do— you know that I myself have options on over three million shares. I'm not going to screw up my own retirement. We absolutely must keep the board of directors out of this. Of course, they understand what's going on, but they don't need to be bothered by the details."

"Yes, yes," replied the visitor. "I agree. That's why we've got to be certain about Reagor." The computer highlighted Reagor's name. It also had picked up a high-pitched cracking sound, probably the rattling of ice in scotch whiskey glasses from Stettler's office mini bar in his credenza. Reagor thought how Americanized they had all become.

"Reagor is *your* man," the visitor emphasized. "The quality of his contacts outside of Germany should be good."

"I've been assured by Peter Volk that they are the best."

"I know he has helped with these kinds of things before, but is he the right person for this?"

"Without a doubt. Hand-picked by Volk himself, you know."

It almost seemed to Reagor that the unknown person in the office knew something about his background with Stasi, although only Stettler was supposed to know.

The conversation wandered a bit.

"How's business, actually?" asked the stranger.

"Shares are up. Our own earnings projections are ahead of the analysts'. We're forecasting some very significant growth over the next several years, especially in light of the ventures into the former Eastern Bloc countries."

"And our little project."

"And our little project. We'll see. We should do well, regardless. The Americans are overanalyzing the market. The British, as usual, are too risk averse. And the French are having trouble putting together the right financing."

"Only us Germans."

"Only us Germans."

There was a pause, a rattling of ice.

The visitor brought them back to the other subject: "I know we need someone like Reagor, but don't you think his background might prove a liability?"

"How so?"

"Well, for one, there's the matter of the suspension."

"Not relevant."

"Not relevant? I think it was relevant to the two innocent women he shot in the forehead, don't you?"

"Not relevant. He did a perfectly professional job. I talked to Peter Volk about it. They saw something they shouldn't have seen. They were where they shouldn't have been. He had no choice. He's got nerves of steel. The fact that he took out two witnesses to an operation that someone else screwed up should be proof of his ability to think quickly. The only reason he was suspended was because those women were Stasi employees. Peter ordered him to take a leave of absence and lie low for a couple of months."

"I suppose."

"Look—it's up to you and me to set this thing up. We can't have any doubt on either of our parts. Let's get this decision behind us now."

"Okay, okay, Hans. I'm convinced."

"All right, then. We'll bring him in on this and then little by little, let him understand the full scope. It's best that we not let him know too much too early in case something goes wrong."

"Nothing's going to go wrong."

"No, of course not. We'll compartmentalize his activities as long as we can, then expose him to the whole thing in a few months from now. I'll talk to him tomorrow and get him started right away. No turning back."

"No turning back now, Hans." The computer screen indicated an end to the conversation.

Reagor deleted the year-old file. No need to keep it. He had memorized the conversation long ago.

8

"Sergeant, take Captain Smith over to the barn and show him how to properly open up a neck, would you? Thanks."

The man in camouflage politely led Greer, dressed in Army fatigues with the name SMITH sewn over his breast pocket, out of the Quonset hut that had been used as a field classroom. They crossed the pine straw yard to the barn.

Only two weeks after the initial meeting with Reed in the Smithsonian safe room, Greer was nervously trying to figure out whether this was a joke or a real test. Somewhere in a Mississippi pine forest Greer had been driven in a windowless van from the small airport in

Tupelo. That much he knew. Turning off the two-lane highway he thought he had seen a military guard with a shotgun wave them through a cow gate. The outside of every building and most of the trees in the compound were splattered with paint. The grapelike remains of the casings lying on the ground indicated that the property had once been used for paint-ball war games. Now it was home to a secret CIA espionage camp.

"Okay. It's simple." The sergeant walked over to a sheep pen and selected a large sheep that had been busy feeding on freshly cut grass. The three of them walked back outside, the sheep happily keeping pace between the two men. "Be quick and be careful. What you don't want to do is slice your fingers off in the process."

He stopped and the sheep and Greer heeled obediently. "Watch how it's done. Sheep's just like a human—I promise you. I'll do it once, then it's up to you."

The sergeant knelt down to sheep level and Greer did, too. "It's important to do it in one motion. Element of surprise." The sheep held its head still, but moved its eyes from side to side looking at the two men. "You'll usually just get one chance, so make it long and clean, ear to ear. Try to use a sharp knife."

The sergeant grabbed the skin and fur at the back of the sheep's head and slit its throat in one fast movement. The animal spasmed, then fell to the ground, blood flowing out through the muscle and cartilage and fat and fur into the pine straw.

"Now *you* try," said the sergeant perkily, holding out the butt end of the knife for Greer.

Greer got another sheep. He tried not to look into its eyes.

"Use the whole blade edge," the sergeant advised as Greer moved his fingers around the sheep's skull.

Greer hesitated, then saw the sheep blink, and cut him clear through to the vertebrae, severing the head completely.

"Sharp knife," the sergeant said. "Drop the head."

Greer's arm was frozen and couldn't let go of the sheep's head.

"Just—let—go, kid."

The sheep assassination turned out to be the grisly highlight of the week at Camp Gilbert, the training facilities for teaching the how-to of espionage. Reed had told Greer that Camp Gilbert was where the

Agency conducted its crash course on espionage. Greer knew from his readings that Camp Perry outside Williamsburg, Virginia, was where the CIA usually sent its trainees. The training usually lasted for six months, but Reed said that he was getting pressured by the DCI to get on with the operation, so Greer's training had been put on a weeklong accelerated schedule. Reed promised to bring him back for the full course after his first assignment.

The last few weeks had been a blur. After clearing out from his Atlanta garage apartment and moving to Washington, Greer had set up shop in the Library of Congress across from the U.S. Capitol. Greer recalled the rush of standing on the white and gray inlaid marble floor in front of an oak door with a brass kickplate on the ground floor of the Thomas Jefferson Building. Room LJ-G07 was next to the Folklife Center Room in a hallway lined with marble walls the color of red velvet cake. Greer turned the key to the lock on the door, turned the brass knob, and entered into a life as a researcher in American government and politics. Reed had hung a framed Ph.D. with his name on the wall. On the book shelf, along with several dozen scholarly works on political science, there was a bound copy of a doctoral dissertation bearing his name on the spine. Reed had also set him up with an E-mail account, complete with a user profile already filled out with his new persona, listing his name, credentials, position, "snail-mail" address and his telephone number in his Library of Congress office. His status as Dr. Whitaker, Research Associate at the Library of Congress was posted on the Internet for all the world to see. The cover was solid, impenetrable. There was also a typed list of background readings waiting for him on his desk, mainly newspaper clippings and articles from academic journals with analyses of American foreign intelligence.

Greer was to meet with Reed every Monday at noon in the Smithsonian safe room. During their meeting prior to Greer's departure for spy camp, Reed quizzed him on his readings and filled him in on minutiae and gossip about key people in the Administration who worked on foreign intelligence matters. The question had crossed Greer's mind several times, but he had never been able to summon up the courage to ask: Why was he spending so much of his time studying the workings of American foreign intelligence policy and personalities? Greer had placed his trust in Reed. The first assignment would certainly be telling.

In the espionage camp, the instructors were all experts in their fields. Everyone wore olive drab or camouflage. No one wore any unit designation, just name badges—certainly pseudonyms—without rank insignia. Greer learned that the property had, indeed, been used for paint-ball war games at one time and the front served as an adequate cover story for men in uniforms coming and going.

Greer received one-on-one instruction during his stay. The emphasis in the classroom sessions was on intelligence-gathering techniques and how to protect a covert operation from being discovered. An audio expert taught him how to install hidden microphones and transmitters and how to tap a phone line and intercept cellular phone calls. There were gadgets of all kinds. The photography instructor brought a dozen different cameras, each with a specialized purpose, from photographing documents to long-range surveillance. Greer learned how to use the latest optical-fiber technology with a camcorder to surreptitiously tape embarrassing moments that could later be used for blackmail. The last technical area covered was secret writing, used to pass information back and forth without being detected. Greer absorbed everything his instructor had to say on microfilming and chemical writing systems. All of this was explained to Greer in a matter-of-fact manner, as if he were the new guy in the office being shown how to operate the photocopy machine.

On his last night at Camp Gilbert, Greer lay on his bed listening to the cicadas starting up in the trees. He wondered how the week of intensive readings at the Library of Congress and the crash course in espionage would tie in with his first assignment.

9 ❑ ❑ ❑ ❑

Randall Jenkins loped past Greer, who was seated in the National Security Council staff waiting room in the Old Executive Office Building. Jenkins wore uncharacteristically casual clothes for a Washington power player—a sport coat, slacks, worn Hush Puppies, and a tie in an unfashionable Windsor knot—but it seemed to fit in with what Greer knew of Jenkins' background as an academic. Jenkins was in his fifties, a little pudgy, and almost completely bald.

Greer had been thinking how things had been moving much faster than he had ever imagined they would. Upon Greer's return from espionage training, Reed had shown him the Executive Finding on White House stationery signed by the President himself.

Reed had filled him in. "Randall Jenkins—the President's college roommate, lifelong friend, and trusted adviser on matters of national security—is under investigation. We believe he's been compromised." Greer read along as Reed recited the particulars of the document. "With the Executive Finding, the President has authorized extraordinary measures not only to confirm the allegations, but to infiltrate the alleged spy ring and find the ultimate source of the intelligence operation. My unit has been given charge of the mission to execute the Finding. You will be the CIA case officer on the line." The Finding was marked TOP SECRET—EYES ONLY STEEPLECHASE. "Only people cleared for STEEPLECHASE know about the operation against the office of the National Security Adviser. I don't have to tell you that this is a highly extraordinary Finding," said Reed. "The CIA—not the FBI—has been ordered to investigate a U.S. citizen on American soil. You can see in paragraph D that the matter has been determined to be so sensitive that the operation required strict compartmentalization to avoid the possibility of compromising this and several highly classified CIA operations. Even the FBI can't be absolutely trusted to maintain the necessary level of secrecy. Very unusual."

Greer was musing about all that Reed had told him as Jenkins made it to his closed office door. He rubbed his bald spot and squinted through his bottle-glass lenses as though in pain.

"Isn't today the interview for the new assistant?" Jenkins asked the secretary sitting outside his door.

"No, sir," she replied, aware that Greer was listening. "Mr. Whitaker is here for his first day." She nodded in Greer's direction.

Jenkins squinted across the room at Greer.

"Oh, I see." Jenkins unlocked his office door and reached inside to flip on the light. "Have we got a folder on Mr. Whitaker, Miss Blevins?"

"Yes, sir, we do." She handed him a file from a pile on her desk.

"Okay, Mr. Whitaker, come on in," Jenkins said, disappearing into his office. Greer got up and looked to the secretary. She cheerfully urged him into Jenkins' office with a nod and a smile.

"Miss Blevins, have you shown Mr. Whitaker where to get the coffee?"

"Yes, sir."

"Fine, fine."

Greer entered the office and stood in front of Jenkins' desk. It must have been government issued furniture from the 1950s, as was the cracked leather high-back swivel chair with the stuffing coming out of the arms where it had rubbed against the desk for years. The desktop was as big as an aircraft carrier deck, but with none of the order or spit and polish. Through the clutter of paper Greer saw innumerable coffee-cup rings.

From his readings and Reed's briefings in the Smithsonian safe room, Greer knew Jenkins' background. Stanford-trained economist. Fellow at the Hoover Institution. Old friend and fraternity brother of the President's from college. Apparently not one of the White House insiders, though. It wasn't clear from Greer's reading if Jenkins had wanted his office situated with his staff at the Old Executive Office Building, or whether someone at the White House had simply assigned him there.

"Man's got to know where to get coffee and where to go pee," said Jenkins, more to himself than to Greer. "Sit down, Mr. Whitaker. Take your coat off."

"Thank you, sir."

Jenkins plopped down into his chair and pushed some papers aside on the desk, making room for Greer's file.

"Miss Blevins?" he called out.

The secretary walked briskly into the office with two other file folders.

"Morning intelligence summaries, sir." She laid the folders on the desk in the clearing and left the room.

"Well, that's real nice. Thank you, Miss Blevins." Jenkins looked directly at Greer for the first time. "Isn't it nice, Mr. Whitaker, that the nice young men and women at CIA have prepared a couple of nice summaries of yesterday's activities for us?"

Greer assumed it was a rhetorical question and didn't answer, but widened his eyes and smiled to show interest.

"It's nice to be nice to nice people, isn't it? See this?" Jenkins held out the two folders, one labeled National Intelligence Daily and the other labeled President's Daily Brief.

"I'm familiar with them but, of course, never had access to current ones in my research."

"Well, every night, bright young analysts in Langley sort through all the incoming cables from CIA stations all over the world and decide what they think is important, then write that down, then show their supervisors, who then makes some changes, then show it to one of the deputy directors, who makes some more changes, who then shows it to the liaison office, where someone takes a few things more out and editorializes and wordsmiths the night's activities and then it's sent here. Couple of dozen people get the NID. The best stuff, though, is in the PDB—only the President, Secretary of State, Secretary of Defense, Director of Central Intelligence, and myself get this."

Jenkins opened Greer's file and read.

"Checking your security clearance. That was going to be the end of our discussion if you hadn't been cleared yet." Jenkins thumped the page. "Says right here you're cleared for the highest level. Doctorate from Emory University . . . Dissertation: 'Filling the Dance Card: America's Search for Partners in the Post–Cold War Era.' Good title. Postdoctoral research associate with the Library of Congress . . . And now you come to us as a White House Fellow. Vice President was one when he was a young man about your age, you know."

Greer didn't really know. "Yes, I know."

Reed, as promised, had taken care of everything. So far, Greer was incredibly impressed with how seamlessly the CIA had moved him into this operation. Reed had somehow known that Jenkins had been looking for an assistant, someone he could train to be his right-hand man, someone with excellent academic qualifications. Reed had supplied the necessary credentials for Greer—a Ph.D. and a vita of impressive scholarly journal articles, which Greer had already committed to memory. Even before Greer had come to Washington for the polygraph and medical exams, Reed had put the paperwork into play to get Greer on the short list of White House Fellowship candidates, then made sure that the committee's selection included the brilliant candidate with the doctorate in political science. Greer's real degrees in political science and his readings at the Library of Congress had given him the confidence to fake it. Greer presented himself as a scholar.

"Hadn't expected you to start today. I sent over a request to the personnel office for an assistant months ago. Can't stand the dance of the interview process. I told them to send me the best. I assumed they'd forgotten about me."

In their last meeting in the safe room, Reed had explained that the White House had become suspicious of Jenkins soon after the President had taken office. Jenkins had been considered a bit of an oddball during the campaign, but once installed as the President's National Security Adviser, he had begun sending really off-the-wall issue papers and recommendations over to the White House. Reed said that Dwight Conrad, the White House Chief of Staff, had done a good job of intercepting Jenkins' communications before they got to the President. It was a very delicate situation, considering the personal relationship and the national security issues involved. But once briefed, the President had done the right thing and signed the Finding authorizing the investigation.

"You can call me Randall or Professor. Just don't call me Sir or Randy. That's what the late Mrs. Jenkins called me."

"Sure."

"Okay, let's make a phone call together."

Jenkins swiveled his chair around to the credenza behind his desk and punched the speaker button on the phone, the only thing remotely high-tech in the room. He adjusted the volume as the dial tone blared out. "Get the door." Greer leaned over his chair and pushed the door closed.

Jenkins punched another button and the phone speed-dialed a number. It rang only once.

"Gibbons," a man answered.

"Ben? This is Randall Jenkins. You're on the speakerphone. How are you, Ben?" Jenkins' voice was smooth.

"Up to my eyeballs, Randall. Briefing the Intelligence Committees up on the Hill later this week. What can I do for you?"

Greer straightened up in his chair. It was Ben Gibbons, Director of Central Intelligence, Reed's boss.

"Well, I've got someone here—a new man on staff we got through the White House Fellowship program—Greer Whitaker. Greer's cleared Top Secret, so we can talk."

"Hi, Greer."

"Hello," answered Greer. The DCI was playing it cool. Of course Gibbons would know Greer's name and the connection.

"Ben, you know you and I have from time to time had a discussion about the National Intelligence Daily and the President's Daily Brief. A lot of fine people spend a lot of time grinding these out every day. They're really very good reports for what their intended purpose is."

"Yes?"

"Well, the last time the National Security Council sat together formally, I asked that I start getting copies of the raw intelligence. If you will recall, the President approved it."

"With all due respect to the President, Randall, the President mumbled something when you brought it up."

"I seem to remember differently. I asked the President point-blank if the National Security Adviser could personally receive raw intelligence on a regular basis. He said yes."

"Randall, take me off the speakerphone." Gibbons was pissed.

Jenkins picked up the handset and pushed the button to deactivate the speaker feature. "Okay, Ben, what is it?" He listened and shook his head slowly side to side.

"Well," said Jenkins, "I've got the staff I need now. Greer is going to start going through the cables. Not everything, just select countries. We'll begin with . . . " He cut off mid-sentence.

"Ben, I understand. But as the National Security Adviser to the President, part of my job is to assess the quality of the intelligence we're getting in and advise the President objectively if I see any room for improvement." He stopped to listen again.

"No, no, no. I don't think it's *necessarily* you. It's the bureaucracy. It's like that everywhere in town. There are people with vested interests who might subconsciously put their own spin on the raw data to protect themselves, for *whatever* reason. Sometimes these analysts are too close to their own work. Nothing outright insidious, Ben. Just human nature." Jenkins paused to allow Gibbons to talk. He listened longer this time.

"Okay, Ben, that sounds fine. Greer's already got clearance. I'll courier you a copy this morning. Let's get back on the speakerphone. You can tell him." Jenkins pushed the button again.

"Greer," said Gibbons.

"Yes, sir?"

"I'd like you to call someone who works on my staff—Kate Mallotte. The two of you set up a meeting to work out the protocol on reviewing the raw intelligence—I assume it's the human sources reports from the stations you're really interested in, isn't it, Randall?"

"Primarily," answered Jenkins. "But it would be nice to take a look at the satellite and communications intercept stuff you get from the National Security Agency."

"Okay. So you two get together and hammer something out, then the four of us will sit down and take a look at it."

"By end of the week, Ben?" pushed Jenkins.

"Sorry. Got to be early next week, Randall. The Senate Intelligence Committee briefing is Friday."

"All right, Mr. Director. We'll be in touch." The DCI's line clicked off and Jenkins hung up.

"*Gibbons* monkey," Jenkins muttered.

"Pardon?"

"I said *Gibbons* monkey. Go to the National Zoo and see them eating lice off each other and playing with their assholes."

"Oh." Greer figured it was a reference to the DCI.

Jenkins swiveled his chair to face Greer. "Get your butt over to see Kate Mallotte immediately to set up that meeting."

What a knockout. An absolute knockout.

Greer allowed the politically incorrect thoughts to percolate as he crossed the wide reception area at CIA headquarters at Langley. He had spotted her even as he was signing in at the front desk.

He knew instinctively which one was Kate Mallotte. Poised perfectly on the edge of the couch, legs crossed like a Vargas girl in a tailored short dark skirt with matching jacket. Late twenties, early thirties. Shoulder-length blond hair. *Very* pretty face. Healthy glow, but not burned or brown. Thin. She could easily have been the new news co-anchor in any major media city who had just been hired from some snowy market in the Midwest. She was gorgeous.

A strange mix of emotions washed over him as he walked across the lobby over the great seal of the CIA on the floor. Here he was back at Langley for the first time since the interview with Reed a month ago in late August. He was a CIA case officer and hadn't talked to another CIA person other than Reed in all that time since he began working under deep cover for the CIA. Now that he was finally meeting with a fellow officer, he couldn't even so much as ask for a little office gossip. He had a powerful sense of affiliation with the people he saw around him and wanted to let them know that he was one of them, but, of course, he couldn't. One of the toughest parts of being a CIA case officer was not being able to share the excitement, Greer told himself.

He looked around casually to see if Reed was lording over the scene anywhere nearby. He didn't see him, but felt he must be watching.

As he approached her the smell of her perfume intensified. It was musky, attention-getting, but not overwhelming. She was taking notes in a planner with an expensive pen. Professional. Obviously career-minded.

She looked up at the ceiling in thought, then cocked her head toward the door and saw him coming. She capped her pen and rose with a warm smile to shake his hand.

"Hi, I'm Kate Mallotte. I recognized you from your picture in the security clearance file that Mr. Jenkins sent over this morning."

Greer shook her hand. It was just right: warm, soft, but firm.

"Nice to meet you," he said. He could tell she was all business.

"Let's go upstairs to take a look at what came in this morning." She led him back to the reception desk, signed him in as a guest, and handed him a visitor's pass to clip onto his suit coat. They silently shared an elevator up one floor.

"Here we go," she said, leading Greer down a hall to a conference room. "Make yourself comfortable. I'll be right back with the reports."

Greer watched her leave the room.

Reed had been on the mark again. Reed had told Greer that if Jenkins continued to push the White House and the CIA, Kate Mallotte would somehow end up being involved. Reed had briefed him. "Ivy League education. Russian language major at Columbia. Recruited out of the Kennedy Center for Advanced Government Studies at Harvard where she got her master's degree. Came into the CIA career officer training program for field officers. Highest marks in her class. Spent three years at the Moscow station where she ran the hell out of her agents. The Russians were tripping over themselves to try to meet her. Ben Gibbons had taken a tour of the major CIA stations just after he was confirmed DCI and met her on his Russian stop. He had been very impressed with her. Everyone is. He asked her shortly afterward to come back to work directly for him as a special assistant at Langley headquarters. She's obviously being groomed for something big. Not cleared for STEEPLECHASE, however. She knows nothing about you or your position with the Agency. And it needs to stay that way."

She returned with a box of file folders.

"The Director said that you wanted to review the daily intelligence that comes in from the field. I thought I'd show you what it looks like in its raw form."

Greer assumed Gibbons had her on his staff to handle headaches like Jenkins and himself. Push it down to a junior officer who'll make it go away.

"These are separated by desk," she began, wedging her hand into the box, pinching a bunch of files together. "This box happens to represent the Far East desk." She pulled one of the folders out and opened it on the table. "Each file contains a computer printout of the cables sent by our station in that country during the last twenty-four-hour period. Unless there's a special situation going on, we usually don't get reports on a daily basis." She seemed to be choosing her words carefully. "The station chief will send a report at the end of every week."

"In a hot region we get a fairly significant amount of information every day. As you can see, the names of all our agents are coded to protect our sources from compromise." She scanned the page with her index finger. "Only the field officer managing the agent and his immediate supervisor know the true identity of the person. In addition to the agents who provide the raw human intelligence, the stations report on ongoing covert operations. These also are coded. What did you and Mr. Jenkins have in mind in reviewing the reports?" she asked carefully.

Greer figured it was a question Gibbons had told her to ask. "All I know at this point is that he wants to look at the raw intelligence. We really haven't had a chance to discuss what he wants to do with it."

"Well," she said, "it's bad security practice to have this level of detail from so many different countries in one place. The Director wanted me to remind you and Mr. Jenkins of that. Massing it together like that would be, in effect, a major breach of the compartmentalization concept."

"I understand, but we've got to work *something* out. Jenkins said the President gave his personal approval of his getting to review the raw data behind the daily intelligence summaries coming out of Langley. I think both your boss and mine are counting on us to find a workable solution that we can both live with."

Greer felt funny about pushing hard to get some of most sensitive information the government had for a man who had been fingered as a traitor to his country. He wondered if Kate was in the loop on that, but Reed had said she wasn't. What would Reed say when he found out what Jenkins had him doing? At the same time, gaining the confidence of Jenkins by doing his bidding was the only way to get close enough to him to find out exactly what he was up to.

"What I suggest is that you come to our offices and review the materials here in a secure environment. In fact, I insist on it. We can get you whatever you want, and if you have any questions, I will arrange for you to meet with someone who can give you more background from the operational country desk."

"So, basically, you're agreeing to unlimited access to the raw intelligence?"

"Yes, the Director has agreed to that, but nothing can leave this room."

Greer winced. "Jenkins is going to want to see this stuff for himself. How about copies?"

"The Director was *very* specific on that point. Nothing leaves the building. He either can come himself or you can take notes back to him."

Greer took a moment to think. He tilted his head toward a mirrored window at the end of the room that caught his eye. What was that? he thought. A two-way mirror? He hadn't noticed it as he came in with Kate. Was he being watched from the other side? Kate didn't know it, but at that instant Greer caught her reflection as she gave him a quick once-over. It was the unmistakable slight lifting of her chin and movement of her eyes in one fast up-and-down motion. For the briefest moment her eyes narrowed and a smile formed on her lips.

Greer started to turn his head back to address her and she just as quickly shifted her eyes back to the file box in front of her. Curious, he thought.

The Agency was giving Jenkins what he had asked for, but they weren't going to make it easy for him. He didn't want to push any harder now. *She* certainly wasn't any pushover.

"Let me talk to Jenkins and get back to you," he said.

Kate Mallotte sat back in her chair, crossed her legs, put her chin in her hand and gave him a smile with eyes that locked on to his.

"Okay," she said, signaling it was his move.

This could get to be interesting, he thought.

Greer was relating to Jenkins the nuances of his meeting the previous day with Kate Mallotte.

"Well, that's fine," Jenkins continued. "If Mohammed won't go to the mountain, then the mountain will just have to go to Mohammed." Jenkins sank back into his chair and jammed one hand into the top of his Sansabelts. "Here's what we do . . . Miss Blevins! Could we see you for just a moment?"

The secretary entered with a notepad and gave Greer a sympathetic smile.

"Miss Blevins, let's get this young man here a laptop computer. See if we can't get one requisitioned by this afternoon." She noted the request and left the office, pulling the door closed behind her.

Jenkins grinned crookedly at Greer and screwed his face up on the left side. "That's just the very point I've been trying to make for months!" he said, using up most of the space in front of him with his waving arms. "No one *is* looking at the raw intelligence across a broad range of geographies. They might be missing some important linkage in the data, something going on that cuts across geopolitical borders. Details that get lost in the National Intelligence Daily and I'm sure in the other internal reports circulating at CIA."

"What about compartmentalization of the work to limit knowledge on a need-to-know basis? That *does* seem consistent with what I know about good security practices."

"In my humble—though learned—opinion"— Jenkins paused to lick his upper and lower lips with one circular motion—"it's *guano* when carried out to extremes like they're doing." The circular slick around his mouth looked like the trail a slug might have left. Greer was distracted. "You know, I'm amazed at the general attitude at Langley," Jenkins continued. "Lots of turf protecting going on, I imagine. Most of the analysts at CIA are very bright. Most of them have graduate degrees. I guess what they lack is a big-picture man over there."

"And Gibbons isn't it?"

"Gibbons *ain't* it." Greer watched Jenkins look around the room as if following a gnat through the air.

"Is there anything specific we're looking for?" asked Greer.

Jenkins turned his attention back to Greer. "What makes you ask that?" He seemed a little defensive.

"I just thought that you might have had something in mind. That's a lot of information to wade through."

Jenkins templed his fingers and his face took on the look of a wizened old Chinaman. "Has someone said anything to you to make you think I might have something specific in mind?"

Greer felt a satisfying rush of adrenaline as he realized the game now had finally begun.

"No, not at all. It's just that there's so much resistance at CIA and you have been so determined to get the raw intelligence . . ."

Jenkins said, "You're very perceptive." He leaned forward. "*Just a theory,*" he almost whispered.

Greer waited for further enlightenment. None came. "What would that be?"

Jenkins sat back in his swivel chair and folded his arms across his chest. "Can't say."

All Greer could do was nod.

"I've got a theory. A hypothesis. Your job is to collect the data that will help me prove that theory. *I* know I'm right. They think I'm wrong. They haven't wanted to give me access to the hard facts that will prove my case. Believe you me, they know what I'm working on. So does the White House."

"So what's my role?"

"Take your laptop over to Langley. Get the daily cables for Europe and the Far East. Key in the data—summarize everything you see. I want to see covert operations, human intelligence gathering, and economic assessments. Keep doing it—every day—until I tell you it's time to stop. Save yourself a trip back over here and modem me the data at the end of the day on a secure phone line. I'll also get you a scrambler for the computer. Keep in touch. Do you already have a government E-mail account?"

"Through the Library of Congress."

"That will do. Send me an update at the end of the day. Nothing classified. Just let me know that you've sent something over, and I'll send you a message back confirming that I got it the night before. The secretary will send you an E-mail message if we need to meet. Check your mail daily."

Greer remembered his upcoming weekly debriefing meeting with

Reed and thought he would try to elicit some indication as to what Jenkins was up to. Reed would be expecting hard information. "If I knew what the theory was, I might be able to help out a little more, don't you think?"

"*Maggots,* Greer."

"Pardon me?"

"Maggots." Jenkins let the word hang for a few seconds. "If I told you, you'd focus on the maggots, not the cause of death." He explained: "When you first walk up to that dead dog lying on the side of the road, you tend to be intrigued not by death itself, but the life that's there, the thousands of maggots that have moved in. Get the data and we can put together a nice little dog-and-pony show for the White House on the cause of death of certain parts of our intelligence service. *And,* what impact that's having on America's interests. We don't want to get up there and just show slides of maggots rippling in a roadkill's belly. See?"

"Got it."

"No way. Forget it."

Kate was adamant. She watched as Greer was unzipping the laptop computer case. He set it on the conference table and pulled out an assortment of cords.

Greer ignored her. "Take notes, of course," Greer said merrily, inserting the mouse cord. "You didn't think I'd be copying things over with legal pads and a number two pencil, did you? We'd be here until midnight every day if I did that. As it is, we'll be here way past dinnertime." Greer plugged the power cord into the computer and held up the business end. "Where's an outlet?"

Kate closed up the top of the file box with the day's raw intelligence reports and pulled the telephone over to her. She dialed, avoiding looking at Greer who was searching for an AC outlet.

"Ben," she said, "I'm sorry to bother you with this. Greer Whitaker —you remember, from Mr. Jenkins' office—is here to start going through the daily intelligence reports. The problem is that he brought a portable computer with him. I thought I'd better confirm with you whether that was part of the agreement."

She listened. Greer tried to interrupt her with a whisper: "Outlet?" She turned her back on him.

"Thank you," she said. "I'll let him know." She hung up and turned to address Greer who was by now out of sight under the conference room table.

"Greer?"

"Down here. I still can't find an outlet."

Greer was, indeed, searching for an outlet, but instead found only her long, shapely legs down below.

"There won't be any need for an outlet," she said. He popped his head up. "The Director said that a computer is totally out of the question."

Greer stood up and faced Kate. "What's the problem?" he asked seriously.

"The *problem* is that the Director agreed Jenkins could review the materials, not copy specific information."

"Oh, I don't know about that. I mean, what's the point of going through all this if we can't take away any specifics? You said yourself that none of the materials could leave the room. We interpreted that as meaning none of the documents or copies of the actual documents. This is the first I've heard about not being able to take notes."

"I'm sorry." The way she said it told Greer she wasn't going to budge. She was doing a good job of standing her ground.

"Well," said Greer, "is there anything—any reason—I can tell Jenkins about why Gibbons won't let me use a computer? He's going to want to know."

"The Director doesn't mind Mr. Jenkins looking at the materials to get a broad impression and to understand in general what comes in. What he insists you *can't* do is take highly sensitive information away to use for some unspecified, unauthorized purpose."

"But the President authorized it."

"I suggest you have Mr. Jenkins take it up with the President, then. Better pack it up."

Greer picked up the phone receiver and looked Kate in the eye. "What's the Director's extension?"

Kate stared back. "You're not going over my head on this."

Greer punched zero and spoke into the phone. "DCI's office, please." Greer looked confidently out the window over the trees.

Kate's finger slammed down the button on the phone, cutting Greer off. "I just *told* you not to call Ben!"

"Look," he said calmly, "you know Jenkins is going to throw a fit if he thinks the Agency is withholding information. He'll just go to the President directly. All it will do is end up embarrassing the Director."

Kate hated like hell to give in and Greer knew it. He gave her another moment. "Well?" he asked.

"I'll be back," she said, turning quickly and leaving the room.

Five minutes later, she returned.

"The electrical outlet is behind the credenza," she said. She clearly wasn't happy about it.

Kate went to the side of the room and pulled the corner of the furniture out. Greer handed her the end of the computer cord and she plugged it in. The computer came to life on the conference table.

"Thanks," said Greer. He pushed a blank diskette into the computer. "You know, we'd better find a way to get along. It's going to make for a lot of long days if we keep this up."

Greer looked at the far end of the room. He saw his reflection in the mirror wall.

"By the way," he said, "what's the deal with that?"

Kate saw he meant the mirror. "This is one of the conference rooms where people from outside the Agency come to meet. Obviously, it's a two-way mirror."

"Are we being watched?"

Kate walked over to the mirror, cupped her hands over the glass and looked inside. "I don't think so. But I don't know for sure. It's out of my hands."

"Don't your own people trust you?"

"Counterintelligence set it up. They don't trust anyone." She was still mad and was working hard to conceal her anger.

Greer needed to smooth things out. "Buy you lunch?" He flashed her an award-winning smile.

Kate took a deep breath and relaxed a bit. Greer saw that her perfect hair had gone a bit loose. Her face was starting to glisten and there was just the slightest whiff of saltiness to her perfume now. A crimson flush was rising up her throat from out of her white silk blouse. Greer thought she looked like a lioness in heat.

"Okay," she finally relented.

10 ❑   ❑   ❑   ❑

Having had a week to think about it, Greer decided that if there was even the slightest chance he'd fall in love with another woman, it would be Kate Mallotte.

It was seven o'clock Friday morning in the Langley conference room on the second floor and Greer was alone. He and Kate had worked together for ten straight days through the previous weekend. For security reasons the rule was, if Greer was reviewing classified material, Kate had to be there as well. Jenkins had insisted that Greer be at CIA headquarters every day to enter overseas traffic and Kate had had no choice but to be there in the same room, twelve, sometimes fourteen, hours a day. Kate had transferred all her calls into the conference room and set up shop to handle the day-to-day business of managing her own work.

She hadn't yet arrived with the previous night's cables. Greer set up his laptop computer and waited. The conference table at which they worked now mirrored the relationship that had evolved between them. Kate now sat across from him, rather than a raised-voice length away at opposite ends as when they had first started working together. She had taken to heart his pleas for cooperation. They had begun exchanging small courtesies. They took turns getting coffee for each other from the pot on the credenza. Kate brought in bagels for the two of them in the morning and Greer ordered dinner in at night as they worked late. The cleaning woman who came in at night gave them knowing looks. Did she know something he didn't?

It occurred to Greer that Kate might well be the love that had been missing in his life as he had clawed his way up the political ladder. He had dated many beautiful women—there were always interesting women of all ages and sexual appetites hanging around the campaigns, the political groupies who could be found stalking any candidate. There were plenty of women attracted to the heady mix of power, money, and fame—a powerful aphrodisiac, as Greer had found out. But there was never enough time to develop a long-term love interest.

Kate came into the conference room, and as Greer saw her for the first time that morning, he felt a twinge of excitement. It would seem the most natural thing in the world to give her a good-morning kiss as he handed her a cup of coffee. She smiled at him, pushing her hair behind her ear, exposing a delicious route to her throat by way of her long neck, and holding his eye ever so much longer than someone really should if she weren't interested in him.

"Morning," she said.

"Morning." Damn, she's beautiful, he thought.

Greer tilted the display on his computer to get rid of the glare from the overhead lights. He watched Kate unpack her briefcase and imagined what she must have been like as a field operative in Moscow. He wondered: This is the hardened CIA case officer who Reed had told me about? The woman who had recruited Soviet agents that penetrated the inner sanctum of the Politburo? Actually, he could see it. She'd lure them in with her looks, hold them with her charm, then she'd buy them or blackmail them into doing her bidding. Who could say no to Kate Mallotte?

Greer clicked the mouse button, and the screen filled with a template ready for the day's input.

The job was fast becoming mundane. It was interesting at first, but quickly became prosaic after he saw the same kind of information over and over again: a new labor leader in a South American country is gaining influence among urban workers; a sex scandal involving a back-bencher in Parliament will become public within a week in the British press; an African chieftain is expected to lead a new assault against a rival tribe, disrupting elections. The kind of stuff that eventually shows up in the international section of a large city's newspaper. The main difference was that the CIA seemed to be getting advance notice most of the time—essentially, doing its job of forecasting events. Greer typed in all the information, then modemed it over to Jenkins' office at the end of the day.

After yet another lunch in the conference room brought up from the cafeteria, Greer stretched and watched Kate as she worked out a memo on a legal pad. They were both relaxed.

"You never mentioned," he said, "about whether you were seeing anyone."

Kate continued scribbling. Not looking up, she answered: "It's a kind of Catch-22. I'm here all day, most weekends, even before you started coming over. The only people I see are in the Agency. But it's bad politics to date anyone in the company. So I don't."

Greer casually pulled the phone on the table over to himself. Kate seemed oblivious as he reached back and got the Yellow Pages from the credenza.

"So what's your favorite restaurant in the city?" he asked. He picked up the receiver and flipped to the restaurant section of the phone book with his other hand.

She finally looked up and shrugged. "The Red Sage. Why?"

Greer found the listing and dialed. He talked as he listened to the phone ring. "Eight o'clock okay?"

Kate finally capped her pen. She looked at him with a slight frown.

"I'm not Agency," he said. It just came out. It felt funny saying it, starting out a relationship with a lie.

Kate nodded thoughtfully, then allowed him a little smile. "So this is the way it starts?" she asked.

"Just like that."

Greer leaned against the copper-and-tile bar at the Red Sage in downtown Washington, waiting for Kate, who had gone by her townhouse before dinner. He had managed finally to reserve a booth upstairs in the Chili Bar. He took a sip from the tumbler of the Herradura Anejo tequila that the bartender had just set down in front of him. He held it in his mouth a moment, then swallowed slowly. It went down as smoothly as a fine single-malt scotch whiskey. He saw Kate come in the front door, a little wind-blown. The maître d' greeted her and pointed to him at the bar. He held his drink up in a greeting.

Greer helped her off with her coat and they took a booth next to the window overlooking Fourteenth Street. Outside the window the store fronts were just lighting up for the evening. Couples were walking by briskly in animated conversation. It was only early October, but the first real cold front of the season had just blown in.

Kate looked beautiful—more beautiful than any woman Greer had ever known. It wasn't just her physical beauty—her figure, her face, her blond hair pushed behind one ear—it was also the way she carried herself. She was confident, yet sensuous, and she had this way of scanning his face before riveting him with her gray-blue eyes. It was—he knew—partly the knowledge of her as the hard-driving professional woman who had ruled the streets of Moscow as a spy runner, the same woman whose eyes were now softening, thanking him without her having to say a word, now smiling at him. Her eyes thanking him for what? For treating her the way she deserved to be treated? How long had it been since she had been regarded as not just an ambitious Agency case officer, but as a woman who might have tired of talking about nothing but operations and agents?

"Hi," said Greer. He was already feeling the warmth of the tequila settle into his chest.

Kate was still slightly out of breath. She inhaled deeply and smiled at him. "Hi."

"I love this place," said Greer, looking around the room. "Good suggestion." The theme was nouveau Southwestern. Bonnie Raitt was playing on the sound system.

The waitress took their orders and they both fell into the groove of the music, nudged along by the drinks.

Kate had already set the ground rules: no office talk. That was fine with Greer. Tonight, his mind was on anything but Bob Reed, or Randall Jenkins, or entering CIA station traffic into the computer. Beyond that, Kate was letting Greer set the tone. It was a rickety bridge over a deep chasm. Greer found himself wanting to trade the intimacies of his life for a deeper knowledge of the woman he was sure he was falling in love with. But he had nothing to offer but lies—lies provided by the fake résumé he was sworn to uphold.

". . . So when my Ph.D. was published I applied for the Presidential Fellowship, and to make a long story short, that's how I ended up in Washington working for the National Security Council."

Kate was listening quietly, hanging onto every word he said. She seemed genuinely fascinated with his stories, happy to let him talk about himself. When he finished, she nodded and smiled and stayed silent. He knew he was talking too much. He babbled some more, part excitement over being there with Kate, part tequila hitting bottom. He squirmed, feeling a little as he did when the Agency psychiatrist was probing him, letting him fill the awkward silence between them. Finally, he shut up.

"And when you were working on your dissertation, did you travel overseas very often for research?" she asked.

The question threw Greer. "Not very." He was stuck. He didn't know the answer he should give. Was he the Greer Whitaker of his true past or the Greer Whitaker as served up by Bob Reed? "Why is it you seem to know a lot more about me than I do about you?" he asked.

"I read your file sent over by Jenkins' office for security clearance. If you had an unpaid library fine, I'd know it." She was a little smug, happy to have something on him.

Greer panicked for an instant. He had seen the file on himself that Reed had concocted before it was sent to Jenkins. He had memorized it, recited it back to Reed over and over again. It was the same information that had been sent to Langley to establish his bona fides for Top Secret security clearance. But had the Agency done any further checking into his past beyond what had been provided to them? Did some clerk in counterintelligence order up a record of his international travel records from the U.S. Immigration computerized data bank? If he answered her truthfully, there was just the one trip to Germany and back. But what traveling had Greer the researcher done? How deep did his cover really go?

"It seems sort of unfair," he said.

"So, what is it you want to know about me?"

"Everything."

Here's an opening, thought Greer. Kate had more wine and Greer stayed with the tequila. Not bad for a Friday night in Washington, D.C., he told himself, as he sat there as a CIA officer with the beautiful Kate Mallotte across the table.

Greer said, "I thought it would be nice if we could spend more time out of the office together. What would you think about that?"

She looked at him as if trying to make up her mind. Greer waited as long as he could, then decided to help her with her decision.

"We could go away for a weekend," he said. "Take me for a test drive. No obligations."

She was amused. But: "That would be problematic, don't you think?"

"How do you mean?"

"Professionally."

"Ah, the bosses. *You're* a professional in the area of covert operations. I'm sure we could figure something out. Assuming, of course, you'd have an interest in pursuing something like that."

She said after some thought, "Ben Gibbons would send me on the next plane to some god-awful CIA station if he ever found out I was dating you."

"You let Ben Gibbons decide who you go out with?"

"My orders were to baby-sit you, not sleep with you, dear." She was quick.

"Of course, I have the same problem, from Jenkins' point of view. The last thing he would want is for me to get cozy with someone on Ben Gibbons' staff." Actually, Greer was thinking more of what Reed would think. "Discretion is the key."

They shared an order of rhubarb and ginger ice cream and finished up with a second cup of coffee after the meal. They were both just a little drunk now.

Greer felt hopeful. Kate had left the door open; she hadn't said no. He motioned to her with his forefinger to lean in across the table. He put his mouth to her ear and whispered. "I've never bedded a spy before."

She pulled back with a slight swagger of the head and a smile that told him that she couldn't make the same claim. "God, you're smooth," she said with a twinkle in her eye.

"Well?"

"Our own little covert operation?"

"Nobody else needs to know," Greer said. "Neither of us is going to jeopardize a career by openly flaunting a relationship and making people on both sides mad. So where do we go from here?"

She was thinking again. Staring at him. Then she put the tip of her middle finger into her mouth, pulling it out slowly. It glistened wet in the light of the candle on the table. She held the stem of her wineglass steady with the other hand as she put the finger on the rim and started to circle it with light pressure. Ripples formed on the surface of the wine and the glass began to sing. Greer could hear the whisper of silk as she crossed and uncrossed her legs under the table.

"We should go," she said.

They walked to the Old Executive Office Building where Greer had got them both passes to park. It was dark by then and the lights were all on inside the White House.

Greer looked around the dark parking lot. Jenkins' car was still there.

Greer felt the full effect of the tequila buzz. It had lowered his inhibitions just enough so that he had let the thought of trying to kiss Kate cross his mind. Then the left side of his brain regained control.

Then the thought came roaring back up his spine and he had to use every bit of self-control he had to be gentle as he pulled Kate against him by her shoulders. She pressed the front of her legs against his. He leaned back onto his car, tipping her weight against him, and kissed her softly—once on the lips and once on her throat. He pulled back and looked at her. Her eyes circled his own face, coming to rest on his lips, then flicking up to his eyes, pleading for more than Greer ever thought she knew to ask. He kissed her again—softly once on the lips—then a long, deep kiss as he slid his arms down her side and pulled her hips into his as she put her arms around his neck. Their movement tripped the motion detectors high above, starting the transformers humming and the sterile white of mercury vapor parking lot lights sputtered on all around them, one canceling the shadows of the other. It was as bright as a prison yard.

Kate pulled back. "Good answer," she said.

Greer was still carnally predisposed. "I don't suppose you'd like me to follow you home, would you?"

Kate never took her eyes off his.

"Greer," she said, "not yet." She leaned in and gave him another long, full-mouthed kiss. She squeezed his shoulder and backed off. "Gives you something to think about while we're sitting together in the conference room all day, doesn't it?"

So this was the way she did it, thought Greer. All those agents in Moscow. Hooked 'em hard, then gave them some line to play with before she reeled them in. Greer would play. She wanted him to work for it. It would be worth it, he decided.

She turned and Greer followed her back to her car. She backed out of the space and gave him a quick look and a wave as she drove off.

Greer looked up at Jenkins' window in the Old Executive Office Building and saw a single light on. He could see the cathode ray glow of the computer screen on the ceiling.

Greer checked his watch: almost ten-thirty. Jenkins was still at work on something. Greer vowed he would find out what it was.

11 ❏   ❏   ❏   ❏

"What's this?" Greer asked. It was the middle of the following week.

"What's what?" Kate answered, looking up from her work.

"In the cable from the Paris station. It references a source named REDWING and an intelligence operation against the United States. REDWING says that it's being run by an ally. I've never seen anything like this before."

"Hold on," said Kate as she walked around the table to look over Greer's shoulder.

"You know anything about this?" Greer asked.

Kate read the cable. "I'm not familiar with it, so I couldn't say."

"Could you get someone from upstairs to give me some background on this?"

"Yeah, we saw it." Greer watched the CIA officer from the Western Europe desk tip back his Styrofoam cup and tap out some crushed cafeteria ice with his middle finger. One odd-looking guy, thought Greer. Short-sleeved shirt and a crew cut. He chewed loudly. "We get reports like that from time to time. I'm sure there's nothing to it, but we always routinely follow up on such things. REDWING is usually a very reliable source."

"Who's REDWING?" asked Greer.

"Someone in European society. We haven't actually been running REDWING as an agent. REDWING comes to us every now and then with information about European politicians and government officials."

"Allies?" Greer asked.

"Yes," answered the analyst, tight-lipped. "Mainly."

Kate interrupted: "You know, of course, that we have intelligence sources in friendly countries as well as in hostile ones. Everyone does it."

Greer thought about that for a moment. "Thanks," said Greer. "I'll be interested to see if there's anything else from this source on the subject."

The analyst held the base of the empty cup up close to his face with his fingertips, examining it as he twirled it around. "So will we," he said.

12 ❏ ❏ ❏ ❏

Kate had been packing up her things late on Friday afternoon, stuffing files into her briefcase, when Greer had the idea. She had already said good-bye, but he followed her into the hallway. He was still wary of the mirrored window in the conference room.

He caught up with her and said, "Just a drive in the country. A picnic. No spooks for miles around."

"Give me one good reason I should spend my Saturday morning tooling around with you in the countryside rather than working?"

"Fun, food, and fabulous company for a day in the Blue Ridge Mountains—away from all this for a few hours?"

"All right, all right."

He had worn her down, after asking her out all week.

She sighed and lifted her briefcase, demonstrating the heft of the paperwork for Greer.

He was unmoved by the display. "Look, Kate. You and I've been grinding away here for weeks. We could both use a break. Whatever that is, it can wait until Monday," Greer said.

"Monday?"

"I'll pick you up at eight o'clock tomorrow morning. Pack for overnight. Bring a sweater—the night air in the mountains is getting cool."

Kate sat in the front seat of Greer's car. The windows were down and the smells of early fall filled the car. The sky was blue enough to punch a hole through. Greer whistled through his teeth, keeping a close eye on the signs going south along Highway 29.

Kate turned in her seat. "Monticello, huh?"

"I remember you told me one of your passions was architecture. It seemed like a nice drive."

"I haven't been there in years. I *love* Monticello."

They arrived in Charlottesville by ten-thirty, had coffee in town, then drove the remaining three miles to the Thomas Jefferson estate. They toured the gardens and mansion, ending up under the rotunda.

"It's still early," Greer said. "Why don't we drive back into town?"

They spent the afternoon in Charlottesville, walking in and out of shops along the cobbled pedestrian mall, finally stopping at an outdoor café for a glass of wine late in the day. They watched the university students and other day tourists stroll by. They had been talking for over an hour about everything but work.

Greer took her hand. "Kate, I know we've only known each other for less than three weeks. I'm a little surprised at myself. Getting this —*involved* so quickly."

Kate squeezed his hand. "I know. I feel the same way. This isn't the way it usually happens with me, either."

"Then you wouldn't object if we were to drive on up into the Blue Ridge Mountains to a charming Revolutionary War–era inn to have dinner and spend the night?"

Kate gave him a kiss. "That sounds just about perfect," she said.

It was already dark by the time they arrived at the inn. The proprietor gave Greer a candle to climb the stairs with. Greer opened the door to their room, which was decorated with period reproduction furniture. Kate slipped from his arm and took the candle, placing it on the bedside table.

She turned back the covers on the bed and Greer hugged her from behind. She turned and kissed him.

"Dinner can wait," she said, pulling him onto the bed.

Naked in the four-poster canopied bed, Kate lifted herself on top of Greer, the quilt falling from her shoulders. Greer used his arms to hold her back as she stretched backward, the upper portion of her body over his legs, tilting her face up toward the canopy, grabbing the wooden posts on either side. He lifted himself up and took her breasts into his mouth.

"Greer!" She was speaking his name to the canopy above, her head thrashing and her hair whipping from side to side. The two of them raced toward the finish. Greer directed the energy in her hips with his hands to the final rapid series of thrusts. She let out a muffled cry heard by no one but the two lovers in their dark room.

"I love you," he said softly, and couldn't believe these words had actually come out of his mouth.

She responded by nuzzling his bare chest. There was no telling what time it was; the candle had burned low and it was too dark to see his watch.

She sat up. "I'm hungry."

Covered in nothing more than the blanket, Greer bent over the rucksack on the floor. From the light of the single candle, he opened the bag and piled things onto the bed. Kate leaned over and watched.

He called off: "Loaf of French bread, smoked turkey breast, brown mustard, a pepper mill, coffee beans, battery-operated coffee grinder, Lebanese cheese cake, persimmons, Bosc pears, navel oranges, and two bottles of Perrier-Jouët champagne, still packed in ice, still steely cold. Could you get some glasses from over there?"

Kate asked, "You brought this for the picnic tomorrow?"

"We'll find something on the road."

Kate set out glasses, flatware, and plates. Greer threw off his blanket and pulled a box of votive candles from the bag. He felt Kate's eyes watching his upright nude form as he set the candles out all around the room—in high places and low—then as he went back to light them, walking as a naked acolyte from altar to altar.

By the time he was finished, Kate had made a feast on the bed. She wrapped his blanket around him from behind and kissed him. They sat cross-legged on the bed with quilts pulled around themselves, set at the center of a flickering universe of their own making.

They were eating the fruit now. "Tell me about the men in your life," Greer said.

Kate sucked the pulp off a persimmon seed. "They're all Russian, all dead," she said.

"I don't mean agents, I mean lovers."

"I mean lovers," she answered seriously.

Greer poured from the second bottle of champagne. "Your agents were your lovers?"

"Other way around. I turned my lovers into agents. The problem was, I didn't know I loved them until after they were gone."

Greer imagined Kate again in Moscow, sitting in the backseat of a chauffeured Volga with a Party official on a snowy night. The car sped through the streets, a law unto its own, running stoplights and ignoring pedestrians, turning a sharp corner. The force of the move left Kate in the lap of a Russian in a bad suit.

"You're being coy."

"It's my job."

"I'm serious."

"I am, too."

"I didn't know that CIA field officers dated foreigners."

"Agent recruitment and management is an intensely human activity. You end up spending hours alone in a safe house with someone. Sometimes things happen. Sometimes they don't. I never went to bed with any of my agents. Where would the incentive be for them to meet me over and over again, each time thinking this might be the night that they'd get lucky?"

"I think I understand."

"But that doesn't mean I didn't get attached. They were humans. I'm a human. Feelings develop over time. You can see that, can't you?"

"Yes."

"Anyone could. But that's not allowed. Not at the Agency. We're taught that if you get too close to your agents, you lose leverage. You lose leverage and you lose control. That's when trouble starts. That's when you start making mistakes. Or your agent starts making mistakes. Things get sloppy. People disappear. People die."

Greer didn't have anything to say to that. It struck him that he was listening to the confessions of a veteran spy runner. Someone who had been in the field and done all the things he still dreamed about doing himself.

Kate spoke again: "If I'm being honest with myself, I have to admit that I did get too close to my agents. I crossed the line. I cared about them too much. . . ."

Greer saw moisture gathering in the corners of her eyes and put his arm around her, pulling her in. He felt sorry for her, for the loss she must have felt. For something she couldn't say any more about. For the feeling that she had lost control of the situation, putting herself and her agents at risk. All she did was make the mistake of being too human, caring too much, he thought. He wanted to hold her forever.

Kate wiped away a tear and looked straight into his eyes. "It's not been easy. The rumors, the jokes. Everyone in Moscow assumed I was screwing Russians to get my agent recruitment count up. I wasn't. Everyone at the Agency assumed I was sleeping with Ben Gibbons to get my current job. I didn't have to. But it doesn't matter. Especially in this line of work, I know that the perception is the reality, so I go with it. I use it to my advantage when I can. The problem's been that I'm considered a user. That's okay in the field, but it's just dirty office politics at Langley. I'm not really close to anyone, haven't been for a while, male or female. The men are afraid of me and my closeness with Ben and the women don't trust me. And to tell you the truth, I don't trust any of them. From the moment I wake up until moment I go to sleep at night, I feel like I've got to posture. I'm either a bitch or Ben Gibbons' slut."

"I had no idea."

"Of course not. You don't talk to people at Langley. It's hard. I don't have anyone to talk to, anyone I can let my hair down with. I'm always on guard. I'm always suspicious of everyone else and they're always suspicious of me. Doesn't make a good foundation for a relationship, does it?"

"No, it doesn't." Greer noticed she hadn't answered his question. "So what about the men in your life?"

"I date. But contrary to what you may think by what's happened here, I don't sleep around."

He didn't really want to know any more. Kate twisted the stem off a pear and held the fruit up to Greer's mouth. He bit into it.

"The truth," she said. "Tell me about the women in your life."

The question didn't bother him as much as he thought it might. He wouldn't have asked *her* if he hadn't expected Kate to turn the question around. Maybe it was time to talk about Stephanie to someone other than the polygraph technician at CIA.

"She was older, a German, a graduate instructor at Heidelberg, while I was doing a year abroad during college. She was the first great love of my life. I totally lost myself in her. We talked about her coming to the States, getting married, you know. I left Germany and she . . . she changed her mind. She was a little crazy, I think. Actually, in hindsight, I'm more sure of it. I guess she took my leaving Germany pretty hard. She somehow got it into her head that I dumped her. She went into a rage. Obviously, it didn't work out."

"She was the one who told *you* that it was over?"

"Yeah. She told me." Greer thought about the phone call from Stephanie when she had freaked on the phone. It still bothered him, although it shouldn't. It just seemed so unresolved. "I guess I took it pretty hard, too. I took a couple of weeks and went out to California. San Diego. I needed time off away, open space. I just drove up the Pacific Coast Highway, stopping along the way, trying to figure out what had happened. By the time I had got to San Francisco, I had decided that it wasn't my fault. I went back to Atlanta and got on with my life."

"You haven't heard from her since then?"

"Nothing."

"Consider yourself lucky. Crazy people do crazy things." Kate started peeling an orange with a spoon. "And the others?"

"There were other women, but nothing serious, nothing lasting. I wasn't ready, didn't have time, whatever." Greer thought about it for a moment. Stephanie had really screwed his mind up like no one else ever did. "I don't know what the deal was exactly. . . ." Exactly, he told himself, you've got fingernail tracks down your back that turned to scar tissue. He wouldn't be surprised if there were bits of her still under his skin. After all these years and all these relationships, it was Stephanie who came to mind first.

Greer poured the last of the champagne. The galaxy of candles had burned to the nub.

"You wouldn't ever lie to me, would you, Greer?"

"No." It was out before his conscience could consider the alternative. "Of course not."

Kate finished peeling the orange. She held the whole fruit in one hand and lifted up the rind with the other hand, one perfect, continuous circular peel.

"I hope not." It seemed to Greer as much a warning as a plea.

13 ❑   ❑   ❑   ❑

Greer returned from the mountains Sunday night, dropped Kate off at her place, and went back to his apartment. Even before turning on the lights, he immediately sensed something wasn't right.

What was that smell? he wondered.

He pushed the thermostat up and the heat came on, quickly filling the living room with hot air, tainted with the smell of gas. It could have been the gas, but it seemed to be something stronger. And now that the lights were on, Greer noticed that things around the living room seemed slightly out of place. Or was it just because he was road-weary?

Greer walked through the apartment, trying to figure out what was different. At first glance, everything seemed the way it had been when he left Saturday morning. But at the same time, little things amiss— the desk chair slightly out of place, the phone on the bedside table a couple of inches from where it usually was—a half-dozen minute differences that gave him the strange feeling that someone else had been there in his absence.

He checked his desk and found everything in order. His briefcase was where it should be by the sofa. He looked closer. Had he really left the combination on his briefcase with the open combination showing? He couldn't be certain. It wasn't like him not to rotate the tumblers off the open combination, but he had done it before. He checked the contents of the briefcase. Everything was still there—his cheat sheets for his computer programs and E-mail, a calculator, a couple of cheap pens—nothing worth stealing, for sure.

In the kitchen the smell was stronger. Greer realized that he had forgotten to take the garbage out before he left for the weekend. There were mildewing coffee grounds in the trash can. He knotted the garbage bag, unlocked the outside kitchen door, and put the garbage in the can.

But wait, he thought. Had he left the latch on the screen door unlocked? That definitely wasn't something he had ever done before. Maybe in his rush to get to Kate's place he had forgotten just this once. It left him feeling unsettled. But he just wasn't sure.

Kate was working on a report for the DCI. Greer scanned a Saturday cable from the Paris station.

"Something *special* going on on the Avenue Gabriel today?" Greer asked. He folded back the page he had been looking at in the reports from the Paris embassy and showed it to her.

Kate studied the document. Five lines in the daily CIA cable from the Paris station—situated in the American embassy on the Avenue Gabriel—blacked out with the hand-written notation in the margin: "See CI."

"I don't know," she said.

"Can we get that analyst back down here from the country desk to talk about it?"

Kate hesitated, sucking in air. She exhaled. "Sure."

The counterintelligence officer came in with the case officer who had briefed Greer on the REDWING operation the week before. The case officer looked troubled. Kate moved to sit next to Greer, facing the other two, and turned to a fresh sheet in her day planner, ready to take meeting notes.

The counterintelligence man never bothered to introduce himself. Greer couldn't penetrate the dark gray lenses of his glasses to get a good read on him. The CI officer recited a statement that seemed memorized: "Our source REDWING has delivered some new information to our people in France about the alleged intelligence operation against the United States that supposedly is being run by an ally. The reference to the new information has been excised from all intelligence reports circulating in the government—National Intelligence Daily, the President's Daily Brief, and all internal communications—pending investigation. We'd like it to stay that way for now."

"What exactly was the new information?" Greer asked.

The case officer sat with his arms folded across his chest and squirmed in his seat, but gave no indication that he was going to be doing any talking. He apparently was there only to listen.

Greer noticed the one with dark eyes turn toward Kate, who nodded her assent ever so slightly before he answered: "The intelligence we received overnight was that the alleged operation is on American soil."

"Is that all?" Greer asked. He looked back and forth at both men. They were reluctant to continue. "Well?"

"The reason the material has been sanitized is because REDWING has indicated that the operation involves a mole in the U.S. intelligence community, someone here in Washington."

Greer's heart skipped a beat, then sank. "I see," he said. So the story on Jenkins was going to come out of another Agency unit, not from Reed's special unit and not through his own efforts. Was he about to suffer yet another defeat, a replay of the Tommy Bickford story? It would be a terrible blow to his pride, not to mention Reed's.

The CI officer continued. "I'm sure you must also be aware that this touches on a rather sensitive political issue for the government, also."

Greer looked at Kate, then back at the officer. "Specifically?"

"Specifically, the pressure that the President's been getting from Congressman Weston on foreign policy and our allies. All that crap he's been spewing about there being analysts in the Agency and at State who are overly sympathetic to the Germans and Japanese. Makes us look bad. We need to keep this situation within the intelligence community. It's not a political issue. The DCI's just trying to make sure that small things don't get blown out of proportion or taken out of context."

"You mean like REDWING?"

"Exactly."

Greer thought a moment. "Any indication in which branch REDWING says there's a problem?" he probed.

"We don't know. It could be CIA, NSA, Defense, State Department, or even someone in the Executive Office. At this point, we're treating the threat as if it were real. The country desk indicates that REDWING has always been accurate in the intelligence passed on to us, so we're handling this with a great deal of seriousness and urgency." The case officer nodded agreement.

"What's your next step?" Greer asked.

"Obviously we want to get back to REDWING to try to get additional information. We're following up over there right now. I'm meeting personally this afternoon with my counterintelligence counterparts in all the other government agencies and departments. Around here the best thing to do is to keep this as quiet as possible and start watching everyone closely. Maybe someone will screw up."

"May*be*," said Greer, with a mental picture of Jenkins being hauled out of his office in handcuffs by the FBI.

Greer checked the time: 6:45 P.M. He took a quick, sidelong glance at the mirrored window at the end of the conference room. He typed a message onto the laptop and turned it around for Kate to see: *I'm about to die for you. Your place? Key? Leave fifteen minutes after I do.*

Kate looked at the screen, but didn't acknowledge the message. She kept working on her legal pad. Greer watched as she doodled in the margin. A door. A pot by the door. Two pots by the door. A flower in the pot on the left. A key under the pot with the flower.

Greer deleted the message from the screen, and modemed the day's entries over to Jenkins' office. He typed in his password and checked his old E-mail address on the Library of Congress system that he and Jenkins were using to keep in touch. There was the usual brief message from Jenkins confirming that he had received all of the previous day's transmissions. Greer typed in a new message to Jenkins, indicating that he was sending another batch. He hadn't mentioned the REDWING reference to Jenkins before and he wouldn't do it now: Greer figured that it was a reference to Jenkins and he didn't want to tip Jenkins off that intelligence was beginning to come in that was pointing the finger at him as a spy. He packed up gear and headed toward the door.

"See you tomorrow," he said.

"Bye," said Kate without looking up.

Stepping outside into the cold air, Greer left Kate's townhouse at six the next morning. Kate was taking the Metro into work and she would follow a few minutes later.

Greer and Kate had stayed up late talking. They were both frustrated by the conflicts of their jobs that wouldn't allow them to be together in a more relaxed, public way. But they had renewed their vows to keep their relationship secret, while at the same time promising each other that they'd find a way to keep things moving along.

Greer's car was parallel-parked across the street. He got in and cranked it. A yellow CHECK light flashed on the dash and the car chimed.

"What the hell?"

Greer looked at all of the gauges to find the problem. The front passenger-side door wasn't properly closed. Greer opened the door to reclose it. When the door opened, a folded piece of paper fell onto the seat from somewhere at the top of the door frame. Greer slammed the door shut and unfolded the piece of paper. Printed were the words: I'VE BEEN WATCHING YOU.

Greer froze. *Who* is watching me? he wondered. He looked into the rearview mirror. Nothing. He looked to his left and right. Still nothing. Everything in the car seemed to be okay. Hell with it, he thought, trying to blow it off. Some kid's prank.

Greer thought about that as he looked at the side-view mirror before pulling out into the heavy morning traffic. The mirror was way out of position from where it should have been. He fingered the switch to rotate the mirror back to the right angle. As the mirror came into place, Greer saw the car. The other side of the street, three cars back, just to the side of Kate's front door. There was someone wearing a hat, sitting with hands on the steering wheel. A hand lifted and waved, then the car pulled out and did a quick U-turn the other way. It was gone behind the cover of the car exhaust in the cold morning air.

14 ❑   ❑   ❑   ❑

Two days later, Greer knew something was wrong when he got to the Smithsonian safe room and Reed was already there. It was dark in the windowless room, as usual, with only the banker's lamp on. Reed never sat during their meetings, but today he was already sitting. He had taken his suit coat off and draped it over the back of a chair at the end of the table. He sat in his vest and shirtsleeves studying an open file folder with his arms propped up on their elbows and his hands folded. It looked like an inquest. Reed lifted his head as Greer walked in and gave him a scowl that would have cowed the dogs at the gate of Hell.

"Come sit over here," Reed said as Greer shut the door. The tone was definitely not friendly. Reed pulled out the chair next to his for Greer and closed the file folder. Reed waited until Greer was seated. "What's your report on Jenkins?"

"Jenkins still hasn't said how much longer I'll be copying daily intelligence at Langley. All he'll say is that he needs more data to prove his theory."

"Has he said what his theory is yet?"

"No. I've pushed him again a few times, but he won't budge. Says it would skew the data collection if I knew."

"What does he do with the information you send him every day?"

"I don't know. I know he's been working late hours every night, but I don't know if he's working on that or not."

"Has he talked to the White House again about his theory?" Reed asked.

"I don't think so. He did promise them that he wouldn't bring it up with anyone until he'd cleared it with the Chief of Staff himself."

Reed made a sour face. "I'm going to be straight with you, Greer. It looks really bad." He opened up the file folder. "I've got a memo here from the DCI that went to the President. Nothing special per se about it. It was a cover memo on some confidential background on the heads of state put together by CIA for the President to help get him briefed for the economic meeting in a couple of months. Basically, they're psychological profiles along with any known aberrant behaviors. Anything that will give the President some insight into the lives of his counterparts that might be used to leverage some advantage in negotiations."

"Okay?" Greer felt defensive.

"The problem is here in the margin. Do you see that?" Reed pointed to scrawled writing to the left of the typed text. "That's a love note from the President. He sent the cover memo back with a love note to Ben Gibbons. Do you see what that says?"

Greer tried to make out the handwriting but couldn't.

"Let me read it to you. The DCI read it to me several times yesterday and I've just about got it memorized. It says, 'Ben—Where the hell is the information from the STEEPLECHASE operation. It's been weeks!' That's a lovely note to get from the President of the United States, isn't it?" asked Reed.

Greer hung his head low and prepared for more abuse.

"Time's running short. We've *got* to deliver. You've got to get Jenkins to fill you in on what he's up to. The President is counting on us."

Greer swallowed hard. "Does the President know what the theory is that Jenkins is pushing?"

"No, not yet. The Chief of Staff has screened everything so far."

"What about the Executive Finding?"

"What about it?"

"How could he have signed it if he didn't know the particulars? Wouldn't he have had to have known the substance of what Jenkins was working on at least?"

"No, no, no. Dwight talked it over with the DCI and the two of them approached the President. It was painful, going to the President about one of his old friends and advisers going off the deep end. It was important to keep the President at a distance in case the thing blew up. The presidency had to be insulated. They quite forthrightly made the case that Jenkins was suspected of espionage. In the end, the President reluctantly did what was right."

"So the President signed the Finding authorizing the CIA to spy on one of his own cabinet members not knowing about this so-called theory of Jenkins, right?"

"That's not at all unusual. There's no need to rock the boat and get the President all upset, especially on the eve of the G7 conference."

Greer remembered reading in Sunday's *Washington Times* about the upcoming economic summit, the so-called Group of Seven, or G7 conference. It was held periodically for the major industrial powers of the world to meet and resolve any big economic issues. The conferees included the heads of state from the United States, Canada, Great Britain, Germany, France, Italy, and Japan.

"In fact," Reed continued, "the reason everyone wants this thing resolved quickly is that the G7 summit is back in the United States next year. Could be embarrassing if the Administration was in the middle of a scandal involving a cabinet-level appointee when the summit was getting under way."

"When's the conference?" Greer asked.

"January, in San Francisco. The White House figured the Japanese would enjoy a visit to California. The thinking is get the Japanese real relaxed and they'll be off their guard. Have them take in a little golf. Drive down the coast to Hollywood. Go to Disneyland."

Greer calculated his next words carefully. "You know what's bugging me?" he asked.

"What's that?"

"I've been working on this case for over a month and I still don't know what this whole thing's about. *You* know, the DCI knows, the White House Chief of Staff knows, Jenkins knows, but I'm the one with my butt on the line here and *nobody's* talking to me."

Reed nodded. "I anticipated that. I understand your frustration. I honestly thought that Jenkins would have let you in on his work by now, but from what you've told me, you won't know anything from him for at least another few weeks until you're done collecting data at Langley."

"Right. Can't you tell me *anything?* I'm working in the dark here."

Reed sucked in his upper lip. "To be honest, I'm just a little afraid that if I tell you what we know about it you might slip up and blow your cover. Unintentionally, of course. We can't have him getting suspicious of you. Remember the talk we had about your having to work in a vacuum? This is it. Life in the CIA *can* be frustrating. You work your ass off on a small but crucial piece of the puzzle and sometimes you never get the satisfaction of seeing the whole picture. That's a fact of life in the Agency. You're doing a good job. But the situation demands more than that now. We've got to respond to the President's demand for action. You're just going to have to push harder."

"Fine." Greer said. It was the adrenaline rush all over again. The CIA demanded blind loyalty; it was the nature of the job. Wherever Reed led, Greer would follow.

They were both quiet for a moment. Greer had really wanted to give Reed some good news, but the only thing new he could think of was the REDWING reference. But it was relevant.

"I did come across something I think you should know about," said Greer. "There's a source in France claiming there's a mole in U.S. intelligence. Supposedly it's an operation run by an ally."

Reed froze. "And?" he asked.

"When I first heard about it, I thought immediately about you."

Reed was defensive: "What's *that* supposed to mean?"

"Jenkins, of course," Greer said. "I think it's the beginning of confirmation that Jenkins is the mole."

Reed's expression relaxed, but his body was still tense.

Greer spoke again. "Am I right?"

"How did you find out about that?"

"It came in a cable from the Paris station. Some source there. Operation REDWING."

Reed looked up at the ceiling, searching for something. Finally he said, "Anything else? How's the rest of your data collection going?"

"Fine. Kate's a great girl to work with." It was already out of his mouth.

Reed took a hard look at Greer, similar to the one he had given him during the interview at Langley. "Greer," Reed began, "don't get too close to Kate Mallotte."

Greer felt himself blush. "What do you mean?"

"We both know what I mean. Kate's a beautiful girl. I've seen other men fall under her spell at the Agency. They lose perspective. They do stupid things. That's why she was such a good spy runner."

Greer thought about the incident with the note in his car that morning. Possibly it was a warning from Reed, letting him know he was being watched. Reed certainly was playing it cool. If he asked Reed about it, then he'd have to explain about being at Kate's house. If it wasn't Reed, then it could turn into a very embarrassing discussion. It definitely wasn't something he could tell Kate about, either. That would take them down the thorny trail leading to Reed. Let it drop, he reasoned.

"I hear what you're saying," said Greer. "You don't have to worry about me."

"I don't want you distracted. We need a breakthrough on the Jenkins case. The President is counting on us. Don't let your relationship with Kate Mallotte screw things up."

"Not to worry," Greer reassured. "I can handle it."

Back at Langley, Greer was settling back into his work. He was deep in thought about all that Reed had said.

Kate was saying, ". . . don't understand why you did that when you knew you were going directly to Jenkins' office."

"What?"

"I said, 'Why did you make an appointment with someone when you knew you wouldn't be here?' "

Greer was confused. "I didn't have any meetings scheduled here. Why would I do that?"

"The receptionist called me and said there was a woman in the lobby who said she had an appointment with you. When I got downstairs, the woman was gone."

"What woman?"

"I thought you'd know."

"I have no idea." Greer shook his head, even more confused. "I don't get it."

"Neither do I."

"Well, obviously it was just a simple mistake," Greer said, more to convince himself than Kate.

The following week, Greer and Kate were at the Sky Terrace on the roof of the Washington Hotel.

"Sit there," she said, motioning to a chair facing south. "That's the best view of the city."

Greer eased into the blue wicker chair and took in the sights. Kate moved the ashtray to a nearby table.

It had been Kate's suggestion to go to the Sky Terrace. It was five o'clock on an unusually warm October day, a break between cold fronts. They drove separate cars into the city and parked again in the Old Executive Office Building lot.

"This is spectacular," he said. "Tell me what I'm looking at."

"The building right next door is Treasury," she pointed out. "And right over there is the east side of the White House." She turned in her chair. "Out in the distance is Arlington National Cemetery. You can see the Lee Mansion on the hill."

A waiter came and he ordered—wine for Kate and a scotch for himself.

Greer looked at Kate. The long afternoon rays of the sun were striking her hair, making it glow golden. She was taking in the whole atmosphere of the city, watching the people down below and the planes approaching for landing at Washington National Airport beyond the Washington Monument and across the Potomac. A VIP transport helicopter in the distance flew through the big red sun.

"You really love it here, don't you?" Greer asked.

"I do."

Greer was content not to talk for the moment, happy to gaze at Kate. He adjusted his chair so that the sun was not blocked by the canopy overhead. The ceiling fans were whirling slowly. The warm sun struck his face. He took a deep breath and let it out. He actually started to relax.

Greer raised his glass to catch Kate before she took a sip of her wine. "A toast?" he asked.

"To?"

"To us, of course."

They touched glasses and drank. It had been less than two weeks since their trip to Monticello and the little inn in the mountains. Kate was wonderful, he thought. He had told himself that a million times since meeting her. Things had worked out so perfectly. First, the best job in the world, then meeting Kate and their falling in love with each other. It was hard to imagine being any happier at that moment. From his vantage on the roof of the hotel overlooking Washington at the end of the day, he felt as if he were on top of the world again.

Greer leaned in. "I meant it, you know. I do love you."

They sat there sipping their drinks quietly, being ignored by their waiter. They watched the sun fall heavier onto the city like a fat red water balloon, the red getting redder and the whole of the sun getting larger as it squashed the horizon. The yellow lights in the brass sconces came on. The breeze picked up as the evening came nearer.

"It's beautiful, isn't it?" Kate said after a while.

Greer curled his hand around the tumbler of scotch on the table and slid it toward Kate's wine. Kate put her hand down and grasped the glass stem. Greer reached out with his pinkie finger and Kate took it with her own, interlocking like a pair of mating sea snakes.

Greer said, "I'm not going to be at Langley forever. We've got to keep our relationship a secret for a little while longer until I'm reassigned someplace else."

"I certainly don't want to give anyone any reason to make things difficult for us."

"It's driving me crazy."

"I was just thinking the same thing," Kate said. "It's all happening so fast. But there *is* the matter of our careers."

Greer raised his glass: "Our careers," he agreed.

There was silence between them for a while longer. It finally got dark and the breeze was getting harder and cooler. Two red lights on top of the Washington Memorial were winking a warning to the landing airplanes.

Kate reached across the table and brushed Greer's right cheek with the back of her hand. "I never noticed that before." Greer had no idea what she was talking about. "What a cute little scar."

"Shaving accident," Greer fibbed. He had completely forgotten about it. He saw it every day while shaving, but no longer paid it any attention.

Kate examined it with her head tilting from side to side. "It's funny—like a crescent moon. It's as white as a pearl. It virtually glows when the light hits it at just the right angle."

Greer thought of Stephanie's fingernails: pleasure in love-making, lethal when she lost control. He saw Kate shiver.

"Ready to go?" Greer asked.

Kate glanced behind her and saw that the crowd had started thinning out. She checked around them again, then reached across the table and took Greer's hand.

"I love you, too," she said. "This will work out."

"It's frustrating, but it's the only way." Greer took a final look from the rooftop out over Washington. "It's a helluva city," he said. He was somber, thinking. "At some point we may both have to make some choices, you know." He was thinking of their careers.

Kate looked out to where Greer was staring. A group of people was just now leaving the White House. Kate gave Greer's hand a squeeze. Barely whispering, she said, "I know."

15 ❏   ❏   ❏   ❏

Erich Reagor sat alone in the corner of the smoking section of the Northwest Airlines club room at Charles de Gaulle Airport in Paris, watching the airplanes taxi back and forth across the tarmac. He didn't smoke and he hated the smell of cigarettes. He was waiting for Congressman James "Jimmy" Weston and the three House Intelligence Committee staffers traveling with him.

The report that Reagor's own staffers at Deutsche Bayrische Werke had prepared for him indicated that Weston always flew Northwest, since his congressional district cut into suburban Detroit, the home base of the airline. Reagor also knew that Weston had a first-class ticket on the eleven-fifteen flight direct to Washington National, that he had a Northwest World Club card, *and* that he was a chain smoker. It was inevitable that the congressman would be making an appearance soon.

Reagor turned the page of *Le Monde* and looked from the smoking room into the main room where Weston would come in. There were two hostesses, one checking club room cards and pouring drinks for the newly arrived, and the other straightening up the room, picking up old glasses and napkins and replenishing dishes full of nuts on the coffee tables. Reagor checked his watch: 10:13 A.M. The congressman was probably still clearing customs downstairs.

Reagor saw Weston's picture on page three of the newspaper. There was a detailed description of his not-so-secret secret mission to several major European capital cities to collect information for a subcommittee hearing he was going to be participating in after Christmas. He was supposed to be on his midterm break, but while every other congressman was home enjoying the long Thanksgiving recess, Weston had scheduled a whirlwind tour visiting intelligence agencies and other government officials of key American allies in Europe.

Reagor scanned the newspaper article to see if there was anything to add to what his staffers had prepared for him. There was nothing new. Although he had been in Congress for only three years, Weston had made a quick name for himself in the States as one of the most vocal critics of the President's foreign policy. It was an unusual position for someone of his background to be in. Before entering politics, he had been a cohost on a nationally syndicated tabloid exposé television program. Weston brought with him a finely tuned sense for the dramatic. He was comfortable in front of the TV cameras. By most accounts, he was a media hog, earning the disdain of his colleagues, especially the ones with more seniority, but the favor of the journalists whom he sought out for late-night card games and rounds of drinks at his well-appointed bachelor's condominium near Old Town in Arlington across the Tidal Basin. Even before he got to Washington, he knew what his strategy would be for gaining national prominence once he was elected. His election from a conservative suburb would be a platform from which he planned to launch a national movement, much in the way Ross Perot had tried in 1992. But Weston didn't need billions of dollars to finance an organization and develop a following. Weston had three things going for him that counted more: he had looks, he had a way with the television camera, and, most important, he was on the right side of an issue that he thought would propel him to the front of the pack.

In its simplest description, the issue that Weston had found and had hammered mercilessly for two years was the decline of America as a world power. As the article in *Le Monde* explained it, Weston attributed this decline to two main factors. The first was the economic rise to prominence of other countries, especially Japan. Weston also pointed to the emergence of the European Union and the growing strength of Germany as potential economic rivals. In his view, it was a zero-sum game: a win by another country or trading bloc meant a loss by America.

The second factor to which Weston attributed America's decline was the new weakness of the office of the presidency as a world leader. Earlier in the century, American presidents threw their weight around and threatened military action if they didn't get their way. The power of the gun—then the Bomb—was the trump card most often played by Americans over the past several decades. But Weston argued that the world had changed. The Wall had fallen, the nuclear threat was largely null, and the world had become more concerned with economic status, now that the threat of being wiped off the face of the earth had passed. He liked to talk about Maslow's hierarchy of needs. It was a simple concept. The civilized countries of the world had moved up a rung on the ladder from focusing on mere survival to improving their economic well-being.

Weston had been first elected in the same year as the President, who, by all accounts, won simply because he was the least objectionable of the two national candidates. Weston cited the President as being a prime example of what a president should not be. The President had come into office on a domestic agenda, he completely lacked foreign affairs experience, and he surrounded himself with boyhood school-mates and college roommates, none of whom had the experience or the spine for confrontational politics with a determined foreign friend or foe. In Weston's view, the President was a naïf who wanted to be loved by everyone—at home and abroad. He tried to please all of his constituencies, and ended up alienating most of them. The President's staff was weak and unfocused, a reflection of the President's own style. While the world was rapidly evolving, the Administration was talking about feel-good domestic policies. Weston specifically cited the Japanese and Germans as countries that had taken advantage of America's generosity, but were now laughing in the face of America's economic woes. The Administration couldn't think about economics in terms of anything other than domestic issues. In Weston's opinion, the President rated an F in foreign policy during his first three years in office. The President and his people didn't even know the right questions to ask in the first place.

Reagor had viewed television clips of Weston and could understand that Weston's true gift was as a communicator. He took important, complex issues and explained them in terms that everyone could understand. The President was no match for Weston in his communicative abilities. On the decline-of-America issue, Weston struck a chord with the American people, not just those in his district. It was a visceral issue. No one wanted to be on a losing team. Weston had ridden the issue and gone from being a neophyte politician, an obscure congressman, to a statesman of national stature. He was now building an international reputation. All in just three years.

But there was something there. The other congressmen knew it, but they weren't so comfortable criticizing other countries, especially American allies. Weston was seen on the nightly evening news alternatively bashing Japan, then the European Union. He started questioning the motives of America's allies. Germany was a particular favorite. Weston saw conspiracies and cover-ups and hidden agendas everywhere he looked. The other congressmen didn't like to talk about it publicly. But in the cloakrooms and over drinks from the desk drawer in a score of private offices tucked away in the Capitol building, the word McCarthyism crept into the conversations of his colleagues. At the same time, however, polls and input from their constituents showed them that Weston was merely saying what a lot of Americans were thinking about and talking about in bars and on golf courses.

The *Monde* article concluded with a description of Weston's last stop in Bonn. While there, he had met with German journalists. In an interview with a reporter from *Der Stern,* Weston dropped a bombshell. He claimed that analysts in the CIA and State Department were either negligently overlooking economic maneuvers of our allies, or— even worse—they were slanting the analysis in favor of the foreign countries at the expense of the United States. It was no wonder, he said, that American policymakers didn't have the correct information and interpretation on which to make good foreign policy decisions. The European press showed Weston as a typical loudmouthed American, totally lacking sensitivity to local concerns. The clips on the evening news only confirmed Reagor's countrymen's worst caricature of the ugly American gone abroad. Run amok, more like it. That was fine with Weston. All three major U.S. television networks and the wire services had tagged along on his European trip. Weston was playing for the audience at home, not the foreign press.

It was when Weston was in London three days earlier that Reagor had been given the order to intervene. The surreptitious recording Reagor had made of Stettler and his office visitor over a year ago finally began to make sense. "An alliance of sorts," Stettler explained before sending him out to do his duty. "This is the new Germany. New friends, new enemies, new economic—*possibilities.*" Reagor understood possibilities. A cold calculation of probabilities. Well-reasoned assessments. No risk, no return. The future was no longer dependent on the past. Stettler had made it clear that the people who had an interest did not find Weston the least bit amusing. He was sniffing around and raising questions about foreign policies of certain friendly countries that the DBW didn't want debated—least of all answered—in a public forum. Weston was becoming too vocal, getting too much attention. "Germany and our friends prefer the American president's approach to America's allies—ignorant and uninvolved," Stettler said. "We cannot risk having these kinds of foreign and economic policies debated in the upcoming Intelligence subcommittee hearings. Weston would turn it into a major media event."

Reagor's DBW staff was the best he had ever worked with, even better than the best of the Stasi teams. They were thorough in their research. And accurate. The one other piece of key information that they had been able to provide him with was that Weston had a passion for Brazil nuts. Plain, salted, chocolate-covered—the guy was just crazy about Brazil nuts. He kept little cans of them in his offices in Washington and back home in the district. The media had picked up on it and it had become a well-known joke. Lobbyists and visiting dignitaries and constituents came bearing Brazil nuts when seeking favors.

Reagor slipped his hand into his side jacket pocket and took out a small Ziploc bag and opened it. He dumped the contents into his hand: a dozen irresistible honey-roasted Brazil nuts. He palmed the nuts, leaned forward and dropped a few on top of the dish of nuts on the coffee table in front of the couch he was sitting on. He got up and walked over to the other side of the smoking room, pretended to pick up a few nuts from the dish on the other coffee table, and dropped the rest of the nuts from his hand into the dish.

Reagor heard the buzzer to the front door of the club room and heard the hostess push the automatic release. He resumed his position reading the paper. He heard American voices loudly coming into the main room. He recognized one of the voices from the news clips—it was clearly Weston's. He heard the group ordering drinks—champagne and screwdrivers—then they came noisily into the smoking section and sat down on the couches and chairs around the coffee table at the other end of the room.

Weston took a sip of his screwdriver, then lit up a Marlboro Light. A couple of his staffers got up and went over to stand in front of the floor-to-ceiling window overlooking the runway. One of the staffers who was still sitting down with him nudged the dish of nuts over toward Weston. Reagor saw his face light up and saw him jab a finger down into the nuts, stirring them around. He picked up a thumb-sized Brazil nut and popped it into his mouth. He nodded enthusiastically, pointed to the dish, and said something to the staffer who shook his head and waved him off. Weston picked up another two Brazil nuts and put both into his mouth at the same time, chewed them up, then washed them down with another swallow of the screwdriver. He wiped a residue of sweet white powder off the corners of his mouth with a small paper napkin.

The sugary powder on the nuts that Reagor had dropped into the dishes was more than a confection, however. Two hours after consumption of the nuts, the eater would develop an acute case of diarrhea that would continue for another hour or until every gram of excretable bodily waste was lost, whichever came first. The body would be acutely dehydrated. Then, the bowels would begin to twist until they were wrung into a knot that would block anything from passing —permanently. Any food, liquid or medicine consumed would be immediately and violently vomited back up. The body would at that point begin to shut down, the person would go into shock, the tongue would expand to four times its normal size, and the brain would begin to swell. The pressure inside the skull would result in massive hemorrhaging and the person would die of a stroke. All within three hours of ingesting the toxin. And all hopelessly irreversible by any known medical practice.

Reagor folded his paper and got up to leave. He smiled at the congressman on his way out of the room. He went into the men's room and thoroughly washed the residue from the nuts off his hands. He smiled to himself in the mirror over the sink as he dried his hands and carefully blotted the spaces between his fingers dry with a paper towel. In about two hours, Congressman Weston would be well over the Atlantic when the severe cramps would begin. The plane would never make it back to Europe in time.

Reagor threw the paper towel into the trash can and pushed through the door. He knew the nonstop to Washington National wouldn't have the drama of some of his other jobs, but the effect would be the same: *shut the motherfucker up.*

16 ❏   ❏   ❏   ❏

Late on the Saturday of Thanksgiving Day weekend, Greer sat in the Main Reading Room of the Library of Congress, surrounded by bound periodicals and notecards. He and Kate had taken Thursday as a well-deserved holiday break. By now, Greer had spent two months going into Langley, transcribing CIA station cables, and modeming them to Jenkins. Normally, he and Kate would have been at the office over the entire weekend, but Greer had told Kate he needed a chunk of time at the library to do research for Jenkins. What he actually had been up to for two straight days was conducting research *on* Jenkins, following up on a hunch. If Randall Jenkins wasn't going to tell him about his theory directly, then Greer was determined to find out for himself.

Greer had been at the front doors of the library Friday morning when they opened and he had worked through closing time. After a second six-hour day in the library on Saturday, he was now thoroughly spent, his eyes bleary and his head aching from the strain of reading. But he also sensed that he might be finally closing in on Jenkins' secret.

Greer had pored over every published piece available written by Randall Jenkins—books, scholarly journal articles, published speeches, conference papers, and obscure monographs. Jenkins had been at the Hoover Institution for fifteen years before being tapped as the President's nominee for National Security Adviser. During that time, he had been a highly productive writer, cranking out dozens of academic works, all of which Greer had read at least once over the past two days. For several years preceding the election, Jenkins had also been the presidential aspirant's primary counsel on foreign affairs. Many of Jenkins' thoughts, theories, and foreign policy biases had wormed their way into campaign speeches and position papers.

Jenkins' specialty was international economics, with a heavy emphasis on global politics. Greer had searched everywhere he knew to look in the library for any single theory that might point to the reason why Jenkins had ordered Greer to spend week after week at Langley entering the CIA cable data. By the end of the previous day, he had chased Jenkins' writings down a series of dead ends, and all he had to show for his efforts was a thick stack of notecards with seemingly unrelated bits of Jenkins' writing. But now, after another day's grueling work, he was beginning to see a common thread running through Jenkins' later writings. Greer scanned the article titles and summaries on the abstracts he had collected. Toward the end of his career at the Institution, Jenkins had focused on issues dealing with America's international trade deficit. There were also pieces examining how America could effectively compete in the global marketplace.

Greer had organized his notecards on the desk from the various articles according to the broad themes that Jenkins' analysis had explored. Greer read through the first grouping of phrases he had written down, which seemed to be laying the foundation for what seemed to be Jenkins' basic argument: . . . *America at risk . . . Especially dangerous situation when the United States has naive, weak leaders unable to see potential for evil from outside . . . American economy worsening . . . Had expected huge economic "peace dividend" following the end of the Cold War . . . lured into complacency . . .*

The next major grouping of cards concerned the international scenario, specifically referring to the Group of Seven nations: . . . *End of threat of Communism means voters in G7 countries feel safe to abandon mainstream political parties/ideas/leaders . . . Voters disinterested in own political parties, much less inclined to listen to supragovernmental organization . . . caustic mix of high unemployment and ultra-nationalism . . .*

Pressure from people to improve their lives . . . international peace and prosperity agreements will mean nothing . . . global free markets a null philosophical concept, not grounded in real-world understanding . . . economic chaos . . . old alliances formed over the past fifty years will be voided. . . .

At the end of two days' work, the jumble was starting to take form, but the specifics were still missing. There seemed to be one last piece to the puzzle.

Greer remembered something, then rechecked the text of a speech Jenkins had delivered to a professional association on America's economic role in foreign policy. Near the end of the talk, Jenkins had thrown out a quick reference to a bibliography he had compiled, something having to do with America's economic allies. It was something Greer had skipped over quickly before, since it appeared it wouldn't contain anything he hadn't already dug up. But now, in the context of what he had learned from his second day of research, Jenkins' offhand remark had taken on new meaning.

Greer checked the time and saw that the library would be closing soon. He would have to hurry. With his workload for Jenkins, he wouldn't have the luxury of another marathon session at the library anytime soon.

Greer ran back into the Computer Catalog Center across the hall. He touched the color screen to activate the ACCESS terminal, then selected Serial Publications. He typed "Hoover Institution." The terminal displayed "Hoover Institution on War, Revolution and Peace" and prompted him to scroll through the listings of publications published by the organization. Greer found the listing for the bibliography and copied the number on a call slip, then crossed back to the Main Reading Room's central desk to turn in his request. The sign indicated that he would have about a thirty-minute wait.

Greer waited anxiously, keeping an eye on the clock. He was the last patron in the library and the bibliography only took fifteen minutes to arrive. He flipped through the pamphlet, scanning the pages furiously, looking for a clue. He mentally checked off all the articles and books he had already reviewed over the past two days, noting all the fruitless trails he had gone down.

But then, under the heading *Unpublished Works,* was a reference to a "white paper" delivered to what looked to be a gathering of high-level political appointees from the previous Administration. It looked to be something used to kick off a discussion. The paper was entitled, *Unnatural Alliance—A Theory of Political and Economic War*. Greer checked the titles in the library catalog and found no listing. Then he searched for it under different key words, coming up with nothing. Just as he was about to give up, he searched under the name of the previous Secretary of State, sponsor of the event. There it was—listed as being part of the library's special collections—an original copy complete with handwritten annotations.

Greer raced back into the Main Reading Room and begged the librarian to get the paper for him. The librarian was already packing up and told him it was too late. He showed his old Library of Congress research associate credentials and pulled every trick he knew to get the document. The librarian finally relented and called to have the paper brought in.

Greer knew immediately he had found the missing piece of the puzzle. It was couched in language less academic than Jenkins' other works, written as if to appeal as much to the reader's emotions as his intellect. Its date indicated that it was among the last things Jenkins had written before leaving Stanford and the Hoover Institution to officially join the President's campaign staff. Taken as a whole with the previous works that Greer had found, Greer could see how the paper was the natural conclusion to the progression in the development of Jenkins' theories.

Greer read every word carefully, trying to figure out every nuance which might give him a clue to the mystery of Randall Jenkins.

The paper referenced Jenkins' earlier thinking on the subject of America's economic vulnerability, but included a much more blunt assessment than his previous academic writing: . . . *open the gates for new powerful economic allegiances that exclude the United States. . . . War conducted on an economic front where America's allies become enemies . . . others now in a position to carve out their own spheres of economic influence . . . Disaster will fall upon America if two or more economically powerful countries decide to form a strategic alliance against the United States. . . .*

Then there was the economic case pointing the long finger at the most likely culprits: *Japan, experiencing a deep slide of Japanese real estate and stock markets . . . looking to other high-return areas so doesn't focus inward.* And Japan's natural partner in the strategic alliance, the new Germany . . . *High cost of German reunification—hundreds of billions into East Germany, a quarter of a trillion total so far . . . The newly enacted immigration laws restricting foreigners . . . The resurgence of National Socialism—the Nazis . . . The burning of homes and murder of foreign workers . . .*

And in his conclusion, Jenkins posited the chilling scenario in the closing passage: . . . *that the Japanese and Germans could catch everyone else off guard in the economic equivalent of Japan's attack on Pearl Harbor and German blitzkrieg into Poland.*

"Quite a theory," Greer said out loud to himself. His voice was lost in the vast space overhead. It could happen, he thought. He read the raw intelligence every day flowing from those countries. He had spent two days working his way through Jenkins' reasoning. It quite possibly *was* happening.

Greer considered with new interest the upcoming Group of Seven conference in January. Germany and Japan. Partners. He could hear the bombs dropping from the Stukas and Zeros. America wouldn't get the news crackling over the radio this time. The news would come in color commentary on CNN with a beautiful backdrop of sailboats and seagulls in the San Francisco Bay behind some windblown reporter. He could hear the sound that the wind makes as it whips across a microphone outside. It was easy to see why the White House wanted Jenkins kept quiet. Everything Jenkins was saying directly contradicted the Administration's assumptions that were guiding their maneuvering for the economic summit only two months away.

But, it was just a theory, he reminded himself.

"I can't go home until I've got a present for Carol," said the CIA director, Ben Gibbons, to Bob Reed. The two stood inside the entrance to Union Station in front of the big black board lit up in red letters and numbers announcing arrivals and departures from the train station. As they stood there, tourists coming in behind them jostled to get past into the refurbished building. There was a loud white noise coming from the voices of the shoppers and lunch eaters echoing in the high vaulted ceiling. Gibbons looked up at the orange digital time displayed on the Amtrak board. "I've got forty-five minutes to get an anniversary present. It's November *twenty-eighth,* not the twenty-ninth. Her birthday falls on the twenty-ninth. I've written it down in next year's calendar already. How could I have forgotten?" He settled down a moment and put his hand on Reed's shoulder. "Thanks. Even *you* know our anniversary."

Reed smiled back. "What are old friends for? I hadn't talked to you in a few months. . . ."

"And the first thing you do is ask me if I remembered my anniversary. Come on," Gibbons said, "let's go find something. We can talk while we look around. I need your advice."

Gibbons led them over to the left to a political memorabilia shop. There were commemorative plates of the presidents and books on Washington. Gibbons spotted a framed collection of campaign buttons from the 1960 presidential election with Richard Nixon and Kennedy slogans. Right next to it was a framed picture of Nixon and Elvis in the White House. He pulled it off the wall and showed it to Reed. "What do you think?" Gibbons asked.

"Carol hates politics. Loved Elvis, hated Nixon."

Gibbons hung the picture back onto the wall and cut out quickly back into the mall. They walked briskly between the shops, stopping in front of the window displays. The DCI said: "Randall Jenkins is *really* becoming a pain in the ass."

"So what's new? You told me that at the beginning of summer."

"Yeah, but it's gotten worse."

"What's the problem now?"

"He's meddling. Thinks he's Henry Kissinger or something." Gibbons tapped his index finger on the glass front of a store. "Do you like that?" he asked, pressing his face close to the window. He was frowning at a gold lamé blouse on a mannequin.

"Carol would never wear anything like that. I don't *think*," said Reed. He led them off to the next window display.

A thought occurred to Reed. A gleeful chuckle: "Hey, how about that Congressman Weston? Tough way to go, huh?"

"Yeah. That was bad. It just goes to show you. It could happen to anyone, anywhere. Death by stomach cramps. I hate to think he suffered much. Son of a bitch."

"There's one headache out of your way. With him gone, all that nonsense about spies in the Agency will go away. Nobody gave a shit about that stuff up on the Hill but him."

"I sent flowers," Reed said.

"I sent a donation to the Communist Party–USA in his name."

They both laughed.

"Bob, I value your judgment. We go back a long way with the Agency. I'd have you on my staff but you're too damned good where you are. We need someone of your caliber in the field, in touch with what's going on. I like having you as my eyes and ears out there."

"Wouldn't have it any other way."

"Anyway, back to Jenkins. He's been leaning on the White House to get a full hearing on that crazy theory of his about economic warfare. Same thing I told you about before. Dwight's put him off, but with his personal relationship with the President, we're afraid he'll go straight to the top. Every time I tell him he's off base on something, he threatens to go directly to the President if he doesn't get what he wants."

They came to the end of the mall and turned around to walk the other side.

"I'm in a tough spot, Bob. The State Department's busting their ass to get the G7 conference set up in January. It's going to be a political coup for the President when he signs the new side agreements with Japan opening up the country to American goods and services. He's the first President to get them to go that far."

"Very favorable terms, from what I've read in the paper."

"Exactly. It's political gold for the President. The economy's the thing that will make or break him at reelection. He can milk this one with labor *and* business. And, it really *is* good for everyone. The President's not going to want to hear all that crap about going to economic war with our allies. It just isn't wise to distract him with some mumbo-jumbo from an economist."

"Economics," scoffed Reed. "The *dismal* science they call it. For good reason."

Gibbons stopped walking. "You've got one of the best political heads in the Agency. I feel that you and I can talk without your bullshitting me. Off the record, what do you think?'

"What are the chances of isolating Jenkins until after the G7 conference?"

Gibbons looked up at the store sign. "Hold on," he said, grabbing Reed's shoulder. They went into the Nature Company and Gibbons led them over to a bin of toys, away from the other people in the store. He picked up a holographic top and gave it a whirl on the countertop.

Gibbons continued in a lower voice: "That's really what I'm asking you. *How* do we keep Jenkins away from the President until after the summit? I frankly don't know if it can be done. To tell you the truth, Dwight Conrad has kind of given me this little project. Find something to occupy Jenkins until after January."

"How about throwing him a red herring?"

Gibbons waited for the top to stop spinning, then picked up a different one and gave it a spin, watching the opal neon colors vibrate. "Know of anything I can use?"

"Let me think about it. There's got to be something to distract him for a while."

They both watched the top spin out to a stop.

"Were you looking for something in particular?" Reed asked.

"Carol keeps talking about a pair of amber earrings she wished she had bought on our vacation to Central America last year. See anything like that in here?"

Reed found the jewelry counter and signaled for Gibbons. "Found it," he said.

"That's perfect," Gibbons said when he saw the earrings under the glass.

Gibbons paid and they headed toward the entrance of the mall. "Walk with me," Gibbons said. They went outside to wait behind a couple at the taxi stand.

"By the way, I've noticed you've been in and out of the country. From reading your reports I know that Germany must be consuming most of your time. It's a real mess over there, isn't it?"

"I can personally testify to that. They're distracted by the problems with the foreign nationals. Lots of political pressure to get something done. It's a real powder keg."

Gibbons peeked into the sack as if to reassure himself of his good gift selection. "She'll like these, don't you think?"

"I'm sure she will."

"Bob," said the DCI, "you'll spend some time thinking about Jenkins, won't you? I'd like some ideas in a couple of days."

"I promise. By the way, have you got anyone else working on this?"

"I've assigned Kate Mallotte to work as liaison with Jenkins' office.

He's got a staffer coming over to look at the raw intelligence every day. Damn waste of Kate's time baby-sitting that guy."

"What's he doing that for?" A taxi sped up to the stand and Gibbons stepped into the door held open by the doorman.

"Something to do with that damned theory of his. I don't know," Gibbons replied. "I'm too weary to fight with Jenkins anymore. He'd win anyway. I ask Kate every now and then what the point is, but the guy from Jenkins' office is tight as a clam."

"What's his name?"

"Greer Whitaker. A White House Fellow. Why? You know him?"

Reed shrugged. "Never heard of him."

The door closed and Reed watched the DCI's taxi screech off.

17 ❏   ❏   ❏   ❏

The man at the sushi bar made the mistake of sitting alone with his back to the door.

A Japanese man in a dark business suit stood on the sidewalk and casually opened the door on the outside of a small restaurant off Union Street in San Francisco. He held the door open and stood to the side.

Fujimata "Jacko" Takiyama stepped through the entrance into the restaurant, followed by the man holding the door and one other. It was six o'clock on Wednesday night, and the restaurant was just beginning to fill up. It wasn't Japantown, but the sushi was unparalleled in the city.

They stood politely just inside the doorway, waiting for the elderly Japanese owner to seat a couple and come over to greet them. The owner's face fell when he saw Jacko, then spread into a large smile as he approached them. Jacko had seen the same reaction a thousand times before.

Jacko spoke quietly to the old man, who nodded silently along. Jacko finished talking and the owner solemnly assumed a position alongside his wife and daughter behind the cash register desk.

Jacko stood back in the small reception area and watched the back of the head of the man eating alone at the sushi bar. He was tipping up a small bowl of miso soup. There was a small fountain in the main dining room that dripped water peacefully onto a flat rock. The sushi chef on the other side of the bar continued to work with his knife, cutting up raw fish and packing rice together in his hands. He was oblivious to anything else going on.

The two men who had come in with Jacko moved quietly through the main dining room, politely—but firmly—telling the patrons that there had been an equipment problem in the kitchen and that they would have to leave immediately. The diners were instructed to see the owner at the checkout desk for a certificate for a complimentary dinner for another night.

Jacko had made the decision that he needed to get out of his downtown San Francisco high-rise office and get out with his men working in the streets to demonstrate the value of one of the most important traits of a successful lieutenant in his organization—discipline. Without discipline, there would be no order. And without order, there would be no organization. Jacko thought it was time to remind the Takiyama organization that he still had the balls to get on the streets, if necessary, and enforce order in the family business.

Everyone was out—except for the man at the sushi bar—in less than two minutes. After the last guest had gone, Jacko signaled to the owner to take his family into the back room. Jacko turned the OPEN sign in the window around to SORRY WE'RE CLOSED and quietly turned the lock to the front door.

The synthesized Japanese music on the sound system and fountain splashing in the main room covered Jacko's steps up to the sushi bar. His lieutenants moved off to the side in a flanking maneuver. Jacko stood directly behind the man who was still unaware of anything going on.

The sushi chef was hunched over a beautiful piece of salmon, making a careful slice into the fish. He stood upright to reach for the rice. He saw Jacko and immediately sensed something was not right. Jacko put his finger to his lips and shook his head slowly. Jacko pointed to the door to the kitchen through a curtain behind the bar. The chef put his knife down and walked out, leaving the man at the counter alone with Jacko and his two men.

There was no one talking in the restaurant. The man finally realized that something was wrong. He looked to his right and saw one of

Jacko's men slightly back, and looked to his left and saw the other. He turned around quickly on his stool to face Jacko.

Jacko smiled broadly. "Enjoying your dinner?"

"J-J-Jacko . . ." the man stammered. He was a chubby Japanese man with a smooth baby face and a crew cut in a blue suit almost identical to those of Jacko and the other two.

Jacko looked over the man's shoulder to see what he had been eating.

"Is this where you shake down our fellow countrymen for a free meal? How much were you planning on paying for that *maguro?*" he snapped. He pointed to the piece of yellow tuna on the rice on the wooden tray on the counter. "Or maybe I should ask how much the old man was going to pay *you* to eat here so you wouldn't trash the place. What do you say, Kiro?"

"It's not like that, Jacko. Really . . ."

Jacko folded his arms and looked down his nose at Kiro. "*Re*-ally," he said.

"Really, Jacko. I was just out this way and stopped in for a bite to eat." He got his wallet out of his jacket pocket and took out two twenties and put them down onto the counter so that Jacko could see the twenty-spots. "I was going to pay and leave a good tip. See?"

Jacko nodded. "I see," he said. "And what I see is a lazy man who brings shame to our organization. Aren't you supposed to be somewhere else?"

Kiro stood up to address Jacko. Jacko put out his index finger and pushed it slowly into Kiro's chest, pushing him back down onto the stool. "Sit—down—scum."

"Jacko, everything's under control. I've got twenty men loading the shipment at the wharf. Harawaki is overseeing the operation right now. I just took a break to . . ."

Jacko flew into a rage and screamed at Kiro, "That's not the point! I gave you personal responsibility for a job and you're here stuffing your fat face while the rest of our men are risking their lives for me and the rest of the organization!" Jacko got right up into his face and yelled: "What are you thinking!"

Kiro shrank back and winced. Jacko smacked him hard across his face with the back of his hand. Kiro grabbed the side of his face in pain.

Jacko was breathing hard. "When I give you an assignment, it's for a reason. If I tell you to personally supervise an operation, it's because I believe you can carry out an order. But because of you, my family is disgraced."

He stepped back away from Kiro and took a deep breath to regain his composure. He stuffed his red tie back inside his buttoned jacket. "There is no place for you with us. You are worthless."

Jacko snapped his fingers and the other two came over and pushed Kiro back against the counter.

"But, Jacko . . ."

One of Jacko's lieutenants grabbed Kiro from behind while the other slipped on a pair of plastic handcuffs, the kind the police use for mass arrests. They held him tightly in place.

"I've given you several chances already," said Jacko. "You will not disobey me again, Kiro. You will not disobey because you are no longer one of us and you will no longer be subject to me and the family. Your services are no longer required."

Jacko pointed with his head to the counter on the other side of the bar. One of the men reached over and got a small blue and white kitchen towel and a ginsu knife.

Jacko picked up off the black and red lacquered eating counter a small Plexiglas display with pictures and descriptions of the different kinds of sushi. "Hmmm . . ." He studied the pictures. "Let's see. You've already had *maguro*. How about . . . *kappa maki?* Have you had cucumber roll yet?"

Kiro shook his head. He had a frightened look in his eyes.

"*Kappa maki*," Jacko ordered.

One of the men reached over the counter and picked up a long roll of rice filled with diced cucumbers that the chef hadn't sliced yet. He put it onto one of the wooden trays and passed it over to Jacko. Jacko sliced the roll into smaller pieces on the tray.

"*Kappa maki*, Kiro."

Jacko took a handful of the pieces and pushed them up into Kiro's face, rubbing it up into his nose. Kiro snorted as he inhaled some of the rice and started coughing and gagging. Jacko let him recover.

"Oh, I am so sorry. I forgot the horseradish."

Jacko reached behind Kiro and got a fingertip of the green spice from Kiro's plate. Jacko smeared the green stuff directly into Kiro's eyes, then pushed his finger up Kiro's nose.

Kiro screamed and started panting.

"Still enjoying your dinner?" Jacko asked.

Jacko picked up the Plexiglas display and looked over the sushi choices again. He shook his head.

"I just can't seem to find what I'm looking for, Kiro. Something *really* special." He looked around the room. "This *is* a nice place, Kiro. You seem to eat well. The food's good here, but the menu is somewhat limited. What say we put together something of our own tonight, shall we?"

Kiro was openly crying and sobbing. All he could do was shake his head. The horseradish was still burning intensely in his eyes and nose. Every few moments he would cough up a piece of rice from his lungs.

Jacko looked over at one of his men. "Some rice."

Jacko took the bowl of rice and scooped out a handful. He pressed it into the bent fingers of his other hand, forming the rice cake that the raw fish is laid onto. He put the rice down onto the wooden tray.

Jacko picked up the knife and held it against Kiro's throat. "Put your tongue out," he demanded.

Kiro was still panting. He had a wild look in his eye.

"Put your tongue out, damn you!" Jacko shouted into his ear.

Kiro hesitantly opened his mouth.

"Out!" shouted Jacko. He slid the knife along Kiro's throat drawing a trickle of blood. He held the blade up to show Kiro the blood.

"Out! Now!"

Kiro put his tongue out. Jacko grabbed the end of it firmly with the kitchen towel and cut off two inches of tongue with the knife.

Kiro screamed again and thrashed, trying desperately to free himself from the two men holding him tightly. He bent over and blood streamed out of his mouth onto the floor.

Jacko smoothed his hair back and watched Kiro writhe for a minute.

"Stand up straight," Jacko said calmly.

Kiro straightened, blood running down his chin over his clothes, spilling onto his shoes. His eyes were clamped tightly shut.

Jacko carefully placed the tongue onto the rice and held the creation up delicately to Kiro's face between two fingers.

"Eat," he ordered sternly.

Kiro opened his eyes and saw Jacko holding something in front of him. He pulled his head back to focus on what it was.

He clamped his eyes shut and shook his head. He started weeping bitterly.

"Eat!" Jacko shouted.

Jacko put the tip of the knife into Kiro's gut and pushed in a little. The jab got Kiro's attention and he opened his eyes again.

"Eat!"

Kiro's face was covered with a mixture of blood and rice and horseradish and tears. He swallowed hard and tried blinking away the tears which the horseradish still forced involuntarily.

"Eat!"

Jacko gave Kiro another jab with the point of the knife.

Kiro responded immediately by throwing back his head and opening his mouth. Jacko laid the tongue sushi into Kiro's bloody oral cavity, the blood pooling and flowing between the spaces in the teeth even as he put the sushi in.

"Now close your mouth and eat," said Jacko.

Kiro closed his eyes slowly as he brought his jaws together, bringing the teeth into contact with the tongue.

"Swallow!" demanded Jacko.

Kiro took a deep breath and tried to swallow, then started gagging again. He seemed as if he might try to spit the food in his mouth out.

"Don't even think about it! Swallow, you bastard!"

Kiro took another deep breath and tucked his chin as he swallowed the tongue and rice whole. Jacko noticed the lump in his throat move down.

Jacko stepped back again to take a good look at Kiro. The bloodied man was shaking with sobs.

Jacko snapped his fingers again. "Outside," he said. "Through the kitchen."

Jacko's two men forced Kiro to walk to the other side of the counter and pushed him through the curtain into the kitchen. Jacko got another bar towel and wiped up the mess he had made as best he could.

Jacko went over to the cashier's desk and took out a tight roll of bills from his pocket. He peeled off five one-hundred-dollar notes and put them under the bell on the desk. He rang the bell twice to let the owner know he was leaving. He pocketed a book of matches with the restaurant's logo and popped a mint into his mouth from the bowl next to the cash register.

"*To-sihu,*" he called out to the back room. Sorry.

On his way outside, Jacko stepped behind the sushi bar and grabbed a squid out of the ice and got down an unopened bottle of sake off the top shelf.

The unlighted alley behind the restaurant reeked of garbage and stinking fish. Kiro leaned back against a Dumpster with his hands bound behind him. The two lieutenants stood nearby smoking cigarettes, but threw them down and stamped them out when Jacko came through the back door.

Jacko threw the arm-length squid to one of the men. It cartwheeled through the air. He caught it by one of its tentacles covered with suction cups.

"You know what they say about oriental food, don't you, Kiro?"

Kiro had his eyes closed. He shook his head.

"They say that oriental food leaves you hungry. I wouldn't want one of my fellow countrymen to go hungry. I am a compassionate man."

Jacko got up close to Kiro. "Have some *tako,*" he said.

Kiro didn't respond.

Jacko punched him hard in the stomach and he doubled over and vomited. Jacko pulled his head back up by the hair and slammed it hard against the metal wall of the Dumpster, making a loud thud sound that reverberated a few moments.

"You will eat when I tell you to do so."

Kiro opened his mouth slightly. Jacko held out his hand and was handed the squid. He pushed a tentacle into Kiro's mouth and Kiro clamped his mouth shut. Jacko punched him hard again and his mouth flew open.

"Hold him," ordered Jacko. They held Kiro's head against the Dumpster.

Jacko kept stuffing the arms of the squid into Kiro's mouth. Kiro started gagging. Part of the squid was down his throat. Jacko took two of the loose tentacle ends and forced them into Kiro's nostrils.

Kiro tried again to thrash. He was getting no air.

"Let him go," said Jacko.

Kiro fell to the ground, rubbing his face on the pavement in an attempt to loosen the squid from his nose and mouth, but the squid was stuck.

The three men watched Kiro struggle for a while longer, flipping around the alley like a fish on a dry dock. After a minute, Kiro was still. Jacko waited until he saw the muscles in Kiro's body relax and saw a telltale puddle of urine spread out from underneath him. He gave the body a nudge with his foot.

The lieutenants watched the ends of the alley to make sure no one wandered upon them. Jacko unscrewed the cap from the bottle of sake and took a slug. He passed it to the others who turned it up for a long swallow.

"*Sayonara,* Kiro," said Jacko, raising the bottle in the air as a toast.

He poured the rest of the bottle over Kiro's body, soaking his clothes and hair. He unfolded the matchbook from the restaurant and struck a match. He stepped back and threw the match onto the body. It burst into flames with a loud, sucking *whoosh.*

Jacko watched the face. Just before Kiro's beautiful long eyelashes caught fire, they curled back upon themselves in the intense heat. The short black hair on the top of his head burnt down to the scalp. Kiro's porcelain face charred like an overdone piece of chicken on the grill.

The heat contracted the fibers in the muscles of the squid's tentacles, making them twist around Kiro's head and face as if it were still alive, sucking the last drop of life out of his body.

The smell of the searing flesh finally rose above the stink of the alley, signaling that it was time to go. Jacko was satisfied. He knew that the word would quickly get out to the others in the organization: *Don't fuck with me.*

"Looks like *unagi,*" observed Jacko to the other two.

They nodded. It would be a long time until they had smoked eel again.

18 ❑   ❑   ❑   ❑

"You cheated," said Jenkins. He narrowed his eyes at Greer sitting across his desk. "I wondered how long it would take you to work your way through my writings." He broke into a wide grin.

"So I'm on the right track?" Greer asked.

"Well, it comes pretty close to the place where the dog is buried, I'll admit."

"You've kept me pretty busy. Now that I've done my homework, are you willing to talk to me about it?"

"Not yet."

"Okay. But what's the deal with my collecting raw intelligence at Langley?"

"*Oh* no. Just keep it up over there. You still have another couple of weeks to go."

"A couple of weeks, huh? Not even a hint?"

"The last administration ignored my warnings. Now that I'm on the inside, I'll be damned if I'm going to be blown off again. It's too vital to the country's interests. That makes what you're doing even more important."

"Promise me that you'll lay out the whole thing when I'm done."

"I can do better than that. I'll let you help me develop the concept for the final analysis. The analysis that Dwight Conrad is afraid I'll rock his diplomatic boat with. I'll not let that weasel of a gatekeeper hold back the truth from the President. I owe it to the President as a duty and as a personal adviser."

Greer felt he was close to securing important information that he could relay to Reed. "So—what's the timing on all this?"

"We're looking at late December."

Apparently, Jenkins wanted to get his theory and proof in front of the President before the G7 conference in January.

Jenkins continued: "We're wrapping up because you and I are taking a little trip."

"Is that the good news you talked about?" Jenkins' secretary had sent him an E-mail message saying "good news" and it was time for a meeting at the Old Executive Office Building.

"I think so." Jenkins pulled down the massive *Times World Atlas* off the shelf behind him and opened it up to where he had inserted a Bazooka Joe gum wrapper comic as a bookmark. He turned the book around for Greer to see.

"Ever been to Germany?" Jenkins asked.

The question flooded Greer with emotions spanning eight years. He nodded. "Yes, in fact, I have. I spent my junior year in college abroad at the University of Heidelberg."

"How's your German?"

"*Ich spreche Deutsch sehr gut.*"

"You'll need it, because we're going to Cologne in about two weeks for the pre-G7 conference meeting. That's why you need to push hard to get as many days in at CIA as you can before we leave. When we leave, that's it. We'll have to find something more productive for you to do around here."

Greer thought about what it would be like not seeing Kate every day, all day. It had been a luxury, he knew.

"What will we be doing over there?"

"Mainly snooping around. The purpose of the meeting is for the staffs of the G7 participants to get together and confirm agendas and protocol for the San Francisco summit. Everyone in the Administration is killing himself to make sure the Japanese sign the side agreement on opening up Japan to American imports. State Department is in charge of the function. We won't have an official role, but I just let them know over at State that we'd be attending so we'll get all the clearances we'll need. License to roam."

"What's my part?" Greer asked.

"Mingle. Hang out at the meetings. Keep your eyes open. These people will be your peers, so you'll fit right in. I want you going to the cocktail parties, dinners."

"And what will you be doing?"

"I'll be around." Jenkins gave Greer a cryptic smile. He pulled the sleeve up of his shirt and looked at his wristwatch. "It's just after midnight in Bonn. Think I'll wait until tomorrow morning to call Herr Kuntze."

Greer recognized the name. Kuntze was the head of Germany's intelligence service. He had been in the news a lot lately because of his hard-line stance in favor of closing Germany to foreign immigration. He termed the immigrants "a security risk." "German intelligence?"

"Yes. Very good. I'm going to see if he'll motor over to Cologne to meet me for dinner one night. I want to feel him out on a few issues."

"Won't the DCI be annoyed again? I mean, won't it seem like you're meddling?"

"Screw Gibbons."

The first week of December arrived along with the first truly awful weather of the season. Outside on the National Mall it was cold with rain blowing off and on. Inside the East Building of the National Gallery of Art, the air was still and warm.

Kate and Greer stood on the inside balcony of the upper level of the museum, watching people crossing the spacious central court on the ground floor below. Greer had out a brochure with the museum floor plan, orienting himself to the different galleries in the contemporary architecture of the building.

"Directly behind us," said Greer, pointing to the entrance of the Twentieth Century Art Gallery. "Through that gallery and up the stairs."

They walked into the first room of the gallery, pausing before Brancusi's *Bird in Flight*. Greer's hand brushed against Kate's as they stood side by side looking at the tall white sculpture. Kate casually intertwined her fingers with his own and gave his hand a firm squeeze.

Greer hadn't had a chance to really get out and see the sights in Washington since moving to the city. He and Kate worked in the office through the middle of the Sunday afternoon, then left for the museum to see a special exhibit of large modern metal sculpture he had read about in the *Post*. There was only a handful of visitors other than themselves.

Greer had spent a lot of time lately thinking about how his professional life was beginning to impact his relationship with Kate. He had to assume that eventually Kate would know everything, but what *would* he tell her? What would she think when she found out that he had been working with her at Langley under false pretenses? As their relationship deepened he was becoming more and more uncomfortable with having to lie to her. But Kate was a professional, too. She would understand, he reasoned. If she were in the same position and knew about Randall Jenkins being a mole, she would do the same thing. He was sure of it. For now, he could still rationalize the deception, his divided loyalties. He would go on with his schizophrenic existence as the lover and the spy.

Greer tugged at her and led her through a passageway into a much smaller room. They looked at the paintings and small sculptures behind glass, then came to the far corner. There was a dark alcove with recessed lights illuminating several tall tropical plants at the base of a spiral staircase.

"After you," said Greer, pointing to the steps.

Kate started up, followed by Greer. As they wound their way up to the Tower Gallery, the sounds of the rest of the museum began to fade. The higher they went, the quieter it got. Just as they got to the top of the stairs, Greer grabbed Kate's arm.

"Hold on," he said in a hushed voice.

She stopped and they both listened.

"What is it?" she asked.

Greer shook his head, still straining to hear.

"I thought I heard a voice I recognized," he said.

Greer motioned for her to keep walking, and they emerged at the top of the stairs into the Tower Gallery. They stepped into the middle of the room.

The special exhibit of sculpture was displayed on low, multitiered risers in front of them. The large pieces looked like totems of some alien civilization. The room was the quietest place in the museum. The only sound they could hear was the movement of the elevators somewhere deep inside the building. Then there was a sharp crack.

Almost indistinguishable from the sculptures was a museum guard sitting on one of the risers. They hadn't seen him in the artificial light when they had first come in. He had just snapped his gum. Greer and Kate smiled at each other.

Then, from around the corner in the adjoining room, came the sound of low, muffled voices.

Greer touched Kate's arm. He had a puzzled, surprised look on his face. He motioned to her to step back toward the top of the stairs and put his finger to his lips.

The voices from the other room in the Tower Gallery began again. Greer listened hard. He couldn't make out individual words, but he could tell that it was two men speaking in German. One of the voices was harsh, slightly more tense than the other. This first voice was unfamiliar to him, but memorable in its intensity and rapid-fire guttural monologue. The second voice broke in sporadically. This other voice was irritated. It was also—familiar.

Greer heard feet shuffling in the other room. The men were coming into the main room where the sculptures were. They were still talking. Greer took Kate's hand and pulled her quickly down the tightly winding stairs behind him before the two men could see them.

"What is it?" asked Kate, trying to keep up with Greer as he rushed down the steps.

Greer had nailed the voice. Even in German, he knew it was Reed. Probably meeting with some German diplomat he was running as an agent. The last thing Greer wanted to do was screw up another of Reed's operations, especially with Kate in tow.

"I'm starving," said Greer. "Let's find something off the Mall. We'll come back another time."

It was just before six o'clock when they left the museum. Outside it was dark and bitterly cold, the rain having taken a break. The steps were wet, turning to ice. Greer hurried them along the sidewalk away from the museum, crossing to the other side of the Mall.

"The thing of it is, we won't be spending all our days together anymore after I get back from Germany. Jenkins says he's pulling me off working on the station traffic. According to him, we're done. I leave in two weeks." He had told her Friday. It was no big deal. He would be back in less than a week, just in time for them to spend Christmas together.

"Your going away for a while may be a good thing," Kate said.

"What do you mean?"

"You know when I was late Friday morning?"

"Yeah?"

"I was in Ben's office. Some guy from the Agency saw us on the rooftop of the Washington Hotel that night."

"That was over a month ago. What did he say?"

"Ben told me that seeing you outside the office was 'high-risk behavior.' He suggested that we not be visible together anymore, for the sake of the Agency and for the sake of my career."

"Dammit!"

"Well, we knew it would happen sooner or later and, actually, I understand his point of view. He has the integrity of the Agency to maintain. There have been security failures before. He's determined it's not going to happen on his watch."

"He sees me as a security issue?" Incredible, thought Greer. And actually a little confusing. According to Reed, the Director was in on Greer's role in ferreting out Randall Jenkins. So what was this all about? Maybe Gibbons was erecting a wall between Kate and Greer to throw any possible suspicion off Greer as someone who was really a CIA operative. If everyone in the Agency saw the Director doing what he could to thwart an outsider such as Greer, it would go a long way to support his cover story. "So what are you saying?" said Greer.

Kate pulled her gloves tighter. "If people don't see us together for a while, maybe it'll blow over. I don't know. I'm honestly not sure how to sort it all out."

It made Greer angry, furious. Now his heart began to overcome his reason. He refused to lose Kate. That was the last thing on earth he was going to allow to happen. That might be what Gibbons and Reed wanted, but it was certainly not what Greer wanted.

"I don't want them to forget! I'm sick of this. I want everyone to know I'm in love with you and I want everyone to know that you're in love with me! Won't it make a difference to Gibbons once I've stopped coming in to Langley?"

"No."

"*No?*"

"From his point of view, I could have been compromised. In his eyes, you're just some guy hired by his main political rival in the Administration to snoop around his workshop. He has no idea how far along our relationship is. He's worried that you might still be pumping me for information, even after you're gone. *Especially* after you're gone. Still feeding Jenkins with information about his agency. I'm just telling you what he said. I thought we should talk about it."

"That's crazy! I've never taken advantage of our relationship. Doesn't he trust you?"

Greer had no intention of sneaking around anymore with Kate after he got back from Germany. It was time for them to come out of the closet. There was something else he had been thinking of. He had wanted to save it until the night before he left. But it was time. "Well, what if he saw us as something more . . . stable? More permanent?"

Kate knew immediately what he was getting at. "I didn't bring the subject up with Ben, you know."

"I know. Well?"

"It could make a difference. People would be less inclined to talk." She stopped him. "It's different for guys. If it gets out that I'm sleeping with someone, it takes some of my power away at the office. It makes me less effective. That's just the way it is. Do you understand?"

It began to drizzle, a fine mist making the lights along the Mall glow big and orange.

Greer understood. He took her in his arms and kissed her hard. Kate matched his passion, meeting every probing kiss, every sweep of his hand over her body.

Greer got them walking again, but more quickly now. They were approaching the steps leading down to the sunken sculpture garden, a collection of modern sculptures set on dormant Bermuda grass. Greer took Kate's hand and led her down.

The garden was below the level of the Mall sidewalk on which they had been walking. There were huge cast-metal balls strewn about the lawn in random fashion, slick with rain, their rough finish refracting the lights from the Smithsonian museums.

Greer led Kate to the base of the wall directly below the Mall. The small rectangular pool was drained for the winter. Around the perimeter of the dead grass were more modern sculptures. In the corner of the garden was an unadorned fifteen-foot-tall sheet of metal set as a monolith into the soft, wet turf. The metal was reddish brown, oxidized, rusting in the rain.

They stood close to the garden wall, just out of casual sight of anyone walking along the Mall sidewalk above. Greer positioned Kate with her back against the sculpture. Greer had no gloves and his numb fingers fumbled to unbutton her overcoat while she unbuttoned his. Kate finished first and unzipped him. She parted for him and he immediately found a path inside her. She sank onto it, lifted up by Greer's hands, pinned to the flat sculpture like a note tacked to the wall. The mist turned into rain again. Kate wrapped her legs around Greer and he drove deeper, then all the way. She went to moan loudly, but Greer covered her mouth with a kiss. They found a rhythm, rocking against the sculpture. The rain came down harder, beating onto the shoulders of their coats, their shoes, soaking them, soaking the sheet of metal, turning it from brown to black. The sculpture responded to the rhythm, buckled slightly in the middle with each thrust. Kate began to hum, to moan, a sound that found sympathy in the gently swaying metal form. A vibration ran through the metal, a note formed inside, and the sculpture began to sing. Kate and the sculpture, driven and bent, a syncopated lovemaking, her hum and its singing, and Greer feeling the note coming out of them both, feeling the tone vibrate out of Kate and the rain-streaked sculpture, a swell in his loins and muscles contracting and up his spine and at last into Kate—

"Now!" she cried—his heels digging into the sod for a hard final thrust after she had said it was his time.

They were still. In the rain, in their overcoats. Utterly wet. Kate's gloved hands around his neck. She slid her legs down and took heavy breaths at his ear. He reached up for balance and touched the metal with his fingertips. The top of the sculpture was still bending back and forth, slightly swaying, still moaning with Kate's love in sympathetic vibrations, channeling dissonant warbling notes through his fingers and into his limbs, back into Kate, like a bow pulled over a saw.

Kate hung on.

"No one's going to keep us apart from each other," Greer said. "We're not through. We're not anywhere close to being through. Dammit, I love you."

19

"We have, as you can see, *disproved* the null hypothesis," said Jenkins, underlining the bottom of the marker board in a broad stroke to make his point and indicate that he was finished with his proof. "By applying standard statistical analysis, we have just shown that it is *not* possible that the Japanese and Germans are *not* cooperating on a coordinated economic plan. Therefore, they *are* operating in concert."

All Greer knew for sure was that he heard lots of double negatives. He looked at the white board in Jenkins' office, smeared in a blur of mathematical calculations. It had been a while since he had taken a class in statistics, but he understood the basic concepts. The bell curves and Greek letters looked familiar. Jenkins could think much faster than he could write, though. The scrawl raced off to the side and turned into an ink study for a DeKooning painting. The writing was hopelessly illegible.

Jenkins saw that Greer was still puzzled. "Don't you see!" said Jenkins. "It's perfectly clear!"

"Let's go through it again, *slowly* this time," Greer pleaded.

"Okay, okay," said Jenkins with fiendish glee. He couldn't wait to go through the mathematical proof again. Three of the four walls of his office were covered with papers tacked to the wall with colored pushpins. From where he was sitting, Greer couldn't read what was on the paper. Jenkins was about to take Greer on another statistical tour of his office, pausing at the groupings of notes like a pilgrim walking the Stations of the Cross at some shrine.

Jenkins took him through the proof again, showed him how the data Greer had been collecting at Langley for the past two and a half months supported his theory.

"I'm impressed," Greer finally said. "An elegant proof."

"Do you see now why I didn't want you to know what we were working toward? Do you see how you could have subtly—subconsciously—altered the facts you were collecting? The evidence would have been tainted. But you collected everything, not just economic data, so your research is more valid."

"Yes, I see that now." Greer felt as if he were sitting at the feet of Plato. The reasoning was brilliant, the implications troubling.

"CIA is great at recruiting and running spies," Jenkins offered. "It's just when all that intelligence gets here to Washington that things sometimes fall through the cracks. The overall management of the analysis stinks. There's no one who systematically sits down and looks at seemingly unrelated events and reports from different parts of the world and asks, What is the possibility that these are related events? CIA would never catch this because they're not looking for these types of cross-regional relationships. I guarantee you—the Far East desk never talks to the Western European guy about this kind of thing."

They both sat there quietly for a few more moments looking at the notes on the board, admiring the logic. There was nothing soft about it. No one could seriously question the numbers or the methodology. Greer was confounded by the implications. Maybe Jenkins was right. Maybe Dwight Conrad and Ben Gibbons and—yes—even Reed were wrong. Maybe the guy wasn't a total nut.

"The implications of this are serious," said Greer.

"Yes, they are."

"I was thinking of the G7 conference."

"So was I."

Greer said, "If Japan is supposed to be signing the side agreements on opening up trade to the U.S., what's all this about? This analysis points to coordination of economic policy between Germany and Japan. There's been no mention of anything like that in the press."

"None," agreed Jenkins.

"So what's the point of their going to the G7 conference if they're cutting some covert deal with each other?"

"You know my thinking on the subject," said Jenkins.

"The theory? A new economic alliance?"

"Yes. All indications are that's what's going on."

"It would totally destroy the world's economic order as we know it today, wouldn't it?"

"Yes, it would. It would mean a return to the isolationism of the beginning of the century. Or worse," he added.

"Damn." Greer thought about Reed and was glad for the meeting already scheduled for the next day, only three days before he left for Cologne. He would have a lot to report. Reed would ask him again about timing. Greer needed to probe.

"I'll be honest with you," said Greer. "There aren't that many people in the Administration who could follow that argument. It's going to be a tough sell. You think the President will understand all this?"

Jenkins gave him a stern look. "You greatly underestimate the President."

"I don't doubt his intelligence. This is pretty arcane stuff. Trying to relate to him on this level with statistics may be a problem."

"Don't forget, the President and I went to college together. What you probably don't know is that we took the same statistics class together. He got the 'A,' I got the 'B.'"

"You're right. I *didn't* know."

"Let's call Dwight Conrad over at the White House to set up that appointment. I want a meeting with the full National Security Council as soon as we get back from Cologne. Be sure to bring your laptop and data disks on our trip so we can work together on the presentation."

Jenkins picked up the phone, dialed the Chief of Staff, and waited for an answer. He covered the mouthpiece. "We'll show those SOBs what real analysis is all about." Conrad's secretary put him on hold as she got Conrad on the line. "Oh, by the way," Jenkins said to Greer as they waited, "since you've put in all this work, I've decided to let *you* give the presentation to the President."

There were no overhead lights in the National Aquarium building and only the indirect lighting from the huge fish tanks lit the room. Greer and Reed stood in the darkest part of the Aquarium in front of tank number 46, *Lepisosteus Osseus,* the American Longnose Gar. Watery shadows wobbled on the floor in parallelograms at their feet.

"They're fumigating the Smithsonian Castle this week," said Reed. "Everybody had to clear out for a few days."

"That explains it." This was the first time they had ever met outside of the Smithsonian safe room. Greer had yet to see Reed in the full light of day, however, and was beginning to wonder if he would recognize him under better-lit conditions. At least half his face was always in shadow. He looked at the tank and saw their faces reflected in the glass five feet away.

The two dozen aquarium filters in the room bubbled a base line to their conversation, just at speaking-voice level. Only an aquarium employee in khaki shirt and pants was nearby working around the tanks.

"You're not going to like it," said Greer.

"Try me. I've been waiting for over two months to get some worthwhile intelligence out of this operation."

"First, Jenkins just got a commitment from Dwight Conrad to set up a meeting the week before Christmas with the President and then the full National Security Council. We'll be presenting the findings on the theory he's been working on. I know what it is now. To be honest, I'm convinced myself. I was the one who collected all the evidence that went into the analysis."

"Go on."

"I researched Jenkins' academic work at the Library of Congress. Jenkins had developed the theory while he was still at the Hoover Institution. He thinks that America would be vulnerable to being isolated economically from key markets of the world if two or more major economic forces cooperated to exclude the U.S. from trading internationally. He refers to it in his paper as an economic Armageddon. Jenkins used a computer and applied a statistical analysis of the raw intelligence I had gathered at Langley and showed quantitatively that Japan and Germany were almost certainly working together on the premise of his theory."

"The analysis looked credible, then?"

"The logic was seamless. It's a solid piece of academic research. The White House won't be able to ignore it."

Reed drew in a slow, deep breath of the humid air. A bare white arm plunged into the top of the tank in front of them from the other side of the glass, stirred up the accumulated muck. The woman on the other side started cleaning the tank.

"What else?" Reed asked dryly.

"I'll admit I'm a bit confused about Jenkins' motivation in this thing. He's put a lot of effort into pushing his theory and gathering evidence to support it. What kind of ulterior motives could he possibly have? Is it possible everyone's been wrong about him?"

Reed shook his head. "You're right. Motivation *is* the crucial question. Remember the Executive Finding. Espionage, but who's controlling him? Our mission was to find out what the whole story is. So far, we've failed."

"What about Cologne?" asked Greer.

"The trip may be the last chance you have to get anything out of him. Gibbons is going to have my head if he walks into that NSC meeting without having anything for the President on Jenkins. The President's reelection may depend on whether he gets the trade side agreements with Japan signed next month. If there is anything possible we can do to stop Jenkins before then to keep him from muddying the waters, I know how grateful the White House would be."

"I haven't given up," Greer said. "I'll keep trying."

"I know you will. And I know you'll succeed. I can easily see how this is going to play out for you. You'll be brought into Langley after this whole thing's over and introduced to your peers in the Clandestine Service as the man who stopped Randall Jenkins. I don't doubt you'll be awarded the Distinguished Intelligence Cross, the highest award the DCI can give. You'd be the youngest officer ever to receive it. It'll be a proud moment for me. After that, you'll get your pick of plum jobs anywhere around the world. I've already resigned myself to losing you, but it will be to the benefit of the Agency as a whole. Do you share my vision?"

Greer was pumped up. "You're damned right I do."

"Let's go get 'em."

"Dammit, dammit, *dammit!*" Dwight Conrad cracked a rolled-up *Washington Post* on the windowsill in his office overlooking the Rose Garden. "Are statistics important enough to go to war over?" he asked. He stood staring out the window shaking his head in disbelief.

Ben Gibbons shared the White House Chief of Staff's frustration. "Congressman Weston is finally gone, and now this. Did you have to agree to a meeting *before* the G7 conference next month?" Gibbons asked.

"I didn't have any choice." Conrad shot the DCI a sidelong glance. "Jimmy Weston. What a trip. I had to beg the President to say something nice about him to the press. Of course, going to the funeral was out of the question."

"Of course."

"Anyway," said Conrad, "enough of that. That problem took care of itself. The President and his wife go to the Renaissance Group outing at Hilton Head every New Year's weekend. Jenkins has also been a member from the beginning, so they'll be spending two whole days together. Jenkins is sure to bring up the subject. If I hadn't agreed, Jenkins would have spent forty-eight hours bad-mouthing me." Conrad started shaking his head again. "Any ideas?"

"I did have one. I solicited input—on a highly confidential basis, of course—from an old friend of mine at the Agency. He thought the idea of throwing Jenkins a red herring to keep him busy was worth pursuing."

"And?"

"Jenkins is going to Cologne to snoop around at the G7 protocol meetings. My idea was to turn him loose on something else while he's over there. Have him visit a few CIA stations. I'd assign a case officer to work with him *and* to keep an eye on him. I think we might be able to pull him away from Cologne for several days. Make him feel important. I was going to ask him to assess our liaison with other intelligence services. I could bury him in minutiae so he'd be too busy to screw things up at the G7 meetings. Ask him to submit a report. Could actually be interesting."

"He's politically insensitive. I don't think he understands that what he's really doing is hurting the President. He's spent too much time at a university. He lives in a fantasy world."

"We might also want to go ahead and draw up a short list of names for possible replacements for Jenkins."

"This soon?"

"I think we need to have it to show the President before Jenkins' scheduled presentation. When did you say it was?"

Conrad walked over to his desk and looked at his desk calendar.

"Jenkins leaves for Cologne on the sixteenth—day after tomorrow—and he's scheduled to get back on the twenty-first. I promised him an hour with the President on the twenty-second. The full National Security Council meets the following day."

"So between now and when Jenkins gets back, we've got about seven days to do something."

Conrad stroked his chin. "What do you think?"

Gibbons answered, "I'm confident the Agency will figure something out. The President will understand the political situation. He'll hate dumping Jenkins, but he'll understand what needs to be done. You can find him a cushy job on some presidential commission that meets a couple of times a year. Let's get that list of new National Security Advisers candidates ready for the President."

20

Already dressed for work, Greer poured himself a cup of coffee. Christmas music was playing on the radio. He finally heard her turn the shower taps in the bathroom and close the door.

Greer went back into the bedroom and made sure that Kate wasn't coming out anytime soon. He went to her vanity and selected a small-pointed, sable-hair makeup brush from the half-dozen brushes sticking up in the vase.

Back in the kitchen, Greer got a lemon out of the refrigerator, cut it open, and squeezed the juice into a bowl. He got Kate's planner from her purse and removed the blank page for the day, December 15. Greer dipped the tip of the brush into the lemon juice and wrote on the planner page. He blotted the paper, blew on it until it had thoroughly dried, then returned it to the planner. He replaced the planner into Kate's purse. He cleaned the brush and bowl and returned the brush to the vase on the vanity. Kate was still in the shower.

Greer put on his overcoat. To help maintain the fiction of their nonrelationship, Greer drove to work and Kate was taking the Metro and Agency shuttle from the city. On the way out he dialed Kate's number at Langley. It rang and he waited for her voice-mail message to come on. Today was the last day he would be working with Kate at CIA headquarters. A quick side trip to Jenkins' office to coordinate their travel plans for the next day, then a short afternoon at Langley to tie up the loose ends and look over any last-minute cables.

He heard Kate's voice-mail greeting begin on the phone. Greer imagined what her reaction would be. She'd be getting his message just about the time he was sitting down to map out his trip to Europe.

Kate hung up the phone in the conference room and opened her purse, just as Greer had instructed. She took out her planner and rummaged around for something else. Yes, she had forgotten about that. At last she found the box of matches from the romantic inn in the Blue Ridge Mountains and put it into the pocket of her skirt.

Also as she had been instructed, she took out the day's page from her planner. She held it up to the light—it was blank. She went down the hall to the women's room and locked herself into a stall. She struck a match and held it beneath the page. Forms began to appear on the page, dark brown letters where the flame almost touched the paper. I LOVE YOU AND WE'LL FIND A WAY TO STAY TOGETHER FOREVER!!—NO MATTER WHAT. BE PATIENT!! She laughed and fanned the match fumes away, then crumpled the note and flushed it down the toilet.

Greer's meeting with Jenkins ran long, and he didn't leave the Old Executive Office Building until after eleven o'clock. He had gotten his marching orders about snooping around the cocktail circuit in Cologne for information that might relate to Jenkins' theory. Their flight left just after eight the next night.

Greer pulled out of the parking lot and turned on the radio. Instead of the NPR station he had been listening to, he heard a click as the cassette tape was being engaged. Funny, he thought. He didn't remember listening to a tape on the way in. Probably the old Little Feat tape he had been listening to after work last night, he figured. He must have tapped it in by accident when he turned the radio off getting out.

There was no sound. He turned up the volume and was suddenly blasted by a voice: "LOVED YOUR NOTE!" It was Kate. Greer adjusted the volume down to the normal level. "Okay, Greer Whitaker, as soon as you get back from Germany, we'll work something out. And I'll wait as long as it takes. I'll see you in the office in a few minutes. I'm breathless. Do you know how fast I had to scramble to get from Langley to your car? Thank God there was an Agency car available for me to use. Anyway, take a look on the floor in the backseat passenger's side. I want you to have something from me to take with you on your trip. An early Christmas present. I LOVE YOU!"

Greer waited until he came to a stop light. He reached behind the seat and felt a small box, about the size of a paperback book. A tidy package in Christmas wrapping. He tore the paper off, slid a sleeve off the box and opened the lid.

"Wow," he said.

A car behind him tapped his horn. Greer saw the green light and pulled ahead. He pulled out the present: a gold Longines tank watch, a genuine period piece, probably from the thirties.

Greer was in shock. The tape was over. He reached to turn it off.

"Don't worry," her voice boomed again.

The suddenness of her unexpected voice made him jump.

"I didn't scratch your car picking your lock. And by the way, there's another of those 'special messages' that came in last night from our friend. I'm sure you're going to want to see this when you get in."

Kate had already anticipated his request. "The Director said that he's arranged for a CIA officer from the embassy in Bonn to meet you and Jenkins," she said. Kate handed Greer a folder marked TOP SECRET. "I thought this is something you need to be aware of since you're going to be in Germany. It's REDWING again."

"I figured," Greer said.

Greer made sure that Kate saw he was wearing his new watch. A quick glance at the mirrored window. "Thanks," he said.

Greer opened the folder and saw a cable from the Paris station. At the top of the page he saw that the transmission had been received at CIA headquarters at 0430 hours, Greer calculated being sent at ten-thirty in the morning Paris time. His eye fell to the bottom of the page where someone had bracketed a paragraph in the margin for emphasis.

He read out loud: "REDWING confirms infiltration of U.S. intelligence, although level and specific agency unknown at this time. Source REDWING also confirms operation being managed in U.S. . . ."

The sentence continued on the next page. He flipped the top page over and creased the top corner back at the staple as he picked up reading: ". . . by Germany." He paused. "Field officer to follow up this P.M. on REDWING's mention of operation's designation as code word STEEPLECHASE. Unknown meaning at this writing."

Greer continued looking at the page. All the words were familiar, but something was wrong.

He reread the paragraph to himself. Then he read it *again*. He became aware of time and how it had seemed to slow down. He lost perspective of time as he read the cable yet another time. His arms were going numb. He was aware of Kate watching him for his reaction. He was taking too long to react. He couldn't talk. It was all happening in slow motion. He slumped into a chair and closed his eyes. He *knew* what was wrong.

"Are you okay?" Kate asked. She touched his shoulder and he nodded with his eyes closed. "Greer?" She made a motion toward the telephone. Greer heard her pick up the phone. "Operator . . ."

"I'm okay," Greer interrupted in a hoarse voice, opening his eyes. He cleared his throat. "Really."

She put down the phone. "What's wrong?"

Greer felt some control returning to his body. He wiped the perspiration from his forehead. "It must have been coming in from the cold. I just felt sick all of a sudden," he said.

Greer lifted the folder from his lap and handed it back to Kate. "Sorry if I scared you. I hope I'm not coming down with anything." He smiled weakly.

Kate gave Greer a worried look. "Are you sure you're okay? You look really pale."

Greer sat up in the chair. "I'm all right now. I promise." He wiped more perspiration off his forehead and neck. He pointed to the folder. "That's explosive stuff."

"The Agency's counterintelligence division has pulled out all the stops this afternoon. The big question being kicked around upstairs is —assuming the intelligence is good—whether the agent was put in place by the old West German government or the East German government. The conjecture is that it's a renegade leftover from the old Stasi before German reunification. It would make a big difference as to how the case is handled diplomatically."

"There *is* one other possibility," suggested Greer.

"What's that?"

Greer was thinking of Jenkins. The reference to STEEPLECHASE *must* have been some perversion of Reed's CIA operation in the National Security Council's office, he reasoned. Somewhere there was a serious leak about STEEPLECHASE. "It could be an operation set up under the *new* German government."

Kate shook her head. "That seems unlikely. The Germans are trying to get U.S. assistance to help defray the costs of reunification. They want part of our 'peace dividend' to subsidize the work. Why would they want to jeopardize American aid?"

"*Why* did Israel run Jonathan Pollard in the eighties?" Greer said, alluding to the Department of Defense employee convicted on espionage charges for spying for Israel. "That was just as stupid."

Kate thought about that for a moment, and decided not to pursue it. "I don't need to tell you that you shouldn't discuss REDWING with anyone on the trip. Ben has asked Jenkins to talk to some other intelligence services in Europe while he's in Germany. He'll be fully briefed by the field officer once you get over there."

Color had returned to Greer's face, although his undershirt was damp with sweat. He would need time to think about the implications of REDWING's report. He needed to get in touch with Reed before he and Jenkins left the next evening on the flight from the airport. He couldn't safely leave a message for Reed, though, from CIA headquarters.

"I think I should swing by my apartment to check on things before coming over," Greer said. "I need to turn the faucets on. I don't want the pipes bursting while I'm gone, you know."

Greer set up his computer and portable printer on the credenza next to the phone. He was whipped.

"Jenkins' secretary is supposed to send me our final itinerary," he said.

Greer entered his password and got into his E-mail. He hurriedly looked at the first page. The itinerary was there, sent only a half hour ago. He typed the command to print out the entire contents of his mailbox, folded the paper and stuck it into his briefcase. He could look at the schedule later.

"I'll be over as soon as I can," he said.

21 ❑ ❑ ❑ ❑

Greer let his fingers slip from the stem of the wineglass to the arm of the Mission-style sofa he was settled into. He rubbed the wood admiringly. It was a world away from the clutter of the sturdy Ethan Allan hand-me-downs of his own apartment. Kate didn't have much furniture, but what she had was beautiful. Two other pieces in the room of the same style reflected a low fire in their polished wood: a high-back rocking chair and a coffee table. A small, hand-tied Persian rug lay in front of the fireplace. The fire was lit and on the mantel flickered candles set in wrought-iron and glass and silver candlesticks of varying heights. Christmas holly with red bows hung over the doorways.

Greer listened to the clatter coming from the kitchen. He smelled dinner cooking, some foreign amalgam of herbs and sizzling meat. He watched through the darkened dining area for glimpses of Kate moving about the kitchen. The dining room was void of furniture except for a huge framed print of a tropical landscape in splashy colors, illuminated by soft spotlights in the ceiling. Looking about the apartment, it was obvious that she had put her money into prints and paintings and other collectibles.

"You okay in there?" she called out.

"I'm doing great." He swirled the wine around its large bowl and took another thoughtful swallow. A lush swell of Chopin came from the speakers.

The kitchen was separated from the dining room by an island with two high stools side by side. The counter was brightly set with linen and sparkling stemware. Two more candles marked the spot where they would dine.

"*Looche pozno chem nekogda,*" she said with a proper Moscow accent. She slipped quickly around the corner from the kitchen. Greer rested his head on the back of the couch and listened to her take half a dozen soft steps through the dining room.

Kate glided from the darkness of the dining room into the shadows of the living room and walked directly behind the couch. Greer tilted his head back farther to see her. She held a spring of mistletoe over his head and bent over to kiss give him a soft, wine-laced kiss on the lips upside down.

She put her mouth to his ear and whispered. "Better late than never," she translated for him. "I thought you'd never get here," she explained. She intertwined her fingers with his. The new watch slid out from his shirt sleeve.

"I love it," said Greer, looking at the watch. "Where did you find it?"

"A friend of mine has an art deco shop on the other side of George-town. I saw it and knew I had to get it for you. I thought you might like it for your trip." Kate moved her head around so she could see the watch. "It looks good on you."

Greer caught Kate's head in his hands and gave her a long kiss.

"We'll never make it through the first course at this rate," she said. She urged him off the couch with a gentle tug on the hand and led him to his place.

On the table were the flowers he had brought. Kate pulled a few stems out and made a few small adjustments. She lifted up the petals of the flowers with her fingertips. "They're beautiful, Greer." She gave him a squeeze of the hand and sat down. Greer poured out more wine for them both.

"*Prost!*" he toasted.

"*Na zdorove!*" They clinked glasses and both took big mouthfuls of the red wine, all the time looking into each other's eyes.

They lingered over dinner. An old Ray Coniff Christmas record was playing. Kate had taken cooking lessons at the American embassy in Moscow from the head staff chef, previously an Italian apprentice chef at a small but excellent restaurant in Los Angeles, brought to Russia by the ambassador who personally subsidized his salary. The meal was as good as any Greer had eaten anywhere.

After dinner they moved back into the living room, taking their wineglasses and the last of the bottle with them.

Greer walked Kate to the couch with his arm around her waist. He seated her, then nudged the logs in the fireplace. He took a closer look at the art objects on the mantel alongside the candlesticks. The Chopin CD came back on. He picked up a frame from among the cluster of photographs and brought it back to the couch.

"This is you?" he asked. He had looked at the photo a dozen times before, but Kate had never commented on it. The heavy winter clothing made the subject almost unrecognizable.

Kate was curling up in one corner of the couch around a point defined by the dregs in the bottom of her wineglass. Red wine made her sad. She pulled the frame closer to see. "My last winter in Moscow."

Greer recognized the background, the familiar onion domes of St. Basil's at the Kremlin. The fur hat and scarf almost completely obscured her face. Her pupils reflected the camera flash through the wisp of blond hair blown across her eyes and she was laughing with her tongue sticking out. The camera caught the instant of a large snowflake landing on the tip of her tongue.

"You look happy."

She lingered over the picture. "It was a rare moment. I felt the weight of the world on my shoulders at the time. There I was laughing it up in Red Square and the fate of five of my agents was being decided behind those walls."

Greer put the picture face down onto the coffee table. He knew it improper to probe and didn't. He also didn't want to spoil the moment by asking who had taken the picture. He sensed that between the wine and the picture, she had slipped into a quiet melancholy and had started to withdraw.

"Time for some Glenn Miller," he said abruptly and changed the music. Tight trumpets punctuated the sudden gloom of the house in a swing beat and the singers followed with the chorus of "Kalamazoo."

Greer stood conducting in four-four time in front of the fire with Glenn Miller's imaginary long baton. The tempo was infectious. The price for Kate's laughing at him was to be pulled up from her position on the couch onto the ballroom dance floor that the living room had become in Greer's mind. Greer led her in a tight motion back and forth with their feet shuffling from side to side in approximately the same position. Kate laughed.

"Give me a minute," she said, pulling away. "I'll get us more wine."

Greer sat down in the rocking chair as Kate went into the kitchen. He took another swallow of the wine. He let his mind free-associate. The wine was good, perfect for the moment. Good French wine he had bought himself. He put his head against the back of the chair and closed his eyes. He dreamed about the sunny slope in France where the grapes grew. He thought about the good life in France. He pictured the markets and wine bars of the early evening in Paris on a narrow street off the Rue St. Germaine . . . Paris . . . the embassy . . . CIA cables . . . REDWING . . . *STEEPLECHASE*. His heart skipped a beat. The fantasy gave way to the realities that loomed.

Kate joined him again. "Kalamazoo" had just ended and the conductor slowed the tempo down with "Moonlight Serenade." Kate put her head onto Greer's shoulder with both hands around his neck. They barely moved with the music. They didn't talk for a long time.

Finally Kate put her mouth to his ear and whispered: "Don't ever doubt I love you. No matter what happens."

"Moonlight Serenade" ended. With hardly a beat between them, the orchestra began playing "Perfidia."

The next night at six o'clock, the taxi pulled up to the south side of the Lincoln Memorial. Greer peered out the window through the dark and saw the cold wind from the Potomac whipping the silhouettes of the bare tree limbs against the backdrop of the lit-up monument. The wind gusts would make for a rough takeoff.

"Wait here," he told the driver.

Greer had everything for the trip in the taxi. He got out and walked along the sidewalk around the base of the monument, then started climbing the granite steps at the front of the memorial. From the bottom, all he could see was Lincoln's massive head. He tried to think if he had forgotten anything. He had his clothes, laptop computer, and copies of the CIA station cable data on diskettes to work on with Jenkins. In his briefcase was his passport, itinerary, and $2,500 in traveler's checks, enough to cover his meals and a week's stay at an expensive hotel that didn't take credit cards. And, of course, a nice Christmas present for Kate. Something really special. Greer stopped midway up where the steps became marble and turned to look out along the length of the Reflecting Pool to the Washington Monument across the water.

At the top of the steps sat Lincoln. The marble panels in the ceiling of the chamber were treated with beeswax, reflecting light onto his white marble face in a translucent glow. Greer came to a stop directly in front of the statue behind the low brass chain. He looked to his left and saw the Gettysburg Address chiseled into the wall. On his right there was another speech, one he wasn't familiar with. He had just started reading it when he was startled by movement from behind one of the vast Doric columns inside the memorial. A figure with his hands jammed into his coat pocket approached Greer purposefully, silently. He joined Greer in front of the statue. They were alone.

"Emergency?" asked Reed.

"Yeah. You could say that."

Greer hadn't slept much during the previous night. After leaving Kate's he packed and worried about what he had seen in the Paris cable.

Greer spoke: "A few weeks ago, I thought that REDWING was fingering Jenkins. Then yesterday the Paris station reported that the Germans are responsible for running the mole in U.S. intelligence."

They both looked up at Lincoln as they talked. Pigeons roosted quietly along a narrow ledge at the top. "Okay. So what's so important that we had to meet on your way to the airport?"

"REDWING said the name of the operation was STEEPLECHASE. I'd say that's too much of a coincidence." Greer turned to look at Reed. "Just what the hell's going on?"

Reed narrowed his gaze on Lincoln and put his head back thoughtfully. "Was there anything else?"

"The Agency people are following up with the source right now. Counterintelligence has made this a top priority."

Reed asked, "What about the evidence? What's the status of the presentation for the National Security Council when you get back?"

For the first time, Greer told Reed an intentional lie, a half-truth really. "Nothing new. As I told you last time, Jenkins has a meeting scheduled and he's going to explain the theory and back it up with proof." Greer didn't want to tell Reed that he was taking copies of the diskettes with him. The only other copies were in Jenkins' office. He had spent a hell of a lot of time collecting that information and now he wanted to see it through. He and Jenkins were going to write the presentation during the trip. Greer knew that wasn't what Reed wanted. But what Greer wanted was to be the one standing in front of the President and the NSC giving the presentation on the theory.

An especially strong gust of wind blew around the chamber. Greer tightened his collar around his throat. "I want to know what's going on," Greer demanded again.

"I'll take care of it," Reed said confidently. "I don't want to compromise the operation by getting into details. Just stick with the plan. Keep a close watch on Jenkins on your trip. I'll talk to the DCI first thing in the morning."

Fine, thought Greer. Two can play at this game. "Anything else?" he asked.

"You're going to miss your plane."

22 ❑ ❑ ❑ ❑

At noon on the second Friday in December, Erich Reagor fastened his seat belt and turned the ignition key to his Porsche with every intention of driving home to Munich at the end of a lousy business trip to Leipzig.

It was sleeting and the headlights sensed the dark sky, popping up automatically and turning on. The automatic seat heater began warming the leather upholstery beneath him. He sat with one hand on the steering wheel and the other on the stick shift, ready to throw the gears into reverse to start the four-hour trip home. He pushed in the clutch.

He just couldn't do it.

He slipped the car into neutral. For a moment he thought about the precious time he had just wasted. He had spent two days poking around an old East German food factory, evaluating the run-down facility as a possible new manufacturing site for DBW's pet food division. It was legitimate company work that he was obliged to squeeze into his other activities. The Vice President for Operations at DBW had been told that a former Communist factory could be had for cheap. That much was true. There were walls, a ceiling, and a floor. There was a two-story-tall wet-mixing station, a packaging line with a canning station and labeler, and a manual roller conveyer belt system. But everywhere he looked there had been rat droppings and paint chips from the peeling ceiling. The machinery was almost forty years old. Fur balls from the factory's dozen cats—Communist pest control —rolled around in the corners, picking up rat hairs from the floor and growing to the size of grapefruit. It was beyond rehabilitation, he concluded. The food that the East Germans used to make and send off to the far reaches of the Soviet empire wasn't fit enough for the least worthy dog in the West.

To the south lay his new world—a nice flat in Munich with a woman who kept him amused and out of trouble, a comfortable job with perks and benefits and now the thrill of the new spy work, and a clean, well-lit, sane city—by all accounts, a nice life.

But to the north, only 120 kilometers away, was Berlin.

The thought of Berlin made his pulse race and his scrotum tighten.

Berlin was really where he belonged and he knew it. There was an edge to living in Berlin during the Cold War that had energized him. As a Stasi officer he had been a member of the elite, a master of the oily, rain-slicked streets. Berlin suited his personality. It was a city of the day anticipating the night. It was a place that looked better long after the sun had set, when the unreal business of the day was replaced by the surreal business of the night.

Reagor hadn't missed the friends he had left behind when he fled Berlin, because he didn't have any. That's how he wanted it. He didn't want anyone getting too close. In his job, he couldn't get involved. It had been that way for the twenty-three years he was with Stasi.

What he *had* missed were his lovers. Not any one in particular, but the general quality of the lovers in Berlin. As he thought about it, he wondered if it might not have been the people themselves, but perhaps the place. Or maybe it was just himself. Or maybe all three things.

In Berlin, no one spoke directly about it, but it was known in certain circles who was Stasi. His rumored position had a curious effect on people, on potential lovers. There were those who were repelled by his profession, thinking him the embodiment of all that was evil with the Communist state. There were others who were drawn to him because they were weaker than he was and they were intrigued by the power he held—they were the submissive ones. Then there was the other group—those who were drawn to him because they were sexually strong and they took pleasure from finding and subduing another powerful animal of the night.

Reagor breathed rapidly, fogging his front windshield. He was sweating. He turned down the temperature and redirected all of the air onto the glass from the top of the dashboard.

Reagor knew that Berlin was the only place he could safely practice the little acts that made him feel alive. The acts whose memory drove him from post to post in life, the acts that drove him into the frenzy that made him want more, that created an appetite that he had to feed or die trying.

There came to mind a funky little club down a poorly lit alley off the Katzbachstrasse in the Kreuzberg district. Before reunification, Kreuzberg had been a relatively poor area in the former western sector, populated by students and immigrants from the Near East. Reagor would sneak over from East Berlin some nights for excitement. He was curious if the old club was still there, how it had done since the new order. There were probably those who remembered him, who remembered what he was like and what he liked. Reagor felt his pulse throbbing in his neck.

Sometimes a guy just has to relax, he reminded himself. Stasi had been a high-pressure job. It was always good to return to Berlin. To be among people you could relax with. Be yourself. Sometimes, it feels good to let go, to let someone else be in control. Sometimes, it feels good to let someone else dominate for a while.

The spy work at Deutsche Bayrische Werke was vitally important to the country. He was beginning to get the whole picture now. What was it Stettler had said? "New economic relationships. An understanding about certain markets and market shares. Merely a recognition of the axis along which the economic realities of the future lie. Japan is, after all, the second-largest economy in the world. It makes sense to come to formalize accommodations with a potential competitor. We don't need to tie up our resources fighting a war on that front."

Reagor was feeling the stress. He would be much more useful if he could relieve some of that anxiety, he rationalized. A couple of nights in Berlin would be dangerous, though. He was still on certain lists kept by certain former colleagues who had never forgiven his leaving Berlin the way he did.

He tried shaking the thoughts off. *Put the car into gear and go back to Munich this afternoon,* he told himself.

But, instead, there came another vision. It was four in the morning outside the little club in the alley and it was misting. He could see himself in a silhouette with his back up against the brick wall of the building. There were two sets of breaths in the cold air. There was another person with him. It was one of his lovers, one of the sunken white youthful faces that hadn't felt the warmth of sunlight for an eternity of Berlin moons. In his mind's eye, Reagor couldn't tell if it was a boy or a girl.

It didn't matter. He needed to go. He *really* did. *Badly.*

Reagor's brain clicked and he set his internal compass on the Brandenburg Gate in Berlin and put the Porsche into gear.

23 ❑ ❑ ❑ ❑

The train lurched forward and an unpeeled tangerine fell off Jenkins' lap and rolled across the floor under Greer's seat on the opposite side of their first-class compartment. The movement of the train also woke Greer up. He looked at his watch: he reset it from 4:20 A.M. body time to 10:20 A.M. local time. He hadn't slept on the flight over. He was a zombie getting his luggage and clearing customs at the Frankfurt airport. He had spent the whole flight turning the REDWING report over in his mind.

"Do you mind?" Jenkins asked. Greer gave him a quizzical look. "Under there," Jenkins said, pointing to the tangerine. Greer picked it up and gave it to Jenkins. "Thanks." He watched Jenkins polish it off quickly on his pants leg, then start to peel it with his teeth.

They were alone in the compartment except for the intense aroma of tangerine peels. The small window at the top was pulled open a few inches to cool the space that had been superheated by a broken lever on the heater. Greer heard the high-end screeching of the train wheels on the metal rail coming in through the crack and felt the rhythmic swaying beneath.

Greer was facing the direction that the train was going. He looked back to try to catch the name of the station they were pulling out of. He missed it. "Where are we now?" he asked.

"Just leaving Koblenz."

Greer stood up and stretched, steadying his legs parallel to the direction of the train and holding onto the storage rack above Jenkins' head. He saw a stack of pamphlets in a dispenser on the wall and took one. On one side he found where they were on the schematic of the

Frankfurt–Cologne train run. Turning the map over he read about breakfast in the buffet car. He decided to pass.

"Looks like another hour or so," said Greer. Jenkins didn't reply— he was involved in separating the seeds from the fruit in his mouth. Greer settled back into the corner of the long seat and closed his eyes, but couldn't go back to sleep. He watched the landscape.

The scenery was different now, a world away from the gray industrial rail yards outside Frankfurt. The rail was following the Rhine River. In the water, large barges pushed coal to the cities. Not long after leaving Koblenz the train was snaking through the hills of the Rhineland, the heart of the region's wine production. Greer noted the steep slopes on either side of the river with the familiar stakes and wires indicating the vineyards. High up on improbable ridges overlooking the Rhine at sharp bends in the river were castles or ruins of castles. He felt as if he had come home.

Greer scrutinized Jenkins through dry, slitted eyes. Jenkins now had his head back on his seat with his eyes closed, warming himself in the sun that had just broken over the high ridges along the river. What was Jenkins' secret? he wondered. Was he the mole that REDWING was pointing to? Why would the CIA let him make this trip if he were under suspicion? Maybe having the Agency field officer working with Jenkins was an attempt to trip him up. And, as Reed had asked, What was his motivation?

Greer thought about Jenkins' theory. It was typical of the kind of speculative work done by academicians who didn't have to answer hard questions in the real world outside of the universities or scholarly journals. Throw a few outrageous ideas out for discussion at some economics symposium that no one other than those sitting around the table gave a damn about. Mad scholarship. All hypothetical. On the other hand, the research methodology was solid and had kicked out Japan and Germany as coordinating economic policies. It certainly raised some interesting questions. Was it really true? If it were true, what difference would it make? Would the results really be so devastating as outlined in Jenkins' white paper?

The mention of STEEPLECHASE in the REDWING report was clearly a problem. From his response at the Lincoln Memorial, Reed apparently knew what that problem was. He was asking a lot of Greer to accept on faith that he would take care of things. But at what point should Greer start to *really* question the STEEPLECHASE operation? Jenkins' activities—although somewhat unorthodox—weren't all that crazy and his theory *was* one that might merit serious consideration at the White House. And then there was the personal element—STEEPLE-CHASE was the cryptonym for the operation that Greer was running. Why should a reliable source in France mention the code name in connection with an espionage operation against the United States? What was the German connection?

Greer wondered whom he could talk to about the situation if it got to the point that he needed to consult with someone other than Reed. Jenkins? He was a possibility, but not while there was even the remotest chance of Jenkins' being responsible for the things cited in the Executive Finding. The DCI? Too risky, Greer figured. Going over Reed's head to the DCI would be a career-ending move if it turned out that the STEEPLECHASE operation was still in good shape. Plus, it was clear that Ben Gibbons was hostile toward the National Security Adviser and anyone from his office. Maybe Kate. Greer decided to think about it over the next week and formulate a backup plan if the STEEPLECHASE references continued to come up in the CIA cables. For now, he was stuck trusting that Reed would, indeed, take care of things.

The train slowed a bit as it approached Bonn. The houses looked clean and prosperous. Greer caught quick glimpses of people crowding lunchtime streets. As the train entered the station, Greer scanned the faces and clothes of the people waiting on the platform. The train was moving too fast and the light in the station was bad. Greer's eyes still hadn't adjusted from coming out of the sunlit countryside.

Passengers were already in the passageway outside the compartments ready to disembark. The train came to a definite stop. Train car doors opened and the people moved through the corridors. Another group of people filled the train, looking for empty seats. They looked at Greer and Jenkins and moved on to the next compartment. Greer took notice of Jenkins. He was clearly asleep: his head fell slowly until his chin met his chest, then rose up to start the whole cycle over again.

The railroad employees on the platform closed the train doors loudly and the train started moving again. The sound woke Jenkins up. He watched a few stragglers walk by the compartment hoping to find a seat.

After a few minutes, the conductor slid the compartment door open, asking for their tickets. Ten minutes later and the train had picked up speed again on the final leg to Cologne. They passed a long succession of grotty villages with coal cars on side tracks. The sun was hidden behind a solid mass of gray cloud cover.

Jenkins seemed too distracted to be bothered with any questions about travel and meeting changes, so Greer thought he'd better take a look at the itinerary himself. He opened his briefcase and got out an envelope. Greer thumbed through its contents—return plane tickets, passport, and his traveler's checks. He thought about what he might buy for Kate in Cologne. Something for the house? A piece of jewelry? An engagement ring? That would certainly be a nice surprise for her. He thought about Kate and how happy she seemed to be that he liked his new watch. Greer found the revised itinerary that Jenkins' secretary had sent over by way of his E-mail yesterday. Greer scanned the two-page schedule. The only change he saw was a later flight out of Frankfurt at the end of the trip.

At the bottom of the itinerary there was another E-mail message tacked on. He hadn't bothered to read it yesterday as he was printing it out. SEE YOU SOON! What a nice sentiment, thought Greer. Jenkins' secretary always sent his messages for him. Jenkins must have typed the greeting himself.

"Thanks for the personalized message yesterday," said Greer. He waved the printout in front of Jenkins. "I guess you know how much I've been looking forward to spending some time with you on this trip."

Jenkins looked over at the paper. He was crotchety. "I didn't send you any message yesterday."

Greer looked out the window again. What? If not Jenkins, then who? The CIA field officer from Bonn? He could have easily got Greer's E-mail address. Maybe the CIA officer had sent both Greer and Jenkins greetings. Greer looked for a return E-mail address, but found none. Just like the Agency, he thought.

Greer heard a tearing sound and smelled chocolate bloom into the air. He turned away from the window towards Jenkins and saw someone just passing by the compartment. Jenkins was breaking off a segment of a Toblerone chocolate bar. The figure walked by again in the opposite direction, giving Jenkins a quick look. He stopped and slid open the compartment door.

It was Reed.

What the hell is *he* doing *here?* wondered Greer.

Reed stepped inside, paying no attention to Greer. "Mr. Jenkins?" he asked, at the same time taking off his glove and extending his hand.

"Yes?" answered Jenkins.

"I'm Bob Reed from the embassy." They shook hands. "I believe that the Director said you would be expecting me."

Jenkins motioned with his head to the space beside him on the seat, then motioned toward Greer. "Greer Whitaker," he said, by way of introduction.

Reed looked at Greer and gave him a wide grin and a handshake. "Yes, I knew that the two of you would be making the trip."

So *that* was it, thought Greer. Reed was the one who had left the E-mail greeting.

Jenkins said, "Ben Gibbons told me you were meeting us in Cologne tomorrow."

"I thought this might be more convenient," Reed said. "I hope you don't mind."

The train was passing through a small station that wasn't a designated stop. It gave a blast with its horn without losing speed.

As Jenkins finished the chocolate bar he turned to the newcomer. "What's your agenda, Mr. Reed?" Jenkins asked, the ambiguity of the question obviously intentional.

"The Director has asked that I brief you on the matter about which he spoke with you on the phone." Jenkins nodded agreement. "After we all check into our hotel, I thought you and I would find a quiet place to go off for a chat." He looked over at Greer. "I understand that Greer is going to be busy with the negotiators, so I'm sure he won't be able to join us." Greer understood.

Reed continued: "I've taken the liberty of changing your hotel reservations."

"Oh?" said Jenkins.

"The Director's office sent me a copy of your itinerary. I've got a more secure facility that also happens to be more convenient to the *Bahnhof.*" Reed looked at the suitcases in the overhead racks. "I can help you schlep your luggage; the taxi drivers would laugh at us if we tried to hire one for three blocks."

Jenkins was picking his teeth with his thumbnail. He was craning his neck looking behind him toward Cologne at the sooted cathedral spires coming into view on the horizon.

Jenkins turned quickly to Reed: "I asked you once, Mr. Reed. You didn't answer me. What's your agenda?"

The pigeons along the west bank of the Rhine River pecked at the winter grass growing up between the cobbles on the quay near the *Altstadt*—the old city—in Cologne. Reed, Jenkins, and Greer trudged through the mass of birds and struggled under the weight of the luggage. The pigeons raced ahead of them, swarming around the men and getting under their feet like beggar children.

The temperature was around freezing. On the right was the river. A shelf of thin ice jutted from the river's edge. On the left was a solid block of houses and flats six stories high, separated from the quay and the river by a busy city street. Greer searched the length of the block for signs of a hotel.

Reed stopped walking. "Here," he said, nodding toward the river.

"*Not* really," Jenkins said.

"*Really*," Reed answered. "Watch your step."

The name on the side of the large boat read *Prinsesse Marianna*. The engines were idling, powering the electric generator. There was an overwhelming smell of diesel fuel. It was obviously some kind of passenger vessel, although it resembled a river barge more than a Caribbean cruise ship. On the level just below deck they could see curtains pulled back in what looked to be a dining room and bar. The next level down had a series of smaller windows, some with curtains drawn to reveal small cabins. On the back of the boat the blue-and-white Danish flag snapped in the wind whipping off the river.

They stepped carefully across the icy gangplank and wound down metal steps into the ship. Reed asked the attendant for their keys.

Reed addressed Greer: "Mr. Jenkins and I are going to spend the rest of the afternoon together." Reed turned to Jenkins: "If that's okay with you, sir."

Jenkins squinted down at the number on his cabin key and tried to figure out which way to go. He started trudging off down the steps to the cabins below. "Whatever," he said. "Just let me hang my bags up."

Reed half-shouted after Jenkins: "Meet you in the lounge upstairs in thirty minutes?"

"Yeah, yeah. Sure." Jenkins was gone.

Reed pulled Greer aside away from the reception desk. "I told you

I'd take care of everything, didn't I? I convinced Gibbons to let me have the assignment. Get some sleep. Have some dinner. I'll handle Jenkins. What time's your first meeting start tomorrow?"

"Eight o'clock. Continental breakfast at seven-thirty."

"Let's meet—say—at seven. You know the bridge?"

"The one leading across the river to the exhibition center?"

"That's the one. Meet me in the middle where that crap metal art is of the guy balancing himself over the water."

"Got it."

"Maybe I can resolve this problem today. Just stay out of the way for a while."

"I can do that."

Greer had been looking forward to coming back to Cologne and was anxious to get out and revisit familiar sights and restaurants in the city. But he was seriously jet-lagged. He wondered what Kate was doing at the moment. It was just after two in the afternoon local time. It was early Sunday morning back in Washington. Kate would sleep in a little, then go for a walk through the neighborhood. She'd stop for coffee and a paper around the corner. Then she would go home and climb back into bed with the paper. He missed her already.

Greer set his alarm clock for four-thirty in the afternoon. Just a couple of hours' sleep would be great. He was hungry, but he needed sleep more. He lay down on the narrow pull-down bed in the cabin and thought of food. He needed to convert some traveler's checks into deutsche marks. He could do it at the exchange bureau in the train station. He remembered there was a favorite restaurant off the *Dom* plaza not too far away from there. A place called the Früh, just around the corner . . .

24 ❑ ❑ ❑ ❑

Clare was standing at the door to the study with a wooden tray.

"Where does Madame wish her tea?"

Marie von Bosacker, the Comtesse de Kaysersberg, closed the estate account books.

"Here," Marie said, making room on the desk. Clare put the tea set down, straightened a frame on the edge of the desk, and left.

Marie put her face over the teapot and lifted the lid. The steam from the Lapsang souchong tea rose up to her, an earthy scent of smoke and old rope. The tea leaves had settled. She replaced the lid and moved the frame back to where she had first put it.

The ledgers were in good shape for the end-of-year accounting for the tax man, she thought. Damn him, as an aside. What did they know in Paris about life on a working estate in the provinces? At least there was something to be paid. The harvest had been good and the new wine had sold well. The land rented to the other farmers had been productive and there was a modest sum from water rights to owners of the adjoining land. After expenses for the workers and managers, the house in Ribeauville and the château here in the vineyards, after all that, there was still money for the future.

Marie adjusted the framed picture once more; the glass was catching the glare from the setting sun. But what kind of future would it be without a family?

She poured the cream, then the tea. She settled into the chair with her cup and saucer.

There were four framed photographs, recently moved from the formal reception room. She was having a hard time finding a place for them where she could look at them throughout the day. Too much sun or too much darkness. But she tried again, testing a new arrangement on her desk. The study was where she spent her time at the château, seated among the ledger books and bills. She needed their help, wanted their presence with her as she carried out the day-to-day duties of managing the estate.

There was a bright picture, the one of her grown son, Paul, and his family. He was gone—gone to Hong Kong as an investment banker with a Paris firm. The vineyards couldn't hold him. He had longed for the city, gone to the University of Paris, and never returned to Alsace. He would not be coming back. The three grandchildren smiled for her, but she saw them only once a year. But not this Christmas, she reminded herself, since Paul's wife had insisted that they host her own family for once in Hong Kong. Paul would inherit the estate, of course, realize that he did not have enough money to pay the inheritance taxes, then sell the whole thing to a large agricultural cooperative. The Bosacker name would be removed from the gate.

There was the picture of her husband, Michael. He had wanted to make it through Christmas, she remembered. He missed by one day. At least it was a mercifully quick bout with brain cancer. That had been five years ago. He was a good man, an adequate husband and father. His fifty-four years on this earth were mostly a waste, though, she thought.

A wartime picture. A sad child, herself at age six, and the sadder mother—*her* mother—a widow at age twenty-five. They stood on the land to which they belonged, the inheritance which they didn't want—not yet. In the foreground were still the marks of tank treads in the mud. Mud to die for. Land was everything. And Alsace was the land. Only six kilometers to the southwest lay Colmar, the wine capital of the region. And only ten kilometers due west of Colmar was the Rhine River, the dividing line between France and Germany. The picture was pathetic. Who could have taken the photo of such a grief-stricken family?

Another wartime picture. Head-and-shoulder shot. A noble warrior in nervous excitement. Her father, of course. He wore a tailored colonel's uniform, Army of France. He was dead, of course. And her mother lived just long enough to raise the daughter to womanhood.

But it just wasn't that simple.

Marie put the tea down and lifted the picture of her father off the desk. She was having a hard time separating in her mind her actual memories of him at six years old from the images in the other black and white photographs in the albums. But she knew the story. Her mother had made sure of that.

Marie felt the rage. She ground the bottom of the cup into saucer until the handle broke.

She swore an oath again. After all these years, it was now in her power to make a difference.

She repositioned the picture of her father on the desk and fumed. Fifty years was a long time to have let the hatred build up.

25 ❏ ❏ ❏ ❏

"Bad boy. *Baaaad* boy." Knowles shook his head as he read the file. "Very, very naughty."

Covey looked up from his own stack of papers. "You think?"

"This one's going in the 'A' pile. Top of the whole lot."

Covey looked at the name on the folder. "We've seen that one before."

"The guy's name is popping up all over the place."

Covey looked up at the grease board filled with two columns of names. The first column was headed GERMANY; the other was headed JAPAN. "Put him down."

Knowles took a red marker and wrote in the Japan column: Fujimata Takiyama, aka "Jacko." "There," he said. Then he put a star by the name.

A star, thought Covey. A very bad boy indeed. "So?"

Knowles read from a memo with an FBI letterhead. " 'Fujimata—Jacko—Takiyama, thirty-five years old, president of Takiyama-USA, the American subsidiary of the Takiyama conglomerate founded and still run by his father Koji Takiyama in Japan. As head of the American unit, controls all of Takiyama's interest's in the country—both legal and illegal. Important businessman in the San Francisco community and don of the Japanese Mafia on the West Coast.' "

"What's he do?"

" 'Represents the new breed of Japanese organized crime in the United States. Extremely well educated, immaculately dressed, financially savvy, politically sophisticated, polite—but ruthless. In the three years he has run the organization, Jacko has consolidated or eliminated most of the rival Japanese gangs up and down the West Coast and instituted a blend of American and Japanese business principles to manage the increasingly sophisticated criminal activities. He has shifted the emphasis of the organization from traditional protection rackets, illegal gambling operations, and prostitution to the much higher-margin—though riskier—business of brokering drugs and laundering money for the growers in Southeast Asia and South

America. Suspected of hiding drug shipments and associated money transfers within Takiyama's huge microchip business. Defense Intelligence Agency currently gathering evidence that—along with the thousands of crates of sensitive electronic parts that the Department of Defense bought from the Takiyama plants in Japan—were multikilo bags of heroin and cocaine. Crates were air-freighted directly from Japan to Takiyama's own warehouses outside a half-dozen military bases and government research laboratories. DIA expects to indict government inspectors and customs officers who were on site—*and* on the Takiyama payroll. Organization uses computers in the warehouses to track inventory of both navigational electronics for U.S. submarines and high-grade heroin from Cambodia destined for the streets of L.A. and New York.' "

"So why haven't they nabbed him already?"

"Apparently everybody wants a piece of this guy. They're trying to build a tax case. Something that'll stick."

"So what's the Agency assessment say?"

Knowles flipped to another page. " 'Only son and heir apparent to the Takiyama fortune. Graduated with an undergraduate degree in finance from Tokyo University, then to America for an M.B.A. from Stanford. Speaks flawless English, but with a British accent . . .' "

Covey interjected: "BBC tapes."

" '. . . acquired from listening to BBC tapes. According to Tokyo agents, father had put him to work in several divisions of the company in Japan after he completed his graduate degree. During this same time, the senior Takiyama started exposing subject to the day-to-day management needed to run a modern criminal organization. Oversaw illegal gambling operations in their private clubs, then moved on to monitoring and improving the efficiency of the drug traffic the Takiyamas controlled moving through the organization. After seven years of proving his value to both his father and to the rest of the business and crime organizations, subject sent back to America, identified by the family as their next big opportunity.' "

Covey looked at the board of other likely candidates. "I think we'd better start our own investigation. Start with his contacts—business, social, whatever. He's definitely someone with enough smarts and resources and total disdain for the law to be managing an intelligence operation here."

Covey stood and took the marker from Knowles. He circled the star. "Make sure the other agencies aren't too aggressive. We don't want him taken out of action before we've had a chance to take a look at him ourselves."

26 ❏ ❏ ❏ ❏

Standing outside the Früh in the early evening darkness, Greer smelled the sausages and beer. Through the dense tinted yellow glass on either side of the door he could see forms moving inside. He heard the clinking of knives and forks against plates. He opened the door and felt a rush of warm air and cigarette smoke. It was noisy. He was ravenous.

The place was filled with university students. Greer made his way through the main room to an empty table on the far side next to the wall. He sat on the bench so he could watch the people in the room.

It seemed that he was being ignored by the waiters. Five minutes passed. Then a sweaty waiter dressed in black and a greasy white apron came to the table bearing a tray of beers. Without even having to ask, he set down one of the small Früh glasses of beer onto his table. That's more like it, thought Greer.

The aroma of searing sausages heightened Greer's hunger. He ordered a large platter of *Bratwurst mit Sauerkraut*. He worked on his dinner along with more of the small glasses of beer. More university students filed in and arranged themselves in large groups at nearby tables to drink and philosophize.

Greer watched one group pull tables together on his right. He tried picking up bits of their conversation in German and became absorbed again in the students' conversation. They worshiped one professor, plotted the murder of another. Greer turned quickly to the sound of his waiter's voice on the other side of the table.

The waiter was gone. And standing in front of him was a woman staring directly at Greer.

It was Stephanie Becker.

"*Greer?*"

"*Stephanie?*"

Greer stared back at her, hardly able to believe his eyes. He was speechless as she came around to his side of the table.

"My God," she said.

Unmistakably Stephanie, he thought.

"Aren't you going to ask me to sit down?" Greer still wasn't able to say anything. "Slide over," she said.

As they continued staring at each other, the waiter set down two beers. Greer looked deep into her eyes to check once more that it was really her. He felt his heart miss a beat, and he gripped the edge of the table for support.

Stephanie said, "What are you doing here?"

"I'm here on business. What are *you* doing here?"

"The thought of going home for the holiday to Bremerhaven depressed me. I was going to spend my Christmas break here with some friends from university."

Cologne was an easy drive from Heidelberg. He and Stephanie had spent some good times in the restaurant.

Stephanie was unzipping her black leather jacket. Greer took a good look at her as she put the jacket over the back of the bench. How could someone so utterly screwed up in the head be so incredibly alluring? She was even more beautiful than he had remembered. She was an exotic blend: half German, half Turkish, with dark skin. Her long black hair was lavishly thick, with beautiful curls falling over the shoulders of her tight black ribbed turtleneck sweater. She wore tight jeans stuffed into short black leather boots. Her facial beauty seemed to derive its underlying strength from the mixture of the competing bloodlines. The only makeup she ever wore was lipstick, a lighter shade now than what she had worn when she'd left her lipstick kiss on his passport.

"I can't believe you're here," she said. She seemed excited to see him, so unlike the Stephanie who had nearly destroyed him seven years earlier with her angry rejection.

Greer groped for words: "This is so . . ."

". . . Unexpected? I know. But I'm so glad to see you!"

Greer finished his beer and slowly recovered from the shock. But what was left in its place wasn't pleasant. A torrent of painful memories pelted him, pushing aside any interest in nostalgia. Hurtful words from her final transatlantic phone call came back to him. He felt himself getting angry.

Greer was overcome with emotion and blurted out: "Don't you think you owe me some explanation? We had plans for a future together! Then without warning you call me up and blew me off from seven thousand miles away and changed your phone number!"

Stephanie looked around to see if anyone had heard him, then she lowered her eyes and turned the beer glass in her hand. She spoke to Greer slowly, calmly. "I've missed you. I realize now that I made a mistake. The biggest mistake of my life."

Greer was still hot: "Seven years later you realize you made a mistake?"

"I couldn't have you. I loved you, but you had to leave me."

Greer said forcefully, "That's as much bullshit today as it was then!"

Greer was exhilarated, finally giving vent to his anger. Stephanie was quiet, seemingly willing to accept Greer's condemnation.

He continued: "I hated you for what you did. I can't imagine anything more cruel. No one deserves to be treated like that! What happened?"

Stephanie put her hand gently onto Greer's, and he instinctively jerked it back.

"Greer . . ."

"*Herr Ober!*" Greer waved his glass and called for a refill.

"Greer . . ."

"What?" he snapped.

"There are things you don't know about. Things you never knew back then . . ."

"Like what?"

"There were reasons . . ."

". . . Name one." He shook his head. "I swear to God . . ."

"I was sick."

The waiter broke the tense silence with more beers. Of course she was sick, Greer was thinking. And apparently she had snapped after he had gone back to the States. At least that was how he had rationalized it over all these years.

The waiter left and Stephanie said, "It wasn't fair to you. I should have told you when we first met."

"Told me what?" he said curtly.

"That I was having . . . women's problems." Stephanie smiled weakly at Greer. "I had been diagnosed as having ovarian cancer sometime before you left. I didn't know how serious it was, so I was still hopeful. I didn't say anything because I didn't want to worry you."

"*What?*"

"I'm so sorry, Greer. I should have told you. No . . . I should have never let you think I was coming . . ."

"Hold on," Greer said.

Stephanie touched Greer's arm and he let it stay.

"No," she said. "Let me finish. You're right—I do owe you an explanation. I made a mistake in not telling you the truth. It was unfair to you. I couldn't tell you about my illness then. I just couldn't let you throw away your life, your career. If I told you how sick I was, knowing how much you loved me, I knew you'd want to stay. I was scared. I had to go through treatment right after you left. The doctors told me that I might not make it. I knew you'd give up everything for me. I told you I'd come to America, but I lied. I wanted you to go. I wanted you to hate me so you'd be free of me. So I . . ."

"My God. Is this true?"

Stephanie nodded. "It's true. Greer . . ."

"Stephanie . . ."

Greer squeezed her hand. He pulled her in and she put her head onto his shoulder. He stroked her hair.

"Stephanie . . ."

She was starting to cry. "I never stopped loving you," she said. "I never have. I'm so sorry."

"Stephanie . . ."

Stephanie wiped away the tears and looked at Greer again. "I'm better now," she said. "All better now, see?" She forced a smile. "There was a rough period after you left, but I'm back to normal. The cancer is gone. I got on with my life."

Everything made sense now. Even the irrational behavior and the trips to a psychiatrist and all those antidepressants. She was living through a crisis and he never had a clue.

She said, "When I got well, when it was all over, I thought about you a lot. But you were already gone. Can you ever forgive me?"

Tears started welling up in her eyes again, and Greer put his arms around her.

Greer quickly figured his bill and left the money on the table. "Come on," he said. "Let's go outside."

Back outside, the night air was cold and clear. The street was quiet. Stephanie took Greer's hand and they walked in silence to the large plaza surrounding the *Dom,* the soaring gothic cathedral that rose up as the centerpiece of the city. Intense floodlights lit up the exterior, highlighting the flying buttresses and carvings around the top.

Near the entrance was a free-standing whitewashed plywood wall. Both sides were covered with photocopied and handwritten messages flapping in the swirling wind of the plaza in a collage of protests, poetry, and remembrances of modern-day martyrs. Peaceniks and antivivisectionists. A nun murdered in South America. A verse from the Psalms over a stenciled dove carrying an olive branch. It was as if here the collective angst of the city was to be vented and dumped neatly onto this place to keep the other parts of the city free from emotional outbursts and unsightly handbills.

Greer steered them to a small door to the side of the massive central doors. The air inside the cathedral was colder than outside and the choir and nave were completely dark except for clusters of candle-light coming from small chapels around the inside perimeter. Greer tightened his grip around Stephanie. The smell of incense was pungent in the high trapped air. Greer led them over to the right and put two fifty-pfennig coins into a collection box. Stephanie took one of the longer candles. They joined three women in heavy coats and scarves wrapped over their heads standing in front of an altarpiece of the Adoration of the Magi, the relics of whom once were supposedly brought to the city. Stephanie lit her candle from the two dozen already burning and set it into the rows of candle sticks.

Stephanie whispered: "This is like a dream. I can't believe that fate has brought you back to me."

Greer squeezed her shoulder and led her back outside.

They walked through the plaza again, this time around the side of the cathedral. They passed by the bronze doors in the medieval southern transept, then went by the modern architecture of the Roman-Germanic Museum. Looking down on them from behind well-lit windows on the higher floors of the museum were broken torsos and vases.

Greer got them heading off the plaza down a steep street leading toward the river in the old part of the city. The lights at the bottom of the hill were magnified in the distance by the fog coming over the river bank. They reached the quay along the river and stopped. The cobbles and rail at the river's edge were wet, coated with a film of thin ice from the dew. A barge passed slowly by, its engines churning upriver against the current of the powerful Rhine.

"The *Dom* brings back memories," Stephanie said.

Greer wiped the top of the rail off with the hem of his coat and leaned against the spot to face back the way they had walked. Stephanie turned and looked, too. The cathedral lorded over the *Altstadt* from the top of the hill.

"Things would have been so different, Stephanie. You should have told me."

"That's all in the past. I'm with you now. That's all that matters."

They walked along the river toward the bridge that carried trains and pedestrians overhead to the right bank of the Rhine. It was the bridge where Greer would meet Reed in the morning. They walked under the bridge and emerged with the Köln Messe—the huge Cologne Exhibition Center—across the other side of the wide river. At the top were the numbers "4711" lit up in large blue neon lights.

Stephanie nuzzled Greer and asked, "Isn't that Siebenundvierzig Elf I smell?" referring to the numbers on the building. "*Evocative*," she said dramatically.

The designation was both the zip code for Cologne and the trademark of the original toilet water with which the city's name was originally associated. The landmark 4711 store nearby had just celebrated 150 years of doing business in the scent trade.

"You always were the drama queen," he said.

He and Stephanie walked along the river, passing several passenger ships tied up along the quay. Before he realized where they were, they were in front of the *Prinsesse Marianna*.

"We need to talk," he said, and led her over the gangplank.

Stephanie clicked on the reading lamp built into the cabin wall. She closed the curtains and fell onto the pull-down bed. The cabin was tiny and warm. The ship rocked slowly in its moorings with the passing of river barges.

Stephanie looked around the cabin's tight interior as Greer hung up their coats. She plumped up the pillows and the down comforter. She pulled off her boots, then rolled sideways onto the covers. She patted the mattress.

"Come. Sit."

Greer sat down beside her. He touched her cheek with the back of his hand and she closed her eyes. He fingered her gold braided Turkish earrings, a gift from her mother—she had worn them years before.

Stephanie said, "I thought I had lost you forever. I've never forgotten. Never fully given up hope."

"Stephanie . . ."

She pulled his head down and kissed his cheek.

Greer said, "What you did . . ."

"Greer, I still love you."

"If I had only known . . . Don't you understand? If only you had told me. I would have stayed. I would have done anything in the world for you."

"I know that. And my whole life would have turned out differently. We could have been together."

"But you didn't tell me . . ."

She kissed him again, lightly on the lips.

"But, Stephanie . . ."

"No one ever loved someone as much as I loved you, Greer. I just couldn't do that to you."

Greer was still trying to take it all in. The sudden reversal of his feelings. He was ashamed now of the hate he had held for her. He had been able to neatly close that part of his life. But now . . .

Greer said, "You did the most unselfish thing anyone could have done. I just wish . . ."

Then she was all over his face with small kisses. She held his head in her hands, and she kissed him quickly on the lips, then she gave him a long, deep kiss, the kind she used to give him when they had been together before.

"Stephanie . . ."

But she wasn't in the mood for talking. She moved on top of him and pinned him with her legs. Greer looked at her face and saw the passion in her eyes. She seemed to want to take what should have been hers years ago.

"Stephanie, wait . . ."

She was pulling the sweater over her head.

"You still love me," she said.

"We need to talk. . . ."

But nothing could distract her now. She unbuttoned his shirt and kissed his chest. She was whispering into his ear: "You're back. I knew you'd come back. Let me make love to you like before. Even if it has got to be just this one last time."

She was tugging at his shirt, unfastening his belt and undoing his trousers. Greer reached up and pushed the bra straps off her shoulders, and she leaned toward him, letting him take her breasts into his mouth.

She bent forward and put her mouth to his ear. "Yes," she moaned.

The sound of her soft voice so close to his ear ignited memories that Greer had been suppressing for years. The old passions came back and he worked to excite Stephanie even more eagerly.

Another barge passed by, rocking the boat again. Stephanie pulled back and held Greer steady with her gaze. She rolled over and stretched out. She passed her hands up over her belly, up to her breasts. She squeezed her full breasts and pushed them up close to her mouth. She licked at her nipples with her long tongue.

Greer unbuttoned her jeans and tugged them off. He caught the edge of her panties with his fingers and slowly pulled them over her legs. Stephanie wet her forefinger and thumb and rolled one of her nipples between her slippery fingers as she slid the other hand back down across her belly, down to the dark patch between her legs. She touched the mound, her hips pressing forward. She spread her legs slightly, moving her fingers deeper inside. All the time, keeping her eyes on Greer's.

Somewhere in his head, he was already saying the mantra: *Don't do this. Stop it now. Run.* But in a deeper part of his brain, Greer was concentrating hard on everything she was doing to excite him. By now she was helping him off with his trousers.

"I remember how you like it," she said.

"Yes," Greer replied, finally closing his eyes and letting it wash over him. He kissed her shoulders. She guided his face down to her breasts again, sucking each breast that she held out for him. Then he moved down, closer to the darkness. There was heat there. He lay his face against the skin of her thigh. She was smooth and hard. He kissed her there, then kissed her everywhere, his mouth searching for familiar places. She arched her back and pressed her hips against his mouth. He found a certain spot high on the inside of her right thigh known to each of them from long ago.

"There," she let out.

He was full of nothing but lust. She urged him on, held onto him, squeezing his upper arms and shoulders. In the morning he knew there would be masterful bruises.

There could be nothing but Stephanie at that moment. The boat rocked and the bed held firm under their motion. It was all so familiar, but so sudden, coming like some drug-induced, hypereuphoric flashback. There was Stephanie and the familiar dampness of her loins, the nectar that drew him in.

He touched the special place inside her thigh again with a kiss.

"Yes, Greer. *Please.*"

She guided his head over the place again. He gently nudged her legs apart and shifted his body to let the light from the reading lamp illuminate the area. He was looking for something. She was quietly urging him on with the upward gyrations of her hips.

There it was. Just as he had remembered it. *The tattoo.*

A red heart encasing a scimitar and a crown with an inscription underneath, *Türkische Königin*—Turkish Queen.

At that moment, she touched him in the identical place. "Yes," he said.

The skin over the tensing muscles of his own inner thigh had a matching tattoo, a red heart and inside, two circles—close together like a figure eight. *Herr Schneebälle,* it read underneath. Mr. Snowballs. The little studio in Heidelberg where the GIs got their tattoos had done a good job. The bottle of schnapps had obliterated the pain. The tattoo was well hidden; Kate had never seen it, but that wasn't on his mind at that moment.

Now, he buried his head in the exotic perfume created by her own body. It was the same ageless perfume she had anointed him with in a dozen other European cities. He found it once again and let himself fall.

27 ❑ ❑ ❑ ❑

Greer's alarm went off at 5:30 A.M. He turned on the reading light and Stephanie stirred, pulling the covers over her head.

In bed with Stephanie Becker.

Greer sat up with a start. What am I doing here with Stephanie Becker? At that moment he looked down at himself, and what he saw frightened him: dark shades of blue and green on his chest and shoulders in the shape of fingerprints.

Oh, my God! he thought. What have I done?

Small things started to come back. The smell of cigarette smoke in the Früh, still in his nostrils. The way the candlewick flared in the cathedral when she lit it. The scent of Stephanie. Asleep with her. Deep inside of her.

This isn't right, he told himself. What about Kate? His job? Everything he had worked so hard for? He was putting it all at risk every moment he stayed there in bed with Stephanie.

He felt like a wreck. The shame seemed worse at this hour, as if someone had suddenly turned a light on in the dark and caught his final, postejaculatory thrust. It was Kate at the lightswitch. *How could he?* He felt terrible.

He watched her back rising and falling as she slept. Then he understood how it had all come about. It wasn't her fault, he reasoned. The only thing she had done was to fall in love with him, then send him away when it looked as if her own sickness might drag him down. It was a tremendous act of selflessness. She had never stopped loving him. How could he fault her for that?

He had to tell her about Kate. Stephanie wouldn't like it, but that's where his true heart lay. Last night was lust, today was reality, and the sudden reemergence of Stephanie could not alter his feelings for Kate. The sooner he told Stephanie, the better it would be for them both.

The first thing to do was to get dressed. Stephanie moved a bit under the comforter, but continued to sleep. They had stayed awake making love all night into the early morning. He was exhausted. His internal body clock told him it was time to go to sleep, not get up. But he couldn't waste any more time or his whole future would be in jeopardy.

Greer showered, dressed, and got the locker key from Stephanie's jeans pocket. Then he left a note saying he would be back in a few minutes, and quietly left to get her bag stored at the train station as he had promised her during the night. She would want her things when she awoke. He wanted her out before he got back from his meeting.

It was still dark outside. The entire city was enveloped in a dense fog. He couldn't see the water, but heard it lapping against the side of the ship as he set off. He was alone, except for a street sweeper.

Inside the station, things were livelier. All the shops were open. It was too brightly lit. People were quietly milling about before going upstairs to the cold, unsheltered train platforms. He went into the news shop and scanned the front pages of a *Herald-Tribune.* The big news in the States was the President's news conference, his last before the Christmas holidays and the end of the year. He was positioning the upcoming G7 conference in a few weeks as a major economic event, hinting that he expected important concessions from Japan. No one in the Administration would talk on the record about the side agreements, but plenty of unattributable "background" briefings by sources high in the Administration made it clear that the President expected Japan to cave. It was a radical shift from the past. More foreign trade equaled more jobs and more wealth for America. And that was something he could talk about to jump-start his reelection campaign.

He stopped by a bakery and bought rolls, went next door for some apple juice and bananas for Stephanie. It was a decent thing to do. He'd feed her, explain things to her, then ask her nicely to go.

He got the bag from the locker, then stepped back outside of the train station.

Directly in front of him as he exited the station was the first light of the day. It was as if someone were turning up a rheostat, increasing the intensity of the light from the city's street lamps that was already there, trapped by the fog and low cloud cover. The sun was not a warm color, but had the effect on the gray sky similar to exciting the gas in a fluorescent lightbulb with electricity. It was a cool light. The sky just got whiter.

Back on the quay, the river was invisible in the fog. Between the

Prinsesse Marianna and the bridge there was a commotion in the water. Unseen from his vantage on the bank—fifty meters away—an engine was revving hard in the current and there was the sound of the hull of a small boat beating against the river. From the place where the sound came, a blue light strobed through the fog a couple of meters over the water. It moved in an elliptical pattern, seeming to circle around a point moving downriver with the current.

Beyond this scene and high up, the first train of the morning crossed the steel-beamed bridge toward the *Bahnhof*. The cold rails screamed under the weight of the train. The bridge, too, was wrapped in fog and invisible.

Greer shivered and boarded the boat.

When he returned, Stephanie was still asleep, one leg sticking out of the covers.

The memories of what he'd done last night were making him ill. He was all too clearly seeing it from Kate's perspective.

He felt terrible. There was, of course, no *good* excuse for what had happened, even though it was understandable. He wouldn't try rationalizing it away. In the end, who would believe that she had made him do it? No one, least of all Kate. What's done was done, he thought. Write it off. Keep your mouth shut. He loved Kate. There's no need to hurt her with this. But he knew he had to settle it now and get back on track. He had important things to do for Jenkins and Reed. They would crucify him if they thought he was spending his time with an old girlfriend.

Greer sat on the edge of the bed and shook her shoulder. She woke up and pushed the hair out of her eyes.

"*Guten Morgen*," she said in a sleepy voice.

"*Guten Morgen*."

Greer offered her the bread and juice. She sat up and drank.

"How are you feeling?" he asked.

"Satisfied." Stephanie kissed him. "How about you?"

Greer smiled nervously. "Hmmm."

"I'm ready for more," she said, running her hand up his pant leg.

"Wait." He stopped her hand. "Let's talk."

Stephanie leaned against the wall and seductively ate the banana. "Okay, talk."

"I tried to tell you last night. . . . You know, a lot has happened over the years. . . ."

"We have a lot of catching up to do."

"Yes . . . Well . . . what I was saying was that it's not reasonable to think that you and I wouldn't have had other—attachments over that time. I'm sure that you've had other relationships, just as I have."

"So, what are you saying?"

"I'm involved in a very serious relationship right now back home."

"Kate, right?"

That threw him. "How did you know that?"

"Oh, I know all about her." Stephanie finished the banana and gave Greer a knowing look. "Actually, I even got a look at her. I followed you to her townhouse one afternoon after work."

Greer was dizzied with a potent blend of terror and confusion.

"Don't you remember?" Stephanie smiled. "I left you that note. I even waved to you that morning from my car."

It suddenly struck Greer what she was talking about. The morning at Kate's townhouse when he had come out to his car and found the passenger-side door ajar. The note that dropped from the door-frame: I'VE BEEN WATCHING YOU.

But none of it made sense.

"*You were in Washington?* What were you doing following me around?"

Stephanie just beamed and snuggled closer to Greer. "I was curious about what you were doing. How you were getting along."

"I don't understand," he protested, as he withdrew from her embrace and stood up, demanding an explanation.

Stephanie's face darkened. "I still love you. I finally made that trip to the States to tell you what had happened, and to tell you how I felt, but you were already with someone else."

"What did you expect?"

"I thought you'd want to see me, but when I found out about Kate, I went crazy. . . ."

Here we go, thought Greer.

The tone of Stephanie's voice had an edge now: "It drove me mad seeing you with another woman. I'm the only one who knows you, Greer. I know all the little things that you want. Like last night. Could Kate do for you what I did last night?"

"Stephanie . . ."

"Not that I ever saw. And believe me, I saw plenty."

Greer was flabbergasted: "You were watching us? My God, Stephanie . . ."

She was staring at him with eyes that had started to glaze, just like when she was starting to have a bad spell in Heidelberg.

"Look," Greer said calmly, "I'm here on business."

She smiled. "I know. I read your itinerary."

She had thrown him again. "What do you mean?"

"I've been reading your E-mail for weeks."

"How . . . So you knew I was going to be . . ." Another thought intruded. "You were the one who broke into my apartment, weren't you? You got my account number and password from the notebooks in my briefcase."

Stephanie just smiled back at him.

Greer said, "You read my itinerary on my E-mail. *You're* the one who left the message. . . ."

" 'SEE YOU SOON!' " she said.

"You knew all along I was coming to Cologne. You knew I'd go to the Früh."

"Just a hunch. Like I said, I'm the only one who really *knows* you."

"*Why*, Stephanie?"

Stephanie seemed suddenly fragile again, as she been had when she had told him of her sickness. "I love you, Greer. Can't you see that? I'll do anything to get you back. If I couldn't tear you away from Kate in Washington, I knew that I could get you back if I just had a chance to hold you in my arms. I knew you wouldn't leave me again if you and I could just be together for a while."

"But, Stephanie . . ."

"Right? Wasn't I right?"

Greer shook his head and turned away from her. "Stephanie."

"I *was* right, wasn't I?"

Greer knew he had to handle the situation delicately if he didn't want her to get totally out of control. He took a deep breath and addressed her directly. "Stephanie, what happened last night was an expression of our love in the past. You know I loved you . . . I can't even describe how much you meant to me. But that was seven years ago and you sent me away and now there's Kate. It's always going to be Kate. . . ."

"Don't say that!" she snapped, turning toward the wall.

"Stephanie, look at me. What we had will always be special. No one can ever take that away. . . ."

Stephanie turned suddenly. "But I'm not content to live in the past!" she said. "I want you now! You're here now and you're mine again!"

"Stephanie . . ."

"I won't have it!" She was seething now: "You can't come back and make love to me like that and just walk off."

"Stephanie . . ."

She was almost yelling: "I can't stand to live without you again! Especially not when I was so close to getting you back!"

Strangely, something Kate had said came to mind. *Crazy people do crazy things.* Kate was certainly right about that. Stephanie had been stalking him. Crossing the Atlantic, breaking into his apartment, following him and watching him making love to Kate. Stephanie had stolen his E-mail password. And now he remembered something else: the woman who had come to Langley claiming to have had an appointment with him that day. It must have been Stephanie, maybe trying to get a better look at Kate at the time. What else had she done? Stephanie was truly unbalanced. She had become obsessed with him again. She was even crazier than he had thought. That *really* scared him. He knew he needed to get out of the situation. *Fast.* Put as much distance between himself and Stephanie as he could.

Stephanie broke down into tears and put her head onto Greer's shoulder. Over her head, Greer saw on the alarm clock that it was already six-fifty. Reed would be waiting on the bridge.

"I know, I know," Greer said, trying to comfort her. "It's hard. All of the old feelings. I can't say there isn't something there. But you've got to understand the position I'm in, okay? You understand, don't you?" Stephanie was still crying hard.

Through her tears, Stephanie was saying, "This will destroy me, Greer. I can't go on. I've come too far to leave without you."

"I'm really, really sorry. I am. If there were any other way . . ."

Stephanie looked up at him and stopped crying. "Leave Kate. Stay with me. Or I'll come back with you. We can work something out. I'll do anything, Greer, anything."

Greer shook his head again. "It's not going to work this time, Stephanie. I'm sorry for all the pain you've been through. And I'll never forget you. I'll never forget what you did. . . ."

She was starting to cry again. "No, Greer."

"It's the only way."

He tried pushing her gently away from him, but she clung tightly and cried harder. He spoke without looking at her. "It would be better if you left this morning."

She cried a while longer, then looked up at him, trying to force a smile. She talked excitedly: "I could stay here in the cabin. I'll wait for you to finish with your meetings. I'll go out later and get some wine and a few things for us to eat. Some candles. It would be romantic."

"No, I'm sorry."

She was crying again: "Oh, Greer."

"It's the only way."

Greer wiped away her tears. She seemed at last resigned and managed a feeble smile. "Checkout time by noon?" she asked weakly.

"Sure. Noon's fine. I won't be back before then. I've got to meet someone in a few minutes."

"Can I see you afterward? Maybe just once more tonight? Dinner?"

"No," he said softly. "We'll just say good-bye now. Okay?"

The tears started again and Stephanie gave Greer a gentle kiss, her tears wetting their lips.

"Okay," she said.

"You'll be all right?" he asked.

"I'll be fine."

Stephanie lay down on the bed. She was moving her head toward Greer and reaching for his trousers.

"No," Greer said firmly.

She smiled up at him. "It was worth a try."

Greer got up and grabbed his briefcase. It was just minutes before seven. He was going to have to hustle.

"Leave the key at the desk, okay?" he said.

"Okay."

With his hand on the door, he took one final look at Stephanie.

It was a mistake.

She was a tangle of flesh in the sheets: a hip, a breast, a calf, her head back on the pillow with her mouth in a pouty half-smile. Part of him said to get the hell out. Another part, he was ashamed to admit, said to stay and make love to her one more time.

She's bad news, he reminded himself.

He bit his lip hard and left as quickly as he could.

The police radio spat out German phrases loudly into the open air in clipped, metallic bursts. The sound traveled almost perceptibly faster through the dense morning air, still heavy with moisture. Except for the radio, though, the scene was eerily quiet.

Greer had heard no sirens. He was hurrying to make the meeting with Reed on the bridge. He assumed Jenkins would catch up with him later in the day.

Greer was relieved to have got through that bizarre ordeal with Stephanie as easily as he had. He had been so caught up in the shock and nostalgia of seeing Stephanie again that he'd allowed himself to be sucked into her crazy, delusional world. Looking back over the past twelve hours, none of it seemed real. He'd forgotten how manic she could get, how obsessive she had been about him. There had been a time when he had enjoyed it and all that it meant. She still needed help, and he hoped she would find it somewhere—at a safe distance from him. It was a heartbreaking situation, he thought, the way their relationship had ended unnecessarily. But it obviously wasn't his fate to spend the rest of his life with Stephanie Becker. Last night had been a close call, one he was determined never to repeat. Maybe it was a good thing, he reasoned. He had been thrown into a bizarre situation and had come out even more committed to Kate. He'd call her as soon as he had a chance. Should he tell her? He should, he decided. And he had better do it soon, in case Stephanie appeared on the scene again in Washington. Just get it all out. Kate would understand, or so he hoped.

Blue lights flashed silently at a point along the quay halfway between the *Prinsesse Marianna* and the high flight of steps leading from the cobbles up to the bridge he had planned to cross. A half dozen white Politzei BMWs—Cologne city police—were blocking his approach. He heard a rumble from behind just as an ambulance shot a burst of siren at him. He jumped aside to let it pass.

Greer walked on toward the scene, intent on not having to retrace his steps and take the sidewalk along the high road up on the bank to the bridge. He didn't want to be late. He saw some other pedestrians slipping quickly through the maze of cars without looking at what was going on. There were no gawkers. The Germans wouldn't do that. They knew that the authorities would take care of everything. Order would be restored.

One of the blue lights—the one he had seen earlier hovering over the water through the fog—was flashing from the top of a muscular-looking river patrol boat pulled up alongside the short wharf normally used by the passenger ferry. The police cars were parked at all angles around the steps leading down to the wharf from the ferry ticket booth on the quay. A hand-lettered sign at the front of the booth indicated that the ferry would not be running until further notice. The police seemed unconcerned with people walking through. The officers were all facing the water, pointing to various spots on the opposite bank.

The ambulance crew opened the back doors, pulled out the stretcher and walked down the steps to the patrol boat. Greer passed through the cars, stopped and turned to watch from the other side. The boat crew of four untied two rope lines from the cleats on the back side of the boat and pulled something heavy on the other end of the lines over their shoulders through the water. They brought it over to the wharf where the ambulance crew were waiting.

The men on the boat jumped onto the wharf, holding onto the lines. They reached down near the water to shorten their grip. One of the patrolmen called out, *"Eins, zwei, drei!"* and they all pulled on the ropes. A large object rolled in the water like a log and briefly lifted up above the choppy water line, then sunk back down. As the object— now obviously a body with clothes still on—rolled, a wooden stick somehow attached to the midsection erected itself then knocked loudly against the side of the wharf as the body turned. The crew tried again, and again the stick struck the wharf and they failed to lift the body much out of the water.

"Scheisse!" one of them swore.

Two of the policemen watching took their hats off and carefully put them onto the dashboards of their cars, then went down to help. The six men finally hoisted the waterlogged body up the side of the wharf and laid it out on its back. Water streamed off the body down through the wooden planks of the wharf to the river beneath.

The head of the corpse was swiveled back at a grotesque rotation. Although the body lay on its back, the face was almost completely rotated downward. From where he stood almost fifty feet away, Greer could see only the back of the head with a few wisps of dark hair plastered against a scalp as blue as the diesel fumes coming from the patrol boat's engine.

The rest of the police went down to the wharf and stood in a circle around the body. The stick in the cadaver's midsection was standing straight up. One of the officers gave it a tug with one hand, then two, but it wouldn't budge. He waved it off. The ambulance crew lifted the body onto the stretcher and threw a blanket over the top half, obscuring the face. They struggled up the steps with the stretcher, the stick still attached to the body. At the top, they snapped the stretcher's frame and wheels into place and rolled it the rest of the way to the ambulance.

A man wearing a parka who had been standing among the officers on the quay stepped over to the stretcher. He took out a pen and notepad from inside his coat pocket and asked questions of the boat crew. It was hard for Greer to translate the German from where he was standing. Greer moved closer, back into the pack of cars to hear what they were saying.

"American, don't you think?" said the man in the parka. He was the detective. He pushed aside the blanket and tugged at the suit coat on the body. He found a label sewed on the inside.

"Cheap suit. See how the water beads up and doesn't soak into the cloth?" Everyone around leaned over and nodded. "Polyester. Not even a blend. Must be a salesman in town for a trade show across the way at the exhibition center. I'll find out what's in town this week." He wrote himself a note. "Was this necessary?" he asked, tapping the stick with the back of his hand holding the pen.

A patrol boat crewman spoke: "He was dead when we saw him. Hung up on some trash along the other side of the river. We were going for him with a pole but the river current caught him and he moved away from the bank into the middle of the river. We snagged him just before he went down."

"Well, I wouldn't take him in like that. Pull it out," the detective said.

The patrol boat crew looked at each other, then took turns rocking the stick back and forth. It wouldn't budge. "It's stuck between his ribs," one said. Another put his boot up against the side of the body for leverage and gave a hard pull that dislodged the stick with the sound of cracking bone. On the end was a metal hook and over a foot of intestines. The patrolman recoiled, cursed, and slung the entrails out over the water in one fast move. They were all quiet, swallowing hard and taking in deep breaths. One of the paramedics pushed a length of intestines back into the cavity between the ribs.

"That's better," said the detective. They all looked at the tool, the kind normally used for moving heavy fish around in the hold of a ship.

The detective pulled the blanket completely off the body. He pushed the head off the stretcher so that the entire face was visible from underneath. The detective crouched down and cocked his own head sideways to look straight up at the dead man's face. Greer walked a few feet closer, unnoticed by the officers. He was now standing only ten feet away, paralytic with horror.

The face was contorted with the mouth open. The right side of the face was split open to the bone starting at the eye socket diagonally down through the upper lip, revealing ugly yellow teeth with silver fillings and gold crowns. The detective got right up in the dead man's face. He tapped the dead man's teeth with his pen. "Too many sweets," he said.

Suddenly a small black eel popped out of the dead man's mouth onto the detective's face.

Everyone jumped back. One of the policemen picked up the eel and tossed it back toward the river. Greer saw it arc up, writhing through the air, basically along the same trajectory as he had just seen fourteen inches of Randall Jenkins' intestines go flying a few moments before.

"I've gotta leave," said Greer. He was moving fast, pulling open drawers in the cabin, looking for something. "You're going with me."

In the minute it had taken to walk briskly back from the crime scene on the quay to the boat, Greer had made a decision: he needed Stephanie's help. As reluctant as he was about any further contact with her, Greer was certain that she was his only chance of getting out of Cologne. Whoever had killed Jenkins might be looking for him, too.

"What's happened? Why the sudden change of heart?" Stephanie asked, sitting up in bed. "What about your meeting?"

"We've got to leave." He pulled her jeans and sweater off the floor and threw them to her. "Hurry up. Put these on."

Stephanie watched him silently as she pulled on her socks. Greer turned around in the small space and pulled open the drawer under the vanity. He positioned his body so that it blocked Stephanie's view of what he was doing; he didn't want her to know about the diskettes. He pulled out the Ziploc bag with the computer diskettes. He got his passport and traveler's checks from his briefcase, then stuffed them and the diskettes into his coat pocket. He picked up Stephanie's bag and looked at her to see if she was ready to go.

"Come on!" he said.

Stephanie was feeling around in the bed for something missing. Greer was impatient. She smiled at him and started pulling on her boots, then jumped off the bed.

"I'm ready," she said. "Just looking for my other earring. I must have lost it last night."

On the quay in front of the boat, Greer could see that the ambulance with Jenkins' body was already gone, but the police were still congregated around the wharf. Greer led Stephanie up to the street level above the quay and hurried her into the heart of the Old Town.

"What's going on?" she asked.

Greer turned them in the direction of the cathedral.

"My boss just got pulled out of the Rhine."

"The President's National Security Adviser?"

Greer hadn't told her. But this time he was all too aware of how she had gotten her information. She'd been following him, she'd managed to break into his E-mail, and he could only imagine what else.

"Yes. Randall Jenkins is dead. Horrible. *Horrible.*"

"So why aren't you speaking to the authorities? Why this frantic rush?"

Greer rushed them into a doorway of a camera shop. It was still too early for the stores to be open. "I need to get away quickly and I need your help." He paused to think. "Let me see your train schedule." Earlier he had noticed it in her bag. Greer turned to the schedule for Cologne departures. "Here's what I need you to do," he said.

"Anything."

"Go to the train station and get us tickets. Put it on your credit card. I'll pay you back before you get the bill. There's an express to Munich. Get it and wait for me on the platform, okay?"

Stephanie seemed reluctant.

"Get us seats in first class. Maybe we can have some privacy in a compartment."

Stephanie took back the train schedule. "You'll explain everything at the station, right?"

"I can't. Not everything."

She was still hesitant. "You now want my help after all that talk this morning about how you didn't need me anymore?"

"Please?" he asked.

Even before she had kissed him and dashed out of the doorway, he regretted having to ask her to help. But he had no choice and now he owed her. Big time.

It was already nine forty-five and Reed would have missed Greer at the bridge, then the exhibition center, and gone looking for him. Greer had moved on after Stephanie had left, and now he was hiding well back in the doorway of the Altstadt Sex Shop, along the wide pedestrian mall of shops that led off the cathedral plaza. The glass front of the store was opaqued with black paint on the inside. It made a good mirror. He looked at the glass and watched the people walking by in the reflection. It was too early for commercial sex in Cologne and the business was closed, but the lights still flashed a reminder to the passersby that they could return later in the day not just for sex, but for *exotic* sex. With his back turned to the mall, Greer was just another traveling salesman from out of town planning his evening entertainment.

The next train to leave Cologne was at nine fifty-five. Stephanie was at the *Bahnhof* now buying them tickets to Munich. He would wait as long as he could, then meet her on the platform. The train station was only a brisk four-minute walk away, he figured. He regretted that Stephanie would now know where he was going, but he needed her help to get out of the city quickly. With her credit card there'd be no record to lead a trail to him. He wasn't sure what he was into, but he knew he was right in the middle and for the time being, he wanted to avoid Reed at all costs. He had to become invisible, and he knew Stephanie was his best hope.

Getting out of Cologne would give him time to think. Jenkins was dead and it was no accident. Too many coincidences. First the mention of STEEPLECHASE in the REDWING cable. Then Reed showing up. And now Jenkins yanked from the river. A high-ranking member of the U.S. government—dead. Whom could he really trust?

At nine fifty-three, Greer had ducked behind a cigarette kiosk just inside the station entrance. He was studying the departing train schedule when his blood ran cold. Just below the large board, he caught sight of Reed scanning the entrances to the platforms in front of him.

Greer saw from the board that the express train to Munich was leaving from platform Number Three. He heard the train doors slamming. He checked the clock in the station. The train was pulling out in two minutes, but Reed stood between him and the platform entrance.

And where the hell was Stephanie?

Greer noticed a porter coming in from the station exit, pushing a cart piled high with baggage from the arriving taxis. As the porter passed Greer quickly fell in beside the cart, hunched over. The porter passed directly by Reed, but Greer was hidden by the baggage. Greer looked and saw Stephanie stepping out from her own hiding place behind an announcement board on platform Number Three, fifty meters away at the other end of the platform. She flashed the ticket so that he could see, pointing to the train next to the platform that was already sounding the signal it was about to leave.

The train master blew his whistle. Greer left the cover of the porter's cart and ran. Stephanie was walking in his direction.

Now the train whistle blew and it made a small motion forward. The train moved ahead slowly, steadily picking up momentum. Greer sprinted up the platform.

He pumped harder. The train was going faster. In just a few moments it would be out of the station.

Greer ran even harder. He was getting closer to Stephanie. Greer waved at her to turn around. "Run!" he called out. Stephanie sprinted toward the train. Greer thought he'd collapse from the exertion as he pushed even harder to make it before the last few cars of the train had pulled out.

Reed had spotted him running: "Greer!" he called out from his position at the platform entrance. But it was too late.

Greer kept his eyes on the train. He caught up with Stephanie and grabbed her hand. Greer was fast enough to overtake a few cars before the train slipped past the platform. He let go of Stephanie and pushed her toward a car door. He didn't have time to look back to see if she had made it. Six cars from the end, he reached up at the coach for something to grab onto. He caught the handle on a coach marked for first class passengers and pulled on it. The door opened and Greer hung on, leaving him swinging over the platform with his feet in the air. He caught a glimpse of Reed running to the platform on the other side of the train. Then the motion of the train swung the door closed again and Greer found the step. He opened the door and pulled himself inside.

Greer ducked into an empty compartment, where he collapsed into the seat, gasping for breath. Thank God, he thought. The train moved steadily on.

As Greer leaned forward for one last look as the train pulled away, he saw Reed's face staring back at him from the crowd. Their eyes met for an instant. Reed looked at a point just beyond Greer. His head turned and followed the train as it passed by at the same moment the door to his compartment was sliding open. Greer reached for his ticket to hand to the train master.

But it was Stephanie coming in instead.

28 ❑ ❑ ❑ ❑

In the cabin on the *Prinsesse Marianna,* the German CIA station chief and a field officer from Bonn loaded Greer's personal things into cardboard file boxes and special vacuum containers under the watchful eye of the Cologne police. After phone calls had been traded at high levels between the Germans and Americans, the Germans finally agreed that the Americans should be involved with the investigation due to the importance of the person and possible national security issues involved. The White House had asked the CIA to handle the liaison. By noon of the day Jenkins' body had been found, it was determined that Greer and Jenkins had checked in together, accompanied by a third man, unidentified, who had not taken a room. Jenkins' bag had been hung up, but otherwise the room was untouched. Jenkins obviously hadn't spent the night.

Greer's room was a different matter.

"Must have been quite a night," said the field officer. The station chief grunted. "Smells like sex," he continued. The field officer slowly untangled the comforter, looking for clues. "*Here* we go." He pulled a pair of latex gloves out of his coat pocket, blew them open, and pulled them on like a surgeon. "Pubic hairs. Want to guess which ones his and which ones are hers?" He picked them up and put them into an envelope. The station chief was looking through the drawers, oblivious to the chatter. "Oh, now, look at *this*, will you?"

The chief glanced over his shoulder. The field officer was holding up a gold braided earring by its post. After he made sure the chief had seen it, he dropped it into another envelope. "It appears he enjoyed some female companionship."

The field officer continued going over the bed. The chief found Greer's laptop computer, opened it up and turned it on. The internal drive hummed and the computer beeped. On the screen the words, "PLEASE ENTER PASSWORD," appeared. He turned the machine off and put it into a box.

The other Agency man spoke again: "Hey, weren't you meeting with Jenkins today? Ironic, huh? Guess you'll still get to see him, but he won't have a whole lot to say. I suppose you can make positive ID. Haven't been to the city morgue in Cologne yet, have you?"

"That's enough," the chief finally said.

The Chief of Staff and CIA Director sat on the opposite side of the Franklin Roosevelt desk in the Oval Office. Three of the four televisions were turned on to the morning news shows with the sound off; the fourth was tuned to CNN's coverage of the death of the U.S. National Security Adviser.

"I don't understand how something like this could happen," the President said, shaking his head in disbelief.

"Yes, sir," the Chief of Staff said.

Gibbons spoke up: "I'm sorry about Jenkins, sir. I know he was a good friend."

"It just doesn't make any sense," the President said.

Conrad cleared his throat. "Ben has got his people on this. They're already on the scene, working with the German police. I thought you'd want to hear the latest." Conrad looked at Gibbons and signaled him with a slight nod of the head.

"Sir, the Germans pulled him out of the Rhine in Cologne just before seven A.M. local time. There was no ID on the body but they had a lucky break. It seems that Jenkins was staying on a boat nearby and as they were about to put his body into the ambulance one of the crew from the boat came over and recognized Jenkins as a passenger."

"What the hell was he doing on a boat?" the President asked.

"We don't know yet."

"Was he killed?"

"It looks that way, but we should know something more definite within a few hours. A team of forensic pathologists is working on the body right now. He *was* in pretty bad shape when they hauled him out, though. Banged up quite a bit. Right now it's hard to say if it happened before he went into the river or after. From what I hear, the Germans mangled the body getting it out."

The President was exasperated. "Horrible, just horrible. How can a simple trip to Germany to monitor economic negotiations turn into such a monstrous international incident? Am I missing something here?"

The Chief of Staff and CIA Director exchanged glances. Conrad realized Gibbons wasn't going to speak first: "Ostensibly he was monitoring the G7 preconference negotiations," said the Chief of Staff. "Ben knew he was going over and had come to me with a request that Jenkins help out with an assessment of foreign intelligence services while he was over there. We thought it would be a good idea. Jenkins was supposed to meet today with the German CIA station chief."

"And?"

The DCI picked up the story: "They never made their connection, of course. Our man was supposed to meet with him at nine this morning for breakfast to brief him on our allies' intelligence organizations. Jenkins never showed for the rendezvous, so the station chief went back to Bonn. He had to turn around to go back to Cologne almost as soon as he had returned after I called him about Jenkins' body being recovered."

"Do you think there's there any connection between this assessment of his and Jenkins' death?" the President asked.

"I don't think so. He wouldn't have known anything yet. Not very likely, sir."

The President was showing the strain. "What about any connection with the G7 conference?"

"I can't see it."

"So what are the next steps?" asked the President.

The Chief of Staff spoke: "Establish cause of death. Work the liaison primarily through CIA, but publicly through the State Department. The Communications Office is drafting a statement for you to read this afternoon just before the evening news. I'll bring it in about an hour for you to approve. I'll draw up a list of candidates for you to look at over the holidays. We're assuming it was an accident for now."

The President sat up and leaned forward across his desk. "Now listen. I want this resolved immediately. Randall was a close friend, and I want to know what happened to him. Do you understand?"

The two visitors answered in unison: "Yes, sir, Mr. President."

The President was looking directly at the DCI: "Do whatever it takes. Do you understand? Let's not be shy about using Agency resources on this one, okay?"

"Yes, sir. I understand."

"Fly his body back over as soon as you can. Send it to San Francisco. He once told me he wanted to be buried at the veterans cemetery at the Presidio."

Conrad said, "I'll take care of it personally. As soon as this meeting's over."

The President eased back into his chair. "Thanks, Dwight. Thank you both."

29 ❏ ❏ ❏ ❏

Stephanie sat across from Greer in the first-class compartment. They were alone. Greer had pulled the curtains closed.

"We're slowing down," Greer said to Stephanie as the train approached the outskirts of Frankfurt.

Frankfurt was the only stop along the way of the express train from Cologne to Munich. It had backtracked along the same route that Greer and Jenkins had traveled the previous day as they had come from the airport. That was less than twenty-four hours ago, but now seemed like a lifetime.

"Are you going to tell me what's going on?" Stephanie asked again.

"Why are you running? Did something happen between you and Jenkins after you left the cabin this morning? Why won't you tell me about it? You're in a lot of trouble, aren't you?"

"Nothing happened. I told you: I saw him being pulled up when I was heading to my meeting."

"So why did you drop everything and take the first train out of Cologne? And who was that guy chasing after you?"

"I have no idea," Greer lied, "but it ought to be obvious that getting out of Cologne was the right thing to do. If Jenkins was a target, I have to assume I might be, too."

Greer wasn't about to tell Stephanie any more than he had to. Given her erratic behavior, he wanted to give her as little information as possible. The less she knew the better. He would have to be careful not to provide her with any further leverage.

Greer was most disturbed by the certainty he felt that somehow Reed was involved in Jenkins' death. It was just too much of a coincidence. Wasn't Reed the last person to see Jenkins alive? After seeing the look on his face on the platform in Cologne, Greer didn't have any doubt that Reed was after him. Bob Reed was the last person in the world he could trust now.

Which brought him right back to the troubling implications of that cable connecting REDWING and STEEPLECHASE. A couple of CIA operations gone bad? The obvious answer to the riddle left Greer queasy. What had he gotten into? Or was this just paranoia gone wild?

The train would be pulling into Frankfurt shortly. He had to think fast.

He turned to Stephanie and asked, "Suppose that guy on the platform wanted to follow me. If he knew I was on this train, he could call ahead and have someone else waiting for me, couldn't he?" He wondered whether CIA would be waiting for him at the other end. The thought was no longer comforting.

Stephanie knew the train routes by heart: "If that guy is following you, he's going to know about the stop in Frankfurt and he might be waiting for you during the brief layover. As far as I know, there's no way for anyone to find out that you have a ticket all the way through to Munich, though."

"What if he took a car?"

Stephanie looked at her map. "If he really pushed it, he might make it to Frankfurt to meet the train before we arrive, but it would be tough."

Greer considered the odds. "The bigger problem would be in Munich," he said. He was thinking there was the chance that Reed would be able to race along the Frankfurt-to-Munich leg of the trip and be there waiting in the Munich train station when they got there.

Greer examined the map again, noting the most likely route that Reed might take if he did drive: due south from Frankfurt as far as Karlsruhe, then southeast to Munich.

As if she were reading his mind, Stephanie explained: "The express train travels fast and the rail is a more direct route than the road."

Greer figured that he could beat Reed all the way to Munich. Reed himself probably wouldn't be a threat.

The train entered the rail yard and headed toward the Frankfurt *Bahnhof.* Passengers were starting to leave their compartments and fill the aisle.

"So what do we do?" asked Stephanie.

"Let's stay on the train." The more miles between Reed and himself the better, he reasoned. Plus, Reed might make the assumption that Greer would get off in Frankfurt to make a detour to throw him off course. "I'm staying put. I'm mainly concerned about when we get into Munich? What if someone's waiting for me there?"

She was grinning at him now. It was disconcerting while he was trying to be serious.

"What?" he asked. He was annoyed.

"You need me more now than you ever did." Of course, she was right. "I know Munich," she said.

While he was still thinking, she said, "And we're not going all the way to Munich."

Greer was a little confused. "There's no stop between here and Munich."

"Exactly. We just leave a little early."

"No." He realized what she was thinking.

"Yes."

"I wouldn't know where."

"Oh, *Liebling.* You really do need my help." She reached across the space between them and gave a soft tug on his tie. "I know just the spot."

• • •

"It's deep enough. Trust me."

The train was approaching the mountain range that separated them from Munich. Greer and Stephanie stood at the back of the coach with the door window down. They were still on relatively flat terrain, but Greer could see where the rail line met up with the mountain. The track clung to the face of the mountain along a path that had been blasted in a rock cliff directly over the Rhine. It was at least a thirty-foot drop from the train to the water below. The barges were maneuvering close to the rock wall.

She was still trying to convince him. "See the barges? They couldn't make it through if there weren't at least ten meters of water in the channel."

"I don't know."

"I'll go first."

The idea of letting her jump and then continuing on to Munich without her crossed his mind. Greer took another look at the situation and assessed the possibilities.

He said, "So you think the train will slow down to about fifty kilometers per hour as it makes the climb along the cliff wall. We'll have to push off far enough to clear the rail guard and make sure that we land at least ten feet away from the cliff face so that we don't break our legs in the shallow water."

"Piece of pie."

"The expression is 'piece of cake.' Then we swim to the other side and follow that little utility road into Munich."

"That's how I saw it."

It was a helluva thing to do. For about five seconds, the view of the Bavarian countryside would be spectacular. Then he'd be stroking through the Rhine.

"How far to Munich?"

"About fifteen kilometers."

"There's no place else we can jump?"

"This is it. Stay on the train or jump." The train was already slowing to take the curve before the grade. "You have about thirty seconds to make up your mind."

They stood in the open doorway of the train. There was nothing between them and the swirling waters below. A barge had just passed, leaving a broad wake.

"Just look at the horizon," he said.

Greer patted his pocket to make sure the Ziploc bag was secure. In it were the diskettes, his passport, traveler's checks, and now his watch.

Greer took her hand. "Ready?" he asked.

She nodded.

Greer could see that the rail line would be pulling back from the edge of the water in just a matter of moments.

"On three," he said. "One . . . two . . ."

Stephanie leaped early, on the count of two, pulling Greer with her. They both pushed off as hard as they could, Greer a split-second after Stephanie, flying away from the train, down along the cliff face, holding hands until they smacked the icy surface of the water.

Greer clawed his way back to the surface. Stephanie was already up, swimming for the other side.

Greer caught up with Stephanie and swam alongside her. The river was colder and stronger than he had imagined. They reached the far side and used the brush along bank to pull themselves out.

"I think I hurt my ankle when I hit," said Greer. He pushed up the pant leg and saw a bruise. It hurt a lot when he tried to move it. "You okay?"

Stephanie was shivering, but otherwise looked fine. The train had already moved around the bend, out of sight.

They stripped and wrung their clothes out the best they could in the shelter of a wooden shrine at the side of the road. There was a ceramic statue of Mary on a wooden shelf and a pathetic, water-stained photo of a young man set in a glass frame. There were flowers in a vase that had been left in the summer, dead and fallen over. A cross marked the spot where he had died in a car accident.

As they dressed, there was the sound of a vehicle coming along the road. A flatbed truck with large white translucent plastic drums filled with something sloshing around inside passed by, leaving in its wake an awful stench. The truck came to a stop a few meters down the road.

Stephanie went over to talk to the man driving the truck.

She came back to Greer. "Hop on," she said. "He's going to the food market to pick up more slop for his pigs. He'll give us a lift into the city."

They climbed onto the back of the truck and rode unceremoniously into Munich sitting with their backs against stinking plastic drums.

"That looks terrible," said Stephanie. "Get it."

The sweater Greer had just pulled on was not much more than an oily rag with holes at the elbows. The used clothing store near the food market in Munich had no mirror. He looked down at himself and was satisfied that he was—item by item—beginning to acquire the looks of a native. He and Stephanie had agreed: he would take on the persona of a German university student—grubby, unshaved, smelling of beer and bratwurst and cigarettes. The old sweater and trousers hadn't been washed before being consigned to the shop and already carried with them the necessary aromas. He picked out a long wool scarf and an old green German Army jacket that would keep him warm.

"Your shoes will give you away. Get rid of them," she told him. She helped him find a scuffed-up pair of brogans that fit reasonably well and he gave her some deutsche marks to pay for everything.

It was late in the afternoon. Outside, they avoided the main streets and searched until they came to a large Dumpster. It was starting to get dark and no one was around. Greer changed into his new German clothes, then tore up his suit and shirt and stuffed them into an empty bag. He tossed in his tie and shoes and pushed the bag down into the trash. He got his watch out of the Ziploc bag and put it back on.

Just a few blocks away was the Hofbrauhaus. The huge vaulted hall on the ground floor was almost empty. Greer led them to a faraway corner bench. He pulled the collar up on his coat and sat across from Stephanie facing the door. She ordered liter mugs of beer for them.

Greer was solemn.

"Why won't you tell me?" she asked.

"It has to do with my work. I can't say anymore."

"I'm a linguist. I'm apolitical."

"I just can't."

"How can I help you if I don't know what the problem is?"

"I'm sorry. If you want to help, then you'll just have to trust me. If not, then we'll just have to part ways."

Greer took another large drink of beer. Just then from upstairs in the banquet hall on the second floor came a rhythmic stomping. A few shouts like barks punctuated the upstairs room and then voices began singing a guttural military song. The stomping got louder and started down the stairs. The singing got louder. It was one of the tunes often heard on the World War II newsreels from Nazi Germany. A group of a dozen tough-looking men in their early twenties marched into the downstairs dining hall in single file. They were singing so hard they were spitting and veins were popping out of their foreheads. Everyone watched silently as they passed through the room and out onto the street.

"The old Germany," said Greer.

"The *new* Germany," replied Stephanie.

Stephanie took a deep breath and looked around the high ceilings. There was a haze of cigarette smoke in the top third of the room. She filled her lungs again with the sooty air. "It's times like this that I wish I hadn't given up smoking," she said.

Back on the street, he felt the exhaustion. He leaned a little on Stephanie, who helped take the weight off the injured leg.

Stephanie knew of a house nearby that had once rented a room to a university friend. The house was fully occupied, but since all the students were away for the Christmas holiday, the rooms were mostly empty. The *Frau* showed them a second floor room of a student from Augsburg who wouldn't be returning for several days. Greer stayed back and said nothing to give away his accent. Stephanie negotiated three nights for sixty deutsche marks. Greer limped up the stairs. The leg was definitely getting worse.

They closed the door and dropped onto the bed—fully clothed— and slept. Around eight o'clock at night, they awoke to the sound of revelers on the street. The room was dark except for the street lights shining through the window. They were surrounded by the possessions of a stranger. The room appeared to belong to some out-of-fashion punk rocker—a girl, they figured. There was a shelf full of heavy metal cassette tapes and posters on the wall. The closet was full of black clothes and leather accessories. There were university books and football posters and a small framed picture of a family. It was all too personal.

"I'm not going to make it very far on this leg," Greer said. The pain was getting worse.

"We can stay here a little while," Stephanie said. "Hopefully the swelling will go down by then."

Stephanie looked at the leg in the strange light. She was very careful in how she cradled his foot so that she could look at the underside. He watched how she took every care not to cause more pain.

"Give it a couple of days," she said. "It may hurt like hell, but you should be able to walk on it."

30 ❏ ❏ ❏ ❏

Two days turned into three. They were running out of time; the *Frau* confirmed that the room had to be vacated the next day by noon. Greer had stayed in the room the entire time. Stephanie immensely enjoyed taking care of him. She had found a new power over him—dependency. He realized she no longer felt the need to overwhelm him with her powerful sexual charms. She already had him exactly where she wanted him to be—under her physical control. He wasn't going anywhere without her anytime soon, and she knew it. But what about afterward when he got better?

During the night, he slept on his side to keep the strain off his ankle. She slept at his back, two spoons in a drawer. He would wake in the middle of the night to feel her stroking his neck, his back, his legs. She made soft cooing sounds as she touched him. He couldn't help but be aroused. But he had sworn never to succumb to her considerable charms again. Nevertheless, it was Stephanie making love to him in her Heidelberg office that occupied his last waking thoughts.

Another night, he dreamed she was taking him into her mouth. She had climbed over him. A glorious, glorious dream that went on and on. He kept his eyes closed and let it play out. In the morning he allowed her casual kisses without strong protestations. She gave him looks as if to say, "Just wait until you're better."

Stephanie would go out daily to get them food and toiletries and to buy newspapers. She came in with a bundle from her morning run to the market.

"Front page picture in the *Herald-Tribune* and all the German papers," Stephanie said. "I'm impressed." She threw down a stack of the morning's newspapers onto the bed where Greer was lying. He sat up and unfolded *Die Welt.* In the top right-hand corner were two pictures: one of Jenkins and one of himself. His photo was the one from his Langley security pass.

"This complicates matters even further," Greer said.

Jenkins' death was a headline story two days ago. Yesterday the papers reported a major diplomatic tug-of-war between the Germans and Americans as the Americans tried to get the body sent back to the United States for a thorough autopsy. The Germans balked at letting go of evidence before the investigation was complete. The Americans prevailed on a technicality, claiming that the body was no longer a person but privileged diplomatic material and therefore exempt from the normal laws of the country according to reciprocal diplomatic agreements. A political cartoonist had satirized the dispute by showing the body in a diplomatic pouch slung over the shoulder of an American diplomat passing by a German customs officer with the caption *"Anything to declare?"*

Today marked the first mention of Greer in the press. He skimmed the headlines and first paragraphs. Any decent journalist would get the essence of the story right up in the front of the article. He read that he was a wanted man. The Germans wanted him for questioning. "Have you read this yet?" he asked.

"No, I brought them up as soon as I saw your lovely face beaming up from the cover pages."

Greer lay back down on the bed. "Would you mind reading to me? I don't want to miss any nuances. To be honest, between those pages and all that hammering out there my head feels like it may crack open."

While most of the student tenants were away on Christmas break, the landlady had decided to do some repair work in the hallway outside their door. Greer and Stephanie had almost killed themselves tripping over loose lumber coming into the room the first night. The hammering had been going on for the entire time during the day. There was no radio or TV in the room and it was the only thing Greer had had to listen to as he lay on the bed letting his leg heal.

Stephanie took the newspapers back from Greer and pulled a chair beside the bed.

She read first from the *Herald-Tribune* first. " 'Aide to Slain National Security Adviser Missing.' " She cleared her throat. " 'The U.S. State Department issued a statement on Wednesday indicating that Randall Jenkins, the National Security Adviser found dead in the Rhine

River in Cologne Monday morning, was traveling with an aide. According to the State Department briefing, Greer Whitaker accompanied Mr. Jenkins on his trip to Cologne as an observer of the pre-G7 conference negotiations being held in that city. Mr. Whitaker has been missing and was last seen in the vicinity where Mr. Jenkins' body was found. The State Department spokesman said that Mr. Whitaker is being sought for questioning. He declined to identify Mr. Whitaker's exact title or responsibilities in his position with the NSC, or whether Mr. Whitaker was a suspect. A source with the German government confirmed that the Germans are cooperating with the Americans in finding Mr. Whitaker, who is believed to still be in Germany. No other information is available on Mr. Whitaker at this writing."

"*Die Welt?*"

She picked up the paper and translated the headline: " 'Colleague Sought for Questioning in Death of American Security Adviser.' " She skimmed the article. "I'm looking for any new information," she said.

"I can't wait."

She saw nothing of special interest on the front page and turned to the back where the story continued. "Here's something. It says that the Cologne police took statements from several vendors at the *Bahnhof* saying that you were there around dawn the day of the death. The newspaper then checked the rail schedule and found out that the next train after that was to Berlin. They interviewed the people at the ticket windows but no one remembered selling you a ticket. There is some speculation that you probably left Cologne for Berlin, though, since you would have already bought a ticket for your escape."

"Good," said Greer with a wry grin. "Let them think I'm in Berlin."

She looked over at Greer. He was staring at the ceiling. "What do you think?" she asked.

"I think I'm screwed."

"Are you going to turn yourself in?" she asked.

"No."

"I just passed the *Frau* on the steps on the way up to the room. She reminded me that we've got to be out of here by noon tomorrow. We'll be on the streets again. What are you going to do?"

Greer stood up and took the copy of *Die Welt* from Stephanie, folding the paper back to the front page with his picture. He pushed up from the bed and walked to the mirror over the dresser. He rubbed his hand over his face. After three days without shaving he was beginning to develop a decent growth of beard. His used clothes added to the shabby look. He decided he could fake it.

"I can't go in until I've figured out what's going on and whom I can trust, not now at least."

"Okay, so now what?"

Greer was sure of his decision. If he did turn himself in, he'd be thrown into isolation for months until the whole thing got settled. The White House would find a way to keep him quiet until after the G7 conference. He owed it to Jenkins.

There was music coming from the street, notes blown from the direction of the city center.

"Only four days until Christmas, you know," said Stephanie.

He looked toward the window. "I'd almost forgotten." Greer thought immediately of Kate. Had she got the news about Jenkins yet? What must she be thinking? He bent his arm to get the light from the window on his watch that Kate had given him. Merry Christmas, he told himself.

Greer tested his weight against the injury.

"You need to exercise that leg a bit," she said, "or it might get even worse."

"Maybe just once up and down the street."

"There's a Christmas market in the Marienplatz. If there's one place to be at Christmas, it's in the Marienplatz. Crowds are safer."

He checked himself out in the mirror again. He couldn't stay in the room forever. He had to find a way out. He needed a chance to evaluate the situation, figure out a way to get back home. Back to Kate, who would straighten this out.

At night, the entire plaza around the column of the Virgin Mary was crowded with stalls strung with white Christmas lights. On the high balcony of the *Rathaus*—the Town Hall—on the north side of the square, a boys' choir was singing carols. People wandered among the stalls, picking out straw and glass Christmas tree ornaments.

Greer pushed the scarf up over the lower half of his face. It was there to hide behind as well as to keep him warm. He winced with every step he took from the pain of the injured leg. He tried to find something else to think about. He pointed to an especially large, ruddy-cheeked woman who was considering a large candle with a gold angel. "I'm so hungry I could eat *her*," he said.

"Come on," Stephanie said. She tugged him in the direction of the food stalls. "I think it's time for some more brats."

The meat sizzled on the grills. They fell in behind a crowd of people with their arms thrust over the counter with deutsche marks trying to get the attention of the vendor. Stephanie caught the eye of the vendor. She got two bratwursts with mustard and sauerkraut and rolls. While she got the food, Greer used hand signals and bought beers at the next stall. They walked over to the side of one of the buildings around the edge of the plaza to get out of the wind.

"*Sehr gut!*" Greer said with a mouth full of meat and bread.

They finished eating and washed it down with the beer. Greer felt more relaxed now that he had eaten. They walked slowly through the stalls, fingering the ornaments and small wooden toys. Suddenly, a mechanical whir and what sounded like the tinkling of a music box filled the air. It was nine o'clock. All the shoppers backed away from the stalls to get an unobstructed view of the *Rathaus*. It was time for the *Glockenspiel*. The small doors high up on the wall opened and out came the painted figures to start the jousting tournament. They circled round tilting at each other, then went back inside. The loud, happy chatter of the crowd resumed.

They turned to leave. Greer ran directly into someone watching the *Glockenspiel* over his shoulder.

"Pardon," Greer said.

It was a German police officer in uniform. Behind him was another policeman watching the shoppers. The officer looked at Greer's clothes then looked at him directly in the eyes. "No problem," he replied in heavily accented English.

Greer saw the expression on the second officer's face change. The officer said something quietly to the other policeman, who was turning to hear what he was saying. Stephanie grabbed Greer's hand and started to lead him off in a fast walk. Only a couple of steps away, Greer heard one of the officers talking into a radio.

"*Halt!*" Greer heard from behind. Without looking back, he and Stephanie started running through the maze of booths, dodging around people in the market. "Stop!" he heard again.

Greer darted behind a row of booths, pulling Stephanie behind him. He stopped for an instant to look quickly in both directions, then cut down a side alley. Another turn and he ran into the chest of one of the policemen, knocking him against a wall. The policeman pushed himself off the wall and at the same time reached to key down on the radio on his shoulder strap. Greer threw a left punch which knocked the officer's hand away from the radio, followed by a quick right which knocked the officer's head back against the wall with a dull thud.

"Come on!" Stephanie shouted, as the policeman slumped.

Greer pulled the radio off the policeman's shoulder and crushed it underfoot, then turned and pushed Stephanie back down the alley. Stephanie pointed to a street which would take them back to their room. They walked quickly away from the Marienplatz.

"*Damn!*" said Greer under his breath. "*Damn!*"

The DCI threw the stack of eight by ten color photos down onto Dwight Conrad's desk and they fanned out like a card trick. Gibbons walked behind the desk and stood over him.

Conrad swallowed hard and picked the top one up to take a closer look. It was a full-length shot of Jenkins' naked body on a stainless-steel table in the Cologne morgue. Jenkins' stomach was down on the table but his head was twisted nearly straight up toward the camera. The body was a horrible array of colors, white and gray and yellow contrasting with blues and plum purples calling attention to the wounds and rough handling of the body. The neck was black and had swollen up almost to the diameter of the head where it had been wrenched around.

Conrad made a face, placed the photo face down on his desk, and picked up the next one. It was a close-up shot of Jenkins' face. The doctors who had performed the autopsy had clamped back the flap of skin from the gash across the face, exaggerating the wound. The right eye was missing the eyelid and was nothing more than a pool of pus. The mouth was rigidly open, looking like a neighing horse's.

"*Damn*," said Conrad. He scooped up the rest of the pictures and handed them back to Gibbons. "I can't show the President *these*."

The Director walked back to the other side of the desk and sat down. "Don't be so squeamish," he said.

Conrad poured himself a glass of water and drank it halfway down. He winced and tried to swallow but something stuck in his throat. He took another drink and sank into his chair.

Gibbons spoke: "They're calling it blunt trauma, but the blood work is still out." He rifled through the stack of pictures and pulled one out. He put it onto Conrad's desk. It was a full-length shot of Jenkins flipped over so that his belly and back of his head showed. "See that?" He pointed to the head.

The Chief of Staff didn't move, but looked reluctantly at the picture.

"Bashed in," said the DCI. This angle doesn't do it justice. The written report says the skin's intact, but the skull is smashed and the brain is mush. On the inside it's like broken eggshells mixed in with the yolk."

"What's wrong with his head?"

"You mean twisted around like that? They don't know anything other than something powerful must have got hold of him. They said a man probably couldn't have done that by himself."

"What about that cut on his face?

"They've determined it's probably not a knife. Something sharp, but bigger. They found metal particles in the flesh around the wound."

"He certainly didn't do that to himself, did he?"

"Actually, they're not ruling out suicide."

"Get serious."

"He might have thrown himself from a bridge or something."

"What do *you* think?"

Gibbons thought about that. "I honestly don't know. Jenkins was a little on the weird side. He's a widower. No telling what he might have got mixed up in. Sometimes people get out of the country and go a little crazy. Maybe he met someone that night. Maybe he went for a walk and got mugged."

Conrad thought for a moment. "What about that aide that went over with him?"

"Greer Whitaker. To tell you the truth, I'm a little nervous about that one." Gibbons lowered his voice. "Jenkins had Whitaker at Langley the past two and a half months reading the daily CIA station cables. Raw intelligence. The most sensitive stuff we've got."

The Chief of Staff's face was pained: "But why?"

"You remember. He threatened to go the President himself if we refused. He made a big deal about being the President's personal adviser and needing the freedom to poke around national security issues. He was working on that *theory* he wanted to show the President. He was a pain in the ass. Remember?"

"Yeah. I do now."

"Well, that guy working for the pain in the ass is missing."

"*Still* missing? I thought all that stuff being put out about him by State was just disinformation. He's *missing?*"

"I'm afraid so. We just got a report that he may have been seen by the German police in Munich. They tried to talk to him and he took off. He knocked out an officer and got away. It's a problem."

"Is he a suspect?"

"Until the Munich incident, we thought he might have come to harm, just as Jenkins did. Certainly we're going to keep pushing hard to find any and all possible suspects, but after he took active steps to elude the police, we had no choice but to put his name on the list. He *knows* he's wanted for questioning."

"Oh shit," said Conrad. He picked up a large magnifying glass off the top of a stack of papers. He held it over his desk so that the lens was oblique to the angle of the mid-afternoon sun coming through the heavy floor-length drapes in a narrow shaft. He focused the light with the lens onto the picture of Jenkins. The concentrated heat caused the print to start smoldering. The room began to smell like photo-developing chemicals.

"What do we tell the press?" asked Conrad. "I can't leave this office until we've got a statement drafted." He held the magnifying glass steadily over the print.

"For now give them the usual bullshit. Say the Germans are cooperating fully. We're working on it. I wouldn't mention Whitaker at this point. We've got to find him before we give the press anything definitive. We've got the Germans looking for him."

A tiny fire puffed up on the picture in the navel of the bloated white belly. Conrad watched it spread to the size of a half dollar, consuming Jenkins' torso. Conrad threw the photo into the wastepaper basket under his desk and let it burn for a few moments more. He splashed the rest of the water in the pitcher into the basket and the fire went out.

Conrad grimaced: "Are we having fun yet?"

31 ❑ ❑ ❑ ❑

On either side of the built-in computer wall cabinet in Erich Reagor's DBW office was a framed and signed print by a favorite Swedish artist. The print on the left showed life at a pond's edge: on weed stems—a moth, a beetle, a grasshopper. The print on the right showed life after death: a grotesque collection of insects chloroformed and stuck with pins to a tabletop. Same subject, different perspective, Reagor mused.

On his computer, Reagor had just accessed the confidential active case files of Interpol. He was paging down through the index of active investigations. He highlighted the name RANDALL JENKINS and clicked the mouse.

The autopsy was incomplete. The Americans had taken the body back to the United States before cause of death could be confirmed.

There were the Cologne police reports. Interviews with the paramedics and policemen on the scene. An interview with a street sweeper who had seen Greer Whitaker in the immediate vicinity before dawn that morning. A summary of interviews from the police canvassing of the *Bahnhof* vendors.

Greer Whitaker was now officially listed as a suspect. Among the nearly two dozen possible sightings was a copy of the report of two policemen in Munich. Whitaker was almost surely seen in the Marienplatz during the previous evening. There had been a woman, probably a German national, but that wasn't certain. The encounter was investigated, and the police were still looking, but no further information had yet been obtained. What the incident had done, according to the file Reagor was now reading, was to officially designate him a suspect.

Reagor scanned the rest of the reported sightings of Greer Whitaker. They were all over Germany, but mainly centered around the Cologne area where the news coverage of the murder was heaviest. Reagor checked the source of the reports. Phone calls into the local police, a couple of tips to the local newspapers. And something new. A handful of leads generated from the WANTED page for Greer Whitaker that had been posted by Interpol on the World Wide Web. Reagor looked at the specifics. All of the Web leads had come from Internet addresses at German universities. It gave him an idea.

Reagor got out the Interpol case database. He checked a list of computer mainframe addresses posted on his cabinet wall. He connected with the central computer at the Free University of Berlin, then accessed the Internet. Reagor typed in the address for the Interpol's page with Greer Whitaker's photograph.

The page scrolled onto his screen. At the top of the page in English and in German were the words WANTED FOR QUESTIONING! Immediately below was a color photo of Greer Whitaker. There was a description of the alleged crime and a physical description of the suspect. At the bottom, the Interpol page requested that any information about the murder or the suspect be sent to the Interpol's Internet address.

Reagor pulled a three-ring binder off the shelf. He flipped to the page headed University of Berlin. The page was full of active student and faculty E-mail accounts at the university.

Reagor picked an account at random. He composed an E-mail message about a possible Berlin sighting of Greer together with a woman in the Tiergarten near the Goethe monument. Reagor sent the message to Interpol under the account's name. He chose four more University of Berlin accounts at random and composed four more messages that he sent to Interpol: a man matching the suspect's description was seen getting off a train at Bahnhof Zoo, the busy train station; the suspect was seen crossing a bridge to the Museuminsel; Greer Whitaker was *definitely* seen sitting alone in a back pew in the Berliner *Dom;* a man who looked like the murder suspect was seen sharing a roll and coffee with a woman at a stand-up cafe near the Alexanderplatz. Apparently Greer Whitaker was all over Berlin.

It wasn't perfect, he knew. The police would contact the system administrator at the university, who would then point them to the students and professors who had answered the Interpol request for information on the murder. They would all deny knowing anything about sending the E-mail. It would take a couple of days. Long enough, Reagor figured, to throw the police off Greer's scent in the south of the country. Long enough to ensure that Greer Whitaker would not be found alive by the police.

After bumping into the police in the Marienplatz, Greer had spent a restless night trying to figure out how he could get out of Munich without being intercepted by the authorities. It was morning now, the sound of a vacuum running somewhere downstairs.

Stephanie was down the hall in the bathroom. Greer looked at his coat hanging on the back of the door. Inside the coat was the Ziploc bag full of computer diskettes. He and Jenkins were supposed to have worked together on the trip to take the raw data on the disks and put together a kick-ass presentation for the President. Jenkins was dead, and now he was the only person who knew how to put the theory together with the evidence. He could do it, but he couldn't do it behind bars. Once he was caught, he thought, they'd take the diskettes away and he'd never see them again.

They got dressed and sat on the bed sharing a loaf of bread and a yogurt between them.

"What do you want me to do?" Stephanie asked.

It had come to this. As much as he hated to admit it, he didn't see any way of getting out of the situation without Stephanie's help. He couldn't have survived the last three days without her. He was scared because he was becoming dependent on her. She looked to be his only salvation now. The close call in the Marienplatz had convinced him of that. The newspapers indicated the extent to which the international manhunt was being conducted.

"Let's talk," he said. "Things didn't go smoothly for us seven years ago, whatever the reason. A lot's happened since then. I'm in love with Kate and you know that. That's not going to change. But I need your help. I want you to stay with me. You've got to help me get out of here. I need to go home."

Stephanie was thinking. "And when it's all over?" she asked.

There was nothing he could say that he hadn't already said. "Kate will be waiting for me at home," he said. "I'm just trying to be honest. If you want to walk now, I understand. But I'm asking for your help. Are you in?"

Stephanie pushed the food out of the way and stretched out beside him like a cat. "*Liebling*," she purred, "I've *been* in."

"Good." That seemed to settle it. "Thank you, Stephanie."

"*But* I'm not going to make any promises. You're not in much of a position now to be setting conditions. When it's done, it's done. I still love you. I just need to make you see that, and I need to make you realize that I'm the only person in the world for you. I can give it time. You'll come around."

"No more games, though," he said. He pushed up his sleeve to remind her of the garish bruises from the night on the boat.

Stephanie scoffed. "No promises."

This wasn't what he had in mind, thought Greer. She's unrelenting. But she was also right. He didn't have much of a choice but to accept her help.

"Just tell me what I can do," she said.

This was it, the turning point. If he accepted and asked her to help, he was giving in. She would have the leverage then. But there were much bigger issues at stake than their relationship. Greer rationalized that he would just have to put up with her so that he could get back to the States and get the story out about Jenkins' theory. And clear his name, of course. God, how he missed Kate. Maybe just a little longer.

"We can't wait, then" he said. "The whole country's looking for me. What they don't know is that I've got you. I need you to do two things. First, rent a car. Something with some zip. You'll have to use your credit card again. Then . . . " Greer looked around the room until he found a phone book. He found the listing he wanted. "Then, go to the Federal Express office on the Ludwigstrasse and pick up an express envelope and an airbill."

"Then what?"

"We're making our move today."

Bob Reed stuck his head into Ben Gibbons' office at CIA headquarters. Ben was listening to someone on the phone and acknowledged Reed with a nod and waved him in. "Okay, gotta go. Call me in an hour with whatever you've got." He hung up.

"Thanks for sending the limo," Reed said. Gibbons got up from behind his desk and walked over to the small conference table in his office.

"I'm glad you're back. I just wish I could have caught you before you left Austria."

"Me, too. I got your message mid-Atlantic. Sounds like I'm just going to have to turn around and go back tonight. Incredible about Jenkins, isn't it?"

"That's what I wanted to talk to you about. Here," Gibbons said, handing Reed the photos of Jenkins at the morgue, "look at these."

Reed looked at the pictures and shook his head. "*Terrible*," he said. "What do we know?"

"I just got off the phone with the station in Bonn. Apparently

Jenkins took a dive off a bridge and got banged up on the way down. They've conclusively matched up metal slivers in his face with the metal on the bridge. Actually on a piece of modern sculpture hanging out over the water. The sculpture is a figure of a guy balancing himself on the beam. It's made out of sheets of metal welded together. The metal had oxidized and some of the rust and small shards came off when Jenkins hit the piece that sliced into his face there." Gibbons pointed to the close-up photo of Jenkins' face.

"Foul play?"

"It's too early to tell. The autopsy team in Cologne couldn't make the call on cause of death. The back of the head was bashed in, but that might have happened during the fall. We're flying the body back tonight for more work at Bethesda."

Reed continued leafing through the pictures and nodded. "What did the President say?"

"He and Jenkins were tight. I could tell he was pretty blown away by the whole thing, but he's not cutting anyone any slack. He wants it resolved yesterday and he's looking to the Agency to make it happen. I'd imagine from a purely political perspective that he's also concerned about the political implications for the economic conference."

"That's not that far off."

"I know, I know. And there's a complication. That assistant of Jenkins went with him on the trip."

"Who was that?"

"That guy named Greer Whitaker. The one who'd been working with Kate Mallotte over the last few months reading the station cables."

"Oh yeah. I remember your mentioning something about him last month."

"Anyway, he's missing. The German police have already found a couple of witnesses that put him near the scene just after it happened. He was seen at the train station early in the morning buying newspapers and coffee, probably leaving town. I was also informed that he was likely seen in Munich."

"How can I help?"

"I want you to go back over there and take charge of the investigation. It's too much for the German station to handle alone. I need someone with experience in Germany. Kate Mallotte's going to coordinate things here, but the liaison with the Germans may get a little tricky, especially with our taking the body out of the country before the investigation is complete. The first thing you need to do is find Whitaker. If you find Whitaker, I think you'll get an answer to what happened. According to all reports, he's still alive. He's missing for a reason. That makes him a suspect."

"Well, its not going to be near as much fun as Salzburg was, but I'd better get a few things together to head back."

"What's up in Salzburg?"

"Just helping out with the recruitment of a prospective agent. I made a decision reading the reports that I should probably go over and try to close the deal myself. You know, some of our younger field officers like bringing in the heavy artillery from Washington near the end to impress the agents. Everything's fine."

"Good. Glad to hear it. Get going. Let me know if you need anything from me, will you?"

"Don't worry. I will."

"Call me as soon as you find out anything. Let Kate know, of course, but make sure I'm one of the first to know, too. And don't come back here without Whitaker. Understand?"

"I understand perfectly."

32 ❑ ❑ ❑ ❑

Erich Reagor happened to be passing by a bright store window while on business in Lausanne, Switzerland. Christmas gifts. Of course. How could he have forgotten?

His staff had already taken one list and sent expensive gifts to former agents, seasonal bribes of a sort for people who might again be of service one day. They generally received bottles of liquor—scotch, champagne, cognac, vintage wines—depending on their tastes; it was all carefully logged over the years. A package without a return address, a card that said simply, "Best wishes, Erich." Just an annual reminder of who their friend was, so that when he eventually came calling one day, the door would be open.

In the store window there was a large working model of a Victorinox Swiss Army knife. Reagor looked with satisfaction at all of the tools moving back and forth. A tool for every need, he was thinking.

In the rush of the season, he had neglected to get presents for his staff and presents for a handful of special agents he still personally ran. It didn't have to be much; they didn't expect it. Just a little something to say "Thanks, job well done."

The sign in the window said gift-wrapping available. This year, he decided, everyone was getting Swiss Army knives.

Greer shifted his weight to his right foot and leaned against the window sill to take the pressure off his throbbing leg. Rushing back from the Marienplatz seemed to have made it worse. He pulled his pant leg up. The ankle was still swollen blue and was extremely tender to the touch.

Greer peered out the window, looking up the one-way street that dead-ended at the street in front of the apartment building. It was already almost noon. Stephanie hadn't left him alone for this long since they had holed up in the room. She had been gone for over three hours and he was beginning to worry that something had gone wrong. She was supposed to walk over to the Munich train station to rent a car, then drive it back to the apartment. She would park the car, then come back to the room to help him downstairs.

Greer wondered if he might somehow have missed seeing her. Traffic on the surrounding streets was light, though, so that seemed unlikely.

Greer looked again down the one-way street and saw a pair of headlights and yellow halogen lamps coming directly at him several blocks away. The car got to a block away at a stop sign and flashed its lights. It drove to the intersection of the street it was on and the street running in front of the apartment and turned right. Greer got a clear look at the driver in the large silver BMW—it was Stephanie. He relaxed a bit. She drove off out of sight to the right.

Greer stayed by the window, watching for Stephanie to walk up to the front of the building. Everything they had between the two of them—which wasn't much—was already stuffed into her bag, which was on the floor next to the door. If she could carry that, he could make it down the stairs and out to the car with a little assistance from her.

After five minutes she hadn't appeared. Then he saw another car coming down the one-way street. As it got closer, he could see that it was Stephanie again. She drove slowly, apparently looking for a parking place. She rounded the corner in front of the apartment once more. She looked up toward the window where he was standing.

Greer thought he noticed something odd. A half block behind Stephanie's car was another car—another BMW, this one smaller and dark green. He immediately realized that it had been following her the first time Stephanie had gone around the block. It moved at the same speed as Stephanie's car, turning at the corner and disappearing down the street.

Greer tensed. Was he just being paranoid? Was the other car also just circling the block looking for a parking place, or was she being followed? Had Stephanie noticed the other car?

Greer waited anxiously by the window, waiting for another sign of Stephanie. He hoped that she had found a parking space nearby this time and was already walking back to the apartment. Several more minutes passed with still no sign of her. He alternated between looking down the one-way street for the car and scanning the front of the building to see if Stephanie was on the way in.

There it was again. He recognized the headlights and fog lamps several blocks away. Stephanie flashed her high-beams at him again. What did that mean? Did she know something? What was she trying to say? She was still too far away to tell if the other car was still behind her.

Finally Stephanie was close enough and he could see that the green BMW was still following her. Stephanie stopped two blocks away to let a car back out of its parking space on the side of the street. She parallel-parked her own car into the space and turned her lights and windshield wipers off. The other car had stopped a half block back and was waiting.

Greer saw Stephanie get out of the car and start down the sidewalk toward him. The other car pulled close to the side of the street, double-parked, and put on its emergency flashers. Two women quickly got out of the car and got onto the sidewalk walking in the same direction as Stephanie.

Greer understood what was going on. Stephanie apparently was oblivious.

By now they were only one block away. Greer frantically looked around the room. Directly opposite the door was the punker's vanity. He pulled out several drawers until he found what he was looking for. He took the cap off the black lipstick and scrawled quickly on the vanity mirror—BEHIND YOU! He threw the lipstick down and rushed over to the window on the other side of the room. He pulled up on it. It had been painted shut. He tried it again, but it wouldn't budge. He picked up the vanity stool and broke the window glass out with the stool leg, then chipped away at the shards around the window frame's edges. He stepped through onto the fire escape and leaned heavily on the railing to take the pressure off his bad leg as he almost threw himself down three floors of steps.

He got to the bottom and hurried around to the side of the building. He peeked around the corner and saw the two women just entering the front entrance to the building. Stephanie would have already gone up.

He ran the best he could to the entrance. From just outside, he recognized the sound of Stephanie's boots taking the steps several flights upstairs. He heard two women talking in low voices, then heard them start up the first flight of stairs. Greer put his head around the door just in time to see the women through the banister, turning a corner to step up onto the next flight of stairs. He also saw that they both had hand guns drawn.

They were walking faster than Stephanie. Greer quietly started up after them. He heard Stephanie stop and heard her trying to put the key into the door. He heard the lock click and the door open. The two women had just caught up to Stephanie, and Greer was right behind them. Stephanie stood in the doorway and saw the mess of the vanity drawer contents on the floors, then saw the message in lipstick on the mirror. Then—in a split second—she sensed something moving behind her in the reflection of the mirror, but before she could refocus her eyes on the image in the mirror or turn around, there was a terrific swift swishing sound as something cut through the air and then a loud cracking noise.

"Get out!" Greer yelled.

He stood over the bodies of the two women sprawled on the floor. He was still holding a two-by-four he had grabbed from the construction outside the room in the hallway. He was gripping the board so tightly that his knuckles were white.

"Go!" he said.

Stephanie grabbed her bag and rushed out of the room. Greer looked at the two women he had just felled with a single blow to the back of their heads. He had taken them out with one hard swing. They both looked to be professional women in their mid-twenties. Who the hell *were* they? One was unconscious and the other was dazed and moaning with her eyes rolling in the back of her head. Greer didn't see their guns. He searched around the area, then saw the guns half hidden by the skirt of the bed where they had slid across the room when the women had hit the floor. Greer got the guns, pushed the safety latches on, and stuffed them into his jacket pockets.

"Greer!" Stephanie called from the hallway.

He took one final look around the room. The room was in shambles. Greer dropped the two-by-four and walked out of the room, locking the door behind him.

"I'm really sorry about having to call you back from your Christmas break."

She had been in his government limousine before, but it was the first time he had ever picked her up from her townhouse.

"Don't worry about it," Kate said. "I'm sure it must be important. What's it all about?"

The DCI kept looking straight ahead. "I'm going to have to ask you some questions that may be a little embarrassing for the both of us."

"O-*kay*?" she urged him on.

"I'd like for us to have a frank discussion. If we can avoid it, I'd like not to have to turn this over to Counterintelligence."

"My God, what are you talking about, Ben?"

Gibbons turned to look Kate straight in the eye. "Tell me about your relationship with Greer Whitaker."

Kate turned her head and stared out the window on her side of the limo at the lane lines blipping past. She knew about Jenkins' death, of course, and had read stories in the papers about his missing assistant. She was sure that she would have heard from him by now. But Greer hadn't called. It was just a matter of time until she got sucked into the whole thing by Ben, she thought. Ben knew she had had—or was having—some sort of relationship with Greer; he had already talked to her about that once.

"What do you want to know?"

"At this point, I'd like for you to start at the beginning. Tell me everything you know about Greer Whitaker. Where he's from. What he does in his off hours. What your relationship really was with him. What you discussed."

"I haven't spoken with him since the day he left for Germany." Kate knew that he must have sensed some deep affection.

"You've been keeping up with the news?" he asked.

"Yes. Before I saw the reports that he was missing, I naturally assumed Greer had been brought back in by the Agency. I even halfway believed he was okay after I read that the Germans wanted to bring him in for questioning. I thought it might have been some sort of deception operation."

"He really *is* missing. My hope is that you can shed some light on what's happening. I think you can play a big role here in getting him to turn himself in." Gibbons hesitated. "There is a possibility, of course, that he's also dead, but I've pretty much dismissed that. I believe the reports of his being sighted around the time of Jenkins' death are credible."

"I pray he's not dead. And I can't believe he's involved. There's no way."

"Why do say that?"

"I know him. We spent a lot of time together. Almost three months."

"Outside the office, too?

"Yes, outside the office, too. I understand the position I'm in here, and I'm not going to lie to you."

"The polygraph would catch you if you did."

Kate nodded. She already saw the path in front of her with the fork in the road and where each branch could take her. Or could go, if she didn't convince the Director she was telling him everything.

"We were talking about getting married," she said.

"Ahh." It was news to him.

"Ben, I'm going to do everything I can to help find Greer," she said. "I'm doing it for you and for the Agency, but I'm also doing it for Greer. I'm going to prove his innocence. I'll find him and find the truth out about what's happened."

"Good. I was sure that you'd feel that way."

The limo was crossing the Tidal Basin. Gibbons pulled the window open to the driver's seat. "Just keep riding around the area. I'll let you know when it's time to go somewhere." He pulled the window closed.

"All right, here's what I want to know first. Was there anything that in hindsight should have tipped you off to something suspicious?"

Kate shook her head. "I've had almost a week to think about it. I've been racking my brains trying to think of anything, but I keep coming up blank."

"Did he ever talk to you about what he was working on for Jenkins?"

"Never. All he ever said was that he was collecting data for a report that Jenkins was working on."

"He didn't indicate what the nature of the report was?"

"No. Nothing. He was always very protective of Jenkins. After all the trouble we had at the beginning, it seemed that he wanted to represent the National Security Adviser's interests. He never had a bad thing to say about Jenkins."

"What about his personal life? Did he ever mention anyone? Did he talk about his past?"

"We're as close as two people can be. There was nothing in his past that would make me think there would be a problem."

The DCI was silent. "Did you ever talk to Greer about confidential Agency matters outside the office?"

"*Never.*" She was adamant.

"You know at some point it still may be necessary for you to take a polygraph. Think hard. Is there anything I should know about? Can you think of anything you have said or done that might have inadvertently compromised the Agency. Did you talk about methods or specific operations?"

"Nothing. In fact, I'd like to take a polygraph as soon as possible. I want you to know for sure that you can trust me one hundred percent." She gave herself a moment to calm down. They sat in an embarrassing silence. "Greer was cleared for Top Secret security clearance," she finally said.

"I know. That may be a problem."

"I'm worried about Greer. I want to know what's going on, too."

"Well," said Gibbons, "I think both our interests will be best served if we can find him and bring him in. The first thing I'd like you to do when you come in in the morning is to retrace the steps taken by whoever authorized him for Top Secret security clearance. I'd like us to take a look at his file tomorrow afternoon together. I want to know everything there is to know about Greer Whitaker. I'm putting you in charge of the recovery operation. I want you to manage it here from Washington. Do whatever you need to, just get him back here alive. I've already put some things into motion that should help out. I've sent Bob Reed to take over liaison in Europe. He'll be our eyes and ears over there. Lots of experience in with the Germans. He's tenacious. Good man, Reed."

There wasn't anything that Ben Gibbons could have said that would have made her even more worried about Greer.

"Thanks."

33 ❑   ❑   ❑   ❑

Here's a girl—at age twenty-five less than half my age—and I'm still more beautiful than she is, Marie thought.

It wasn't conceit; it was a fact. Marie von Bosacker was the same age as Catherine Deneuve. In her youth, she had been told that she was as beautiful as the movie star. Only last month someone had made the same comment.

On the coffee table in the reception room in her house in Ribeauville was a cassette recorder. On the other side of the table was the plain-faced, earnest graduate student from Strasbourg University. She was completing the interview for her dissertation on the history of Alsace during the last war. The session had gone on for an hour and was coming to an end.

"Do you mind if I ask you a few personal questions?"

"Please."

"The name Bosacker is synonymous with the large land holdings and wine producers of Alsace." She was writing as she talked. "And the title?"

"The Comtesse de Kaysersberg? It's been in the family for hundreds of years. A bit pretentious, but useful for promoting the vineyard, especially overseas."

"Your father, Henri Bosacker. He chose not to join the Germans when they came to liberate Alsace?"

A telling question. "You are not from Alsace?"

"Freiburg, actually."

"Well, as you know, history has not been able to decide whether we are to be a German or French province," Marie answered. "This strip of land—along with Lorraine—has been caught in a centuries'-old tug-of-war between France and Germany. . . ."

"Yes, yes," the student interrupted.

The impatience of youth.

"But what about your father? Was he an ardent nationalist?"

"My mother used to tell me how my father would repeat my grandfather's story about the time when Parisians draped the statue of Strasbourg in the Place de la Concorde with black crepe in 1871 after Bismarck forced France to give up the provinces. It's my own, less academic understanding of history that from then until World War I, French foreign policy was dominated by a single passion—the desire to recover Alsace-Lorraine. The Alsatians of the day had given up the hope of independence and were resigned to the fact that they would be punted back and forth between the two countries."

"So when Hitler crossed the Rhine and entered France in 1940, your father had already been called from the estate to a command in the defense of the country? He was already in the field fighting?"

"Yes. Apparently as Hitler's panzer divisions cut the country in two in their race to the Channel in May of that year, my father's unit was cut off from communications with French military headquarters and the family heard nothing from him. You know, of course, that by the middle of the next month, the French government left Paris for the south of the country. Within two weeks, France had surrendered to the Germans in Compiègne Forest. . . ."

". . . in the same railway car that Germany had surrendered at the end of World War I."

"Yes. Well, by then, my father was already dead. It took until the end of summer for the full story to make it back to Alsace, from a returning fellow officer who had served under my father. Apparently my father had been trapped with his back to the Ardennes when the Germans broke through. Rather than surrender, he and his men fought on. Eventually, they were overpowered and he surrendered rather than throwing his young men into another battle and certain death. The German officer who accepted his surrender noticed his peculiar accent and quickly determined that he was from Alsace. The German was so incensed that my father—as an Alsatian and, in the view of the officer, a German—would take up arms against a fellow German, he summarily shot my father in the head with his side arm, making him an example for any other Alsatians in the unit who might again contemplate such treasonous action."

The student scribbled furiously. "And your mother?"

"My mother . . ." Yes, my mother, Marie thought. But what about my father? Will what you are writing simply be a footnote in the history books of your generation? Did you not hear what I just said about my father? Did you not hear how the Germans took him from a young wife and child? "My mother was a widow at the age of twenty-five. She took over the responsibilities of caring for the vineyards and running the château. All of the other men in the family had either been killed or forced underground to join the Resistance."

"I see."

Did she? Marie wondered. Did she really? It was all a scholarly exercise. Transcribing the wartime memories of the survivors before they themselves succumbed to death. Fashionable in academic circles. A rush to gather the oral history of the nearly dead.

"Is there anything else I can tell you?" Marie asked.

The student turned the cassette player off. "Tell me how you really feel about it all."

Marie thought about it a minute. The girl was eager, the age her mother had been when she had assumed sole responsibility for running the business and raising a child by herself. What in the girl's own life would allow her to relate to what Marie might say? How could she possibly convey the depths of her emotions about what impact the German's act of violence against her father had made?

Save it, she told herself. Channel your emotions into the other thing.

"I can think of nothing else."

Marie walked her guest out and said good-bye.

She climbed the steps to the living quarters on the second floor. The first door in the hallway was locked and cold to the touch. Her parents' bedroom hadn't been used since her mother had died over forty years ago. Marie unlocked the door and walked to her mother's dresser.

Marie opened a jewelry box. She had long ago removed the simple necklaces and earrings and bracelets. The only thing left in the box was a pendant.

On a length of gold chain was attached a miniature crystal vial, its contents perfectly sealed now with wax. Marie held it in her fingers. She turned the vial upside down and the liquid inside turned over upon itself.

Fifteen years of her mother's crying for her dead husband, grief for the loss to the wife and child. Fifteen years of tears collected in the delicate vial. She must have loved him very much, Marie thought. Her mother must have missed him as much as she missed him now herself.

34 ❏ ❏ ❏ ❏

Greer filled out the Federal Express air bill as they sat in the car with the engine idling. He wrote so that Stephanie couldn't see.

Stephanie observed, "You certainly have made some powerful enemies over the years. What was that all about?"

Everyone was suspect at that point. Even the teenaged kid having a smoke outside the coffee shop across the street. Shouldn't he be in school at this time of the day? "Someone's trying to stop me. That surely wasn't the police coming after me back in the room."

"No," she agreed. "That wasn't the police."

"How did they know where I was? How did they know to follow you?"

"I didn't even see them. How long had they been following me?"

"At least three times around the block. You didn't see them behind you after you picked up the car?"

"I was so intent on getting back to you, I could have easily missed them. I don't know where they picked me up."

Greer slid the computer diskettes into the box and sealed it.

"What's that?" Stephanie asked. "Were those diskettes?"

Greer didn't want to tell her everything. There was no need for that. "They're just something I was working on. I'm afraid they'll be lost or damaged. Back in a moment."

He jumped out of the car and deposited the package into the Fed Ex drop-off box outside the Ludwigstrasse office.

He got back into the car and hit the electronic door locks to seal them into the car.

And man, what a car, thought Greer.

Greer craned his neck behind him and tapped the accelerator lightly, gunning the engine as he waited for traffic to open up. He listened to the twelve-cylinder engine rev and watched a panel of amber gauges and LED displays respond. He was in the cockpit of a luxurious fighter jet, not a mere car. It was the biggest BMW Greer had ever seen. Stephanie had definitely chosen well. This kind of car wasn't even available in the United States. It was much too powerful for American roads. It was a machine made for the autobahn, where only a driver's car and nerve determined his speed. On the wide-open German roads or twisting through the forest or scaling mountains, Greer would be less conspicuous in this than in a lesser car.

He looked in front of him and on both sides and saw no signs of the police.

"Any problems?" she asked.

"It went as smooth as a baby's . . ."

"*Behind*," she finished.

"Thank you."

"You're welcome."

Greer checked the rearview mirror and the sideview mirrors, then cut sharply into the fast-moving traffic.

"Did I see California on the label?" Stephanie asked.

Greer started to answer, then caught himself. The diskettes were the only way of proving Jenkins' theory. He now knew that he would be guarding them with his life.

"A friend," Greer answered.

"I've never been to California. What part?"

Greer nervously tapped the turn signal with his finger as he kept checking his mirrors and watching street signs.

"On the coast," he answered. He looked at Stephanie. She seemed to be expecting more. "Just an old friend on the coast." He concentrated on getting them through the busy city center traffic.

"I still don't know where we're going," Stephanie said. Greer steered them into a turnabout.

"Oh, come on. Can't you guess?"

"I haven't a clue, really."

Greer smiled smugly. He had to concentrate on getting over to the outside lane so he could make his exit.

"On this trip," he said, "I'm the pilot and you're going to be the navigator. Get the map out of the glove compartment."

Stephanie obeyed and folded it so that Bavaria was on top. "I'd like to buy a clue, please," she said.

"You've been spending too much time watching American television. Bad habit."

She gave him a squeeze on his inside thigh. "*You're* my only bad habit."

Greer tensed. They hadn't made love since the night in Cologne, and he wanted to keep it that way. He just needed to keep her on an even keel long enough for him to get out of the country. "We want to take the Romantic Road."

Stephanie traced a route on the map with her finger from Munich. "North or south?" she asked.

"North."

Stephanie took another look, then put the map down into her lap and sunk into her seat. "Just follow the signs for Augsburg," she said. She closed her eyes.

They left the city behind surprisingly quickly. Greer turned on the stereo. It was preset to a station playing Christmas music. The sun was shining brightly on the countryside. Stephanie fell asleep in the big leather womb of a seat.

In less than an hour Greer saw the sign for the turn-off. He was at the Romantic Road that led from the Bavarian Alps in the south up to the river Main to the north. To the left, the quick jaunt to Augsburg. To the right, a hundred-kilometer dash to the endpoint of the trip— Rothenburg ob der Tauber. He leaned into the turn and banked the car like a jet to the right without slowing down.

He let her sleep another half hour. When they approached Donauwörth he shook her. She stretched in the full sun coming in her window.

"We're crossing the Danube," he said.

She leaned over and gave him a kiss on the cheek. "*Danke,*" she said. She looked about to get her bearings.

They crossed over the river and Greer felt a twinge of nausea. He was seeing Jenkins being rolled out of the water.

"Good nap?" he asked, shaking the image from his mind.

"Umm. I was having a dream. Do you remember the first time we saw each other?"

"At the coffee shop at the Heidelberg student union. I was supposed to meet my academic tutor."

"Yes. I was dreaming just now about a nice cup of coffee and it reminded me of how you shyly flirted with me."

"In hindsight, I guess I shouldn't have done that."

"You were *endearing*, darling. You were handsome and a little cocky. You kept looking at me. Didn't you know that I knew what you were doing, or didn't you care?"

"I didn't care."

"Did you flirt like that all the time?"

"Only with you."

"You're such a good liar, Greer." She reached over and pinched his arm.

The car swerved across the center line, then back into its lane. "Hey!" exclaimed Greer. "That hurt!"

Stephanie patted his arm. "My dear, dear Greer." She encircled her knees with her arms and curled up into a ball.

They were getting close. Greer slowed as they passed through Nördlingen. Thirty kilometers farther along the road they saw the Romanesque tower of St. George's as they approached Dinkelsbühl. Within a few minutes they were through the town and back onto the open road.

"What we had, Greer, I haven't experienced since you left. I've had lovers, of course, but nothing like you. You set out to capture my heart and you did."

"Let's not start that again now, if you don't mind."

Stephanie watched Greer as he drove. "I don't want to lose you again. I know you still feel something for me. Tell me you do."

Of course he still felt something for her. How could he not feel *something*? But what was once an exhilarating mixture of love and passion had been replaced by merely pity and a lust he was at a loss to understand or contain. Not a good basis for a relationship. He ignored her prodding.

Greer gripped the steering wheel hard with both hands and looked straight ahead at the road. The Christmas music on the radio from

Munich was beginning to fade in and out and nearby frequencies crowded the reception. Greer tried changing the station, but the complexity of the stereo thwarted him while driving.

"Would you mind finding another station?" he asked.

Stephanie fiddled with the buttons and infrared adjustments, scanning the airwaves for a strong signal. "Well, what do you think?" she asked.

"About what, specifically?"

Stephanie answered: "About us." There was a slight hurt tone to her voice. "What do you *feel?*"

Greer didn't answer. Was he afraid of the truth? He was thinking of Kate. Stephanie, his first real love, had been an all-consuming passion. He had neglected his studies in Heidelberg to be with her every possible moment of every day for nine months. But Stephanie had deceived him, broken her promise. Screwed up his life for a long time afterward. He understood now, of course, why she had done it, but the hurt was still there. Kate was what he wanted now, to hear her voice. He needed to find some way to get through. If Stephanie wanted to help him out, he would let her. That was it. But not for the price of betraying Kate again.

He heard a "beep" from the dash. He glanced at the clock readout on the dash. It was exactly 5 P.M.

The LED frequency readout Stephanie was playing with cycled back down to the bottom of the spectrum. It found a solid band, locked in, and the eight stereo speakers hummed.

The brief silence was broken with eight bars of martial music, followed by four beeps. "This is the BBC Worldwide Service," the announcer said.

"Turn it up," he said. Stephanie adjusted the volume.

"The news, read by Ian McGowan. The *New York Times* is reporting in today's issue that unnamed intelligence sources have confirmed the cause of death of the U.S. National Security Adviser, Mr. Randall Jenkins, as blunt trauma to the head. The President's chief intelligence adviser was pulled dead from the Rhine River in Cologne, Germany, on Monday. The body of Mr. Jenkins has been flown back to the United States for further forensic examination. Although neither German nor American officials would comment for the record, sources in both governments have indicated that evidence suggests the National Security Adviser was murdered. The story went on to quote the same unnamed sources as saying that the prime suspect is now an aide who had accompanied Mr. Jenkins to Cologne. The aide, Mr. Greer Whitaker, has been missing since the day the body was discovered. He is still believed to be in Europe. The White House has had no comment on the *New York Times* story. In a related development, several members of the U.S. Congress have asked for a formal inquiry into the circumstances surrounding the death. Some members of Congress have expressed their belief that the President may be trying to cover up facts relating to Mr. Jenkins' visit by returning the body to the United States before a full investigation can be made. The White House also had no comment on the Congressmen's statements. In Israel today . . ."

Greer reached over and turned the volume back down. "The 'Beeb,' " he said. "I've really hit the big times now."

"A dubious honor I'd say," Stephanie answered.

The car scooted up a hill and crested the top. As the road dipped down suddenly, Stephanie grabbed her stomach.

Before them lay the high walls and spires of the medieval city of Rothenburg ob der Tauber. A Teutonic flag was flapping over the entrance gates, welcoming them back.

35 ❏ ❏ ❏ ❏

Jacko Takiyama and Kevin Hatu throttled down their matching Suzuki motorcycles at the sight of the diner and slowed to a stop at the intersection nearby. It was seven-thirty on a cool Saturday morning. They were just south of San Francisco on Skyline Road, the two-lane highway that ran along the top ridge of the Santa Cruz Mountains through the redwood forests overlooking San Jose and Silicon Valley. They turned in, parked their motorcycles, and took their helmets off. They unzipped the top of their matching one-piece silver riding suits to let a little air in, then stepped up onto the porch and brushed the dust off their legs.

It was Alice's Restaurant, the first stop most Saturday and Sunday mornings for a certain group of motorcyclists heading south out of the Bay Area for a day's excursion through the shadowed mountain redwood forests. Jacko and Kevin were among the first there this morning. The motorcycles parked outside were sleek, expensive, almost exclusively high-tech Japanese bikes in bright Day-Glo colors and BMWs in black. They went inside, waved to a couple of tables of other cycling enthusiasts, then took a booth, ordering coffee and bran muffins.

"I miss California," said Kevin. He broke open his muffin and took a bite. "Not too many redwoods back East," he said.

Jacko looked across the table at his old graduate school roommate from Stanford. They were the same age and for the two years they were in school together they had been best friends. Kevin had got his M.B.A. in international management, then taken a job heading up the import department of an electronics firm in the Valley. His mother and father were third-generation Japanese-Americans. He had majored in Japanese as an undergraduate at Stanford. Three years ago, at just about the same time Jacko had moved back to the United States, Kevin wrote Jacko that he had taken a government position with the Department of Defense in Washington, D.C. It turned out to be a lucky break for Jacko.

Jacko smiled at Kevin. "You're very valuable where you are, my friend. But it's good that we can talk freely now that you're back for a few days." Using the phone to make contact with Kevin was, of course, not a possibility.

Jacko mused on the complex set of relationships that bound them together. Friendship. Stanford. Their Japanese heritage. Jacko's father's close ties to Japanese intelligence. The Tokyo government's need to know what was going on in the heads of American policy makers. Kevin's real job as an analyst at the CIA and Jacko's de facto role as his spy runner.

Kevin munched on his muffin. "I don't know how much longer I can keep this up," he said.

Jacko looked thoughtfully at his old friend. Kevin was home in San Francisco visiting his parents over his Christmas vacation. Jacko had bought the motorcycles, suits, gloves, helmets, and other motorcycle paraphernalia just so that he and Kevin could spend a couple of days tooling around the area together. And, so that they could talk.

"I checked before you got into the city. Your bank account is growing very rapidly," said Jacko.

The Japanese government's payments that passed through Takiyama to the secret Tokyo bank accounts of its paid informants supplemented Kevin's relatively meager salary as a U.S. government employee. In the private sector, with his credentials, Kevin could have been making at least three times his government salary.

"You know that's not it, Jacko."

They both knew that the money wasn't what motivated Kevin. Kevin and Jacko had been meeting once every six months in San Francisco ever since Kevin had begun his job at CIA. As soon as Jacko had found out what Kevin's real position was in Washington, he had mentioned it to his father. The Takiyamas had assisted Japanese intelligence many times before. The Takiyama business groups had provided cover for government operations outside of Japan, usually when the Japanese bureaucracy demanded information on American developments in a variety of scientific fields—electronics and bioengineering, for the most part—which could have significant application in the Japanese business sector. Most of these activities centered around small venture companies in Silicon Valley. Jacko assisted by planting Japanese agents inside the companies or obtaining information from unwitting employees. The criminal side of the Takiyama family's operations provided muscle and a way to move large amounts of money around to finance Japan's covert operations and secretly purchase weapons systems that would ensure Japan's national security, a program contrary to Japan's public position and stated foreign policy.

It had taken less than a week for Jacko to receive word from his father on how to begin managing Kevin. There were two objectives. First, arrange regular meetings with Kevin so that Jacko could pump him for whatever information there was on U.S. intelligence operations against Japan and to determine what alternatives U.S. policy makers were considering regarding Japan. The second objective would be much more difficult to achieve. Jacko was to persuade Kevin that he should "color" his analysis of Japan's activities so that it appeared that Japan was less of a threat to U.S. economic security than it really was. As leader of the team analyzing raw intelligence from the CIA field officers, Kevin was in a superb position to influence the way analysis was conducted on the CIA's Japan desk. Jacko's father had made it clear that Kevin was potentially Japan's most valuable intelligence asset. Jacko knew without asking that these orders had come from the highest level within the Japanese government.

Jacko answered Kevin. "You know that what you're doing is important. The country's at a crossroads."

Kevin stirred a packet of sugar into his coffee. "You don't have to tell me. I live this stuff every day."

To convince Kevin to work for him and for the Japanese government, Jacko had relied on their friendship and Kevin's sense of obligation to Japan. Kevin at first was reluctant, although he agreed philosophically with Jacko on the need to help protect Japan's fragile economy. Kevin knew from the reports he was seeing that the economic situation in Japan was much more precarious than most business analysts had figured. Jacko was also authorized to offer to set up a secret bank account in Japan in the name of Kevin's parents who— even though they had worked hard and did all right in a family-run food brokerage—were far from well off. Kevin accepted the offer and returned to Washington after that first meeting with Jacko. Kevin Hatu had become a witting spy.

Jacko had told him that it would probably only be a short-term assignment, that Kevin just needed to help out until the current economic difficulties had passed. That had been three years ago. Japan's economic position had continued to weaken. The real estate market was shaky, the yen had become strong, and exports began to slide. There had been constant turmoil and turnover among the ruling parties in parliament, which had unsettled the financial markets. Kevin was anything but naive, thought Jacko. Kevin understood that he was being strung along.

Kevin looked out the window. There were more bikers arriving, gliding their machines in pairs into the gravel parking lot.

Jacko leaned across the table and tapped Kevin on the wrists, waking him from his day-dream.

"Hey," said Jacko. "It's me. Jacko. Talk to me."

Kevin turned away from the window and looked at Jacko.

Kevin spoke. "I feel trapped, Jacko. I never imagined myself in this position. It's one of those situations where I feel strongly both ways. No one is more respectful of his Japanese heritage than I am. You know I'd do almost anything to help that I can. And I think I have. I honestly believe that I can help Japan by letting the government know what steps the U.S. is planning to take. Like with this Group of Seven conference coming up out here next month. I don't like seeing my ancestors' country being screwed in the deal. On the other side, I feel a great sense of obligation to the U.S. This country gave my parents and my grandparents a good life. And me. The best education in the world." Kevin looked down at the table and shook his head. "I don't know if what I'm doing is immoral or not. I've thought about it a thousand times since I agreed to work with you on this. I just can't come to a resolution. But I do know that what I'm doing is illegal. It's treason. If I get caught, I could be given the electric chair. At the very least, I'd spend the rest of my life in prison. I'm only thirty-five. This isn't how I'd envisioned it. Do you know what I go through every day?"

"I can only imagine," said Jacko.

"You can't, really. I don't know from moment to moment if my time's up, if I'll be caught. There's a knot in my stomach that won't go away. It's like my adrenaline gland is stuck open. Some days I'll be sitting at my desk, and I'll just start hyperventilating. I've started having panic attacks at the office. I go to the men's room and lock myself into a stall for half an hour trying to get a grip on my sanity. I'm scared to death, Jacko. I don't think I can go on much longer."

Jacko sat in silence looking at his friend. He would let him say whatever he wanted to say. He understood that Kevin didn't have anyone to talk to about what he was doing. The meetings every six months had started becoming traumatic about a year ago.

Kevin spoke again. "And do you know what the worst part is?"

"No, what?"

"The worst part is imagining the shame my parents would have to endure if I were ever caught. Did you know that my parents and grandparents were prisoners in the American concentration camps during World War Two? Did I ever tell you that?"

"Yes, I think you did," Jacko answered quietly.

"Can you figure it out? My father was imprisoned by his own country because of his race, and now he flies the biggest American flag in the neighborhood. Have you seen him lately? What's he got on his lapel? An American flag. Can you believe it? He didn't do a damned thing to earn his way into that camp, but he's the proudest American there ever was. But look at me! Look at me! I know what I'm doing. I'm spying on America for Japan! It's ironic, isn't it?"

Jacko lifted his hands and motioned Kevin to quiet down.

"Why am I doing this? Why, Jacko? Can you tell me why I'm doing this? Is it because I feel an affinity with Japan, or is it really because I want revenge for what America did to my family during the war? What do you think, Jacko?"

36 ❏ ❏ ❏ ❏

Erich Reagor stood at a large window on the second floor of the Upper Belvedere Palace and watched helplessly as a Viennese traffic policeman lifted the windshield wiper from his Porsche, which was illegally parked on the curb of Prinz-Eugen-Strasse, and inserted a parking ticket onto the glass. This was the curse of being an industrial spy, he thought. No more diplomatic protection to cover an unlimited number of criminal offenses in any city of the civilized world. Crumpling up parking tickets and throwing them to the ground had been his favorite perk of being on Stasi's payroll. But then again, Stasi never provided him with a Porsche.

His contact was very late. Reagor checked his watch again. Three thirty-five. The museum would close in less than half an hour. This was the first time in over twenty years that his agent had kept him waiting for more than ten minutes. As a professional courtesy he should have been there, regardless of the reason. Mutual respect of one spy runner for another. It certainly shouldn't matter that Reagor was no longer working for Stasi. His new employer played an equally dangerous game. Deutsche Bayrische Werke knew which strings to pull to make the marionette dance a Viennese waltz or a Bavarian polka.

The museum guard kept glancing over at Reagor, so he decided to go back into the Austrian Gallery of Twentieth Century Art. He looked around the room. There were works by Gustav Klimt, Egon Schiele, Oskar Kokoschka, and others of that school. It was his favorite gallery in Europe. On the same walls he could find the extremes of love and death.

He walked over to the large dark canvas by Schiele of *Death and the Maiden*. Poor Egon. The maiden represented, of course, the mistress his wife would never let him really have. She clutched a wide-eyed corpse in the fetal position; the corpse was the artist himself. He couldn't have her and she couldn't have him. Too bad for them both.

Schiele fascinated him, but ultimately depressed him. His subjects looked like residents of Nazi concentration camps. His women were severe. He sought relief on another wall.

He was searching for Klimt. He passed over *The Kiss*. It was too saccharine, too commercialized. *Judith* caught his eye. This was what he wanted. Klimt was the master of respectable soft pornography in his day. Judith enticed him with her dreamy gaze, her head slightly back and her red lips parted showing white, glistening teeth. She was a fantasy. Her hair was pulled up away from her face. Her cheeks were pink. She was clothed in gold. Her bare stomach muscles were taut and her left breast was exposed, perfect in its roundness. He wanted to reach out and take her nipple into his mouth.

"Sorry I'm so late." It was Bob Reed. Reagor hadn't noticed that he had come up beside him to look at the painting.

Reagor took a long look at Reed's face and nodded. "Good to see you, old friend," he said. He took him by the elbow. "Let's go for a walk."

They went down the marble steps and strolled leisurely outside like tourists along the gravel path connecting the Upper with the Lower Belvedere Palaces.

"Here," Reagor said, motioning to a bench. They sat facing a pleasant view of St. Stephen's Cathedral in the distance.

"So tell me," said Reagor, "what is going on with our young friend Greer Whitaker? Things are not going as we had planned, are they?"

"I believe he's still ours, Erich."

Reagor arched his eyebrows. "You *believe* he's still ours," Reagor repeated. "You don't sound nearly as confident as the last time we met. My frank assessment is that you have lost control over the recruit. Unfortunately, that's a belief that I've had to share with my superiors."

Reed was shaking his head. "I've gone back over everything in my mind, trying to figure out if there was any point where I may have lost him."

"From what you've told me, I suspect he may have begun to sympathize with Jenkins. It's a classic case of falling in love with your subject. Whitaker got caught up in what he saw as a just cause." Reagor fell quiet as two men passed by. "Using your contact in the Vice President's office to get Whitaker the White House Fellowship was a stroke of genius. It provided the perfect entree into the National Security Adviser's office. The room you were able to procure through the CIA in the Library of Congress basement was a nice touch, too. You are very skillful, but you must admit that you were very lucky, also."

"I'll take my breaks wherever I get them." Reed thought for a moment. "It wasn't easy, you know. I had to jump through a lot of hoops to make the scenario seem credible to him. It was a lot tougher than I expected."

"He's very clever, Bob. You knew from the beginning that Whitaker would be an unusual challenge."

"One wrong step, one small miscue, and I knew he would have been spooked. There were a couple of times when I thought he was just about to figure out that something wasn't quite right. He started getting more aggressive, asking too many questions. . . . "

"Just like a good intelligence officer."

Reed turned on the bench to face Reagor: "It's like being hypnotized. You've got to be open to it in the first place. There's never been a person who wanted to be a CIA field officer as badly as Greer Whitaker did. In many ways, he was no different from the dozens of other young CIA recruits I see every year. Idealistic, zealots for their country. Greer just seemed to want it more than most of the others. Of course, he questioned things. But he believed in the Agency and he believed in me. That's why I think we can get him under control again."

"But, Bob—*really*. He's sharp enough that now he's gotten away from you and you have no idea where he is." Reagor looked out over the Palace grounds and considered the question that he had been musing all day. Does he tell Reed about his ace in the hole? Does Reed need to know how deep the organization runs? No. As fond as he was of Reed, he was still his agent, not his equal. There was no difference between this operation and the ones he used to run for Stasi. Everything should be compartmentalized. No one should have too much information in case something went wrong. Having Reed and his own DBW people both working to find Greer Whitaker was the best approach, he concluded. Take the information from one and feed it to the other. But never the two shall meet.

Reagor spoke. "I think we need to review the operation's objectives, don't you? Perhaps that will help get us refocused. Okay—you initially learned about what Randall Jenkins was up to through your chat with Ben Gibbons at the beginning of the year. First, you were supposed to determine exactly what Randall Jenkins was working on. Fine—you did that. We know about his so-called theory. Next, you were to determine if he had been able to support his idea with evidence. Well, Greer Whitaker helped that cause along, so we now know the answer to that. A presentation was scheduled with the President and NSC." Reagor smiled at Reed. "But that's not going to happen now."

"Jenkins refused to cooperate," Reed said.

"You nudged him. Well, I suppose you were right. If he refused to cooperate, then he's better off dead. But the final objective is still hanging out there, isn't it? You were supposed to find out what Randall Jenkins was really up to, then you were supposed to shut it down. Jenkins is gone, but now we have a much bigger problem with Whitaker. Our own agent, the subject of an international manhunt."

"How was I supposed to know he would run?"

"You thought you still had him under your control. You were wrong. Why *did* he run?"

"He got spooked. There's a leak, Erich. Someone is leaking information about this operation. Greer saw a cable from the CIA station in Paris. STEEPLECHASE was specifically referred to in connection with a mole in the Agency. Frankly, *I'm* spooked."

"Not good." This was the first Reagor had heard of it. Stettler knew all about the cryptonym STEEPLECHASE, of course, and Reagor assumed that the operation had been fully discussed with Stettler's own contacts in the German intelligence service. It did, indeed, seem as if there were a leak. It would make for an interesting conversation back at DBW headquarters.

Reagor was thinking out loud. "If Greer Whitaker has specific knowledge of how the theory fits with the evidence, he could easily make the case himself to someone in Washington. The G7 conference is just over a week away. That's cutting it a little close. The key question now is, Has Greer Whitaker done anything on his own to advance the theory inside the Administration already? Even if he were killed, he might have already communicated with someone about it. It's something my superiors are going to need an answer to."

"I have no way of knowing that."

"Greer Whitaker must be eliminated, but first we must be certain —be *absolutely* certain—that the theory and evidence are eliminated, too. It's time to tidy up this operation and bring it to a conclusion."

Reagor thought through the next steps. Of course, Reed knew nothing of his having sent the two DBW women to Munich after Greer. They were supposed to have forced information from him. Reagor, too, had underestimated Whitaker's resourcefulness. And now he had two of his top field people in the hospital with critical head injuries. But there was more than one way of getting answers out of Greer Whitaker. It appeared the more subtle approach wasn't working, either. He'd give it a little more time and if he got a favorable update, fine. Maybe, thought Reagor, he should try sending someone in just one more time to force a confession. But he'd have to be quick before Reed caught up with Whitaker. Reed would without a doubt kill him on sight. Of course that was in the plan. So if Reagor had any hope of finessing one last move, he'd have to get to Whitaker before Reed.

"He's slipping through our fingers, Bob."

"He'll surface. His face is plastered all over the newspapers and television. And as soon as the Germans or anyone hears anything and gets in touch with the CIA, I'll hear about it."

Reagor nodded thoughtfully. He looked out over the city. "You and I go back quite a few years, don't we Bob?"

"Twenty-two, twenty-three years, last time I reckoned."

"Do you ever regret making the move?"

Reed looked down. "It's not something I think about anymore. It's something that happened. It's part of my life now."

Reagor continued to find points of interest on the horizon. He watched the pigeons assemble on the iron fence around the palace gardens.

Reed continued: "No one likes to be blackmailed, but that's what got us to where we are today, isn't it? Is that what you're asking?"

Reagor cracked a little grin. "That's harsh, isn't it, Bob? I mean, our relationship has—*evolved* over time. It may have started out a bit strained, but I was just doing my job, just as you were doing yours. It's just that I happened to catch you doing something embarrassing before you caught me. I consider it to have been a purely professional matter. Anyway," he said, turning to Reed, "we don't talk about things like videotapes these days, do we?" He asked in a tone that demanded an answer.

"No."

"You and I operate on a much different level these days. We're comfortable with each other. We respect each other. I respect and value your talents and pay you accordingly. I understand your need for security."

"Let's not get too deep, Erich. You and I both know that as long as you are holding certain materials over my head, I don't have any choice but to work with you. The money you pay me is good, but you know I'd walk in a minute if I could."

Reagor nodded. He enjoyed the leverage he still had over a high-ranking CIA officer. "You must have been nervous when the Wall came down." He was tightening the screw. Reagor reached over and patted Reed on the leg. "Robert—"

"Dammit!" Reed exploded "Don't call me that! And don't touch me like that again!"

Reagor withdrew his hand slowly into his own lap and smiled condescendingly at Reed. "Relax, Bob. There's no reason to get excited."

Reed took a deep breath. "I'm not sure that I wouldn't have been happier if you had been caught and confessed to running me as a spy," he said. "To tell you the truth, it would have been a relief to have this over with. I never dreamed that I'd still be working for you when you went to the private sector."

"You remain very valuable," Reagor agreed. He tapped Reed quickly on the knee. "Let's walk," he said, standing up.

They headed off slowly together toward the Lower Belvedere. The only sounds were the nearby end-of-day traffic and gravel crunching under their feet as they walked through the bare-treed Orangery.

Reagor spoke: "What's the latest with Kate Mallotte?"

"Sore point, Erich. What's your interest in her now anyway? You don't have the Russians to report to anymore."

"Kate has always been a special interest of mine. Of course, she is one of the most *charming* of the CIA's officers. I am certainly glad that you arranged an introduction at the American embassy in Moscow a few years back. I've been carrying her memory with me ever since."

"She was just a kid."

"A very beautiful woman, Bob. KGB was not very happy with her activities while she was posted there. You were very helpful in pointing her out to me as the new spy runner."

"You're welcome."

"You're still very touchy about her. I told you that you need to let it go. You need to learn to relax. She got the job in the Director's office and you didn't. She's young, she's beautiful, and she's intelligent. Of course the Director of Central Intelligence would choose her to work with. Do you think he is a fool?"

"I don't want to talk about it anymore," Reed said.

"Just because you give twenty-five years of your life to the Agency doesn't mean it owes you anything, does it? You don't still feel slighted by the Agency, do you, Bob? You don't still think that your old friend forgot you when he got the Director's job, do you?"

Reed stopped walking. "I didn't come here to talk about Kate Mallotte or Ben Gibbons. What do you want me to do about this mess with Greer Whitaker?"

Reagor smiled smugly and continued walking with Reed at his side. They reached the top of the steps leading to the lower part of the garden in front of the Lower Belvedere Palace. Next to the steps were a fountain and terraced pools surrounded by statues. They went down and Reagor stopped them at the bottom. They were out of sight of the street and the museum guards of the Upper Belvedere Palace on the other end of the Orangery.

Reagor handed Reed a small bag with the logo of a Viennese coffeehouse. The label indicated a cheap blend of African beans.

"I've just wired a bonus payment to your Lichtenstein bank account. It's triple your normal monthly deposit."

Reed tested the weight of the bag in his hand as he listened.

Reagor continued: "You must find Greer Whitaker before he does any more damage before the economic conference. There's an old Russian Nagant revolver from World War II in the bag for you. It can't be traced. It will look like some crazy old Nazi who ripped the gun off a Soviet corpse did him in. Finish the job."

Reed shoved the bag into his overcoat pocket. He wasn't happy.

Reagor heard Christmas music. It reminded him. He dug into his coat pocket and handed Reed a small gift-wrapped package. "Merry Christmas."

Reed took it.

"Open it." Reagor was especially cheery.

Reed snapped the ribbons off the box, tore off the paper, and opened the box.

"A knife?"

"Not just any knife, Bob. A Victorinox Swiss Champ Army knife."

Reed was a little flustered. "Thanks," he said somewhat confused. "I'm sorry I didn't get you anything."

Reagor waved it off. "It's nothing. Okay, you have the gun. And now you have the knife. I'll need proof of Greer Whitaker's death for my superiors. From the copy of his file you gave me, I know he has a tattoo on his leg. Use the knife. Cut out the tattoo and bring it to me."

"*What?*"

"Just as I said, Bob. Bring me the proof."

"Erich . . ."

"And don't forget," interrupted Reagor, "there's the other big payoff at the end when we've set everything in place. There's a place for you in the new economic order," he said, pushing a finger into Reed's chest for emphasis. "But performance is everything, Bob. The bottom line *is* the bottom line these days. No new economic order, no payoffs for you and me. Think of it as a long-term investment. A comfortable retirement plan."

Reed stood frozen in place.

Reagor turned away, talking: "What are you just standing there for? You've got work to do."

Reed watched Reagor walk through a wrought-iron gate next to the Palace and disappear around the corner into the evening pedestrian rush hour.

Kate tilted her head back and put in eye drops again in the women's room down the hall from the Director's seventh-floor office. She checked her makeup, but she couldn't hide the fact that her face was still puffy from a bad night. Not very professional, she told herself. Use people, defend institutions, wasn't that the proper perspective? She had secretly cried for her Russian agents when they had been taken away in the middle of the night never to be seen again, her operation undoubtedly compromised by a mole still in the Agency. She could certainly shed a few tears for the man she loved, regardless of the fact that he was a mere pawn in the operation. How could she have let this happen? Let personal considerations get in the way of her professional responsibilities? She had heard the rumors circulating at Langley— that she had been so good at recruiting and manipulating agents in Moscow because they had all fallen in love with her. Now the tables were turned. *She* had fallen in love this time. Kate Mallotte, rising star at the CIA, reduced to a softie. It was true.

The report from Bonn that she had been given earlier in the morning about Greer being seen in Munich with a woman hadn't helped. But wasn't that what the plan had called for? Now was the time to pull it back together. If she could maintain her cool, REDWING might still be salvaged. She owed it to the Agency. And besides, there was still a chance—ever so slight as it was—that Greer might make it home alive. It was ironic, she told herself, that Ben Gibbons had asked Bob Reed to get involved with the case and act as CIA liaison in Germany. Ironic in a deadly kind of way.

The whole world was looking for Greer Whitaker. Of course, Kate knew exactly where he was. At present, he was in someplace called Rothenburg ob der Tauber. She had looked it up in the Agency library. A romantic medieval city. She needed to let him stay out there just a little longer. Long enough for him to attract as many of the conspirators as possible. Above all else, REDWING must go forward, she told herself. Even if it meant the man she loved had to be put further at risk. There were others who had already died, others who *might* die. Just a little longer, she told herself again. *But what was he doing in Rothenburg?*

The old doubts returned. Things she had thought about a thousand times during the nights since Greer had left. How could she have done it? She was angry with herself. She had never counted on falling in love with Greer. She had made a choice and put the Agency in front of him. She could have called it off, of course. It still wasn't too late. It was true: her love for Greer had clouded her commitment to the Agency. She knew it. She was afraid everyone else knew it, too. No, she said to herself in the mirror. REDWING definitely *must* go on. For now, at least.

Kate looked again at the file on Greer, the one that Ben Gibbons had asked to see. Everything was in order; she had seen to that. Everything in the file confirmed Greer's background for his Top Secret security clearance. Ben would see it and feel good that the Agency had done its usual thorough job. It would put Ben at ease, she knew, give him a sense of well-being about the Agency's role in the Jenkins matter. He would back off a little, giving her just a little more time to pull the operation together.

Kate took a deep breath through her nose, cleared her head, and headed to Ben Gibbons's office to tell him some more lies about Greer Whitaker and herself.

37 ❏ ❏ ❏ ❏

Greer looked down from the window of their room in the Hotel Adler. Directly below was the patio. It was closed, of course, since it was winter, so Stephanie would be at this moment in the bright breakfast room on the main floor, getting food she could sneak up to him.

It was quite a change from the shabby accommodations in Munich. The Adler was a sixteenth-century former monastery that had been fully modernized on the inside. Their room was on the second floor, overlooking the patio and the walled gardens atop the steep hillsides sloping down to the river. The only room left had been the grand honeymoon suite. Stephanie had told the receptionist that she would take it, but that it was only for a single. She had paid with her credit card again. As soon as she had checked in, she called out the window to where Greer was hiding and summoned him upstairs.

Greer thought about the big bed and the antiques in their room. "Just hold me," she had said. They slept together, exhausted from the escape from Munich. Greer had his arm over her on the bed and she seemed happy. Keeping Stephanie calm would help. Surely Kate would understand that.

He had spent a lot of time thinking about his next steps. He knew he needed to get in touch with Kate as soon as possible. But what could he tell her? What about STEEPLECHASE? But what if his suspicions about Reed were pure paranoia and Reed *was* legitimate? Not likely, but didn't he still have an obligation to keep the operation secret in case Reed wasn't responsible for Jenkins' death? How far did the operation go? Was it Reed or the entire operation that had gone bad?

He was restless and eager for Stephanie to return. She had been gone for twenty minutes and he was ready to go. Being confined in the hotel made him nervous. His leg had improved considerably. He could walk well enough alone now. But where was Stephanie? Against their agreed-upon plan, he took her bag and left the room to find her.

Greer checked the breakfast room downstairs before he entered. It was empty. He peeked around the corner of the doorway leading to the lobby. The receptionist was filing forms in a drawer. The telephone rang in a back office and she left to answer it. No one was there.

Greer crossed the lobby and headed toward the front glass door, quickly dropping the key onto the front desk. Stephanie had to be outside.

Greer slipped out and turned to shut the door, catching a glimpse of Stephanie just coming out of the telephone booth off the lobby. He quickly stepped to the side before she saw him looking at her, then waited outside. She had seen him, though. Stephanie opened the door, joined him outside, and led him away by the arm.

"Where have you been?" he asked.

"Where have *you* been? I went back to the room and you were gone."

"I was worried something had happened," he said. "You were going to get some food for us and bring it back up to the room."

"Breakfast." Stephanie pulled out a small bundle wrapped in a napkin from her coat. "I had to visit the little girls' room while I was downstairs," she said.

Greer had just caught her in a lie. Why hadn't she told him she was going to make a call? Who had she been talking to? He felt a wave of paranoia wash over him.

Greer took the bundle and ate the muffin he found inside. She was leading them toward the plaza in the middle of town. It was cold and gray, the wind swirling around the narrow street.

"This makes me nervous as all hell," he said.

They had arrived on a Friday. It was Saturday morning and the streets were filled with tourists. Colored Christmas lights were strung across the streets.

"No one would ever think of looking for you here. They're looking for you in the major cities. Not in Grimm's Fairy Tales countryside."

"This was a mistake."

A couple passed, then another. Greer froze and pulled Stephanie into a doorway.

"Did you see that?" he said.

"No. What?"

Another couple passed by. The man had a very short haircut and distinctive clothes. Greer overheard the other couple talking.

Stephanie spoke: "How did you know that half the families from the nearby U.S. Army post would be here? Only two more shopping days until Christmas. You'll blend in here."

Greer caught his reflection in the window of the shop front. It wasn't the same Greer who had come to Germany five days ago. The beard was coming along. He had never grown a full beard before. It was coming in red and brown, darker than his hair. The coat and the sweater from the used clothing store were shabby. Greer smoothed out the wrinkles at the shoulders. He ran his fingers through his hair. A new part, he decided. He separated the layers of hair and moved the part from the right to left.

Around the medieval city was a high stone wall. Greer remembered a gate near the street they were on. Greer kept his head down and hurried them along the cobbled street, avoiding looking into the eyes of the shoppers.

Through the gate, there was a path outside of the wall. Without the wall's protection, the wind whipping up from the hills was punishing, freezing the moisture in their noses. They walked along the path over-looking the river Tauber.

Greer spoke as they followed the outside perimeter: "You know, I can't stay on the run forever over here. Eventually I'll get caught."

"You can't leave me again, Greer." She seemed serious.

"I've got to get back to the States. I can clear things up for myself."

"How are you going to do that?" she asked.

Should he ask her? Who was she talking to on the telephone?

She asked another question: "Does it have to do with the diskettes?"

Had he mentioned the diskettes? He had made a special point of keeping them out of her view, but she had seen them when he was putting them into the Fed Ex packet. That must have been it. But why would she ask that? Questions from her that would have seemed normal, innocuous, thirty minutes ago now seemed full of innuendo. Was he just being paranoid? Maybe it was nothing. Maybe he should keep it to himself and see what she was up to, he finally decided.

He shook her question off. "No," he mumbled. "Not just that."

"It's going to be hard finding someone who will listen to a murder suspect," Stephanie said.

They trudged along the narrow dirt path, hugging the wall. The water was rippling loudly below at a bend in the river. The wind was ferocious.

Stephanie stopped and grabbed Greer by his sleeves. She was almost shouting when she spoke. "I don't want to do this, but I think I know a way I can get you back. If that's what you want, I'll help. I'll help you get back so you can do what you have to do."

"What did you have in mind?"

"In Salzburg. Can we make it to Salzburg?"

"We can if we have to. But why?"

"There's a community of Turks here. My mother's family has friends there. I'm sure they can help."

"Sounds like we should try to make it."

"It would probably be better if we stayed in a nearby town and I went into Salzburg to make arrangements first."

"What are you thinking?"

"I don't want to scare the Turks. If they're not expecting us, they might think you're just there to spy on them."

"*That's* funny."

"All non-Germanics living in those countries are especially sensitive now about emigration issues. They think that everyone from the politicians and police to the skinheads are out to get them."

"They're right."

"It would work out better if I went in first and prepared your way into the Turk community. I know they can help."

"Okay. The sooner we leave the better."

They came to another gate in the wall. "We've got to get out of this wind," she said.

They went through the wrought-iron gate and emerged onto a

cobblestone street decorated for Christmas. It was packed with people with shopping bags going in and out of shops.

"Let's get the car," said Greer. "I'm ready to go now."

They headed back in the direction of the hotel, Stephanie hanging onto his arm. There was the smell of fresh baked goods in the cold air.

"Look," said Stephanie. She slowed them down. Stephanie pointed to a hand-lettered sign taped to the window of a pastry shop. Beneath was a wicker basket full of fist-sized round pastries coated with powdered sugar.

Schneebälle.

"I know, I know," he said. He got them going again. "We've got to hurry."

"Sure thing, Herr Schneebälle."

Greer and Stephanie walked close together along the narrow cobbled streets back toward the hotel. The swelling in his leg had gone down and walking had become less painful.

Suddenly, up ahead, Greer saw two cars rumbling along the cobbles to a quick stop in front of their hotel. Greer moved Stephanie to the side of the street and pushed her back into a doorway.

"What is it?" Stephanie asked.

Greer shook his head and squinted at the cars—a pair of unmarked black Saab Turbos. Police? Someone sent by Reed? A man got out of each car and rushed quickly inside. Greer stiffened.

"Damn!" Greer said. It must be *them* again, he thought. Just like in Munich. And he didn't even know who *they* were. Greer instinctively felt for the gun in his coat pocket.

Their car was only a block away, but on the opposite side of the hotel from where they stood. They would have to circle back around the block to avoid the front of the hotel to have a chance of getting to the car and making a getaway.

"We're going to have to run," said Greer.

"I'm getting used to it." She grabbed his hand. "I'm right behind you, *Liebling.*"

Greer noticed the black Saab behind them on the autobahn just west of Lake Constance, some forty kilometers from the Berchtesgaden exit. Was it one of the cars from Rothenburg? He checked his speedometer. The cruise control was holding them steady at 175 kilometers per hour, not unusual for the more powerful cars on the wide-open stretch of E11 between Munich and Salzburg.

After leaving Rothenburg, they had forsaken the Romantic Road in favor of the much faster motorway, driving northeasterly to Nuremberg, continuing on in a southeastern direction to Regensburg, then dropping south to a point west of Lake Constance along the main highway to Salzburg.

There was something still bothering him. "Who did you call back at the hotel this morning?" he asked.

Stephanie sat with her head against the back of the seat. "What do you mean?"

"Didn't I see you making a phone call this morning when you went downstairs to get my breakfast?"

She didn't answer right away. Greer looked at her, then back at the road. He checked the sideview mirror. Greer pushed the control lever on the steering column forward, and held it until the speed reached 190. The car behind him matched his new speed.

Stephanie eyed the needle on the speedometer nervously. *"Liebling.* Let's not give anyone the satisfaction of our killing *ourselves.* I was just checking phone messages at home. I'm invited to a New Year's Eve party. Think I'll make it? I'm supposed to bring the marzipan pigs."

Marzipan pigs were the traditional gift for good luck in the new year, Greer knew. He wished he had one at the moment. He saw movement in the rearview mirror.

"We've got company again," he said.

Greer turned the cruise control off and took control over the accelerator. He pushed the speed up to 200, and the black car matched his speed again. They were both going over 120 miles per hour.

At this speed, Greer figured it was about ten minutes to their exit.

When he got to the exit ramp he purposely didn't put on his turn signal and didn't slow down. He cut off the road at the last possible moment. The black car swerved to match his maneuver and followed him to the top of the ramp to the stoplight. He was right on Greer's tail, revving his engine.

Greer studied the driver of the car behind him in his rearview mirror while he waited for the light to change. It was definitely one of the men who had run into the hotel in Rothenburg.

The light turned yellow, then green. "Hang on," Greer said. He floored the pedal and threw the back end of the car around the corner heading up the road leading into the mountains around Berchtesgaden. The black car followed close behind.

The four-lane road turned into two lanes and began cutting back and forth as it climbed up into the mountains. They reached a long stretch of a climb up the side of a mountain. Greer saw the other car closing the distance.

"He's making a move."

They were still on the straightaway section of the road with the Saab right on their tail. Greer pushed his car harder, but the Saab kept up and suddenly pulled out into the other lane up alongside their car; the driver took a long, hard look at Greer and Stephanie. Just then, Greer caught a glimpse out of the corner of his eye of a sign indicating they were fast approaching another hairpin turn in the road.

The driver raised a gun at them. Greer took his foot off the accelerator and they fell back as the other car zipped around them and back into the right lane turn just as a large oncoming truck was rounding the corner, blasting its horn.

"Give me the gun!" shouted Greer.

The Saab slowed down, forcing Greer to slow down, too. Finally, Greer rounded a particularly sharp curve, drove another ten meters and stopped the car with the engine running. The Saab stopped, too, about five meters in front of him.

On the left was the other lane, then a straight drop down to the valley floor. On the right was about two feet of road shoulder, then a sheer rock cliff where the road had been blasted into the side of the mountain. Greer watched the head of the driver ahead of him swivel around to see what was going on. Greer put the car into gear and moved the car forward slowly, then floored the pedal and raced around the Saab before the other driver had time to react.

In the lead again, Greer raced up the winding mountainside road, slamming the car from side to side, the other car matching him turn for turn and losing no distance. Greer took another hairpin turn and decided that was the one he was waiting for. He stopped his car suddenly and the car behind him almost ran into the back of him.

Greer watched the driver in his rearview mirror reach over to the passenger seat for something. Greer put his car into reverse, but didn't let off the brake or clutch yet. He was waiting for just the right moment. Just then, the driver rolled down his window and started to position his gun.

Stephanie shouted, "Greer!"

At that instant, Greer revved the engine and popped the clutch, and the BMW went hurtling back toward the Saab. In a blinding second, Greer heard the shots gotten off by the startled driver as their BMW slammed with full force into the other car, which bounced backward like an eight ball off a solidly played cue ball, off the road and over the side of the mountain.

Greer waited for the sound of the Saab hitting valley bottom, then pulled to the side of the road and got out to look at the damage. Only then did he notice the pain in his wrist. He had banged the hell out of his arm in the collision.

Pushing back his sweater sleeve, he saw the shattered remains of his watch, including the crystal that had fractured and was digging into his wrist. He unfastened the watchband and applied pressure to his wrist to stop the bleeding.

Greer turned the watch over and discovered the casing was also cracked. He prodded the back with his finger and popped out a microchip and subminiature electronic components soldered to the other side of casing. There was some kind of electronic mechanism that drove the watch hands. There was something else, too, apparently undamaged. It looked remarkably similar to something he had seen before. He reached back into his memory. Something he had seen in spy training camp maybe? A transmitter of some type. Actually, the exact same type used in conjunction with Global Positioning System satellites to locate downed fighter pilots.

And missing CIA operatives.

Stephanie called out from the car, "Everything all right?"

"Yeah, fine."

Greer quickly scooped up some snow. He made a snowball and pushed the transmitter into it. He lobbed the snowball over the edge of the road toward the valley floor below.

The back end of their car was in no better shape than his watch. Greer kicked the dented wheel well away from the tire, then got back into the car.

"On the bright side," Stephanie said, "I signed the collision damage waiver."

Yet Greer was so lost in thought, he didn't hear her.

Nice sentiment, Kate. What the hell were you up to? And just why did you think you needed to be tracking my whereabouts with a GPS satellite beacon?

38 ❑ ❑ ❑ ❑

The President knocked back his third bourbon. It was three-thirty in the morning, two more days until Christmas. He sat in the Oval Office in his sweats and running shoes. He got the bottle of Maker's Mark out from the credenza behind his desk and poured himself another.

He picked up the report again from his pollster that the Chief of Staff had brought over just before the end of the day. He looked first at the verbatims from the voter focus groups conducted the week before. He was a caretaker. His administration hadn't accomplished anything significant in three years. He hadn't proved himself exceptional. The dozen people in each of the four focus groups in different parts of the country seemed to understand that he hadn't had the opportunity to lead them through a foreign crisis. But that also meant he was untested. He was a nice guy, but someone else might do a better job for the next four years. The President winced.

The hard numbers from the telephone surveys were what should have really counted, but the personal words of the individuals in the focus groups hurt most. These were the unvarnished sentiments of real people. These were groups that had voted for him the last time, but now they were considering a candidate from the other party. He flipped the page and looked at the polling results. His overall approval rating was at forty-seven percent and falling. On foreign policy he scored a dismal thirty-five percent. On domestic policy, forty-five percent. The pollster noted that the domestic rating was probably more of a "sympathy" score, since he was generally perceived to be a sympathetic person.

He turned the page and looked at the question typed in bold face at the top: *If the election were held today, would you vote for the President or someone from the other party?* Fifty-six percent of the voters polled sided with the other party. Thirty-nine percent answered for the President and the rest were undecided.

The President picked up the phone. "Get me Dwight Conrad," he told the White House operator.

He waited for half a minute, then pushed the speakerphone button. He pushed his swivel chair back and put his feet up on the edge of the desk. The operator came on: "Still trying, Mr. President. I've called him on his beeper."

"That's fine. I'll wait."

The operator came on again two minutes later. "Here's Mr. Conrad, sir."

"Mr. President," said Conrad.

"Dwight, I've been looking at the pollster's report. It doesn't look good."

"It's salvageable, Mr. President. The election's still eleven months away."

"Shit, Dwight. That's not much time to turn this around. You've read the report. You know what it says to me?"

"No, sir. What?"

"They're lukewarm toward me. They're already looking for the next hero. The electorate is bored, Dwight. What do you suggest?"

"I'd like to call a meeting right after Christmas, sir. Get the top advisers in. We'll meet off-site somewhere. I've been working on some ideas. . . ."

"*After* Christmas? We need to do something now!"

There was silence on the other end of the line.

"Dwight? Dwight? Are you there, Dwight?"

"Yes, Mr. President."

"What are we going to do?"

"Well, sir, it's been my belief all along that the economic conference next month is our opportunity to put the screws to the Japanese and score some points with the voters. The voters are tired of the Japanese taking advantage of Americans. If we can stick it to them in San Francisco, I believe—and our pollster believes—that the numbers will turn around rather dramatically. It'll make you look strong."

The President played with his empty bourbon tumbler. He mellowed. "You think so, Dwight? You've got data to support this hunch of yours?"

"Yes, sir. If you turn to the second to last page of that report, you'll see the numbers. The collective American ego has been bruised by what they see as years of abuse by foreign countries. They see outsiders as taking advantage of us. We give them huge handouts while we still have lots of problems at home. We let them come over here and sell us their products while at the same time our own manufacturers can't compete over there because of protectionist tariffs."

"So what you're saying is that we've got an exceptional opportunity for turning this around by coming away with a home run at the G7 meeting?"

"Absolutely."

The President looked around the Oval Office. "Dwight?"

"Yes, sir?"

"What do we do to make sure this thing with Jenkins doesn't overshadow the conference or the work we're doing around here?"

There was a moment of silence.

Finally Conrad spoke. "We have to do our best to keep it back-page news."

"Dwight?"

"Yes, sir?"

"I want you to talk to Ben Gibbons and tell him not to push too hard on the investigation on Jenkins. Do you understand? Let's get him in the ground. The last thing we need is the media running wild with speculation over Jenkins while we're pulling off this deal with the Japanese. If this is our best shot, Dwight, we've got to make sure we've got the attention of the country where it should be."

"Yes, sir. I understand."

The technician in his white lab coat wiped off his workbench again and straightened the rack of test tubes. He had been told that someone from outside would be coming to look at his work. He rarely had visitors from the clients. He was told not to ask any questions, but to cooperate fully and supply any answers he could. He kept an eye on the door that led to the hallway. Through its window he could see the assistant director of the firm escorting a pretty woman in a bright red suit down the corridor.

The assistant director pushed the door open for Kate. He gave a nod to the technician. "Call me when you're done and I'll come back to walk you out," he said to Kate.

"Good morning," said Kate brightly, holding out her hand.

The technician shook her hand. "Good morning. Nice to have you with us today."

Kate got right to the point. "I understand you've finished with the samples. I was hoping that you could brief me on what you found."

"We worked through the night to complete the report." He picked up a half-inch-thick bound report off the bench. "It's just preliminary," he said. Kate took it and opened up the cover. It was entitled, "Forensic Examination of Materials from Jane and John Doe." She flipped through without focusing on the material.

Jane Doe, she repeated to herself. So it was true. The report of Greer traveling with a woman in Munich.

"This looks very thorough," she said, recovering herself. "I certainly appreciate the time you've put into this. I'll read it later. What I'd really like is for you to actually show me the evidence—the samples. Walk me through how you arrived at your conclusions."

The technician moved to a bench that held an assortment of glass and cardboard containers with code numbers on them in black marker. He pointed to the samples. "I should tell you that the only thing I was told about these was that they came from the same scene. I wasn't told anything else so that I wouldn't be influenced by what might be preliminary conclusions. My job is to provide as much information as possible from the samples utilizing scientific methods."

"I understand," said Kate. "Please continue."

He picked up a box and took off the lid. "One of the first things we determined was that there were two subjects." He held the box for Kate to look at. "This bed sheet provided us with most of the information we have."

Kate felt an involuntary shiver run through her.

He continued: "A sheet is always a prized discovery in such an investigation."

"So what have you learned?"

The technician put the lid back onto the box and set it aside. The CIA station in Bonn had cabled a message to her saying that the evidence was on the way. She made a decision to have the samples sent to one of the CIA's outside private research laboratories rather than to the FBI. If the test results yielded anything that might jeopardize REDWING, she didn't want it circulating around the J. Edgar Hoover Building.

The technician was picking up a piece of white cardboard with several strands of hair taped to it. "You can clearly see—even with the naked eye—that there are two types of head hair here." He pulled a mechanical pencil out of the pocket protector in his shirt and pointed to the hair. "On this side you can see the shorter of the two types. It's relatively straight and dark brown. Under a microscope it's easily identified as a male's."

"Greer's," Kate mouthed silently.

"On the other side we have somewhat long, black, curly hair that further microscopic examination identified as belonging to a woman."

"Son of a bitch," Kate murmured.

"Pardon me?"

"Nothing. Just thinking out loud. Please go on. This is all *very* fascinating."

"Now, then, if you'll step over here." He turned on a large microscope with a video monitor beside it. The screen was filled with what looked to be an enormous bulb on the end of a shaft. "This is a pubic hair removed from the sheets. It's the female's." He flipped a switch on the machine and there was a similar picture. "This is the male's." He adjusted the microscope and zoomed in. "You'll notice, I'm sure, that there is a substance adhering to the shaft."

"Yes?"

"You may have guessed it's a mixture of dried bodily fluids. Our analysis show that it's a combination of his sweat and semen and *her* sweat and mucous secretions.

Kate drew in a deep breath. "Yes. Go on."

"To give you an idea of how good our techniques are here, we've even isolated the female subject's mucous secretions and further differentiated them into oral and vaginal secretions."

"Amazing."

The technician leaned against the work bench. "This was pretty straightforward. What we basically did was separate all the samples by male versus female then perform DNA analysis. You take the results from these tests plus the other information available, compare them to known human descriptors, and you get quite a picture of the subjects. It's what we specialize in here. No one's quite as advanced as we are. I can tell you stuff about them that they probably don't know about themselves."

"Tell me what you found."

"The guy? He's in his late twenties. Caucasian, with a mixture of Anglo-Saxon, Germanic, and Celtic bloodlines. No major predispositions for diseases—cancers, heart attacks, things like that. He ought to live a long time."

We'll see, Kate thought.

"What about the woman?"

The technician reached for the report and opened it up to read. "*She* was quite a bit more complicated." He turned several pages until he found what he was looking for. "Here it is. An interesting mixture of German and Turkish blood, evenly split."

"Anything else?"

"One other thing." He walked over to another counter and turned on a full-sized TV and VCR. "I took these shots yesterday with a camcorder on the microscope." He pushed the PLAY button and the solid gray screen suddenly came alive with squiggling lines. The picture focused itself.

"What is it?"

"*That's* the guy's *sperm*. I had to call the client liaison who brought this stuff in to give me just a little bit of background because it is almost unbelievable. Apparently the male subject was cleaning up with a hot washrag and threw it against a radiator in a bathroom. The combination of heat and dampness kept the sperm alive. The washcloth was sent to me in a vacuum bottle, so it was still warm. You know, sperm can live up to three days in the right environment. This guy must have . . ."

"What?"

"It must have been a long night. It's hard to say for sure, but due to the low sperm count on the sample, I'd speculate he probably ejaculated several times in a relatively short period of time."

Kate stared at the screen. The technician looked a little embarrassed, but proud of his work. The sperm were dancing furiously on the monitor.

Kate knew she shouldn't have come. Didn't even have to. She had a file on her desk with the name and photograph of the woman Greer was with. So why *had* she come?

Something finally snapped. She couldn't go through with it. REDWING wasn't as important to her as Greer.

"Thank you," Kate said. "I think I've seen enough."

Kate called from the lobby of the laboratory.

"I'm not hearing any arguments," she said. "I've made the decision. . . ."

Kate listened, her anger rising. "No! It's too dangerous. I'm calling it off." She looked around the lobby and lowered her voice. "That's an order, or have you forgotten my position in the organization. You're not just talking to some junior-level assistant to the DCI. Find out where Greer is and bring him in. Now!" She slammed down the phone.

To hell with them all, and to hell with what they might think. Of course they knew the real reason she was shutting it down. But she wasn't going to lose another one. Not Greer. No way.

Greer watched the road beneath him from his vantage near the top of one of the highest mountains in the Berchtesgaden area. He could see cars below winding slowly up the mountain roads. It was already three-thirty. Stephanie was supposed to be dropped off by her friends from Salzburg any moment.

He spotted the gray Ford Fiesta and saw a puff of blue smoke as it shuddered to shift into lower gear to take on the next part of its ascent. Having timed other cars, he calculated it would take them another ten minutes to make it up.

The car rolled up from behind. Stephanie got out and said good-bye to her friends, then the car quickly left.

Greer was anxious. "How'd it go?"

"Fine. It went fine. They're willing to help. They said they can get you out of Europe. They've done this sort of thing before."

"Thank God." It was the first good news he had had since Cologne.

"They're coming back tomorrow night. They'll meet us here again and take us both into Salzburg."

"What time?"

"One-thirty in the morning. They figure there will be people returning from midnight Christmas Eve services so we won't look suspicious driving around at that time of the night. They said it's best if you come into Salzburg under cover of night. Don't take any chances."

"Good." Greer gazed out over the mountain valley. "I've been thinking," he said. "I'd like to get a read on what's going on back home. I've got to make a call."

The room was dark, except for the green glow of four computer screens set into a console along the wall. On each screen there was a different map, each in more detail than the next, and an icon in the shape of a small red wing quickly flashing. The first screen was a Mercator projection map of the world. The second screen showed Europe. The third screen was a close-up view of the German side of the Bavarian Alps. Over a zoomed-in detailed map of the Berchtesgaden Basin, the silhouette of a hand traced a road leading toward the town on the fourth screen. A set of latitudinal and longitudinal coordinates were superimposed in the corner of the map.

"He's no longer tracking," Covey said. "The flashing icon means that's the last position from which a transmission was received."

Roller chairs moved forward and two faces moved a little closer into the periphery of the screen's glow, but the features were still hidden in the dark. All that could be seen of the two was the light from the computers reflected off a pair of glasses and off a shiny forehead.

Knowles spoke. "Calling the operation off just got—problematic."

"Impossible," added Covey with confidence. They were collectively trying to make a point.

The third person in the room leaned over the last screen. Kate's face was lit up, a luminous green.

She had known exactly where Greer had been at any given moment since December 15, give or take the several yards accuracy rating of the GPS satellites that had been tracking him from 11,000 feet up in space. She had plotted his every move on a map, tracking him since he had left Washington. She felt she had been in control of the situation. But now he was lost.

"Look, Kate. This is Greer," Covey said. "He's not your ordinary operative. You've developed him on the basis of a solid relationship."

She knew what he was trying to say. They were trying to make it easier for her. If she weren't his superior, he would have said it outright.

"I can't lose this one," she said. "This time it's personal." There was no sense in trying to pretend with these guys anymore. Anyone else in the building, but not them. Now they could get on with the business of figuring out what to do next.

"I know," said Covey quietly. "And we're going to do everything we can to help."

39 ❑ ❑ ❑ ❑

At that moment, Marie von Bosacker stood in the central aisle next to the front pew in the old church in Kaysersberg. She looked up at the crucifix over the altar, crossed herself and genuflected, then sat down near the end of the empty pew. She left a space on the seat beside her open next to the aisle.

Marie pulled the kneeler out and slid down to pray. She fingered an antique ivory-and-gold rosary as she remained with her head down and eyes closed. Finished with her silent prayers, she crossed herself and sat back on the hard wooden pew.

The church—for centuries the focal point of the town's life—was now itself nearly empty. On her way in from the narthex, Marie had seen only a handful of old women scattered throughout the sanctuary, each sitting alone. They were bundled against the cold in the unheated church. There were no men to help keep them warm. The turn-out, even for the special pre-Christmas service, was typical. France, like most of the rest of Europe, had largely turned from the Church. There hadn't been a service attended by more than a dozen people for several years.

Marie was a link with the past. She looked around the church and reminded herself—completely without any sense of self-importance—that if it were not for the Bosacker family, the old place would have been shut down and collapsed decades ago from neglect. The Bosackers had given generously to the church for at least the twenty-two generations recorded in the official church record book kept in the sacristy that recorded the births, baptisms, marriages, and deaths of the family. Over the past ten years, she had paid to replace the roof, install a drainage system to protect the walls from mildew and erosion, and clean the sooted-over stained-glass windows in the narthex and nave. Ever since the Second World War, the Bosackers had also paid the full salaries of the priest, the sexton, and the organist. And, a year after her husband's death, Marie had spent over 750 thousand francs as a memorium to replace the organ.

Marie heard hacking coughs and sniffles coming from the widows behind her. She waited for the beginning of the service and thought about the history of her family connected with the place. Lining the walls on either side of the church were the crypts of some of the prominent members of the Bosacker family, their names cut into the marble wall plaques. The dead were the only family with her today. The pew used to be full. Now Michael, her husband, was gone. So was her son.

Marie had faint memories from her childhood of a time when the pew she was sitting on was crammed tight with the Bosacker family. Her father would sit on the end of the pew next to the aisle—in the space that she had purposely left empty—and she would sit between him and her mother. The aunts and uncles and cousins would fill out the row. Her father was a working landowner. The whole family would scrub the night before the weekly Sunday morning service, but Henri Bosacker could never get the smells and stains of the grapes out of the pores of his skin. During the week, Henri was busy tending to the fields and supervising the wine making at the château and rarely had much time for the family. He left before dawn and returned well after the sun had set. But on Sunday, he dressed in his Parisian suit and devoted himself entirely to his wife and his daughter, Marie, his only child.

She put her hand down onto the pew in the place where her father used to sit and rubbed the rough wood. Over fifty years ago, she was sitting in church on that very same pew, holding his hand during the homily, turning his fingers in her hand. It was her fondest—and last—memory of him alive.

A loud, dissonant organ chord suddenly filled the air, breaking her concentration. The organist played around with several chord progressions in a minor key before resolving into a crescendoing major. He lifted his hands dramatically off the keys at the end, and the sound of the music continued echoing around the nearly empty church.

The priest emerged from a side door. He made eye contact with Marie von Bosacker—his patron—nodded slightly, and began the service.

Marie mouthed the words of the liturgy she had memorized as a child. But she wasn't thinking about the words. She was thinking about her father, trying at that moment to summon all the memories of him that she could from her childhood. As she got older, the images of her father became fuzzier, muddled. All but two, that is. These two images were strong and grew more vivid as time passed. The one was of him sitting next to her in church, holding hands. It represented the happiest moment of her life. Of all the truly wonderful things she had experienced—her marriage, raising her son, playing with the grandchildren —still nothing compared to the happiness that overwhelmed her when thinking about those precious Sundays on the pews, squeezed tightly between her parents, with Henri indulging his little girl's curiosity about his large, calloused, grape-skin stained hands.

And the other vision—the one that had assumed such a horrible vibrancy—was of the German tank officer pulling the trigger of a gun pressed against her father's head, robbing her forever of the company and love of a father whom she could sit with in church on Sundays. *That* vision was permanently screwed into her consciousness. It was in the front of her brain and rattled her head like a throbbing bass note from the organ.

40 ❑   ❑   ❑   ❑

Greer and Stephanie drove back to the General Walker Hotel in Berchtesgaden. It was a U.S. Army facility run for soldiers and their families in Germany who wanted to get away from their Army post for a while and enjoy the scenery and recreation of the Bavarian Alps. Earlier Greer had noticed a phone booth on the grounds. The U.S. troops had retained rights to a number of properties after capturing the area during the Second World War. There was no security at all to keep them from driving up. People were home for the holidays and the parking lot was empty, ringed by snowdrifts that had pushed to the edge of the asphalt.

It was late morning in Washington. Stephanie made the phone call and charged it to her home number. She waited until she heard the number ring and handed the phone over to Greer.

Kate answered.

"Kate, this is Greer." He was talking fast. "Don't try tracing this call and we can talk. Okay?"

"Greer!"

"Kate. I need your help."

"Are you all right?"

"I'm not hurt. I'm going to talk fast, so listen. I'm timing this so you can't trace the call."

"I'm listening."

"First, I want you to know that I didn't kill Jenkins. I saw him being pulled from the water by the German police."

She sounded worried. "Greer, why are you running?"

"Because whoever killed Jenkins is also after me."

"Well, I'd like to kill you, too, but that's a different matter." She said it matter-of-factly.

"What?"

"Never mind. It's just that I know about your Turkish girlfriend. It's . . . it's something we can sort out later. We've got to bring you in."

"My *what?*"

"Oh, stop it. The woman you've been with since Cologne. It doesn't matter now. Just tell me where you are."

Greer was tongue-tied. "How do you know anything about *her?*"

"We can sort all that out *later* . . . this isn't the time."

"Look, Kate . . ."

"Not now, Greer. We've got to stick to the business at hand."

Greer looked outside the phone booth to see if Stephanie was listening. Things were flying apart. He had to reassure Kate, even if he wasn't completely sure about her own motivations. He turned his back to Stephanie and lowered his voice. "Kate . . . I *love* you. I can explain it all later. I've got to get off this phone. I'm in a jam and I need your help. You want to help me, don't you?"

"Of course I do. The best thing for you to do is turn yourself in. You'll be safe in custody. I can arrange for a liaison to pick you up almost immediately afterward."

"It's not that simple. If I just surrender, I'll be arrested and the whole truth will never come out."

"What's that?"

"It's too long a story to get into now."

"I have a suggestion. Let me have one of our people meet with you directly. No intermediaries, no foreigners. You can talk. I can arrange for you to be brought in safely, discreetly. The Germans will never know."

"I don't trust anyone."

"You can trust me."

There's irony there, Greer thought. "I don't know that."

"Look . . . I'll send someone who's authorized to deal."

"It needs to be you."

"I can't, Greer. I have to stay here to coordinate your return. Where are you?"

Greer paused. Things were really closing in on him. He really did need Kate's help. But how could he trust her now? "Kate . . . I know about the watch."

There was silence on the other end.

Her voice went up. "What about the watch?"

He could tell she was surprised. "That's why you're asking me where I am now. I found the transmitter. You've been tracking me all along. If there's a manhunt for me, why didn't you just tell someone where I was? Why didn't you send someone to help me already?"

Even without his watch, Greer knew that precious seconds were ticking away.

"The tracking device was for your own protection. . . ."

"My *protection?*"

"We both obviously have things to explain when you get back, but for now you have no choice but to *trust* me, Greer." She was deliberate in what she was saying: "We *have* to trust each other. It's not safe for you to be out there. Do you understand?"

She was right, of course. He was running out of options. He would need someone to help him once he got back to the States. What was the *real* reason she had tracked him? And how did she know so much about Stephanie? Why would she still be willing to help him if she *knew* about Stephanie?

"I can send someone to help you now," she pleaded.

He was feeling desperate. But he had to ensure his own safety. "Only you."

More silence on Kate's end of the line.

"I can't."

"I insist."

Greer was determined. If anyone was going to bring him in, it was going to have to be Kate. "If it's not you, I won't be there."

She finally spoke. "Okay. When? Where?"

"We meet on my terms. Only you."

"I swear."

Greer looked at Stephanie. "You'll have to take an overnight flight *tonight*. . . ."

"But . . ."

"We're going to do it my way or not at all." Kate was listening. "Take an overnight flight to Munich. Drive to Berchtesgaden. I'll meet you tomorrow night—Christmas Eve. There's a little church in the middle of the village. Stand in front of the main door at eleven-thirty and stay there for a five full minutes. I'm just giving you one chance. Miss the meeting and the whole thing's off."

"I'll be there."

"Just you, Kate."

"I promise."

"I'll be watching."

Stephanie banged on the door of the telephone booth. Greer held it closed with his foot. She was pointing to her watch. Greer knew that he needed to get off the phone to avoid a trace.

Stephanie was pushing through the door.

"I'm counting on you," he said. He whispered: "Kate, I . . ."

Stephanie put her finger down on the button, cutting him off. She gave him a stern look. "Time," she said.

Stephanie was shrieking, "She can't come back like this! *I'm* the one who's helped you. *I'm* the one who looked after you while you were hurt. *I'm* the one who loves you. She can't take you away!"

They stood outside the phone booth, dwarfed by the mountains, alone in the snowdrifts of the parking lot.

Greer had already asked her once to keep her voice down. But, he supposed, better to have her wailing in the open mountain air than in the hotel room.

"It's the only way," he said. "She's the only one I can trust to bring me back in."

Stephanie scoffed. "She'll turn you over to the police as soon as she gets her hands on you. There'll be a hundred FBI agents waiting for you in the airport in the U.S."

That may be true, he thought. But he believed Kate, despite the doubts. He *had* to. He believed that she would be there tomorrow night. He believed that she would be alone and he believed that she would, indeed, bring him in so that he wouldn't be turned over to the police. His story would still get out. It was the only way now.

"It's a chance I have to take."

"I know," she said quietly. "I know. It's just that it's so terrible to be losing you again. But I know you need to go. I'll help you."

Greer held her tightly and kissed her hair.

The stiff sea breeze blew the American flag off the coffin onto the ground next to the freshly dug grave. A camera flash caught the awkward moment. An embarrassed Marine guard in full dress uniform walked stiffly over and picked it up. Another Marine joined him and the two of them folded the flag into a triangle. The first Marine walked to the two nearly empty rows of metal folding chairs on the grass where the families and friends of the veterans usually sat. He presented the flag to a nephew of Randall Jenkins, who sat unemotionally watching the seagulls hovering not too far above the corporal's head.

The Vice President stood and turned to address the group. There were only seven other people present, not counting the Marines and cemetery workers standing to the side. There was the nephew—the only family member attending—a member of the Vice President's staff, two Secret Service men, a reporter from the *San Francisco Chronicle* and the newspaper photographer.

The Vice President looked out over the group. The day contrasted sharply with the event. The view from the little veterans cemetery at Inspiration Point at the Presidio in San Francisco was unparalleled. It was sunny and the wind whipped the water in the bay into white caps.

The Vice President smiled at the group, then returned to an appropriately serious face. He raised his eyebrows and took a deep breath.

"Friends," he started, "today we come to pay our tributes to a great man, a servant of our country—Randall Jenkins. The President of the United States personally asked me to represent him here, at the funeral of one of his closest friends and advisers. He had wanted to be here himself, but he is—as you probably know—preparing for a major economic summit in a few days. He sends his heartfelt condolences to family and friends gathered here today."

The newspaper reporter scribbled notes onto his notepad.

He continued: "Today we come here to honor one who has contributed much to our country." He reached into his coat side pocket and pulled out an index card to look at. "He was a navy veteran, a college classmate of the President and a key member of the President's campaign team. He received undergraduate and doctoral degrees in economics from Stanford University and made major contributions to that field as a university professor and fellow at the Hoover Institution. Most recently, he served as the President's National Security Adviser. In that capacity he helped steer the Administration through the tangled web of national security and intelligence issues. He was married to his late wife, Helen, for over twenty years. Among us today is his nephew, the son of Helen's sister." He paused to look down at the nephew, who was still watching seagulls swooping down above the assembly.

"It is most unfortunate that Randall Jenkins' life ended so tragically. We all mourn this loss. He was a husband, scholar, friend, and loyal public servant. I know that you will miss him as the President and I shall. I ask you to bow your heads in a moment of silent prayer for the dear departed soul of the patriot, Randall Jenkins."

The Vice President waited with his head bowed and eyes closed for a few moments. He gave a brief nod of the head and walked to the chairs. He shook the nephew's hand and sat down.

One of the Marines raised a bugle and wet his lips to play "Taps." The first note wavered before it found its confidence.

Everyone got up and the group began to break up and walk slowly away. The workers lowered the coffin with straps and dumped the first few shovels of dirt into the pit. After everyone had gone, one of them climbed onto a backhoe—previously hidden in a nearby shed—and finished the job.

41 ❏ ❏ ❏ ❏

At eleven-fifteen on Christmas Eve, the bells of the Berchtesgaden churches were calling people to midnight services.

Stephanie had her hand on the doorknob in their hotel room. Greer was waiting for her to go so he could lock up behind her. She turned and put her arms around his neck. She put her head on his shoulder. Greer put his arms around her and held her tightly. They had already said their good-byes. They agreed that it would be better for everyone if she and Kate didn't meet. Stephanie would leave, then Greer would get Kate and go. No looking back.

"It's going to be all right," he said. She was crying softly. "I couldn't have got this far without you. You'd better go." He thought he was going to start crying himself.

Stephanie dried her eyes on his shoulder. She avoided his eyes. "I love you," she said. Greer nodded and kissed her forehead. She left.

Greer locked the door and turned out the lights. He walked to the double window and parted the heavy floor-length curtains, but left the inner lacy curtains pulled together. He opened both windows and pulled a chair up from the writing desk. He turned the chair with its back facing the window sill and sat down.

Their room was on the second floor of the hotel that was on a small hill overlooking the street and the small church. The room had an unobstructed view of the front door of the church where the people were already gathering. He parted the inner curtains and watched the townspeople, dressed in dark green Loden coats and snow boots, converging at the church doors. A group of men came noisily out of the church, wearing Bavarian hats and carrying muskets on their shoulders. They slapped each other on the back and pointed to the guns. He saw Stephanie cross the street and go in without turning around.

Ten minutes later the crowd was still flowing into the church. Greer could see the inside every time the door opened. He could see the front altar lit up in golden candlelight, a crèche under a Christmas tree.

At eleven-thirty a couple of stragglers pushed their way into the packed nave and stood against the walls. He heard an organ playing now. The doors shut for the last time.

The bells stopped ringing. Inside the church, the service would be starting. The snowy streets were deserted. Greer watched the area in front of the church intently. Out of the corner of his eye he saw something move. It was time. A figure walked through the shadows on the sidewalk to the left where the street light wasn't shining. From the sound and rhythm of the footsteps, Greer determined it was a woman. She walked slowly toward the church and stepped into the cone of soft light from the lamp over the church's front door. It was Kate. Greer felt his heart jump. *No, it wasn't.* In his excitement, he had made a mistake. It was a young woman walking a small dog. The animal stopped to sniff at the corner of the church.

The woman moved on. Greer waited, listened, straining for sight of Kate. Several more minutes passed. Dammit! he thought. Where is she?

There was still no sign of Kate as a church bell rang once, marking the quarter hour. She was fifteen minutes late. How much longer should he give her?

The streets were utterly deserted. No cars, no people. Everyone was either at home or in the middle of a Christmas Eve service. Greer was nervous, holding his breath to listen for any little sound. He was startled when the church bell began tolling the midnight hour. Half an hour late. She wasn't coming.

Thank God for Stephanie, he thought. He was almost overcome by emotions, something that must have been stored away. He was more grateful than ever that Stephanie had set up the contacts with her Turkish friends. Greer took a moment to congratulate himself for not canceling the trip to Salzburg later in the night. It never hurt to have a good backup. He would need it now that he wasn't going anywhere with Kate.

Greer zipped up his coat and headed toward the door. He needed to let Stephanie know. In the dark, he startled himself with his own reflection in a mirror. He stopped to look. He looked haggard. The beard made him look ten years older.

There was still no traffic on the street. Greer stepped off the sidewalk and onto the packed snow in the road.

Greer was halfway across the street when he heard a sound coming down the sidewalk to his right. He froze. He was in the full light of the streetlamp, but he couldn't see who was coming through the shadows. The person hesitated. Before he could move, the woman walking the dog appeared again. The dog hesitated at the same point where it had stopped before at the corner of the church.

As soon as the woman walked away, Greer relaxed and put a foot out toward the far curb. He was still only halfway across the street. He froze again. He heard something. From the side of the church stepped a figure. It wasn't Kate. Greer couldn't see clearly, but it appeared to be a man. The figure moved out of the total dark to a position just outside the cone of light from the lamp over the church door. He seemed to be looking away from Greer at a huge cross outlined in lights on a nearby mountain slope. Greer turned sharply to go back to the hotel, but as soon as the man heard Greer's footsteps in the snow, he turned toward the noise in the street.

Greer looked back. The man stepped directly under the light. His head was bent down and covered with shadows. Greer took a couple of steps closer just to make sure.

It was Reed.

Reed squinted at Greer standing in the middle of the street. Reed seemed not to recognize him at first. Then his eyes flared slightly and his jaw locked.

They stood ten feet apart and said nothing. There was just the muffled sound of voices inside the church collectively reading a Psalm.

"*Guten abend*," said Reed. Good evening. Greer sensed that Reed still wasn't totally sure he was talking to Greer.

"*Fröhlische Weihnachten*," answered Greer in perfect German. Merry Christmas.

Reed walked a few steps closer.

"Stop right there," Greer demanded. Reed froze.

Reed spoke: "We were getting very worried about you. We didn't know if you were dead or alive. I didn't know what to tell the Director when you didn't show for our meeting in Cologne."

"Cut the crap, Reed. You and I both know why I didn't stick around town."

"No. You tell me."

"The dead body of a National Security Adviser. Seen one lately?"

"Ah—you apparently lost your nerve when you saw Jenkins dead."

"I didn't lose my nerve. I gained a sense of perspective. You killed Jenkins, didn't you?"

Reed gave him a tight-lipped smile. "Didn't I warn you about not getting squeamish when things started getting interesting?"

"This wasn't in the game plan. You're not going to tell me the CIA is going around murdering top presidential advisers."

"You forget the special nature of the situation. Jenkins was under investigation for being a spy. The President authorized extraordinary measures to deal with the problem."

"I doubt he authorized killing Randall Jenkins."

"You saw the Presidential Finding signed by the President himself."

Greer was unconvinced. "Where's Kate?"

Reed looked over Greer's head to the summit of the Watzmann. He took in a deep breath and blew it out into the chilly air through his nostrils. Inside the church a bass note from the organ vibrated the stained glass windows in their leaden casings. After the introductory measures on the organ, the congregation joined in the singing of "O Holy Night" in German.

"She couldn't make it."

"Then I want to speak to the Director."

"I'm afraid that's not possible now."

"Why not?"

Reed answered in measured phrases. "Because you blew your cool when the pressure was on and ran away from a difficult situation. Ben Gibbons doesn't travel in the company of cowards. Not only have you proved yourself unworthy as a CIA field officer, but you've embarrassed the Agency and the whole U.S. government. Ben has already taken the appropriate steps to distance himself from you and the operation."

"What do you mean?"

"Plausible deniability. It's simple. He just denies he knows anything about you or STEEPLECHASE."

"You're lying."

Reed smiled. "Who's more believable? The Director of Central Intelligence and the President or a fugitive murder suspect?"

Greer had no response.

"You see, you did yourself in. You violated the cardinal rule of espionage. You brought attention to yourself. Now you're totally ineffective. You're nothing but a liability now to the Administration. Let's do this quietly. Come back with me and we'll make sure that it's handled without a fuss."

"Forget it. My deal was to go with Kate."

"And why do you think I'll just let you walk away?" Reed asked.

"Kate Mallotte promised me a deal."

Reed chuckled. "Kate Mallotte." He shook his head. "Nice girl. If you make this difficult, it's going to reflect badly upon her. Kate's in charge of the damage control at the Agency concerning you. If she gets you back in, she's a hero. If she doesn't, her relationship with you becomes an issue for counterintelligence and she's thrown to the dogs. She'll have to take the blame for what's happened." Reed shrugged. "The Agency will need a scapegoat. Her career's over at that point."

"This discussion's over. See you back home. I'll give you a call."

"Greer . . ."

"I'm not going anywhere with you. Tell Kate I'll be in touch. *Maybe.*"

As Greer was turning, Reed pulled his hand out of his overcoat pocket. He held the old Russian Nagant revolver that Reagor had given him. "Enough games," Reed said. "Let's go."

Reed motioned with the gun to the side of the church that faced away from the street. Greer obliged.

The area on the side of the church was hidden from the streetlights, but the snow was lit up by the light coming through the stained-glass windows. Reed stood to the side of a window in the shadows, but his breath was illuminated by the shafts of colored light. On this side of the church was also a small old cemetery surrounded by a stone wall with paths running between the rows of headstones. On the graves were small glasses holding votive candles lit for Christmas Eve.

"Now what?" Greer asked.

"We're going for a walk." He pointed the gun at one of the paths leading through the cemetery toward a gate made of iron bars in the wall. Greer started out in that direction. He stopped when he got to the gate.

"Where?"

"Through the gate. Go," he ordered brusquely.

Greer looked around. Although they were in a dark cemetery on the side of the church away from the street, at least they were in a fairly open area. If he went through the gate, they would be completely cut off and out of sight from anyone who might happen by. It would be certain death if he went through with Reed.

Greer turned around. He faced Reed, who was holding the revolver barrel pointed at his gut.

"Let's talk about this for a moment," Greer said.

"There's nothing to talk about at this point. Move it."

Greer held his ground. "You're going to have the whole weight of the CIA on you. Kate won't let you get away with killing a fellow CIA officer."

Reed smirked. *"You're* not CIA. You're an asset being run by me."

"What are you talking about?" Greer asked incredulously.

"Your application to the Career Training Program was rejected. The CIA doesn't know anything about you except what they've seen on the evening news. All the Agency cares about now is wiping you off the front page of the newspapers."

"What do you mean, *rejected?"* Greer demanded again.

"Simple—you didn't make the cut. You had an ass-kicking résumé and you knocked the socks off everyone during the interviews, but you failed the polygraph. I saw you as you came through and realized you might be useful to me. I lifted your file and decided to let you *think* you had made it into the elite Directorate of Operations. You would have made a helluva field officer."

Greer was flushed and visibly shaken, looking at Reed in disbelief. "The Executive Finding? The note on White House stationery?"

"Faux, my friend," said Reed. "It was all a fake."

Reed wagged the gun at him. "I'm not wasting any more time. I've got a report to fill out that says I found you dead. Walk!"

Greer turned back toward the gate and lifted the latch. He pulled the gate open and walked through. Greer heard the gate behind him creak as the spring in the gate started closing while Reed was passing through. Reed put his hand out to catch it from slamming into his face and stuck his other hand holding the gun through the opening in the gate to keep the weapon trained on Greer. Greer knew the gate was swinging shut. He ducked down and pulled the gate closed hard, catching Reed's forearm with the gun. The revolver dropped to the ground and went off loudly in the direction of the street. Greer picked it up quickly and pulled back the hammer. He leveled it at Reed's head.

"Don't move, you son of a bitch!" Greer shouted.

Greer stood on one side of the iron gate and Reed stood on the other. Greer was breathing hard and the hand holding the gun was shaking. He looked around quickly to see if anyone was watching.

"Step back!" Greer demanded.

Reed moved a few steps backward.

"Farther!" Greer said.

Reed moved farther back along the path between the tombstones.

Greer carefully opened the gate and came through.

Reed spoke calmly: "What do you think you're going to do now?"

"Shut up," Greer snarled. "Who do you work for?"

Reed was stonily silent.

"Why did you set me up to spy on Jenkins? Was it because of the theory he was working on?"

"You're pathetic," replied Reed.

Greer walked a little closer. "Tell me, you bastard!"

Just then there was a loud boom from somewhere in the surrounding mountains. Greer kept his gun aimed at Reed, but looked around. There was another explosion, clearly the sound of a gun going off, echoing through the mountains range. Then there were several shots together, followed by a constant succession of more explosions coming from all around them in the mountains around the town. Greer realized it was from the men who had taken the muskets into the mountains in the old tradition of firing the special guns to announce the coming of the Christ child on Christmas Eve.

"Merry Christmas, Greer," said Reed. "Now what?"

Greer moved closer, holding the gun on Reed with both hands. The muskets were booming in the air. Greer felt the powerful percussions in the cavities of his body.

Just then, Reed lunged forward. Greer stood his ground and hissed between his clenched teeth: *"Eat shit and die!"*

Greer squeezed the trigger and Reed froze.

There was a metallic click as the hammer fell on an empty chamber. Greer felt a pang of terror as nothing happened. Suddenly another volley went off in the mountains, closer by. Greer flinched, thinking it was the gun in his hand. Reed rushed him again.

"Die, dammit!" Greer said, squeezing the trigger again. This time the gun exploded with a deafening flash. Greer was momentarily blinded and heard Reed hit the ground before he saw him.

Reed was slumped over a tombstone. Blood was spilling out of his side and running down his leg to the ground. A few drops fell onto the votive candle on the grave, extinguishing it with a hiss and small puff of smoke.

Greer gave the body a shove with his foot and it fell onto the stone grave plate. The muskets were still booming. The force of the gun's explosion left his hand feeling numb. He wiped the gun off and threw it over the cemetery wall.

The muskets stopped firing. Greer walked back to the church and opened the door. Everyone was singing a hymn. Something was wrong. He saw people's lips moving and the organist playing, but couldn't hear very well. He became aware of a loud ringing in his ears. He looked for Stephanie and found her on the end of a pew near the back, then slipped in beside her.

Stephanie was startled to see him. "Greer . . ."

She offered him the open hymnal she was singing from and he took it. He gave her a soft kiss on the cheek. Greer saw that his sleeve was blackened and he knew she must be able to smell the gunpowder.

The song ended and the lights were turned out. The only light was from the candles on the altar. Men walked down the aisles carrying wicker baskets full of small candles, passing them to the people along the pews. The priest came down the aisle lighting the candle of the person on the end of each row.

A peaceful end to the Christmas Eve service.

Then suddenly the doors burst open.

Greer turned quickly to look, sure it was Reed, up from the dead, coming at him again.

In came all the men who had been shooting the muskets in the mountains. They were rowdy, joyful. They joined their families in the pews and held the lit candles. They, too, reeked of gun powder.

Stephanie put her arm around Greer's waist. The priest led the singing of "Silent Night."

42

Rauf drove and Suleyman kept a nervous lookout from the passenger side of the Ford Fiesta. They had already dropped into the hills on the Austrian side of the border.

Slumped in the backseat, Greer was reviewing his situation. First, Kate not showing up. Then the confrontation with Reed. Greer obviously had misjudged them both. Kate was in on it, whatever *it* was. She'd sent Reed, which made her involvement perfectly clear. It was also clear now that if she had wanted to help him, she could have rescued him at any time. Instead, she had sent someone to kill him.

Stephanie was quietly triumphant, enjoying her victory.

They approached the outskirts of the city. Suleyman motioned for Greer to stay down out of sight. Stephanie hovered over him.

The car rumbled over cobbles. Greer lifted his head and peeked out the window. They were crossing through the slush of the cathedral plaza. They were entering Salzburg during the magical few hours between Christmas Eve and Christmas morning—sleeping children and empty streets, the gaudy colored lights unplugged for the night. Greer wiped the condensation from the window. A single white lamp weakly illuminated the front of the huge baroque cathedral, creating a muddle of shadow and light. It was as still as Mozart's city ever got.

The car dropped them in front of a dark high-rise apartment building on the other side of the river and left. They were under a canvas awning out of the weather. No lights at the entrance. Stephanie had a key to the front door.

But before she could use it, Greer pushed her against the wall in the doorway and kissed her hard. She dropped the key and held onto Greer as tightly as she could.

Greer felt her hands move down, unzip and release him. He unbuttoned her jeans and slid them off, then supported her back end as she lifted her legs up high around his waist before settling onto him. He drove her back against the wall, giving himself something to push against. She gasped.

He stayed still and she moved around him. He let her set the rhythm. Something fired inside of her. She started the roll of her hips back and forth and he joined in. He became the piston, perfectly fitted for her. She sucked in short breaths and smothered his face in her leather jacket. "Greer," she let out.

A frozen mist became frozen rain, beating onto the awning overhead. He breathed hard, held his breath, and pumped some more. His hot, wet breath froze in her hair.

They were slamming the wall, using it, making it work for them. She let him set the tempo now, driving deep and hard—the rise, hesitation, and accelerating fall of a sledgehammer, over and over again. She let him have it all.

He was in a race—running, running, running. Faster now. This wasn't what he wanted—this wasn't what he wanted.

But this was the way it was going to be.

He bit into the leather of her jacket to muffle the shout. She slid down and kissed him for a long, long time.

43 ❑ ❑ ❑ ❑

It was the most depressing place he had ever spent Christmas Day.

Greer turned from the window and looked around the room again. It reminded him of a dorm room at a small state college. The two single beds and other furniture were institutional. It was clinically bright from the bare overhead fluorescent lights. The walls were painted a light shade of gray and between the beds was a framed print screwed to the wall of a Pierrot staring sadly back at Greer. They both wanted to cry.

Greer took stock of his present situation. Not good, he told himself. He had put his faith in a woman who first spied on him, then tried to have him killed. Now he had put his life into the hands of a psychologically unstable woman who had stalked him across an ocean.

He looked out the window of his sixth-floor room in the apartment building. All he could see of Salzburg was the high-rise building next door. Down below was the roof of a shorter building and its air units stuck into the tar. He couldn't see the street. The sky was about the same color gray as the walls of the room. He had nothing to read, no television, and no one to talk to. He hadn't eaten breakfast and it was lunchtime. He was hungry, but there was no food. He couldn't sleep and he was bored to the point of screaming.

He heard the elevator doors open and several pairs of feet walking up to the outside of his door. He heard a key being inserted into the lock and turned. The handle turned and Stephanie stepped halfway into the room.

"I've brought friends," she said in a half-whisper. Greer nodded.

Stephanie came in, followed by two unsmiling, bearded men about his own age. They were the same two who had picked them up in Berchtesgaden the previous night. One carried plastic grocery bags and the other an athletic bag over his shoulder. She pointed to one of the beds and said something in Turkish. They dumped their load onto the bed, then stood flanking her.

Greer and the two Turks eyed each other suspiciously. During the trip from Germany into Austria and Salzburg, no one had spoken. They had dropped off Greer and Stephanie in the dead of night and spoken in Turkish to Stephanie about coming back the next morning to get her.

Stephanie spoke in English: "Greer, this is Suleyman and Rauf." They all shook hands. "We have just had a long talk. I'm sorry it took so long. I know you must be starving."

"I could eat," Greer agreed.

"Let's all sit down and talk. We picked up some food on the way over."

Greer's face lit up. The two Turks saw his expression and they smiled. The one named Suleyman came over to Greer and put his arm around Greer's shoulders and led him to the food on the bed. Stephanie sat on the floor and leaned against the opposite twin bed. Rauf opened up the grocery bags and pulled out an assortment of cheese and bread with fruit juices. Greer ate hungrily.

"Suleyman and Rauf understand English, but don't speak it very well," Stephanie explained. The two of them nodded in agreement. "They've worked out a plan to get you back to the United States."

"I'd like to hear it," Greer said with his mouth full.

"First, we get you a Canadian passport and other supporting documents. You will fly into Mexico as a Canadian citizen who is returning from a European business trip via Mexico. The Mexicans are highly unlikely to question either your passport or your reason for being there. Okay so far?"

"Good so far."

"You can't leave from any city in Germany or Austria. From the news it appears you are still believed to be in the country." She nodded to the Turks. "They will arrange for you to take a train from here to Rome. The Italians make a big show of security at the airport, but it's really just a big joke. From there you will fly to Mexico City."

"Then what?"

"You will have to get onto a flight going north from there. The easiest point of entry into the U.S. would be at the Tijuana border crossing back into California with the hundreds of other Americans.

You'd go over as a tourist. There are several small companies that make the flight out of Mexico City."

Greer thought about that for a moment. He swallowed a mouth of food. "When do I leave?"

"There are trade-offs. If you leave when there aren't many tourists traveling—such as over the next couple of days—you'll spend less time waiting in lines in clearing immigration and therefore you will reduce your exposure. They tell me that standing in the customs and immigration lines is the time of greatest risk of something going wrong."

"And the alternative?"

"Go during the peak tourist travel times so that you're just one of hundreds jamming the airports getting back to the U.S. They figure that the day before New Year's Eve will be the next extremely busy day."

"What's their recommendation?"

"Leave in a few days to join the other tourists traveling back on New Year's Eve. That would also give them several more days to work on your passport."

Rauf spoke up: "We can assure you that you will be safe here. We have used this place for many years to hide many of our own people. We will treat you as we would one of our own. Stephanie is family. We will help."

"Thank you," said Greer. "I don't know how or when I can repay you."

The Turks both looked at Stephanie.

Stephanie spoke again: "In return, Greer, they've asked that you leave your American passport with them so that they can use it to help forge other American passports for fellow Turks trying to get into the United States. I told them that you would do that."

Greer sat on edge of the bed and took a last swallow from the orange-juice bottle. He got his coat from the closet and got out his passport. He opened it up and looked at his picture on the inside cover. It had been taken just before he had left for Germany eight years earlier. The picture looked nothing like him now. That was the old Greer. This was the new, cynical Greer. He took a final look at Stephanie's kiss among the stamped visas, then handed over the passport to Rauf.

"I hope you make good use of it," Greer said.

"Thank you."

Suleyman unzipped his athletic gear bag and got out a Polaroid camera. "We need to get a picture for the passport," Rauf explained. Rauf looked around the room and seemed to have trouble choosing which blank spot on the wall would be best for a back drop. "Over there," he said, pointing to the space just inside the door.

Greer stood with his back against the wall. He took a swipe at his hair with his hand and tugged at his sweater around the collar. "This all right?" He looked at Stephanie who was still sitting on the floor. She bit her lower lip and nodded.

Suleyman fiddled with the camera in front of Greer. Suleyman finally spoke up: "Say Merry Christmas!" he said.

Greer said "Merry Christmas" halfheartedly, and the camera flash went off. Suleyman snapped the picture out of the camera and looked at his watch to time the development.

Greer chuckled: "I had almost forgotten." Greer looked around the depressing room. He looked at Stephanie sitting on the floor. She smiled and shrugged her shoulders. Her eyes started to tear. "Merry Christmas, *Liebling*," she said sadly.

"Merry Christmas," he said again.

Dammit, Bob, he thought. Late again.

Reagor's Porsche idled outside in the snow as he flipped through postcards in the tourist shop in Obersalzberg. Not too far away was the cottage where Hitler had finished *Mein Kampf.* Nearby also were the ruins of Hitler's Berghof, where he had given the British prime minister his "autograph" to secure "peace in our time." Four hundred feet above on the Kehlstein Mountain was the Eagle's Nest, closed until May. Inside, a few off-season tourists looked for souvenirs of the Third Reich.

Ironically, now Reagor hoped Reed actually *wouldn't* show with the proof of Whitaker's death as Reagor had ordered in Vienna. Since he had last talked to Reed, Reagor had received new information. There was the matter of the diskettes. What was on those diskettes? Until he knew for sure, he needed to keep Whitaker *alive.* He also needed to make sure the diskettes never got to anyone who could do anything with them.

The agreement was to meet in the shop at noon. At fifteen past the hour—if Reed hadn't appeared—he was presumed to be not attending and the meeting was off. It was twelve-twenty. There was a problem.

Reagor paid for the postcard and got back into his car. He had driven two hours from Munich for this meeting, just to be stood up. What a waste. What a way to spend Christmas Day. Greer Whitaker was playing havoc with his holidays.

Maybe he had been a little rough with Reed in Vienna. Nevertheless, Robert had better have a damned good excuse this time.

44 ❑ ❑ ❑ ❑

Marie von Bosacker watched him sop up the last morsel of his food with a piece of bread, pop it into his mouth, and toss back the remaining drops of the Gewürztraminer from the small green wineglass. It was the same each time they came to the restaurant. He would order the huge plate of sausages and potatoes with a bottle of the local wine, and end up with just enough wine in the glass to polish off the meal. He pushed back his plate.

"*Wunderbar,*" he said slowly in a deep, low voice. He had a slightly drunken cast to his face. He looked through the candlelight on the table and seemed to have a hard time focusing his eyes. His head wobbled a bit. He smiled kindly at her.

She smiled back and patted his hand in a comforting way. He was still handsome at sixty. His face was fleshy, but he still had a strong stand of dark hair with some salt-and-pepper graying. He dressed well —conservative and expensive. She actually did still like him a little. He was exceptionally bright and funny and was a good conversationalist. He was no longer trim, though. He had eaten too many sausages and drunk too much beer. But he had come to her that way.

"*Allons-y?*" Shall we go? she asked.

"*Oui, oui,*" he replied slowly again. His accent was thick with German. He seemed reluctant to move. He looked at the proprietress behind the bar who had been waiting on them. They were the only ones left in the restaurant. She brought the bill and went back to the small bar. He pulled out several one hundred franc notes and left them on the table. She returned with the customary two double cognacs for them to take upstairs to their room with them. *"Merci,"* she said to him. *"Joyeux Noël,"* she said without emotion. She never looked directly into the eyes of the woman dining with him.

Kaysersberg was always the same. Quintessentially Alsatian. So close to the German border, yet adamantly French. The hotel and the room were always the same. And they always kept the lights off in the room. She opened the window to the side of the bed. The view brought her a small measure of happiness. She pulled back the covers on the bed. He sat down heavily on the edge and undressed to his tank-top T-shirt and boxers, then fell back onto the pillows. He propped the snifter of cognac up on his large belly and watched through half-closed eyes as she undressed.

She unbuttoned her white cotton blouse and pulled off her skirt. She folded her clothes and put them carefully over the back of a chair. She left on her slip and her bracelet from Hermès on Rue du Faubourg St. Honoré, bought on her last trip to Paris. She climbed into bed next to him.

He put his cognac onto the bedside table and moved next to her. He slid down so that his head rested on her breasts. He held onto her like a child. She petted his head and he nestled against her.

He seemed asleep. She looked out the window. The view was an illustration for a fairy tale. She could see the ancient castle ruin on the hill nearby, lit up by an almost full moon. She remembered that the calendar on her desk at home told her that there would be a perfectly full moon on the last day of the year. Of the castle, all that was left was a roundel and turret, but it stood proudly over the town. It was ironic, she thought. That was *her* castle—although no one lived in it anymore —yet here she was sneaking around at night in a hotel.

Of course, management at the hotel was discreet. They all knew her. Her family had the largest land holdings in Alsace and some of the choicest vineyards. She had a chateau in the countryside and a great house in Ribeauville. Even though she was widowed, there were still people who mattered on the estate. It was seamy, but it was better this way.

He stirred. She looked down and saw him staring at the ceiling.

"What's wrong?" she asked in French. There was hardly a trace of her native Alsace.

"Can't sleep. I'll have to go soon."

She knew what this meant. His home and his wife were sixty kilometers away in Strasbourg. He had taken an exceptional risk to see her Christmas Night. She tried to delay the inevitable.

"When is parliament back in session?" she asked.

"Soon. Too soon," he replied wearily. He inhaled deeply, then let out a large alcohol-tinted breath.

She stroked his head. *"Mon petit chou."* My little cabbage. She wanted to go ahead and get it over with.

Her words excited something in his brain. He turned over on her and kissed her breasts. She let him pull the slip over her head. He took off his shorts and T-shirt. She lay down flat on the bed, arms to her sides, and he climbed on top of her. He mistook her shudder for passion.

She turned her head to the side and looked out the window as he moved on her.

It was a necessary thing. For now.

45 ❏ ❏ ❏ ❏

The four days of waiting in the awful apartment had passed excruciatingly slowly. Now Greer and Stephanie sat silently crammed together in the backseat of the tiny two-door Fiesta. Up front were the two Turks, Rauf and Suleyman. Rauf drove fast through the night city streets, pushing the little car hard around the curves. Every time Rauf accelerated, the car would backfire and Greer would jump. He wasn't sure if they would make the train station.

The car stopped at the passenger drop-off in front of the *Bahnhof.* Rauf kept the car idling, gunning the accelerator every few seconds to keep the motor from dying.

Neither of the Turks said anything. There was nothing left to say. All of the Canadian documents had been handed over and the train ticket to Rome purchased. The Turks had supplied Greer with a suit of well-worn clothes—a pair of gray slacks, an unremarkable blue blazer, and a lined overcoat; he was the picture of a weary Canadian on the way home. He had trimmed his beard to look more businesslike, less of a student, and dyed his hair a much darker shade. He carried with him the Alitalia airline ticket for the nonstop flight to Mexico City. They had all gone over Greer's itinerary in detail, rehearsing where he should go and how he should act. The Turks were experienced at running people into other countries. For them, this was nothing unusual. They had reckoned Greer's chances of successfully making it all the way through to freedom in Mexico City as "good." When Greer pressed them for more specific odds, Rauf just shrugged his shoulders and said "good" again.

The car was beginning to fill up with exhaust fumes, since it was sitting still. Greer knew it was time to go. Greer was more than just a little grateful to Stephanie for everything that she had done. The last four days and nights together in the Salzburg apartment had been transforming, a kind of love they had never known together. Not the manic sex of eight years ago. Not the excesses of the night on the *Prinsesse Marianna*. The roles strangely reversed: Greer given over to pleasing *her*, giving her what she wanted in a tender, but passionate, way. Kate had been right. He still did love her a little. He reached down and squeezed her hand.

"I think it's time to go," Greer finally said.

Stephanie nodded in agreement.

"When I've taken care of everything in the States, I'll come back. I promise."

Stephanie's eyes were filling with tears. She took Greer's hand again and squeezed it hard. She put her head onto his shoulder and wiped the tears.

"It'll be okay," he said. "I'll be in touch as soon as I can."

Greer looked at the rearview mirror. Rauf had his eyes cut watching him.

"You're strong. You'll be just fine," Greer continued. "Just stick close to your friends." He nodded with his head to the front seat. "And keep the gun close by." He had given one of the two guns to Stephanie and the other to Rauf. "Use it if you have to," he said.

Rauf spoke: "It's almost eleven."

Stephanie let go of Greer's hand. "You must go now," she said.

Greer kissed Stephanie, a long kiss to say good-bye for a long time again. It was a kiss he could never have imagined possible. With the kiss he gave her love and gratitude and a new understanding of what they could be. He was now glad she had not forgotten him. She had set out to capture his heart again and—against all odds—had been successful. There was something to be said for that.

Suleyman got out of the front seat and helped Greer get out of the back. Suleyman closed the door and Rauf revved the engine again. The two Turks looked impassively ahead.

Stephanie was in the backseat with her hand pressed against the back window. Greer put his hand up on the other side of the glass against hers and mouthed the words "Thank you."

The car lurched forward, then they were gone in dark. Greer heard the echo of the car backfiring somewhere down the block.

46 ❑ ❑ ❑ ❑

Lunch hour in the downtown business district in San Francisco. On one level of a converted underground garage was a new club, invitation only, five thousand dollars a year initiation, a thousand a year membership, where the hippest people of the city's business world spent their lunch hour. Men and women facing a sloped-back wall, standing erect in a two-handed Weaver stance, wearing ear protection. Jacko Takiyama was among them, standing at Position Number Six at the Bay Town Indoor Shoot and Lunch Club.

Jacko pulled off three quick shots at the silhouette, holding the semi-automatic pistol steady. He was sharp at seventy-five feet, deadly at forty-five. He sighted the target again and pulled off three more quick shots into the center of the paper man. Jacko punched the target return button and rolled his sleeves back down as the target flew toward him like a ghost.

Off came the headgear. He buttoned his cuffs and got his Presidential Rolex watch and Stanford class ring out of his pants pocket.

The ring. A reminder.

Kevin Hatu was losing nerve. Jacko pulled his tie out of the inside of his shirt. He put his suit coat back on and made a quick executive decision.

Jacko unclipped the target and threw it away. He ordered a turkey club sandwich to go. He'd eat it on the way to the airport. There was a late-afternoon flight to Washington, D.C., that he could just barely make.

47 ❏   ❏   ❏   ❏

It was eleven-fifteen at night in the White House. The Chief of Staff looked at the rusty Nagant revolver on his desk but was afraid to touch it. "You're sure Greer Whitaker killed your officer?" he asked Ben Gibbons.

The DCI deferred to Kate. "I had arranged for Greer to meet Bob Reed on the night he was killed," she said. "The FBI has positively identified this as the murder weapon. The gun had been wiped, but there was still a partial thumb and finger print on the barrel, probably from where it had been thrown. It matched Greer's." She felt like dying when she said it. There was no way to cover up what had happened. Any more lies to CIA management and the Administration would only make the situation worse at this point. She would say as little as possible, hoping neither of them would ask the right questions. From now on, it was a matter of damage control.

Gibbons added: "It was fired at point-blank range. Reed never had a chance. Seven point six two millimeter. The bullet tore through his gut like a cannonball. Bloody mess."

Dwight Conrad waved his hands in front of him. "Please, please! No more pictures from the morgue!" He took a pencil and nudged the gun. "This thing loaded?"

Gibbons picked the Nagant off the desk and palmed it like a pro. He gave the old revolver a spin, showing there were no bullets in the chambers. He pointed it at the window and pulled the trigger. *Click.* He pulled it again. *Click, click.*

"Damn it, Ben! Put that thing down."

The Director elaborated: "From the FBI lab reports, apparently the gun misfired before it went off. The bullet that the pin on the hammer hit the first time didn't fire. Must have been quite a surprise for him when he pulled that trigger and nothing happened the first time."

"No doubt," replied Conrad.

He addressed Kate: "What do you suppose he's doing now?"

Kate had thought about nothing else since the report had come in confirming Greer as the murder suspect in Reed's shooting. What could have gone wrong? Why would Greer kill Reed? Where had the gun come from? The truth was, she had no idea where he was. She had been counting on the beacon in the watch. Ben Gibbons had no idea what he had done when he refused to let her bring Greer in herself. Then, worse, when he insisted she send Reed.

She answered: "If I were in his position, I'd just try to get lost in a big city somewhere in Europe. He knows he's wanted, so he'll have to be extra cautious. He'll hide out for a while, but I'm sure he knows that eventually he'll be caught."

Gibbons spoke: "That's why we're going to try to keep the lines of communications open between him and Kate. He and Kate had a good relationship that we think we can use to draw him out. We think he'll try to get in touch with her again."

Conrad eyed Kate. "Use her as bait, huh?"

Kate nodded.

"What about the girl he was with?" Conrad asked. "Any truth to those reports?"

Kate had tried not to think about that, pushing it to the back of her mind, but the thought of Greer with another woman was making her crazy. Knowing who it was made it worse. Kate envisioned Greer in the pull-down bed of a passenger ship with the exotic black-haired German. The vision sent a chill up her spine. Knowing that she had a role in throwing them together again made her even crazier.

Kate took a calming breath. "There was just the one report from Munich. I wouldn't make any assumptions about whether there's someone with him or not. If there is, though, he'll have much more flexibility. Especially if she's someone who knows her way around and has contacts."

"The press won't link Reed with Greer Whitaker," said the DCI. "The Germans don't want a fuss either. They turned over the body and the gun without any hesitation."

The Chief of Staff thanked them for the briefing. They rose and started toward the door. "Ben, could you stay behind for just a moment?"

Kate closed the door behind her, leaving the two of them alone.

"Well, I've got some FBI reports of my own," said Conrad.

"What do you mean?"

"I've got a summary from the FBI on their sweep of Jenkins' office yesterday.

"Oh?"

"They didn't find anything that might help them to solve Jenkins' murder."

Gibbons nodded along.

"They thought the office was *too* clean," Conrad continued. "Looked as if someone had wiped the place clean. You need to know."

"Anything else?"

"That's enough, isn't it?" Conrad said irritably.

Gibbons and Conrad looked at each other for a moment.

"We did the best we could, Dwight," said the DCI. "The FBI was already on the way over. They were going to seal Jenkins' office and I was afraid we'd never get back in. I had to have a couple of my guys stall them while I went through his things."

"Well?"

"I found the diskettes and notes and a report on that theory of his he was going to give the President when he got back."

Conrad rolled his eyes up at the ceiling. "Where's it all now?"

"Destroyed. I took care of it."

They looked at each other again.

"Be careful, Ben."

They opened the door and shook hands. Kate rose from an armchair next to the secretary's desk.

"My purse," she said, smiling. She brushed past them and picked her purse up from beside the chair in front of Conrad's desk, where she had left it.

Conrad thanked her for coming.

"I'm here to serve, Mr. Conrad."

Kate and Gibbons walked down the carpeted hallway toward the southeast White House entrance.

A Marine guard held the door open for them. Gibbons was cheerful. "Good meeting," said the DCI on their way out.

"Did you get all that?" she asked.

Covey and Knowles sat in the backseat of Kate's car. At five o'clock in the morning, the downtown Washington streets hadn't come to life yet. Taxis were lined up in front of the American History Museum on Constitution Avenue, waiting to be called for the first fares of the day. A street sweeper ground through the intersection ahead of where they were parked. In front of them at the end of the Mall the sun was lighting up purple clouds from behind the Capitol building.

Kate pushed the rewind button on the microcassette player standing on end on the dashboard.

"It was a little muffled, but I think we got it," said Covey. The gray lenses of his glasses seemed even more impenetrable in the dark, when the telling whites of his eyes should have shown through. He reflected the taillights of a National Park Service patrol car that had been circling the streets around the Mall. "Recorded pretty well in your purse, didn't it?"

"This changes everything," said Kate. "I had simply wanted to see if they had heard anything about the operation that we hadn't. I had no idea of *their* involvement."

Knowles was bitter. "They're so naive. They think they're just trying to stop a kooky idea from reaching the President. It's all politics to them. They have no idea that they're unwittingly abetting a major spy operation against the U.S. They're just making it more difficult."

"Or, perhaps," said Kate, "they've inadvertently given us more time to take care of this the right way."

Knowles was still hot. "It just proves what we've said all along. You can't trust political appointees with sensitive information, not even the Director. Not when the whole Agency is at risk. Some operations are just too sensitive for outsiders to have access to. Your boss—our *leader* —just proved the point. Thank God none of them have been briefed on REDWING."

Kate was already thinking ahead to other issues. "How did I know Greer would kill Reed?" she asked. "There was no way I could have known that Gibbons was going to insist that Reed go in my place. I pleaded. I begged. It didn't make any difference. All that was supposed to happen was Reed was going to bring Greer in. It was simple. I was prepared to shut down REDWING at that point. Can you imagine what must have been going through Greer's head when Reed showed up? After I had promised to come personally and not tell anyone else where he was?"

Kate knew that Greer would never trust her again.

"You couldn't help it," Covey said.

Knowles said, "Now Reed's dead. He was key to this part of the operation. What do we do now?"

The sky had brightened enough for the photoelectric sensors to turn off the streetlights. It was drizzling onto the car windows. The world outside the car began to blur.

"Stephanie Becker," offered Knowles. "Still the missing link?"

"Greer's the missing link," said Covey. "Stephanie's a couple of links removed from the end of the chain."

Kate thought again of Greer with the woman in the photo.

Covey hung his chin over the front seat. "She was a damn good recruiter for Stasi at the university, wasn't she?" he said. "Greer wasn't the first bright young American to come under her spell. We've got a file an inch thick to prove it."

"She's as good as our own best recruiters," said Knowles. "A book, a beer, a bed. Then if Stasi were interested, she'd make the introductions to one of her old friends, then one of their officers would make a subtle recruitment pitch—just like the we do it. Apparently either Stasi wasn't interested in Greer or he didn't realize he was being recruited. I had my doubts initially, but his polygraph cleared him on that."

Kate knew the truth. She'd known it before the thought of joining the CIA had even crossed Greer's mind. "I'm sure," she said, "that after Stasi determined he wasn't going to become an asset, they instructed Stephanie to throw him back. She needed to troll elsewhere. We've got an excellent profile on Stephanie Becker. She really hooks them hard. Greer must have been crushed when she blew him off."

"I've heard the tape," volunteered Knowles. "NSA still had it in the archive from seven years ago. She's *really* good. She can play the seductress or psycho or damsel-in-distress—whatever it takes to get the job done."

Kate shook her head slowly.

Covey asked, "He told you he didn't care for her anymore?"

"He said it was over a long time ago," Kate said.

"I'm afraid everything dovetailed even better than we had even planned," said Covey.

Knowles spoke. "Unfortunately for us, Greer had to go and kill

Reed." He leaned over the seat. "You know the rules, Kate. Lose control over an agent and it's time to shut down the operation. We can't predict what Greer's going to do next. He seems to have acquired an agenda of his own."

Kate wiped the fog off the inside of the windshield. The drizzle was turning to rain. "I already tried shutting it down. Right now, I just pray he makes it back alive."

Knowles added, "He said in his interviews that he wanted adventure—he got it. He knew the risks."

Covey gestured over the seat. "We can't just shut down this part of REDWING because Reed's out. We've still got Greer. He's in play. Let's keep him in."

"And do what?" asked Kate, irritated. "We don't even know where he is."

Covey answered. "Shame about the watch. I thought he'd take better care of it, coming from you, but don't worry. He'll call back."

"I wouldn't count on that," Kate said.

Knowles said, "Eventually he's going to realize he needs your help now more than ever. Follow Greer and we'll find the girl. Follow the girl and we'll find what we're looking for. Let him dangle. He seems to attract the kind of people that REDWING was set up to flush out. Let's not waste an asset."

Kate turned around quickly in her seat and looked at them both. "He's *not* just an asset!" she said angrily. "He came into this thinking he was joining the CIA. He's more than an asset. He should be given every consideration that any other employee of the Agency would be given."

The only sound was the wind whipping big raindrops in waves against the car. Kate could read their minds.

"Where's it going to lead?" asked Kate. "I can't see where it's going."

Kate started the car up and turned on the wipers. Greer hated her, she thought. Anything could happen. And there were still Agency lives on the line. There were still moles buried in the building at Langley.

"We don't have any choice," she said. "REDWING goes forward as planned."

48 ❑ ❑ ❑ ❑

Greer stood nervously at the line marked on the floor at the Mexico City International Airport and watched the police with their machine guns scanning the passengers from their positions around the perimeter of the room. Fifteen feet in front of him was the immigration officer talking to the person in line ahead of him. Greer was next.

Greer had been standing in line for over twenty minutes. He had been one of the last to get off the plane. Several international flights came in just as his had landed, crowding the baggage claim and Immigration booths.

He was weary of traveling and he leaned against the column next to the line. It was 10 A.M. local time on the day before New Year's Eve and he had been traveling nonstop for a grueling thirty-six hours since leaving Salzburg. He hadn't really slept, didn't feel that he could. The train trip from Salzburg to Rome was without incident, but had taken nine hours on the overnighter. The train stopped at every pig path on the route to drop off mail. Getting to the airport in Rome from the train station had required a wait, a transfer, and another train ride. The airport in Rome was packed with people traveling home from the holidays. He had spent the entire seven-hour flight from Rome to Mexico City scrunched down in his window seat, covered up to his eyebrows with a thin in-flight blanket. The grandmotherly Mexican woman sitting next to him on the aisle had wanted to start a conversation just after the Alitalia flight took off, but Greer told her in German that he didn't speak Spanish or English. Fortunately, she didn't speak German.

As he waited to be motioned forward, Greer looked at his passport. It was odd to see the Canadian crest instead of the American eagle on the front. Rauf and Suleyman had done a good job of it, though. He flipped through the pages. They had aged it and filled its pages with immigration stamps from cities all over Europe and South America. He opened the front cover. He was now Peter Billings, resident of Vancouver, British Columbia. His picture showed a full-bearded face. It wasn't a happy face. He remembered how sad Stephanie had looked as Suleyman took the picture. It made him sad again to think of her hiding out in that drab room, waiting for him to return. Who knew how long it would be?

The line moved forward a few feet. Greer discreetly looked to the sides, then did a double-take. Hanging on the side of the custom booth was a poster with his name and picture.

Greer heard the immigration officer say something and wave him forward. Greer presented his passport, along with the Customs and Immigration card he had filled out on the plane just before landing.

The image of the poster was vivid in his mind. Two pictures of himself, one a copy from his NSC badge and the other a sketch of what he was supposed to look like with a beard. He had seen his name in bold letters, but in the brief moment he had turned, he was able to read nothing else on the poster.

The officer took the card out and laid it aside. He looked perfunctorily at the passport. He addressed Greer in English: "How long will you be staying, Mr. Billings?"

"About a week, then I go home."

"And what is the purpose of your visit?"

"I'm returning from a business trip by way of Mexico. I'm going to have a holiday in the sun before going back to the cold."

"Do you have anything to declare?" He looked at Greer's sides to see if he was carrying any baggage.

"No. Not this time."

The officer seemed unconvinced. He said nothing and just looked at Greer. Apparently he was waiting for Greer to say something else. Greer was about to die.

"I've shipped everything back to Vancouver," Greer volunteered. "All I need for this week are a bathing suit and a toothbrush." Greer reached into his jacket pocket and pulled out his toothbrush and laid it on the counter in front of the officer. The officer looked at it, then scrawled his initials on the Customs and Immigration card and threw it into a cardboard box.

"Where in Mexico will you be going?"

"Cozumel."

The officer opened up Greer's passport and stamped it. He forced a big, toothy, smile at Greer. "Have a nice stay in Mexico, Mr. Billings," he said, handing the passport back to him.

Greer followed the signs out of the room, past the dozens of waiting relatives stacked three deep outside, and found the currency exchange bureau. Since Stephanie had paid for everything in Germany with her credit card, he still had almost all of his twenty-five hundred dollars in traveler's checks left, minus a few deutsche marks. He looked at the signature scrawled on the left-hand side of the checks—he had signed the checks in a hurry in a totally illegible hand at the bank in Washington. He couldn't even read his own writing. He told the teller that he wanted to buy a hundred dollars' worth of pesos and the rest in dollars. Greer countersigned the traveler's checks in the same illegible handwriting—the teller certainly wouldn't be able to read his name, but he could plainly see that the two messy signatures matched. He said it would be a moment while he counted the cash.

Greer leaned against the booth wall and watched the people going by. He was desperate for sleep. He closed his eyes and dreamt someone was calling his name.

"Sir," someone called. Greer opened his eyes. "Sir . . ." It was the teller. He turned to the window.

There it was again. His name. Peter Billings. On the loud speaker. In English. *"Paging Mr. Peter Billings. Please contact the Federal Express representative in the main concourse."*

What was that? Did he hear it correctly? How many Peter Billingses were there in the airport?

He was flustered. The teller counted out the money for him. Greer didn't even bother to count along. The teller put the money into an envelope and handed it to Greer.

Greer was shaken. Was that really a page for him? Stephanie was the only one who knew where he'd be traveling and the assumed name he was using.

Greer followed the signs again, out of the International concourse to the main terminal. He spotted the Fed Ex sign along the wall. He approached slowly.

He stopped at a newsstand about twenty yards away. He picked up a Mexican football newspaper out of a rack and held it up as if he were reading it. He looked around the terminal for anything suspicious.

He put the paper back and walked slowly toward the Federal Express sign. As he got closer, he saw a woman at the counter in a Fed Ex uniform. She lifted a telephone and punched in a number. She read from the airbill on a Fed Ex box. As she spoke, her voice boomed through the terminal: "*Mr. Peter Billings, passenger on the Alitalia flight just arrived from Rome, please contact the Federal Express representative in the main concourse. Mr. Peter Billings, please contact the Federal Express representative in the main concourse.*"

Greer looked up and down the concourse. He saw the sign he was looking for to his left. He walked quickly into the men's rest room. All of the stalls except the large handicap stall were occupied. He went in, locked the door, then climbed back out under the stall. He washed his hands and checked himself out in the mirror again. He *did* look a lot like the bearded face in the poster on the column at passport control.

Greer searched up and down the concourse. He remembered seeing someone when he had come through Customs. He went back to the area where passengers from the international flights were coming through. He spotted the man in livery and cap, apparently a chauffeur. He was holding a sign with someone's name and a company logo.

"*¿Habla Usted inglés?*" Greer asked.

"Yes."

Greer gave him a fifty-dollar bill and handed him his Canadian passport. He took the sign out of the chauffeur's hands.

"I'll wait here for your ride. Go to the Federal Express desk and pick up a package for me. Take it into the first men's room down the concourse in that direction and push the package under the handicap stall." The man opened the Canadian passport and looked at Greer to confirm who it was. "I'll be waiting here," Greer said.

The chauffeur was looking at him dubiously. Greer held out another fifty. "Take this and there's another fifty when you get back. I'm not going anywhere without my passport."

Greer held the sign up for the passengers to see. The chauffeur seemed satisfied and left. As soon as Greer saw the chauffeur was out of sight, he threw the sign into the trash and followed the chauffeur toward the Fed Ex counter.

Greer hid in the newsstand again. The chauffeur spoke to the Fed Ex woman and showed her the passport. He signed on a clipboard and she gave him the package.

The chauffeur was slowed moving through the concourse by a pack of disembarking passengers from another international flight. Greer walked fast around the group, moving ahead of the chauffeur. Then

Greer turned into the flow of people, elbowing his way toward the chauffeur. The chauffeur was straining on his toes to see if Greer was still where he had left him. As he swiveled his head to look for Greer, Greer ducked beneath the mass of heads, made a push through the crowd toward the chauffeur, and snatched the package and the passport away. Greer stayed low, hidden in the middle of the passengers until he got to the end of the concourse. The chauffeur was nowhere in sight.

Greer ducked into a phone booth, shut the door, and tore open the package. The routing slip indicated that it had been sent from Salzburg the same day. He dumped the contents out onto the small shelf beneath the phone. There was a videotape and a small Tupperware container. He shook the container. Something rattled dully. He looked inside the box for a note, but found nothing else. The videotape was unmarked.

He opened the container and was immediately struck by a powerful stench. He closed the lid back quickly. He held the container up to the light, but couldn't tell what was on the inside. He held his breath and opened it again, knowing to expect the smell. He dumped the contents onto the shelf.

There was an ear and another grisly chunk of flesh. His heart skipped a beat, then it went racing off. He immediately recognized the earring attached to the ear as Stephanie's.

He held his forearm to his face and breathed through his coat sleeve. Greer rolled the lump of flesh over with the container lid and saw the tattoo—*Türkische Königin*. He quickly scraped the ear and flesh back into the container and sealed it. He felt a cold sweat break out and he slumped dizzily to the floor.

They've got to Stephanie. It must have happened just after he had left Salzburg. But what could he do to help her now? He was desperate to get to a place where he could play the video, hoping against hope he could find some way to help.

Greer walked shakily to another concourse, reading the departing flight schedules of the airlines. He was looking for a small Mexican airline.

"May I help you, sir?" said the man at the counter. The flight schedules were handwritten on a marker board on the wall behind him.

"I need a ticket to Tijuana, please," answered Greer.

"Will that be round trip or one way?"

"One way."

Greer huddled by himself in a corner of the gate waiting area in the terminal reserved for the small airline services. It was just after one o'clock in the afternoon and he had another two hours to wait. On the chair next to him was a stack of old magazines and newspapers. He dug through the pile, looking for something in English. He caught a glimpse of a headline.

He pulled the paper out and folded it back to the first page. It was a *Dallas Morning News* Sunday edition from the previous week. At the bottom was a color photo of a brilliant blue sky set above a white-capped sea. In the foreground was a grassy hill and a Marine in full dress uniform bending over to pick up an American flag off the ground next to a silver coffin. The caption read: President Mourns Loss of Close Friend, National Security Adviser.

Within the space of one minute after stepping out of the terminal in Tijuana, Greer had been offered a shoe shine, a switchblade, a fake Rolex watch, a gold chain, firecrackers, a taxi ride, and a lay. He chose the taxi ride.

"First time in Tijuana?" asked the driver.

"Yes it is." They bumped along in the gritty taxi down the Boulevard Agua Caliente.

"Are you here on business or pleasure?"

"Perhaps a little of both."

The taxi driver adjusted his rearview mirror to look directly at Greer.

"So maybe you are looking for a little something to do in the evening, no? Maybe take in a little jai alai? A little gambling? Pretty girls always at jai alai."

"Probably not tonight."

The driver nodded. "Tomorrow night will be the big night. New Year's Eve is very spectacular in Tijuana. Lots of fireworks. Will you be here tomorrow night?"

"I'm not sure."

The driver pointed out the open window. "There is what you asked about." He pulled the cab to the side of the road, just before the place where the traffic started backing up. The street ahead was splitting from two lanes into eight where he was pointing. "That's the crossing. It is the most heavily crossed international border in the world. On the other side is San Ysidro. The United States of America." He turned around in his seat to face Greer. "Will you be walking or driving across?"

"Probably walking."

Greer was surveying the checkpoint. Cars were inspected by guards. They checked the trunk, then waved the cars through. He also saw people filing into a passageway on the left-hand side of the street.

"Okay," said Greer. "I need a hotel."

"Sure thing." The taxi driver spun the cab into a U-turn, blasting other cars out of his way.

The driver said, "I take you to a nice hotel downtown. The Fiesta Americana. It's beautiful. Thirty-two floors high. That's where all the businessmen stay."

"No . . . nothing that nice." Nothing that exposed, he was thinking. "I have a question."

"*Si?*"

"I need a hotel with a VCR."

"VCR?"

"Videotape players."

"*Oh,* I see. You are right. The Fiesta Americana is not the hotel you want if you want to watch videotapes. I take you to another one you will like. Some businessmen stay there also. They are also in Tijuana for a little business and a little pleasure."

The taxi turned sharply at the next street. The area quickly turned seedier as they headed away from the Boulevard Agua Caliente. There were few shops for the tourists and more cantinas. There were few children in this part of town. Greer saw several *putas* walking along the sidewalk. Lots of leg and lipstick. Not much to look at. They turned and watched sadly as the taxi with the gringo in the backseat passed by.

The taxi slowed. The driver swept his hand across the street. "Take your pick." On both sides were one-story buildings painted in garish colors with big lettering on the outside. Greer couldn't make out all the Spanish but he understood the neighborhood and the triple Xs over the doorways.

"Maybe you have heard about La Couahuila, Tijuana's famous

entertainment district? No? All of the hotels have videotapes. You rent a room that has dozens of videos and a machine in the room. You can watch them as many times as you want. You can even rent a camcorder and tape yourself or with a friend. Whatever you want. You can call down to the front desk and they will get you anything you want. Food, beer, tequila, marijuana, women, condoms. You never have to leave the room. I bring many customers here from America. I drop them off on Friday night and pick them up on Sunday afternoon. Are you sure this is where you want?"

Greer hesitated. But he had to see the tape from Salzburg.

"Which one do you recommend?" he asked.

"I think you would like Felix El Gato."

"Felix the Cat?"

"*Si.*"

The driver pulled up to a one-story cinder-block motel painted bright blue. Around the outside were large cartoons of Felix the Cat chasing around and engaging smiling girl cats in different positions. Over the doorway was a sign painted in English in white block letters: WELCOME TO HOTEL FELICITY. Greasy black smoke rose from behind the building.

"Nobody calls it Hotel Felicity," explained the driver. "No one knows what it means. Everyone calls it Felix El Gato. It's clean inside. Run by a nice couple. Not many roaches."

"*Gracias,*" said Greer. He paid the driver and pushed through the knee-high gate up the walkway.

The cat theme of blue walls was carried through on the inside. The lobby was decorated with matching blue vinyl-covered chairs and a sofa. Felix the Cat was everywhere: on needlepoint throw pillows, stuffed dolls, framed prints, a telephone on the corner table. There was a Felix the Cat *piñata* hanging from the ceiling. In a dish at the registration counter there was a bowlful of Felix the Cat wrapped candies.

A man was sitting on a stool behind the registration desk watching Felix the Cat cartoons on a TV on the counter. There was a VCR on top of the TV set. He saw Greer coming in and turned the volume down.

"Yes, sir. May I help you?" he asked.

"I'd like a room. I was told I could get one with a VCR."

"Oh, *yes,* sir. That is our specialty." He punched the EJECT button on the VCR and pulled out the cartoon tape. He got a tape off the shelf on the wall and inserted it into the machine. The tape came on in the middle of a hard core sex scene. Two women and a man.

The man saw that Greer had no luggage. "Is this just for the afternoon?" he asked.

"No, no. I'll be staying the night."

"*Very* good, sir." He pulled a clipboard off the wall and looked at a chart showing the layout of the rooms. "Any special interests? We stock all of the rooms with the standards, but we also have specialty rooms." He turned the clipboard around for Greer to see. "The Scandinavian Room has a good collection of blondes and the African Room specializes in black women. I might suggest the Variety Room if this is your first visit. No?"

"Yes. It's my first visit. Really, anything will do. I brought my own tape."

"Okay." The man pulled a key off the board behind the desk. "The Variety Room then it is."

Greer looked at the TV. The three people were changing positions. The sound was down, but he could imagine the noises.

"And how will you be paying for this—cash or credit card? If you want to use a credit card for business expense purposes, I can run it though any of several names we use for imprints. You choose—a restaurant, a regular hotel, whatever you want."

"I'll pay cash in advance."

"*Very good,* sir. We find that most of our customers like to stay right up to our checkout time—eleven A.M."

"I plan on leaving early."

"Will you be joining us for breakfast on the patio, sir?"

"I don't think so."

"Okay." The man held the key up for Greer and pointed down a blue hallway. "Your room is just down the hall. Enjoy your stay."

The Variety Room was small and dark. The Felix the Cat theme was gone. The furnishings consisted mainly of cheap Art Deco–style furniture painted black. A gorgeous bronze-skinned nude with black hair and blue eyes smiled out of a black velvet painting on one wall. There were a toilet and a sink in the corner. At the foot of the twin bed was a cabinet holding a twenty-four-inch color television and a VCR, both Korean imports. On a shelf at the bottom of the cabinet were three dozen videotapes, all of them copies, with handwritten labels—*Debbie Does Dallas, The Russians Are Coming, Behind the Green Door.*

Greer turned the power on to the TV and VCR. He put the Salzburg tape into the machine and took the remote control over to the bed and sat down. He sank low. The springs under the mattress were shot. He started the tape and heard the tape heads whir.

The screen was black, but he could tell the tape wasn't tracking right. Greer pointed the remote and made the necessary adjustment. He turned up the sound.

The picture was grainy and still didn't seem to be tracking perfectly. What had he expected? The tape was made in Austria, played on a Korean machine, running on Tijuana electrical current.

The black screen snapped into an overexposed head-and-shoulders shot of a woman sitting with her head bowed down. Greer saw immediately it was Stephanie. From offscreen, someone thrust a newspaper in front of the woman's face. The camera zoomed in and the picture took a moment to refocus. Greer could see that it was yesterday's edition of *Salzburger Nachrichten.* The hand let the paper drop.

A voice came over the tape in English with a German accent: "As you can see, Greer, we have Stephanie. She would like to say a few words. . . . Stephanie, wouldn't you like to say something to Mr. Whitaker?"

Stephanie lifted her head. The camera zoomed in tighter on her face. It looked like an overripe eggplant. It was purple and one eye was completely swollen shut. Her lips were split and bleeding. Her hair was plastered to the side of her face with blood.

"Greer . . ." she said in a whisper.

"Louder, my darling. He can't hear you," said the voice.

She tried licking her lips and winced. "Greer . . . I'm alive . . . They will kill me if I don't talk to you. . . ." She spoke slowly.

"Please, continue," the voice urged.

"Greer . . . I had to tell them that you were on the flight from Rome. . . . They know about the computer diskettes. . . . They want you to give them up in exchange for me. . . . They're very serious about it. . . . I'm in pain, Greer. . . . Please help me."

Greer hit the PAUSE button on the remote. It was more than he could stand. He hit the PAUSE button again and the tape resumed.

"Greer . . ." she said. "Please . . ." She couldn't finish the sentence. She was in too much pain to talk anymore.

The tape kept running for a couple of minutes. Greer watched her writhing, her body jerking every few seconds with a spasm of pain.

The voice came on again: "Greer, we obviously know that you are in Mexico. It is only a matter of time until we catch up with you." The video stayed in a tight shot of Stephanie's ghoulish, contorted face. "She told us about the diskettes you sent from Munich. We want the diskettes."

There was something familiar in the voice, but Greer couldn't quite place it.

The tape ran another minute without sound, holding steady on the close-up of Stephanie. Greer could hardly bear to watch, but he couldn't take his eyes off Stephanie. "It's very simple, Greer. Turn over the diskettes and Stephanie lives. No diskettes, and she dies."

Greer was overwhelmed. He punched the wall next to the bed, exploding through the thin Sheetrock. Stephanie was a victim and he was to blame. His mind flashed back to the last time he had seen her. She had looked so sad in the backseat of the car in Salzburg as she had been driven away from the train station, with her hand pressed against the window. Now she was beaten to a bloody pulp and it was his fault.

Greer was overcome with grief. He felt something he hadn't felt in a long time. There welled up inside of him an intense sadness with a physical pain. He started to cry. He hadn't taken his eyes off the TV. He tried to disassociate what he saw from reality so that he could think rationally again. What he saw on the screen was no longer Stephanie. This was a dying thing. It was a nature film on television showing a frightened animal that had been beat out in a run across a dry flat range. This is what the dead thing looked like just before it became dead.

"Get the diskettes, Greer. Stephanie has told us that you sent them to a secret location on the California coast. Get them—wherever they are—and do not move. Do not do anything with them. Do not talk to anyone about them. Get them and sit on them. We will be in touch. Without the diskettes, there will be no hope in ever seeing her alive."

The tape ran for another minute without a voice. Stephanie moaned in pain. The motion of her head seemed to split an especially large swollen patch under the eye that was closed.

"It's up to you now, Greer." The man on the tape gave an order in German to someone off tape to shut the recorder off. The screen went black.

The voice.

Greer sat straight up in bed.

Where had he heard that voice? There was something familiar in the intensity, the pitch, and the halting rhythm. Was it the voice he had heard speaking with Reed in the Tower Gallery in the art museum in Washington?

49 ❏ ❏ ❏ ❏

Greer stood at the sink in his motel room, holding to his throat the straight razor borrowed from the front desk. The fugitive poster he had seen in the Mexico City airport portrayed two likenesses of him: one the clean-shaven Greer of his NSC ID and the other an artist's conception of what he might look like with a beard. The artists had been close, the beard full as it had been before neatly trimmed in Salzburg. What was needed was another new look.

Greer winced as he shaved. The straight razor was dull, there was no shaving foam, and the water was tepid. He scraped at his throat, then his cheeks. He left hair on the upper lip, the chin, and around the sides of his mouth. He wiped his face with a thin towel and felt tiny air currents on his face. It was, he decided, just the look he had anticipated. The goatee made him look like any kid who might be found up and down the coast. Definitely "beat."

Greer experimented with the part in his now black hair. Earlier that morning he had sent out for hair dye.

Greer held his breath and opened the Tupperware box, removing the ear. He removed the earring and rinsed it off. He put the earring into his pocket, returned the ear to the box and finally exhaled.

All that was left was to find a discreet way of getting rid of Stephanie's flesh. There was a rubbish fire in a metal drum behind the motel that had been burning ever since he had checked in. Horrible, but discreet.

• • •

It was four o'clock in the afternoon on New Year's Eve. Greer lined up with the other American day tourists who were waiting to walk back through the border crossing to San Ysidro at the end of the day. Earlier in the morning, Greer had bought fake Levi's, a piñata, and a pair of small-lensed sunglasses. Afterward, he had eaten a quick lunch and bought a T-shirt at the Tijuana Hard Rock Cafe. In the bathroom of the restaurant, he had changed into his new clothes. He had his Canadian passport in his hip pocket, but he had already decided that unless he was asked, it would be better to try to sneak back across the border as a regular American tourist. The fake passport had got him this far, but this was the first time he had confronted American border control. He looked ahead and saw that the guards weren't checking ID. No one looked more American than he did in his new clothes.

Greer took a look around the room. Behind him in line were more Americans and a few Mexicans. One of the Mexicans quickly looked away as Greer looked toward him. Greer moved forward another few steps, then turned and looked again. The Mexican who had turned away was silently mouthing something to another Mexican farther back in line. The one farther back saw Greer looking at them and gave a signal with his head to the other in Greer's direction.

Were they talking about *him?* Greer wondered. Greer stepped up to the guard.

"Anything to declare?"

Greer put his souvenir down on the counter.

"Piñata," Greer answered.

The American customs and immigration officer gave Greer a quick look-over. The officer shook the piñata.

"Is that all?" asked the officer.

"Yes, sir."

He waved Greer through and looked to see who was next in line. The low sun coming through the exit door glass nearly blinded him.

"Stop!" The voice had come from the border-control office on his right. Greer kept moving.

Surely that doesn't mean me, Greer thought. He didn't look toward the voice and walked on.

"Stop!"

There was commotion all around. There were people, Mexicans by their look, breaking out of line behind him, jumping turnstiles, and running toward the exit doors on the American side. Greer looked in the direction of the voice. A guard was looking directly at him. "I said *stop!*" Greer caught a quick look at the wall in the office directly behind the guard. It was lined with fugitive posters.

Greer threw down the piñata and sprinted out the door. There were a dozen others running, each thinking he must have been the one being yelled at to stop. Greer joined the pack, racing into San Ysidro. There were too many of them for the guards to chase. Greer had seen it before on the evening news—a handful of Mexicans making a run for it at the Tijuana border crossing. They ran in random directions, like cockroaches being surprised at night by a kitchen light turned on. Except that Greer knew exactly where to scramble.

Greer pushed through the people on the sidewalk. The California side of the border in San Ysidro flashed by. He was pumping his arms hard, darting in and out of the pedestrian traffic.

He glanced over his shoulder and saw someone running behind him. Then he saw a second person moving through the crowd in his direction. They were the two Mexicans who had been behind him in line at the border crossing.

Greer ran harder along the sidewalk down Central Drive, running out into the street and ducking around stopped cars to keep moving. He looked back again. The two men behind him were matching his speed. One of them appeared to be talking into a radio as he ran. Just two more blocks, he told himself. Finally, a half block away, he saw his objective. There was a bus pulling out of the lot ahead. The motel manager had told him the next shuttle to downtown San Diego wouldn't be for another hour. That wasn't even a possibility now. He ran harder, waving at the bus to stop before it turned onto the street. The driver didn't see him. He ran diagonally across the street ahead of the bus, stopping on the pavement only ten feet in front of the still moving bus. The driver stomped on the brakes, bringing the bus to a stop at the end of his outstretched arms.

Just as he was about to step up onto the bus, there was a small, tight explosion that sounded like a gun from behind. Greer flinched and instinctively crouched down. The bus door opened. Without looking back, he jumped onto the bus. "Just go! Go!" he shouted at the driver. "Go!"

The door closed behind Greer and the bus lumbered onto the street. Greer fell into the seat across the aisle from the driver and looked outside the window, searching for signs of his pursuers. The two Mexican men were standing in the street, watching the bus go by, the one still talking into a radio.

Suddenly there was the explosion again. Greer swiveled his head around to see where it was coming from.

Once again, he heard the sound. He pinpointed it as coming from the alley that ran behind the bus station they were passing by. Greer heard two more bangs again in rapid succession and saw two Mexican boys crouched in the alley, tossing little Black Cat firecrackers in the direction of a mangy dog who appeared too chewed up with vermin to move. Greer slid down in the seat and closed his eyes. It was, after all, Greer reminded himself, New Year's Eve.

"You gonna pay or what?" he heard.

Greer walked forward to pay the driver the fare.

"What the hell was all that?" the driver asked.

Greer didn't respond. He was still winded from the half-mile run from the border crossing.

50 ❑   ❑   ❑   ❑

It was already late at night on New Year's Eve in Munich. Reagor sorted through the mail that had been held for him while he had been traveling. Among the stacks was a package so small that he wondered how it had ever made it through the mails.

Reagor got the computer humming for a late night's work. He checked his voice-mail messages. There was one that had come in earlier in the night.

The package was wrapped in brown paper and taped shut. He shook it, but heard nothing. Ordinarily he would have had such a package X-rayed first before he opened it, but the San Francisco postmark and use of the children's sticker on the back depicting a lion told him it was okay. HAVE A NICE DAY, the lion was saying. Well, he certainly hoped so.

Reagor hit the button for the speakerphone and retrieved the voice-mail message. As he waited, he carefully slit open the package with his Swiss Army knife. There was a box inside.

On the speakerphone was a warbling tone, then static, then white noise. Reagor rerouted the phone into his computer and started the descrambler program.

He opened the box. In its molded velvet compartment was a fountain pen and a card. Reagor took out the pen. He read the note, a scrawling flourish of someone with big hands and a native alphabet something other than the English in which it was written: MERRY CHRISTMAS AND HAPPY NEW YEAR! The card wasn't signed.

Reagor held the pen in front of him in the tips of his fingers, his elbows propped on the desk. A cheap imitation of black lacquer. He pulled slowly on both ends of the pen. He concentrated hard on sliding the cap smoothly off. The more he pulled, the broader the grin on his face.

There was a beep on the computer, indicating the descrambler program had finished. It would have to wait a moment.

He swore he wasn't going to flinch. A final millimeter more, and the pen exploded in his face.

Reagor was laughing.

What a cheap son of a bitch, he thought. Less than two U.S. dollars for a toy fountain pen that set off child's caps. He chuckled, recapped the pen, and threw it into his top drawer.

One spy to another. Friends across the water, friends across the years. The bottle of cognac would have arrived sometime after the pen was sent. It pays to keep in touch, Reagor reminded himself.

He swiveled to the computer to read the converted message. A smile of satisfaction: HE IS STILL OURS. Reagor snapped shut and pocketed the knife.

It wasn't for nothing he had set a backup plan into motion.

51 ❏　❏　❏　❏

Greer got off the shuttle at the San Diego bus station. After the thirty-minute ride from the border, he was still trying to cool down from his run. He oriented himself facing east, and saw the flashing lights against the darkening sky that the Felix the Cat motel manager had told him to look for. He set out toward the beacon.

Greer walked up and down the aisles of the used-car lot, peering inside the windows and stepping back to inspect the puttied-over body damage.

A man in short sleeves wearing a turquoise-and-silver-tipped bolo tie came out of a small building on the lot. He was chewing on a fat unlit cigar.

"I'm looking for a car," Greer told him. "Ramirez at Felix the Cat told me to ask for Jose."

"I'm Jose," the man answered, extending his hand. "Look no more. What kind of car do you need?"

Greer turned around to take another look over the cars. He pointed to a white VW van. "The van," he said. "Does it run?"

Jose went back into the building and came back with a key, then got in and started it up. Greer opened the back up and watched the fan belt turning. Jose cut the engine and got out.

"How much?"

Jose motioned to the large fluorescent orange numbers on the windshield. "Eight hundred," he said without flinching.

Greer shook his head. "Ramirez told me you could do something special for me." He pulled out a wad of bills. "I'll pay cash tonight. What's your price?"

Jose walked around the van, looking serious. "How much money do you have to spend?" he asked.

Greer shook his head again. "Unh-uh. What's your price on the van."

Jose looked thoughtfully at the vehicle. "Six hundred," he said.

"C'mon. This has got to be over twenty years old!"

"A classic," agreed Jose seriously. "You could apply for antique car plates."

Greer counted out several crisp hundred-dollar bills. "Here's four hundred dollars. Take this and I'll drive it off the lot right now."

Jose took the money, folded it and put it into his shirt pocket. "I'll be right back," he said, and went again into the shed.

Greer got into the van and cranked it up again. It sounded good. He tried the brakes—they were a little squishy, but workable. The rearview mirror was held in place by rubber bands. He pulled the headlight knob and looked at the illuminated panel. It was a world away from the BMW he had driven through the Bavarian Alps. There was a full tank of gas—unless the gauge was broken. The odometer read 565,232 miles. Over half a million miles. More than twenty times around the world. If, of course, the odometer hadn't been rolled back.

Jose came back and Greer forged a signature on the vehicle registration and the title.

"How's the best way to pick up the interstate going north?" Greer asked.

"Take a left out of the here and follow the street until it dead-ends. Then take a right and follow the signs to Interstate 5 to Los Angeles. Need a map?"

"No, thanks. I know where I'm going."

52 ❑　❑　❑　❑

Kate rushed into the room where Covey and Knowles were examining a fax. "Let's see it," she demanded. She snatched up the report.

"Positive ID, Kate," said Covey. "Finally, after hundreds of dead-end leads."

Kate was scanning the report as Knowles added, "Immigration spotted him at the San Ysidro crossing in Tijuana with their new computerized facial recognition system. They photograph the people coming through, then check the digitized faces against a database of over ten thousand criminal suspects. It even identifies people wearing disguises."

"There was also corroborating identification by an eagle-eyed border guard," Covey said. He pulled down Greer's fugitive poster from the wall and thumped the section below the paragraph citing allegations. "Distinguishing marks," he read. "Kate, you told us about this yourself." They both looked to her.

Knowles looked over Kate's shoulder while she read the fax out loud: " 'Subject was also identified by the scar on his right cheek.' It says here he saw a crescent-shaped white scar that glowed like a light when the sun hit it. Wearing a goatee?"

Kate flipped the page. There was a picture of a piñata in shape of a bull. "What's this all about?" she asked.

"Hair samples," said Covey. "They found hair samples on the piñata. I had them send it to a lab in San Diego. They're comparing it to the samples from the boat cabin in Cologne. We'll have the analysis completed in a few hours."

Kate said, "I'm not waiting until then. That's him. We'll look at the lab results when we get out there. I think I know where he's going," she said. "After Stephanie Becker blew him off, he went to California to get his head together. He told me all about the trip he took up the coast. I'll bet he's following the same route again."

Kate pointed at Knowles. "You stay." She pointed at Covey. "You and I will go. I don't want the entire federal government getting in our way. We can bring him in ourselves."

Kate pointed again at Knowles. "Contact the credit-card companies and have them pull their records on Greer going back seven years. I want to know every stop he made on his trip up the coast—hotels, gas stations, whatever. Fax it to me on the company plane as soon as you get it. We can be in Tijuana by nine-thirty tonight. Tell the San Ysidro Immigration people we're on the way."

Kate and Covey looked at the videotape again in the U.S. border control office in Tijuana. It had recorded everyone who passed through the turnstiles going from Mexico to the other side. The tape recorded from four different hidden cameras, each shot holding for five seconds before moving to the next.

The head of the local U.S. Immigration office explained. "The digital facial recognition system program indicated a probable match between the person in line and a suspect in the computer's database. We don't check everyone coming back across. We usually don't ask for passports or any other ID. It's impractical. We stop anyone who fits the profile of a drug smuggler or illegal immigrant. Or anyone who trips the computer program. Officer Bledsoe was on duty when the silent alarm went off and he was on his way to check. That's when all hell broke loose."

Kate hunched over the TV screen. A man wearing a Hard Rock Cafe T-shirt and sunglasses stood in front of the camera aimed at the border guard's desk. He had black hair and wore a goatee. He carried a bull piñata. "That's him?"

"Officer Bledsoe saw the scar just after he passed through the turnstile. The light coming through the exit door struck his face just right. He doesn't look *just* like the pictures in the wanted poster, but close enough. The goatee was a nice touch. But Officer Bledsoe is very good at what he does."

There was commotion on the tape. A shot from a different camera angle, head-on as the people had just passed through the turnstile and headed toward the exit door. The suspect was walking directly toward the camera. Then confusion as a dozen young men break line, jump the turnstile, and push through the door. The suspect runs like hell. Greer looks unknowingly directly into the hidden camera.

"That's definitely him," said Kate. She turned to Covey: "We've got a long night ahead of us."

"Look, Kate. All we have to go on is this list of hotels and gas stations he stopped at seven years ago."

"We've got to go with what we've got," Kate said. "He's got a six-hour lead on us if he's really headed up the coast as he did before. We'll take the plane to L.A., then pick up the trail north of there."

53 ❑   ❑   ❑   ❑

Jacko Takiyama poured out the steaming sake from the large ceramic bottle into the cup for his Uncle Hiro. They sat at the back of a Japanese restaurant in Nihonmachi, San Francisco's Japantown, located about a mile to the west of the fancy stores around Union Square. On the television screens in the corners of the room, Sumo wrestlers on videotape bounced off each other and fell into an audience like a bad train wreck.

Except for their ties, the two Takiyamas were dressed identically—dark blue suits, starched white button-down shirts, and highly polished black wing tips. Jacko wore one of two dozen red silk Burberry ties he owned. It was his trademark—he never wore any other tie. The uncle wore a conservative rep tie from an expensive shop in the Ginza district of Tokyo.

"*Kanpai,*" toasted the uncle. He was in his late sixties.

"*Kanpai*," answered Jacko. They each took a large sip of the hot rice wine.

The uncle spoke in Japanese in a hushed voice: "Your father sends his regards." He patted Jacko on the shoulder. "The family is very proud of you." He beamed.

The elder Takiyama had arrived just that morning on an overnight flight from Tokyo. It was his custom to come to the United States once a month to discuss business with Jacko and pass along messages from his brother. He especially liked coming to America around the holidays. Koji Takiyama, Jacko's father in Japan, still held a grudge against the United States from the war and had never visited America.

The younger Takiyama nodded thoughtfully. He looked at the night's patrons, all Japanese. They were mainly businessmen seated together in groups of four or six at tables facing a small platform to his right. A few couples. After karaoke there would be a new crowd and a large New Year's Eve party.

"Business is good," Jacko said, shrugging. "You ought to know—you keep the books at home."

A waitress cruised by to check their drinks. She took the sake bottle away and brought another one back.

"What news of home, Uncle?" Jacko asked.

The older man drew up closer to Jacko. "There is a problem that your father was recently made aware of." He looked to see that no one was within earshot. He switched to English, knowing that the clientele was more fluent in Japanese. "The government in Tokyo has asked us to help out discreetly in a matter that strikes at the heart of our national economy. Your father—as you know—has a great number of friends in the government. They have been involved in painful negotiations with the Americans about imports. If we let the Americans in, they will flood Japan with cellular phones, Jeeps, cheap rice. Our own manufacturers will suffer greatly. Our economy and the Japanese people will eventually suffer greatly, too."

Jacko was distracted by a man in short sleeves stepping onto the small platform. The man turned on an amplifier behind him and watched the console lights come to life. He set a microphone stand out in the middle of the stage and tapped the mike. The thumping came out of the speakers behind him.

Uncle Hiro continued: "The Americans are pushing to have a new agreement signed at the Group of Seven meeting later this week here in San Francisco. The Americans have been holding out, delaying. The Americans are now threatening sanctions, which may harm our national economy even more than opening up to American imports. We will sign the trade accords under duress." He paused dramatically and leaned into Jacko's face. "The Americans will think that we are caving in. But actually, the government has another plan," he whispered loudly.

Jacko looked at his uncle. "What kind of plan?" he said coolly.

"A plan to make Japan a strong, proud nation again. It is a plan that will ensure our economic well-being for a thousand years." The uncle spoke with wonderment. "We will never have to bow down to America again!"

Jacko didn't respond. He lit up a Dunhill cigarette, inhaled deeply, and blew the smoke up toward the ceiling.

"What's that got to do with us?" Jacko said.

"You know that we have always helped the government out with intelligence and security matters."

Jacko nodded. He himself had placed many agents for the government in Silicon Valley companies. And, there had been his greatest success, Kevin Hatu.

The uncle continued: "Our government has already signed a secret treaty with the Germans. There will be a division of the world's markets along economic lines. The Germans will get exclusive influence in certain countries and product categories and the Japanese will get the rest." Hiro sat back in his seat, finished with his revelation.

Jacko looked at his uncle as if he were looking at someone in an insane asylum. The lights in the restaurant dimmed and small spotlights came on from behind their heads, shining onto the stage. Jacko blew another lungful of smoke up toward the ceiling through the shaft of light.

Jacko said, "Are these the ideas of old men who lust for the old empire? We are doing well here in America. All of us. Things have just begun to go our way. Why do we want to jeopardize that?"

The uncle leaned back in. "Because we will prosper as the nation prospers. But there is a potential problem."

"What sort of problem?"

"For now, let me just say that we've been getting bad vibes from our German associates. The people in our government who have been coordinating this pact have become anxious, nervous about certain aspects of the situation."

"What situation?"

Uncle Hiro looked worried. "A potential crack in the intelligence end of things that the Germans have been handling." Hiro waved it away: "It's nothing we need to get involved with now, but . . ."

The man who had set the stage up returned. It was precisely ten o'clock at night. He spoke into the microphone in Japanese, calling for the night's first karaoke participant. Around the restaurant, the groups of businessmen nudged each other, urging one another to perform. Finally, one of the men got up from a table covered with half-eaten steaks and half-empty bottles of scotch whiskey.

"But what?" Jacko said.

Hiro continued. "I'm staying in the States for an extra week through the G7 conference. Just in case I'm needed to relay information to you about certain—operational aspects of the situation."

"Stop playing games, Uncle. Tell me how I'm involved."

Hiro pulled a file from his briefcase and slid it across the table. Jacko looked at a photocopy of a *New York Times* article on Greer Whitaker, including his picture.

"What's this?" Jacko asked.

"This is the young man who could be standing between our people and prosperity. We've been in close contact with our German counterparts throughout this entire episode. Until recently, we've trusted that the Germans have taken care of everything, including Mr. Whitaker. Just familiarize yourself with the particulars of the case. I'm waiting for the signal from Tokyo. I don't want to tell you any more than you need to know—you understand. We don't want to jump the gun. There's too much at stake to risk upsetting our new German allies unnecessarily. If the time comes, I'll supply you with all the information you'll need." Hiro smiled knowingly. "Our intelligence network runs very deep here in America."

It occurred to Jacko that there must be many other Japanese running agents like his friend Kevin Hatu.

Hiro added, "Just as the Germans have a special group to handle things discreetly, the Japanese government has us."

Jacko lit up another Dunhill. "Of course, I'll do whatever is necessary," he said.

Uncle Hiro beamed again and squeezed Jacko's shoulder. "My nephew . . ."

He was cut off by the opening measures from the preprogrammed karaoke machine. The Japanese businessman held onto the microphone stand unsteadily. He squinted in the spotlights at his table of comrades. He was serious as he started to sing the opening measures of the Elvis Presley version of "My Way."

54 ❏ ❏ ❏ ❏

At midnight, Greer passed the white dunes of the Pismo Beach promontory shimmering in the moonlight a half mile off the highway. A dune buggy soared over a dune with its headlights on, cutting a path against the starry backdrop set above the ocean. A wave started a domino roll and crash on the beach while the vehicle was still suspended in the sky.

He saw small fireworks rocketing up from somewhere hidden down in the dunes, bottle rockets exploding in a little star, the moist sea breeze pushing the explosion inland for a few feet, then quickly dampening the sparkles.

"Happy New Year," he said to himself.

He had stopped only once since leaving San Diego seven hours earlier. In Santa Barbara he refueled the van and found an office supply warehouse just off the interstate. He bought a low-end computer and printer, diskettes, paper, and other supplies. He had phoned ahead to reserve a room at an out-of-the-way place he had stayed at once before.

His constant worry was that he would be stopped by a highway patrol car. If he showed his driver's license or was uncooperative, he'd be immediately arrested and it would all be over. He was afraid the condition of the old van would get him pulled over for driving an unsafe vehicle. Every time he saw a patrol car with blue lights on the top or on the dash, he got a nervous rush of adrenaline that took fifteen minutes to work its way out of his system.

• • •

An hour and a half later Greer was well into the Santa Lucia mountain range, driving the winding road atop the cliff face and the crashing ocean below. It had been twenty minutes since he had noticed the car behind him, somewhere along the rolling stretch of highway in the foothills just past San Simeon. The other car's actions fed his paranoia: Greer had given the person behind him every chance to pass, but the other car hadn't taken it.

There were a few other cars on the highway at one-thirty in the morning on New Year's Day, a couple of obvious drunks and even several trucks. Greer wanted to test the car behind him, which was matching his speed while keeping a constant distance of twenty yards or so. Greer saw a sign for a scenic roadside park at the top of the next hill. He pulled over, stopped, and let the other car pass. Greer waited a couple of minutes, then started north again.

Five minutes later, he passed a car with its lights off on the side of road. He watched in the rearview mirror as the car turned on its lights and pulled onto the highway behind him. It was the same car. He was definitely being followed. Was it someone sent by the German on the vidcotapc?

Greer gauged his location. He was only a half hour away from his intended destination. How was he going to evade the car behind him? The condition of the van meant there was no chance he could outrun the other car. Greer hoped his advantage would be that he knew the area better than the other driver.

Greer started seeing more signs for Big Sur. By now, there was a large truck in front of him, causing Greer to drive even more slowly around the road which had become more and more winding. The truck all but stopped to make the hairpin turns. For a few moments at a time, Greer noticed he would lose sight of the other car's headlights as he picked up a little speed going downhill on a steep grade, then cut sharply around a corner in the road.

Greer saw the landmark he had been waiting for fly by—the Henry Miller house. Greer checked the traffic in front of him: fifty yards ahead, there was a car approaching. On the next sharp turn, Greer pulled out around the truck and gunned the van to take the lead position, cutting back into his lane. He looked back and saw the car behind him try to do the same thing, but having to drop back just in time to avoid a head-on collision with the oncoming car.

Greer steered the van around another sharp turn, accelerating as much as he could, losing sight of the car that was still behind the truck. There came a quick succession of entrances to hotels and gift shops that he passed. Then Greer cut the lights on the van, pushing the accelerator to the floor, trying to put as much distance between himself and the other car as possible. The road was absolutely dark, except for the light of a full moon just rising over the ocean shining onto the asphalt. Finally, he came to a hidden driveway on his right. Greer spun the steering wheel and threw the van down the gravel driveway, taking the van quickly to the back side of a compound of rough wooden buildings. As he rumbled on, he saw in his rearview mirror the truck and other car pass by on the highway.

The driveway made a circle through the compound, really a series of one- and two-storied cabins. Greer drove the van onto a rougher path next to one of the cabins leading into the woods. He cut the engine and let the van coast off the road through the dense growth. Bushes and tree branches scraped the sides of the van, then finally there was a sudden jolt as the van hit a stump and stopped. He was well back in the woods, hidden from the highway and driveway running through the compound.

Greer rolled down the window and listened. He could barely hear the sound of the breaking surf on the other side of the highway. A few cars passed on the highway. He watched for headlights coming around the driveway. He'd give it another fifteen minutes, then he'd go inside. There was work to be done tonight.

55 ❏ ❏ ❏ ❏

Greer had arrived at the rustic cedar buildings that comprised Lund-quist's Big Sur Inn. Seven years earlier he had stayed here on his weeklong trip up the coast. It looked as if nothing had changed.

He had bittersweet memories of Lundquist's. Before, he had come to sort out his feelings about what had happened between Stephanie and himself. By the time he left, he still didn't understand what had happened, but he carried with him a new sense of peace. Spending a few days in Big Sur had allowed him to get on with his life after Stephanie.

Greer walked quickly from the hidden van, carrying computer equipment toward one of the cabins. He pushed the door open with his foot and unloaded the equipment onto the kitchen table. There were no locks on the doors at Lundquist's, only a latch on the inside. Greer pulled the curtains closed and kept on only the one dim light from the bedside table. At this point, all he could do was hope that whoever it was who had been following him had assumed that he had been able to speed away while the other car had been stuck behind the truck. All Greer needed was an hour or two to take care of what he had to do. He'd have to work fast, then find a way to get out.

He had called from Santa Barbara to reserve the cabin. And, as he had requested, they had brought his FedEx package to the room for his arrival. Despite his considerable fatigue after the grueling eight-hour drive up the coast, the adrenaline was still pumping from the chase on the highway.

He took a moment to think. He knew the moment he handed over the diskettes to anyone, Stephanie died. If he withheld the information, then no one in power could do anything about it. What was more important? The life of Stephanie Becker or the economic well-being of the country? Suddenly, he felt a chill. If the German on the tape were right, there was someone already on the way. Probably the car tailing him.

Greer turned toward the door to get the rest of the equipment and felt a painful jab in his pants pocket. He got the object out and held it up in front of his face.

It was Stephanie's earring.

A little gust of wind pushed through the door and jingled the earring like a small wind chime.

Greer closed his hand around the earring and closed his eyes. He squeezed the earring so hard his eyes teared.

Greer dragged the kitchen table in front of the fireplace and set up the computer equipment. The room was freezing. He brought in wood from outside and lit the fire.

He sat staring at the bright cobalt blue computer screen as the kindling caught fire and crackled.

Where to begin?

The blank screen had a hypnotic effect. There was too much to say. He had to organize his thoughts.

A dozen three-and-a-half inch black squares with colorful tabs. Two and a half months of raw data from the daily CIA cables. There were also the diskettes that Jenkins had given him with the statistical proof of his theory. He set them aside for the moment.

After seeing the videotape of Stephanie suffering, Greer had fooled himself into thinking he wasn't going to carry out his original plan, the one devised on the flight from Rome to Mexico City. Even if he did turn over the diskettes, there was no way of knowing whether Stephanie would be released. Maybe there was still a chance of saving Stephanie. The best thing he could do now was to push ahead. If things went according to plan, he'd have even more chips to bargain with to get Stephanie back alive. There just wasn't any time to waste.

The sound of the stream outside the window over his bed distracted him. A night bird's call echoed off a thousand trees before being absorbed by the lush undergrowth in the forest. It was already 2:30 A.M. He began to type.

56

By four in the morning, all the work was done. Greer had been able to get the van out of the brush. He had already walked down the compound driveway to the highway and found no signs of the car that had been following him. He had hidden copies of the diskettes in the van, bargaining chips if he needed them. He slipped an envelope with cash under the office door of the manager's cabin to pay for his room, then headed north again on the Pacific Coast Highway.

There was still the matter of the box of printed materials and diskettes he had generated that needed to be sent off. Rounding the curve on the way out of Big Sur, Greer saw the parking lot full of cars at Nepenthe. He looked at the full moon and smiled. Of course, he said to himself. Greer hid the van behind a larger truck so that it couldn't be seen from the road, then walked quickly up the steps around the outside of the restaurant.

The traditional Full Moon Party at Nepenthe brought out all the hippies and bikers in black leather from the redwood forests around Big Sur. There was a reggae band on the stone patio at the edge of the ocean cliff. There was the telltale whiff of something bittersweet in the air. The restaurant was closed to tourists passing through Big Sur and the locals had reclaimed the chilly lookout for their pagan feast.

Greer was looking for someone in charge, someone he could trust to send the box of materials off the next day. With a twenty-dollar tip, Greer convinced the manager tending bar to call Federal Express the next day to pick up the preaddressed box of materials Greer had just finished preparing.

Greer was in a hurry to get out of Big Sur. Seven years ago he would have lingered. The place was called Nepenthe, he reminded himself—named after the drug in Greek myth. The name meant "no grief." Anything that made someone forget his sorrows.

There was still no sign of anyone coming for him or the diskettes. He ran over the plan again in his mind. What else could he do? What if Stephanie were already dead? What good would it do him to wait indefinitely? He'd push on with his plan, then do whatever he could to help Stephanie.

He was resolute in his determination to carry forward his mission. Not too far out, Greer saw an errant humpbacked whale break the surface of the water and send a spray up through its blowhole, then disappear beneath the silver surface. A good omen, he thought. Time to go.

He headed toward the steps that would take him back down to the van in the parking lot. He stopped in the middle of the patio to look at a wooden statue of the Phoenix bird carved out of a large piece of driftwood.

The Phoenix, thought Greer. The bird who rose from the ashes—symbol of resurrection.

Greer had died a spiritual and emotional death over the last two weeks. His faith in his country was gone. Reed had betrayed him. Jenkins was dead. Kate had left him. He was wanted as a traitor and murderer. He thought about Stephanie's cut and bloated face in the video. He imagined the pain she had suffered as the ear was cut off and then the chunk of flesh gouged. He felt as if he were being chased by some unknown force that wanted to draw him back into the conspiracy or maybe just kill him off too. Oh, Kate, he thought. Why did you abandon me?

But here he was at Nepenthe. He *would* forget his sorrows. He wouldn't feel sorry for himself. He owed it to Jenkins and Stephanie. Now was the time to focus on what had to be done. Kate and Stephanie couldn't help him. It was something he had to do himself.

He turned his back to the Phoenix bird and left the patio. From the ash heap, he figured, there was no place to go but up.

Greer felt the pressure in his bladder growing and ducked into the men's room on the first landing down.

The light was poor, with one dim bulb over a chipped porcelain sink filled with cigarette butts and ashes. There was someone locked in the stall. He was snoring, probably passed out. A Full Moon Party neophyte. He should learn to pace himself, otherwise he'd never see dawn at Nepenthe. Greer read the graffiti on the wall over the urinal as he relieved himself. It was pretty much the same everywhere, he thought. Maybe a bit more contemplative in Big Sur, with a folksy, philosophical bent.

Behind him, Greer heard the door open and the reggae music came in. There was a shuffle of feet and the door closed. In also came the pungent smell of marijuana. More Rastas, Greer surmised. The person in the stall snored on. Greer flushed and reached to finish and zip.

There was sharp steel pressing at his throat, the blade still cold from the nighttime Big Sur air.

"Lover," she said.

That voice. The throaty, sensual voice—again. He felt himself shrivel in his hand.

"Give it another shake and let's go," she said.

The knife led and Greer followed over to the sink. In the scratched polished aluminum mirror, Greer saw his own wide alert eyes. At his throat a trickle of blood flowed over the top of the knife blade. Behind him floated the head of Stephanie Becker.

"This switchblade has never been used," she said. "Just recently bought in Tijuana." Her voice turned harsh: "Don't make me dull it cutting off your head."

In the mirror they stared at each other. Greer had kept a distance from the crowd at Nepenthe, so he wouldn't have seen her from a distance in the dark. If he had looked directly at her mingling with the crowd of partygoers, he wouldn't have been able to distinguish her from the leather-clad bikers. Stephanie shifted slightly to the right and Greer could see her entire face now. It was as beautiful and flawless as when they had first met. She tilted her head back and Greer saw that she was wearing new silver earrings in both ears.

Stephanie opened the door with her free hand. "Miss me?"

"Pig's blood and makeup. You forgot that I was involved in theater as an undergraduate?"

Greer was lying on his bed at Lundquist's with his feet and hands secured with duct tape. He was blind and mute. He could barely hear or breathe through the tape wrapped around his head covering his eyes and mouth. He was also bound to the bed itself, the tape wrapped over and under the bed several times so that he couldn't move.

"The ear I got through a friend at the city morgue, pierced with an ice pick to take my earring," she continued. Greer heard the crash of furniture turning over. Stephanie's voice moved around the room. "The tattoo artist in Heidelberg had never worked on shaved pig's flesh before. A belly of a dead pig, a woman's inner thigh. It's all the same under the needle, my dear Herr Schneebälle."

Cabinet doors flew open and things spilled to the floor. A tray of flatware. Glasses tumbling and smashing onto the kitchen counter. Greer listened to Stephanie's boots circling the room on the wooden floor, then walking toward him.

She sat down suddenly next to him, bouncing him on the bed. "You've made this much more difficult on yourself than is necessary, darling." She got up just as quickly. The sound of the bedside table being overturned. "You'd think that you would be happy to see me. I don't understand this refusal of yours to please me. You know how I've always taken a professional interest in your work. I'd really love to take a look at those diskettes."

Greer heard her walk to the middle of the room and stand still. She sighed loudly.

"Don't go anywhere, sweetheart. I'll be right back."

Stephanie walked to the door and closed it quietly behind her.

Greer lay on the bed, trying to interpret any small sounds he heard. He felt a draft from over his head. He had opened the window over his bed slightly earlier in the evening to let some fresh air into the room.

She was at the van, opening and closing doors. He thought he heard the sound of upholstery being shredded. He imagined the stuffing being pulled out of the van's seats. He envisioned her prying apart the dashboard. It seemed that she had been working on the van for half an hour.

"Thank you, darling," she said, coming back into the room. "I enjoyed the workout. Hiding the diskettes behind the radio in the dash was very clever. Sorry about the van."

Greer heard Stephanie turn on his computer, heard it beep and grind as it booted up. Stephanie typed in commands and tapped her long fingernails on the table as she waited for the program to start running. He heard her push in a diskette into the machine and the computer grabbed it. Another set of commands.

"Ah, yes, very good, *Liebling*." More typing. "This looks like everything." Greer heard her push the eject button and the diskette popped out. He heard her push in several more, in turn, and review them. "You are very thorough. Everything is organized so well. Just like the anal retentive you always were."

Stephanie popped the final diskette out. He heard a zip that sounded as if she was putting the diskettes into the pocket of her jacket. The next thing he heard was a crash and the spillage of computer chips and monitor glass on the floor.

She walked to him and stood next to the bed. He thought he heard her jacket creak as she bent over. She hadn't said anything. There was a swift whipping sound though the air, then he immediately felt the sting of being struck across the face. He tried to yell, but his mouth was taped shut and the cry stuck in his throat.

Another stinging blow crossed his face again as she screamed at him: "I should beat you to death for not cooperating!" She threw the whip onto his chest. He thought he recognized it as the power cord from the computer. She was calm again. "But I really need to be going."

Greer felt Stephanie's fingers pressing hard into the flesh of his thigh. In the morning—if there *was* a morning, he thought—there would be bruises the color of moss. She scratched lightly at the denim of his jeans. She trailed her hand up to his crotch, unbuttoned and unzipped him, pulling away his boxers. She hesitated. Then he felt something hard and sharp moving along his shaft. He sucked in a breath and held it, waiting for the pain. At first he thought it was her knife, then he recognized it as what it was. It was the edge of one of her long fingernails.

"You would have let me die, wouldn't you, darling? Weren't you told to get the diskettes and wait here or something bad would happen to me? I came here to do a job, but your insensitivity has enraged my passions." She kept running her fingernail up and down the length of him, with just enough pressure to cause him a little pricking pain, but the result was instead involuntary excitement. She knew what she was doing and so did he. He hardened unwillingly. She had stroked him like this many times before as a prelude to lovemaking, something she had learned from the *Kama Sutra*. Leave marks, but don't break the skin, the book said. The perfect amount of pressure, a sharpness on the underside that stimulated him into taut hardness, preparing him to enter her. He kept perfectly still, afraid of what would happen.

"It's a good thing your filthy mouth is taped shut. That way I don't have to listen to your lies about why you didn't wait as you were told. The lies about why you would let me suffer. Now it is your turn. Except there will be no acting. This is for real."

She removed her hand. He heard a swift snap. She had opened her switchblade again. Stephanie wasn't speaking, wasn't moving. Greer tensed, not knowing where the pain would be. Was she going to slit him under the chin, watching him suck air through a bloody gill in his throat? Or just remove his stiffened member, leaving him bound helplessly on the bed, dying slowly from a pulpy, gushing bloody stump?

She pushed the blade into his chest over his heart, just enough to tear through his shirt and steady the point in the flesh. She twirled it and Greer flinched.

"While you were taking the slow overnight train from Salzburg to Rome, we taped my bit of acting—not bad, if I may say so—then I flew from Salzburg to London, then on to Mexico City. I arrived there before you did. I watched you in the airport as you retrieved the Federal Express package and boarded your flight to Tijuana. I was on the next flight out. I had people in Tijuana follow you when you arrived. They were at the border when you made your run and they saw you get onto the shuttle for San Diego. I beat you driving into the city and watched you buy that old van. And I've been right behind you ever since. At least until you gave me the slip for a while back down the road." Stephanie shifted her weight off the bed. "But I don't know why I'm telling *you* this. I'm talking to a dead man."

Stephanie lifted the switchblade, then snapped it shut.

There were so many questions he wanted to ask her. He tried forming the words in his mouth, but the one question that summarized all the others only came out as a throaty complaint, recognizable only to himself: *Why?*

Greer heard the curtain covering the window over his head flutter. Stephanie slammed the window shut. Then he flinched again at hearing another familiar sound, the tacky scream of duct tape being ripped off a roll. He imagined Stephanie biting a length off, as she had done when she had bound him. She was walking quickly around the room, pulling off the tape, placing it on a window. Moving to another wall, she taped another window, then another. He heard her go around the room one more time, the panes of glass rattling as she patted the tape down. When she was done, she threw the empty cardboard roll into the fireplace.

Stephanie left the room. Then, in a minute, Greer heard her kicking the door back open. She dropped an armload of wood into the fireplace. She made four more trips for wood, each time adding to the pile on the grate. She crumpled paper and stuffed it under the wood. Then Greer heard a sound that made his heart skip a beat. Greer had left the chimney damper in the fireplace open earlier in the night. What he heard was the sound of the damper being *closed*. Did she think she was really opening it? Would she discover her mistake before it was too late?

Greer heard the rattle of a match box from the mantel. A match struck and there was the hiss of the head flaring up and the acrid smell. There was nothing, then the paper ignited suddenly and the bark on the wood crackled. Greer wondered how long it would take for the fire to consume all of the oxygen in the sealed room. Would he die of lack of oxygen or smoke inhalation first?

Stephanie walked over to the bed. Greer sensed her face hovering over his, felt her breath on his cheek and smelled the firewood smoke mingling with the scent of marijuana in her hair. Her breath was sweet; she had had nothing to smoke tonight. Even from across the room, he could feel the heat of the roaring fire on his bare arms above the tape at the wrists.

Here comes the kiss of death, Greer thought.

She kissed him tenderly on his penis instead.

"*Gute Nacht,* my dear Herr Schneebälle. When you awake, you will be dead and I will be having a cup of coffee back in my cozy office in Heidelberg. *Auf Wiedersehen.*"

Her boots clicked to the door and stopped.

"Miss me," she said. Then he was alone.

57 ❏ ❏ ❏ ❏

Greer awoke, still blind, bound and gagged, breathing heavily through his nose. He knew that he had blacked out several times already. The room was hotter than any place he had ever been. He took a long breath through his nose, filling his lungs more with smoke than with usable air. He coughed violently. He took in shorter breaths, trying to get enough oxygen. He coughed and strained again so hard that he thought his eyeballs would pop out of his head.

He had stopped struggling; the tape wrapped over and under the bed wasn't going to give. His throat was dry, with a sooty, gritty taste in his mouth coming with the sputum up from his lungs. How long had he lain there? How long since Stephanie had left? Fifteen minutes? Half an hour? Two hours? He had lost all track of time during his blackouts.

The fire was not as loud as when Stephanie had first lit it. It had consumed all of the paper and kindling and was burning the large logs now. The fire felt larger and hotter to his skin. He seemed to have stopped sweating—a bad sign. Didn't that mean that the body had given up? That it had shut down in a final, desperate attempt at conserving energy to keep the vital organs alive?

Did he hear voices? Angel voices? Where were they coming from? Above? Outside the window? Now outside the door? They were coming for him, he reasoned. He tried making his own noises, but the sound of the fire was louder. He tried again, but nothing came. He fought hard against blacking out again.

In his delirium, he thought he heard the door hitting against the inside wall and felt a rush of cold air. But the bed was moving. Was this how it felt at the end? Now his entire body was shaking violently. Was his soul fighting the smoke for possession of his body? He sucked air where there was none. He tried forcing himself to stay awake, but at last felt the pressure of his eyes rolling into the back of his head. Something was going on in his throat. He knew the symptoms.

This was the end. He couldn't help it.

He was swallowing his own tongue.

But the she-devil had come back.

Greer felt her long fingernails prying for an edge to the tape over his mouth. There was her knife, too, sawing at the tape binding him to the bed.

Why had she come back? Had she changed her mind?

He felt his body moving effortlessly off the bed. Had he already died?

The next thing he knew was that she had pulled the tape from his mouth. He still couldn't see, but somehow he *could* see. Someone was beating on his chest. Or maybe it was something beating inside his chest. He still felt nothing. She reached down his throat and retracted his tongue.

She placed her mouth over his and blew air into his sooty lungs. They expanded, raising his chest, and filling his body with life-giving air. She rolled him onto his side and hit him on the back and he coughed up a mouthful of thick, gritty mucous.

She started breathing into him again. Then there came from the distance a bass beat and the high notes of a singer. Was he dead? Was this what heaven was like? A Full Moon Party with a reggae band?

She was yelling to stop. Stop what? The pounding on his chest stopped. Was it his heart stopping?

He took his first breath of fresh air since he had died. The sweet, pure air of Big Sur, tinged with the smell of salt from the sea and the redwoods of the forest.

She pulled the tape slowly off his eyes. The adhesive stuck to his eyelids and tugged hair off his eyebrows. Greer strained the muscles in his face to get his eyes open. It was still dark. The first thing he saw was the blazing full moon directly overhead.

An angel, not the devil? When he saw her he was sure he was in heaven.

"Kate?" he croaked. He coughed again, then turned his head and retched onto the soft pine straw.

A man's voice from nearby said, "He's alive."

Greer lay on the ground trying to orient himself. He looked to be outside his cabin. The man who had spoken moved from his head to where Kate was standing by his side. Greer tried to sit up but was too weak. "I was dead?"

Kate wiped his face and mouth with the collar of his shirt. "You had stopped breathing. That's about as close to dead as you can get and live to talk about it."

The smell of smoke in Greer's nostrils sent a wave of nausea through him. He was shivering. Kate took off her coat and laid it over him.

Kate looked at him strangely. "What I want to know," she said, "is what you were doing with your pants undone."

The cabin stank of wood smoke, but with the windows open again the air blowing through was fresh. Greer slumped in an armchair. Kate sat beside him in a straight-backed chair, the only one without broken legs. Covey looked around at the damage in the kitchen.

Kate was wiping Greer's face with a washcloth. "Did she get what she came for?" she asked Greer quietly.

"I suppose she did."

"What was that?" Covey asked. From all the way in the kitchen he had heard them talking.

Kate had already introduced Covey as being from the Agency, but hadn't mentioned him by name. Covey walked back over and stood in front of Greer wiping off his glasses.

"What *was* she looking for?" she asked.

Greer was breathing deeply, forcing oxygen into his lungs. He was weak, but the secret of the diskettes would remain his. Kate might have saved his life, but she still had a lot to answer for. "I don't know," he answered.

Kate surveyed the room. "She really did a number on the place, didn't she? And did you get a good look at what she did to that van?"

Covey parted the curtains and looked at the van again. "It's almost five A.M.," he said. "You said that she took you from Nepenthe sometime after four. She's got a good jump on us. Where do you think she's going?"

"Back to Germany," said Greer. "She's probably headed up to San Francisco to catch a flight out from there."

"We need to catch up with her," said Kate, "and tail her as far as the airport."

"And after that?"

"Have someone we can trust follow her after she gets to Germany."

"You're going to let her go? We could have her arrested for attempted murder." Covey gave Kate an odd look, then nodded at Greer, thinking Greer didn't see it. Covey motioned Kate to the kitchen and they conferred in low voices. They came back over to Greer.

She addressed Covey. "Why don't you stay here with Greer while I go to the pay phone and call the office. My cellular phone won't work out here." It sounded too scripted, Greer thought.

Greer started to get up. "Don't you trust me alone?" he asked.

Kate gently pushed him back down. "Just sit still," she said. "You need to rest. I'll be right back." She left him alone with Covey.

Covey paced around the room, kicking through the rubble on the floor, eyeing Greer suspiciously. "You doing okay?" he said.

"Doing great," said Greer. "Thanks for asking."

It was a moot point. Greer heard a car door shut, and Kate came back with a map. She and Covey traced likely routes up the coast into the Bay Area and to the San Francisco airport. "Greer said she's got a rental car," Kate said. "Why don't you see about getting some people waiting at the different rental car returns. It will be important for us to follow her from there so that we know which flight she gets onto. Leave a message at my Washington office as soon as you spot her. I'll check in every few hours."

"Are you *really* sure?"

"It'll be okay." Greer saw Kate touch her purse.

Covey nodded knowingly. He waded through the debris to the door and left.

"What was that all about?" Greer asked.

"You and I need to have a little talk," she said.

Greer sat up. "Starting with why you didn't show in Berchtesgaden."

"Ben ordered me not to go. He insisted Reed go instead. I didn't have any choice. And I wanted you home."

"I had to kill him, Kate. He would have killed *me*. Do you know about Reed?"

Kate let him continue.

"Bob Reed recruited me to work for the CIA. Has anyone told you yet that I'm CIA? I was brought in to infiltrate Randall Jenkins' office. Reed told me that the President had signed an Executive Finding authorizing the operation. My job was to keep an eye on Jenkins. As it turns out, the evidence I gathered and the statistical work Jenkins did support his theory that the Germans and Japanese are working together to dominate the world economy at America's expense."

Greer could tell from the look on Kate's face that is was all news to her.

"So then I start reading about an operation called REDWING in the station cables. There's a spy in the U.S. government. Okay, it makes sense. It fits with what Reed had been telling me all along about Jenkins. Then REDWING's source drops a bombshell: the name of the operation in the U.S. is STEEPLECHASE. That's *me. I'm* STEEPLECHASE. *That's* the cryptonym for Reed's operation against Jenkins. I freak. I'm on a train on the way to Cologne. And guess who shows up? Reed, of course. We get to Cologne and Reed takes Jenkins away. I think he killed him, Kate. Jenkins wasn't the kook everyone in the Beltway thought he was. I know it sounds paranoid, but someone—maybe more than one person—wanted to shut Jenkins up because he was getting too close to the truth."

Kate asked, "So what is it that Stephanie's got? What is it she came all the way over here for?"

Greer still wasn't sure if he could trust Kate yet, but figured he'd have to tell her to get her help. "She's got the diskettes with the statistical proof of Jenkins' theory."

"This actually is working out very well. She's got the diskettes and she'll make a beeline to her controller. I've already checked into arranging something like the Federal Witness Protection Program for you, except better. You'll have a new identity, a new life. We'll go away from all this when it's over."

It was the first time she had acknowledged her relationship with Greer since she had come.

Kate said, "But first we need to finish up this business." She folded the washcloth to a cleaner side. She started to get up.

"I don't want a new identity or a new life," said Greer. Kate sat back down. "I want to clear my name and make sure that these people are stopped. I don't care if we are talking about our supposed allies. I don't care what it does to the Administration's political agenda. Friends don't conspire to disrupt the American economy, spy on us, and kill the President's National Security Adviser. You and I seem to have a difference of opinion on how this thing should be handled."

"To be handled effectively, it needs to be handled quietly. There may be more moles that need to be flushed out. The best way to do that is let them think that it's business as usual. Let them keep on making contacts with their German and Japanese controllers and we'll eventually catch them. I don't want to blow this operation. I frankly no longer know whom to trust at the Agency or in the Administration. And I'm worried about you, Greer."

She gave him a long, steady gaze. Then it hit him and he pulled away.

"What operation?" he asked. "You mean STEEPLECHASE?"

Kate moved her chair directly in front of Greer. "You're not going to like what I have to say. First, let me say that I love you, and I was doing everything I could to help you."

Kate had a look on her face that Greer couldn't decipher. She lowered her eyes and said in a whisper, "I was the one responsible for throwing you in front of Stephanie again." She looked up, but couldn't look him in the eye.

Greer was stunned. "How can that be possible?"

Kate lowered her eyes again. "I've deceived you," she said.

Greer sat up straighter in the chair. He glared at her. "Tell me," he said.

When she looked up at Greer, her eyes were clear and unflinching. "I'm not just a staff officer working in the Director's office for Ben Gibbons. I'm section chief of a special internal counterintelligence unit in the Agency. It was set up back in the fifties when career CIA officers were really running the Agency, not political appointees. They were concerned that the Agency might be infiltrated through the Administration and wanted to maintain an investigative unit that was independent of any political influence. Our main objective is the preservation of an uncorrupted American intelligence organization. When there's a turnover of administrations after a presidential election, the new appointees—DCI, his staff he brings with him, the deputies that are appointed—aren't briefed about our existence. Ben doesn't know anything about it—or me. It's sort of like a secret fraternity, a self-perpetuating group. People at the Agency hear rumors about it, but, of course, it's unofficial and only the current members know who else is in the unit. The group is made up of individuals from all over the Agency. The best and brightest, if you'll allow me. I was tapped to join while at the Moscow station, then asked to take over the whole group when I returned to Washington. That officer you met, Covey, is my right-hand man. We set up a task force to investigate the REDWING information when it started taking on aspects relative to U.S. domestic politics and infiltration of the Agency."

Greer looked at her skeptically. "So how does that concern me?

"We'd had our eye on Bob Reed for a long time—since before the Wall came down. Back when I was still in Moscow. We got word that he was barely passing his regular polygraphs. We'd never been able to nail him on anything, though. I was just starting to get information from one of my own Russian agents about a high-level mole in the CIA being run by Stasi, when all of my agents suddenly disappeared. I didn't have a positive identification yet, but the description and facts matched Reed perfectly. I believe it was Reed who tipped KGB off to the identity of my agents. He had access to their names as a higher-ranking officer, even though he was working in Germany. He could have justified looking at the operations' files on the basis of his involvement with running operations against the East Germans. I know he's responsible for my agents' deaths. The ones I had promised to protect, promised that nothing would ever happen to them."

Kate stopped and looked into Greer's face, looking for signs of comprehension, as if she wanted to know if she really had to explain the rest, or if he could figure it out for himself.

Greer just stared back at her. He wanted her to say it all, hold back nothing.

"You mentioned the REDWING source," she started out. She was speaking in a more detached manner, as if recounting the plot of a boring movie she had just seen, rather than the story of how Greer had come to be an international fugitive wanted for espionage and murder.

"Yes?"

"Among other things, REDWING was letting us know that there was some kind of new German intelligence organization, some sort of quasi-official successor to Stasi that was operating not just throughout all of Germany, but was using the operations and agents it already had in place throughout the world. We hadn't been able to figure out what they were trying to accomplish. That's the whole purpose of REDWING. Of course, when we found out about the German organization, we immediately wondered if Reed was still involved. His polygraphs over the last two years still indicated deception, so we suspected that he was. We wanted to catch Reed but, more important than that, we wanted him to lead us to the source of the intelligence operation that he was working for, this new organization."

"So the Agency hires me and assigns me to work with Reed. What was the purpose of that?"

Kate shook her head. "You were never hired by the CIA. We used you as bait for Reed. I made sure that you didn't get accepted into the Career Training Program. I changed your polygraph results to look as if you had failed. I also made sure that Reed saw your rejection. Your application was otherwise so strong you were perfect to dangle in front of him in the hope that he might see you as a potential asset—an agent—of his own that he could run. By watching how he ran you— where he sent you, what kind of information he had you collecting— it would lead eventually back to the German organization that was running him."

"Then why send Reed after me in Berchtesgaden?"

"It was Ben Gibbons' decision. I tried to argue him out of it, but he wanted his old buddy on the scene. Sending Reed out to get you was the last thing in the world I wanted to happen."

"And STEEPLECHASE?"

"Fiction. Reed made it up to try to impress you. There's no such CIA operation."

"And Stephanie?"

"Stephanie Becker was a known recruiter of American students for Stasi. We also knew that she was still involved in recruiting and assumed that it had something to do with the new German intelligence operation. One of the officers in my counterintelligence unit who knows about the German organization spotted her name while vetting your CIA application and brought it to my attention. At first we thought that you might have been a spy recruited by and working for Stephanie Becker who was trying to infiltrate the Agency. After the polygraph showed you hadn't been compromised, we thought you could be very useful to us in helping to figure out who was running the organization and what their objectives were. We felt that Reed would have turned over information about you to his controller—especially a copy of your detailed Personal History Statement. We wanted to see if the organization running Reed was the same one running Stephanie. If they were, we figured that Stephanie might try to contact you, especially if you ended up going to Germany. It would be too tempting not to try to further compromise you—unwittingly, of course. We assumed that when the organization found out that you were in a sensitive intelligence position, they would take a run at you through Stephanie Becker." Kate hardened. "We were right. So very, very right, Greer. I'm sorry."

Greer hadn't taken his eyes off Kate since she had started talking. This was unbelievable, he thought. He could hardly comprehend it all. Of all the deceptions that he had been subjected to, which was the worst?

Greer asked, "So you knew about Stephanie Becker and me all along? And you deliberately set me up so that she'd take another run at me? And you just assumed I'd fall under her sway a second time?"

Kate looked sad, tired. "Yes. But I guess I also wanted to believe that you would have resisted."

"I'm sorry."

"Me, too."

"I thought she was just sick in love with me. She had had so many problems. She *was* a little crazy, you know."

Kate shook her head. "No. That was all an act, back in Heidelberg and now. She faked her mental illness—her stalking, her irrational behavior—to make it look as if that were the reason she suddenly appeared on the scene after all these years. That, and to play on your sympathies. Her intention was to run you as an agent, just as I was. But the same thing may have happened to her that happened to me. She might have fallen in love with you."

Greer felt too conflicted to know how to respond. He struggled for words. "I felt protective of her. I thought she was vulnerable, weak. I wanted to take care of her. Just as I wanted to take care of you. You told me how you cared too much about your agents. How you cried over them. You told me I was the only one you could talk with. You opened up to me and left yourself be vulnerable, too. That was all an act, too, wasn't it? You made your own play on my emotions."

"No."

At almost five in the morning, Greer was watching the new realities buzzing around him like a swarm of angry, bloodsucking mosquitoes. He was trying to figure out which one to knock down first. He took a swat.

"So you dangled me in front of Reed and then you dangled me in front of Stephanie, is that right?"

Kate nodded yes.

"How could you do this to me?"

"I *do* love you, Greer. But this was all in motion before we fell in love. There were lives at risk that are my responsibility. I didn't want to see them killed off like my agents in Moscow. The Agency had to come first."

"I see. That's exactly what Reed said you would say."

"But things changed. Once I saw that you were in real danger, and once it hit me that you really were with Stephanie, I had had enough. I tried to call it off."

Greer's strength had been gradually returning. Now with the jolt of her revelations, he felt reenergized. He wanted to kill someone.

"So that explains the watch, too," he said. "You tagged me like some animal, then threw me back into the woods. Just to see where I'd run. Just to find out who would hunt me down."

"But we also did it so that we'd know where you were in case you got into trouble."

Greer was skeptical. He spoke in slow, measured phrases between clinched teeth. "Reed used me, Stephanie used me—and now I find out that the Agency and you did, too." He couldn't hold back his rage any longer. He kicked a broken chair leg across the room from his seated position.

Greer gathered a breath to say something more, but was struck with a sudden, deep cough that brought up more of the black phlegm. He got up weakly and slowly made his way to the door, sticking his head outside to spit. He leaned against the doorway, staring up at the sky. The stars were fixed and twinkling.

He turned back into the room, leaning on the doorway with the other shoulder. "There's no reason I shouldn't just walk right out of here. There are people who need to know about all this. I also think they need to know about Jenkins' theory."

"Your proof went with Stephanie. She took the diskettes and trashed everything else, right? No one's going to listen to you without proof."

"Jenkins had copies," Greer said cautiously.

"The FBI did a sweep a few days ago. They didn't find anything about the theory. You're a fugitive, considered armed and dangerous, and you'll be shot on sight if you make a move. That's not just me talking. That's the opinion of the U.S. government."

He had nothing to say to that.

She said: "You have no idea the danger you're in, do you?"

"I think dying gives me some idea, Kate. But now Stephanie's gone. The danger has passed."

"The Germans will come back, Greer. Once they find out you're alive, they'll come back."

Greer didn't have any answers.

"Come with me, Greer. *Please.* Together we can put the pieces of the puzzle together and do this the right way. Here's your chance to be the hero in this story for real this time. Come with me and you can live to tell it."

"*You* don't even know who to trust. Not in the Agency, not at the White House. What guarantees do I have that my story will ever be heard?"

Kate just looked at him. He figured she must have been out of reasons.

"You don't have much confidence in me, do you?" he said. "How do you think I've made it this far?"

Kate had a tired, disappointed look on her face. "Greer, don't you get it? You made it this far because Stephanie and her controllers allowed you to," she said. "They obviously were waiting until you retrieved the diskettes, then they were going to waste you. If they had wanted, you would have been bobbing in the Rhine alongside Randall Jenkins."

Greer noticed that the reggae band down the road at Nepenthe had stopped playing. A bird warbled frantically from a place deep in the woods, setting up a chorus of responses.

"Greer, it's late."

Greer turned to her voice and caught her reaching into her purse and pulling out a small handgun. "If you're not coming voluntarily,

I'm taking you into protective custody. I'm sorry, but this is for your own good."

"Oh, cut it out, Kate," he said wearily.

"If I let you go, you'll be found and killed. I won't let that happen."

Kate walked to him in the doorway. "Please don't make this difficult," she said. Kate held the gun steadily on Greer. "Outside to the car. This is business, now. You're driving," she ordered.

As he walked toward the car, he thought about how Kate had deliberately thrown him back in front of Stephanie and watched him on the satellite as he squirmed. She let him dangle. Now she had a gun on him. Greer decided he wasn't going to let Kate Mallotte or anyone else stop now.

Kate motioned him to the passenger side: "Get in and slide over," she said.

Greer got into the car behind the steering wheel and Kate handed him the keys, still holding her gun on him.

Greer said, "That's not really necessary, you know."

"My professional judgment says it is. You'll thank me later."

Greer started the car and the warning chime sounded for the seat belts. Kate was dialing a number on the cellular phone with her free hand. "Buckle up," he said.

Greer reached quickly over his shoulder with his right arm to grab the seat belt, then brought the arm back with a sudden blow to the gun in Kate's hand. In one fast motion, he pulled open her door and pushed her out of the car.

"Greer!" she shouted as she hit the ground.

Greer threw the car into gear and sped out of Lundquist's, the force of the momentum slamming the door shut. He hit the automatic door locks and glanced quickly into the rearview mirror as he turned onto the highway. Through the moonlit dust, he could see Kate slowly getting off the ground. She would be all right.

58 ❑ ❑ ❑ ❑

Marie von Bosacker plucked the two wires supporting the row of bare Riesling grapevines. The wires were taut and they sang like a harp. Two canes from each of the plants hung intertwined with the wires like the arms of Christ crucified.

"Your fields are in good shape," said her companion.

January was pruning season. She moved down the row of vines, testing the strength of the wires and inspecting the stock for damage from insects or mildew. Here and there she snipped some wood back with her pruning shears where her workers had missed.

The two of them were silhouettes against a low sun on the south face of the hill. The vineyard was perfectly situated, sitting to the east of the Vosges Mountains at a perfect altitude. She had always thought that the property perfectly embodied the Latin poet Virgil's maxim that "Vines love an open hill." For as far as they could see, the late afternoon golden winter sun flooded row upon row of dormant grapevines.

"Bernhard," she called to him. He had wandered a bit. He came back to her side.

"*Oui?*" he said.

"I just wanted you nearby," she said. He laid his hand gently onto her shoulder. She continued walking along the row, bending over every now and then to push some dirt up around the base of a vine or prune an errant cane.

They finished the row they were walking on and strolled arm-in-arm back to her Range Rover at the edge of the field.

Bernhard opened the back of the car. He got out a bottle of wine and two glasses. He uncorked the bottle and poured them both some wine.

"A toast," he said, handing her a glass.

She leaned lazily against the car and raised her glass.

"A toast to my Marie on this New Year's Day." He lifted his glass in a sweep to the countryside and said, "And a toast to another fine year for the finest wines in Alsace." They touched glasses and drank.

They drank in silence and watched the sun moving almost perceptibly to the horizon.

Marie pushed the mud clods off her high green rubber boots with her other foot. Bernhard refilled their glasses.

"I'm sorry about last night," he said.

"It's nothing."

"I had thought I could get away, but she wanted me home. What could I do?"

Marie continued working the mud off her boots. "A wife has a right to expect her husband to be home at night with her," she said, avoiding his eyes. "Especially on New Year's Eve."

"But we had planned to spend last night together. I was disappointed."

"Think nothing of it," she said.

"But, Marie, I know you must be upset. . . ."

"We'll not talk about it now." She looked up again. "Tell me how your work goes."

Bernhard shook his head. He gulped down his third glass of wine and poured another for himself. "Work . . . always work. Service to my country. I am bored."

"Why bored?"

"The longer I am in Strasbourg, the more certain I am sure that what we are doing there is a waste. It will all be for nothing."

"Bernhard, how can you say that? You are an important member of the European parliament. You are helping to rebuild Europe. A unified Europe will become an economic power to be reckoned with."

"Ha!"

"Why do you laugh?"

"Because soon Europe will not need me. Soon there will be no more European Union."

"Why do you say that?"

"Because soon the power of nationalism will again sweep over Europe. Only fools think that the European Union has a chance."

"Are you already drunk? I don't understand, Bernhard. What nationalism?"

"Do you not read the papers, Marie? Do you not know what is going on in my own country? And in yours? We are closing the door to immigrants. You are, too."

"I suppose. But Germany has always had a tradition . . ."

"What? Of hating foreigners? I agree. And for good reason. They are sapping our national resources. They will ruin our economy. Paying for unification is costly enough. We don't need the added burden of taking care of foreigners. Mind you, I'm not like one of those skinheads, though."

"Of course not, Bernhard. But why should the European Union fall apart?" she asked.

Bernhard drained the last of the wine into his glass. He was flushed with alcohol and excitement. She was still sipping her first glass.

"Because," he said, "Germany will soon be striking out on its own again."

Marie asked carefully, "Is this related to STEEPLECHASE?"

Bernhard picked a speck off the rim of his glass with his forefinger and flicked it away. "Yes," he answered.

"But what does that mean?"

"It means that the next big lie will be told within a few days. The Germans will tell the world with a straight face that they support the Americans in their efforts to force Japan to open up trade. Watch the television news for all the happy, smiling faces. Between their clenched teeth, the Germans are saying, 'Go to hell, all of you!' "

"And that is not the truth?"

"Of course not," he scoffed. "The Germans don't want to cooperate with the other Europeans. They want to *dominate* them."

"How so?"

"*Economics*," Bernhard emphasized. "That's where the next war will be waged. There will be no tanks rumbling through the beautiful valleys of Alsace this round. By the time the German parliament has moved from Bonn back into the Reichstag in Berlin, the secret war will have begun. Germany and Japan—the new partnership." He lifted his glass to the horizon. "Cheers to the new imperialism."

"And what of my France?"

"*Your* France? *Your* France, Marie? *You* are Alsatian. You are more German than French. You tie up your grapevines like the Germans. The grapes you grow are from German stock. You eat like a German. Alsace is German. It lies in France through an accident of history."

"I am French, Bernhard. *You* are a German."

Bernhard said, "I hate politics. Why do we have to talk about politics?"

"Politics is your life, Bernhard. Not me, not your family. It's important to you. That's why we talk about it."

Bernhard didn't answer.

Marie talked. "So what about the Americans? How do they figure into this? Do you think they will stand idly by as Germany marches?"

Bernhard scoffed: "The Americans are naive. They think only of themselves. They think that if only Japan will buy some American cars and rice, all their problems will go away. The American President is so busy concentrating on bashing Japan that he doesn't see what else is going on in the world. He jumps from one crisis to another. The only thing he's worried about is getting reelected. Well, let them find out what it is like to be an island. Let them see what happens when they find that their export markets have dried up."

"What do you mean?"

"Market share, my dear Marie. No more bloody wars for a treeless hill or a maze of muddy trenches. Forget dirt—market share is the new prize." He was getting drunk quickly. "Just wait until they find out one day soon that Germany has excluded them from one half the world's economies and Japan the other half. By then, it will be too late for them to do anything. The world economy can crush any army. The American century is coming to a close."

"Bernhard . . ."

"Yes, Marie?"

"Do you think that we shall be together this time next year?"

"That depends, Marie."

"On what does it depend, Bernhard?"

"It depends on what you will think of me as a German in a year's time, and not just as a lover."

59 ❑　❑　❑　❑

Between Big Sur and San Francisco, Greer was forced to make one stop. His old clothes—the fake Levi's and Tijuana Hard Rock Cafe T-shirt—had been so filthy from the smoke that he needed to change before he got into the city. Looking like a traumatized homeless person, he had found a Salvation Army store in Saratoga and bought a loose pullover shirt with bright green, orange, and turquoise stitchery and baggy cotton pants. He thought the outfit appropriate for a young northern California dropout, a member of the new lost generation.

He drove to San Francisco International Airport and parked Kate's car in long-term parking. No one would bother checking on it until many days had passed, so there was little chance that it would be found and traced as stolen. If the car *were* found sooner, there would be no way of knowing if Greer had stayed in the city or found a way to catch a plane to some other location. He took with him Kate's portable cellular phone, which she had dropped as he shoved her out the car, then he boarded the shuttle to the main terminal. From there he found a seat in the back of the bus that took him to the heart of the city.

Greer walked over to Grant Avenue to one of the few stores open on New Year's Day in Chinatown. The windows were crammed with electronics behind large Going Out of Business signs. The same store under the same management had been going out of business eight years earlier when he had been there on his previous visit.

Although it was located in the heart of Chinatown, Greer thought it odd that everyone working in the store was Mexican and the merchandise was almost exclusively Japanese. There was every conceivable kind of electronic equipment: cameras, video games, computers, stereo equipment, calculators, TVs, VCRs, camcorders, and any kind of gadget imaginable.

He got out his list and found a stray shopping cart. He walked up and down the aisles filling his basket with boxes, methodically checking items off his list.

The man at the checkout called out the equipment as he rung them up: "Binoculars, twelve-band scanner, extension cords, adapters, multiband transceiver. Anything else, sir?"

Greer checked his list then looked over the man's head at the case behind the counter, scanning the merchandise behind the locked glass doors.

"The rifle and scope," he answered. "Throw in a couple of ammo clips. And call me a taxi."

The Director of Central Intelligence and the White House Chief of Staff stood in the freezing empty library room of Randall Jenkins' Chevy Chase house with their overcoats on. The heat hadn't been on since Jenkins had left for Cologne. The housekeeper had returned to her family in Guatemala. All the furniture was gone. Everything else was packed in boxes stacked up in the living room.

The room smelled like wet ashes. It was drizzling just above the freezing point outside. There was a drip in the fireplace.

Gibbons instinctively inspected behind the curtains for microphones. He examined the perimeter of the walls for wires. He was saying, "So what's the President's problem?"

"He's beginning to lose confidence. He thinks if he doesn't pull off the Japanese deal that he's a goner. And he's probably right. His ego's shot. He can't stand not to be universally loved. The polls just get worse and worse. I'm the one who has to give him the bad news every Monday morning."

Conrad stooped over the fireplace and tried to close the damper. "Any new intelligence on what the Japanese are up to?"

"Nothing. All we can get is that they're pissed off, but they're going to suck it up and sign."

"Good," said Conrad. "I'll let the President know this afternoon."

"Not much time."

Gibbons took a look around the room. "What do you think? Can we close it out?"

Conrad nodded. "There's nothing here. The FBI's been through and found nothing. Contrary to his reputation, Jenkins was a boring guy. A little eccentric, but basically a boring guy. I'll tell them to go ahead and turn the place over to his estate. We're done with it."

Gibbons nodded. "Going to San Francisco?"

Conrad snorted. "Are you kidding? I wouldn't miss that show for anything."

60

"Sloppy. Very Sloppy."

Stephanie lifted her head and looked around. Her wrists and ankles were tied to a chair. Only the closest wall was visible. Everything else was pitch black. In the light of a kerosene lantern she saw Erich Reagor standing in front of her holding a long black flashlight. She saw the narrow-gauge track and the small, open railcar that she had come on. The wall glistened with a crystalline sheen.

Rauf and Suleyman—the two who had brought her forcibly to this place—were at her sides. How could they do this to her? They all worked together with Reagor. They were Turks. And she had thought they were her friends.

"No one can hear us here," said Reagor. "An abandoned salt mine. We're a almost a thousand meters inside this mountain. Don't even think of trying to escape. There are a countless number of tunnels running between Germany and Austria in this mine. Your only hope of getting out alive is to cooperate with me."

Stephanie looked him in the eye and pleaded, "What do you want? I've done everything you've ever asked of me."

Reagor reached into the side pocket of his coat and pulled out a handful of diskettes. He threw them at Stephanie. "Garbage," he said. "Worthless garbage, just like you. You bring this back. I think that you decided to collaborate with Greer Whitaker. I think you still feel something for him after all these years."

Reagor stepped close and kicked the chair hard from the front. It fell backward and Stephanie hit her head hard on the floor. She let out a moan.

"Get her up," Reagor ordered. Suleyman tipped the chair back up. "I'd like for us to get this over with quickly, *Fräulein*. I want to know why you left him and brought back these diskettes with meaningless information. Didn't you bother to check them before you came back?"

"I *did,* Erich! I looked at them on the computer and it looked like what you had told me Greer had worked on. I had to assume that was it."

Reagor didn't respond. Stephanie closed her eyes and shook her lowered head slowly from side to side. Was it even worth reasoning with him? she wondered. "I called you as soon as we got to Munich and told you where we were, Erich. I even led your two women to him in the boardinghouse. I called you from Rothenburg. *I* was the one who told *you* that he had sent the diskettes from Munich."

"But you couldn't even get him to tell you what it was all about. You and your supposed power over him. It wasn't working. I knew you weren't going to be able to make him crack even as early as Munich. That's why I sent those two others after him in Munich—to force the information out of him. And then outside of Rothenburg on the autobahn. I'm dealing with incompetents and liars! Now I don't believe anything you've told me about Greer Whitaker. You're going to tell me how you let him escape and where he's going!"

"No! You're wrong, Erich!"

Reagor raised the flashlight over his head. Stephanie had closed her eyes again, so it came as a total shock when he brought the flashlight down hard with a glancing blow off the side of her face with a loud crack.

Stephanie was still dazed from the fall on the back of her head. Her mouth opened as if she were yawning. It was a silent scream. The shock of the pain was too intense to make a sound this time. She started to shake as the pain enveloped her whole body.

Reagor was unfazed. "You stupid bitch! I'll break every bone in your body, starting with your face, and work my way down if you don't start talking."

Stephanie rolled her head from side to side.

"Tell me how you have helped Greer Whitaker to escape with the information you were supposed to bring back. Tell me why you promised that if we let him leave here and go back to the United States, you could get the diskettes back." He scoffed, " 'HE IS STILL OURS'— your message to me. But he wasn't."

Stephanie lifted her eyes up to Reagor. She tried yelling at him, but the cheekbone was already swelling, her speech was garbled: "Erich . . . you can do what you want with me, but there's nothing to say! I have been loyal to you! I just made a mistake!"

Reagor pulled around one of the other chairs and sat down facing her. He crossed his legs and folded his arms across his chest. He checked his watch. "It is now almost eleven P.M. Based on my rather substantial previous experience, I estimate that you will be willing to talk candidly to me within half an hour. Certainly no more." Reagor pointed with the flashlight to Rauf. "You go first, Rauf."

Rauf unfolded a large blade from a Swiss Army knife. He put the point of the blade against Stephanie's throat. He put his face right up into hers and smiled. She could smell his last meal of something meaty on his breath. He pricked her lightly and she flinched. A tiny trickle of blood started flowing down her throat to the top of her turtleneck sweater. He let out a short laugh and grabbed the top of her sweater roughly. He put the blade into the fabric in the collar and started pulling it down slowly, cutting open the front of the sweater. When he had cut it all the way to the bottom, he parted the cloth and looked at her breasts.

"Easy, Rauf," warned Reagor. "Slowly. Leave something for Suleyman."

Rauf pushed the torn sweater off Stephanie's shoulders and pulled out the corkscrew on the knife. He stood over her and got a firm grip on the corkscrew, placing the tip of it on the fleshy part of the shoulder. He pushed down until it went into the flesh and drew blood.

Stephanie winced. Then he hit muscle. "Erich!" she screamed. "I didn't help him!"

"Here we go," said Rauf. He pushed down with his body weight and screwed the tool into her shoulder.

Stephanie let out another scream. Rauf let go of the tool. It stood up on its own. He readjusted his grip and bore down with another hard twist. She let out another scream and tried thrashing, but the duct tape held her arms and legs in place. Suleyman made sure the chair didn't turn over.

"Once more with the corkscrew," said Rauf. . . .

On the other side of the Bay in Berkeley, Greer was violating a half dozen ordinances of the local fire code.

On the third floor of a run-down hotel on Shattuck Avenue a couple of blocks from the downtown Berkeley BART station, Greer plugged in yet another electric cord into the adapter in the wall behind his twin bed. There was only one outlet in the room. Thick orange extension cords crisscrossed the bed and floor. The plug was loose in the socket and every time he touched a cord, sparks sizzled and flew out of the hole, scorching the wall. The lights flickered. Greer waited for a fuse to blow somewhere in the hotel.

Greer had taken the taxi to Berkeley from the electronics store in Chinatown. It was in a perfect location. He peeked through the sheer acetate curtains. He had unobstructed views up and down the Shattuck Avenue shopping and business district. One whole block on the other side of the commuter rail station was closed off to traffic, with police barricades set across the wide street. Most of the activity flowing to the summit in the other part of town passed near his hotel.

There was commotion in the area. The national TV networks were setting up their relay units in preparation for the summit conference nearby starting the next day. There were big trucks with generators humming loudly and large satellite uplink dishes on top.

Greer checked the electrical connections in the room. Everything was finally in order.

He pushed some of the cords aside on the bed and sat down. He got a pad of paper and a pen out from the bedside table. He turned on the twelve-band scanner and watched the LCD display start to automatically scan radio frequencies.

The scanner covered the frequencies for all of the police, fire, and emergency medical bands. It also picked up a lot of other two-way radio communications.

Greer leaned his head against the wall. There was no headboard on the bed and there was a greasy spot on the wall from the previous occupants. The trick with the scanner was figuring out exactly where the local transmissions were. To find out which channels the local police were using, for example, he had to punch in an upper and lower limit for the search within a band, then press another button on the scanner for the equipment to search for an active frequency within the limits.

Trying to find a specific frequency for a specific transmitter could take days. Greer eyed the rifle leaning against the wall in the corner near the window. He didn't have that long.

Reagor was still sitting in the chair with his legs crossed. He checked his watch again and frowned. "Eleven forty-five," he said. "We're not making very good progress."

He looked pitilessly at Stephanie, now lying on the ground. Her dirty face was streaked with tears from earlier. But she had no more tears left. She was naked except for the shredded sweater and cut apart jeans and panties. Her body was weeping blood onto the hard-packed salt floor in small streams from dozens of wounds. The Swiss Army knife lay beside the chair, a bloody mess.

"Pretty tattoo, don't you think?" asked Rauf.

Reagor nudged her torn jeans aside with the flashlight to look at the tattoo again. She moved her head slightly and moaned.

Reagor said calmly, "One last time. Tell me what you have done and where he is."

Stephanie looked at Reagor through eyes that were swollen almost completely shut. Her voice was a harsh whisper: "Erich," she said. "I have served only you."

Reagor was incensed. "Where has he gone? I find it totally inconceivable that you—my best agent—allowed him to deceive you about the diskettes, then escape being killed! You fell in love with him, didn't you? You're trying to protect him, aren't you?"

Stephanie shook her head. She could no longer speak.

"Waste of time," Reagor said. "He never did give a damn about her. Maybe she did help him, maybe she didn't. Get the lamp," he said to Suleyman. "We're leaving."

The three men walked back to the rail car, leaving Stephanie in the dark.

Reagor turned the flashlight on. "On second thought . . ." he said.

He walked back to Stephanie. She didn't move, but he could see her chest rise and fall as she breathed.

Reagor took another step closer and gave her a hard kick to the head.

Stephanie's body convulsed violently on the packed salt floor. Then she was still.

Reagor walked through the dark and climbed into the rail car. Reagor pulled the control back and the train started moving out the way they had come in. As they were leaving the excavation room, Reagor flashed the light over Stephanie's body. Faulty signals from her brain caused her muscles to jerk, the body's last futile attempt to spasm itself back to life.

They left her body twitching in the absolute dark, a half mile below ground in the Salzbergwerk inside the Watzmann mountain.

61 ❑ ❑ ❑ ❑

Marie von Bosacker entered Au Bain Marie on rue Boissy d'Anglas, shutting the door behind her against a bitterly cold but brilliantly bright January day in Paris.

"*Bonjour, madame.*" The woman who usually worked downstairs greeted her casually, taking a moment to look up from the silver she was polishing on the counter and giving her a familiar smile.

"*Bonjour,*" answered the Comtesse.

She unbuttoned her heavy topcoat and took off her sunglasses. She pulled off her doeskin gloves and put them into her pocket. She left the printed silk Hermès scarf tied loosely around her head.

The store lay in a famous shopping district in the eighth arrondissement, just around the corner from the Place de la Concorde. It was a world-famous store, specializing in expensive and hard-to-find tableware. On the first floor of the spacious, high-ceilinged open area were silverware, linens, china, and specialty items for the table such as wine coolers, salt wells, nut crackers, and napkin rings. Some of the things were new and some were very old, pieces acquired from some of the great estates of Europe that had fallen on hard times. On the second floor was a vast cookbook collection. Au Bain Marie was a Paris institution, attracting chefs, restaurateurs, and home entertainers from around the world.

The Comtesse wandered to the back of the store where much of the antique silver was displayed on tables. She picked up a few small items—a candle snuffer, a menu-card holder—then put them back. She browsed along the back wall to the right side of the store where the new china patterns were displayed. There was another shop girl there, carefully stacking the plates and cups and saucers for dusting.

The store was very quiet, with the feel of an old public library. The only sounds were the Comtesse's footsteps on the wooden floor and the occasional passing of a car outside in the narrow street.

The Comtesse made the three and a half hour trip from Alsace to Paris in her Range Rover on the first Tuesday of every month. She left Kaysersberg early and arrived in the city by nine-thirty or ten, depending on the traffic.

Her schedule had varied little over the past three years. Her first stop was always at a small cafe off Rue St. Honoré where she parked her car for the day and had a coffee and pastry. From there she made her way south along the street, shopping at the dozens of boutiques, crisscrossing from one side of the street to the other as she headed toward the Place de la Concorde and the Crillon, the end point of her day.

The ritual was not complete without the stop at Au Bain Marie. She usually spent a half hour downstairs looking at things, turning them over to see their price, and replacing them. Then she climbed the wide wooden stairs to the second level to browse through the cookbooks.

The Comtesse went upstairs.

Among the more interesting, older books was a 1933 copy of Mrs. Beeton's *Household Management,* the four-inch thick guide to proper cooking and servant management for English gentlewomen between the world wars.

If she only had a written message to leave, she would pull the book off the shelf and open it to Chapter One, page nine—entitled "The Mistress"—putting her note between the pages and replacing the book in its position on the shelf.

If she needed a face-to-face meeting, she would leave the scarf on her head while inside and browse through the cookbooks for a few minutes, then leave the store to meet her contact at the Crillon for a late tea.

Today she skipped over Mrs. Beeton and pulled the scarf knot a little tighter under her chin. She walked slowly down the broad stairs to the first floor, passing the shop manager on her way out. She made sure that the girl working in the china department saw her so that she could relay the signal.

"*Au revoir,*" she said.

"*Merci.*"

He was already waiting for her at the table set for two next to the wall, half hidden from the view of the rest of the restaurant by a tall red leather screen with a gold fleur-de-lis design. In the center of the L'Obelisque restaurant hung a Lalique crystal chandelier. The chairs were red velvet. The table looked as if it had been set with the most expensive items from Au Bain Marie only a block away. She saw him watching for her in the mirror-lined walls. The empty chair waiting for her was out of sight behind the screen, out of angle for the mirrors.

They greeted each other with kisses on the cheeks and sat down. There was something businesslike about how they interacted, but there was also a familiarity.

Marie addressed him in English: "We needed to meet."

She got a cigarette out from a gold and lapis lazuli case in her pocketbook and waited for him to light it. Officially, smoking had been banned from all Paris restaurants, but the owners of the Crillon—and every other restaurant in the city—ignored the law to keep their patrons happy.

She inhaled deeply and blew the smoke off to the side. She gave him a smile with her crisply colored lips. "How *are* you," she said.

"I'm fine," he answered. His accent was unmistakably American. He was in his mid-fifties. "How are *you?*"

He had acquired that European look somewhere along the way, something cosmopolitan in the cut of his clothes, a luxurious tie from Hermès.

"Oh, you know," she said. "The usual."

Over the past three years, he had played the role of her friend, therapist, language tutor, spiritual adviser, and messenger. At this point in their relationship, she thought that she needed him more than he needed her. She was wrong.

"How long do you have?" he asked.

She gave him a weary smile: "We can talk as long as you want. If I have to, I'll stay here tonight."

He ordered tea and sandwiches for them. They ate unhurriedly.

"Bernhard is heading toward a nervous breakdown," she said.

"Why do you say that?" He didn't want to rush her. He would draw the information out of her in a civil, leisurely manner. "Is that why you wanted to meet today?"

She shrugged.

"He's gone off talking about the Germans again," she said. "He hates his work in Strasbourg. He can't handle the stress of maintaining two lives anymore. His father is pressuring him to come into the business. He's moved past middle age. You name it, it's stressing him out."

He nodded sympathetically. "How are the two of you getting along?" he asked.

She shook her head and stubbed out the cigarette. "*I'm* torn. *He's* torn. I love him—you know that. I can't help it. I don't know why. It's his core being, not what he parades around as that I love. Strip away everything that has made him a success, and what is left is what I love."

More sympathetic nodding from the American.

She had met the American at a dinner party thrown by someone from the American embassy just over three years ago. He had just been assigned to Paris and she didn't recognize him as one of the regulars. She had been a frequent guest of the Americans at diplomatic functions and knew many of them. He exuded a determined, but quiet eagerness to get to know her better. He found out that her husband had died. The American's approach was asexual, but the attention was appealing nonetheless. He had introduced himself as the new political officer. She knew immediately that he must be CIA.

"What's he saying about the Germans? That's why you wanted to talk today, isn't it?"

She picked at her food, but drank the tea quickly. He waved the waiter over and ordered another small pot.

"Mostly it's more of the same. But I sense a fervor I hadn't seen in him before. He's obsessed with German nationalism. He says that the Germans' participation in the European Union and the trade talks as part of the Group of Seven conference are a front, a sham. He says that Germany is moving ahead with plans to create a new superstate, a Germany that will dominate Europe again. He carries on and on about economics. God, I hate politics and economics. . . ."

She almost said his name. One of the rules was that when they spoke in public, they would never call each other by their real names. For three years, she had left him notes and met him in the Crillon, but never had she spoken his name.

He got out a pen and jotted some notes on the back of his embassy business card.

She continued talking, slowing down a bit so that he could capture what she was saying in writing: "He mentioned something the other day that I thought was curious. He said that the Germans and the Japanese were coordinating economic policy and had already decided on how to divide up the world's markets. It's the first time he's mentioned the Japanese. It sounds crazy, doesn't it?"

The American nodded, raising his eyebrows in agreement, and kept on writing.

"According to Bernhard, the Germans and Japanese are planning what will be, in effect, an economic blockade on American exports. The Germans and Japanese will so dominate the world's economies that the Americans will have no more export markets. They intend it to be a subtle takeover of the world. No bullets, no tanks. Only the guiding hand of free economics. The Americans say they want open markets and a free market world economy? Bernhard says that it will be the Americans' ruination. The Germans and Japanese are convinced that *they*—not the Americans—can give the people of the world a better product, whether that be a car or loaf of bread. In a new world of free choice, the world's consumers will buy German or Japanese."

The American looked more serious than usual. "What else?" he said.

That weary smile again. "What else," she repeated. She looked up at the ceiling, looking for the proper English words to express the complex thoughts and feelings that engrossed her. "What else," she said again softly.

She cleared a space on the table and propped an elbow up, resting her chin in her hand.

"Everything I've done, I've done for my country," she said. "My dear Alsace . . ."

The American cut in: "You've been a tremendous service to your country. Don't ever underestimate your contribution."

"I know, I know. You more than anyone know that I put my country, my land, above all else."

Another delicate question from the American: "Even Bernhard?"

"Yes," she said. "Even now Bernhard. And that is the real reason we are talking today. I sense that it is just about over with Bernhard and me. When it is, I don't think that you and I can continue our relationship. It's not just that I won't be able to tell you anything anymore. I think I've already told you everything there is to say. For my part, I've accomplished what I wanted. It's also that if we continued to work together, it would remind me of my time with Bernhard, and I don't want that. It has been a sad time for me. This will be our last meeting."

She poured herself another cup of tea.

She spoke, "I know that you have worried about my getting too attached to Bernhard. You never said so, but I knew. I surprised myself. I hate everything he represents. He's German, he's *nouveau riche,* he's a married man." The thought of those things made her angry and disgusted with herself. "And somewhere along the way, somewhere over the last three years, I fell in love with him."

"You two have become very close," the American agreed.

She lowered her voice. "I've got to rationalize my actions over the past three years somehow. In the beginning, you sought me out. You wanted someone to help you get information on members of the European parliament. I circulated in the Strasbourg society and knew a lot of Euro MPs. You knew I hated the Germans. They took away my father and the happiness of my childhood. 'Alsace is German,' Bernhard would insist at the Strasbourg parties. He laughed loudly, spilling wine on his tie. Wine from my family's vineyards. The irony was not lost on me. He made my blood boil. I was ecstatic about helping you. Anything to keep the Germans off my land. Anything to make them pay for what they did to my mother and me."

The American stopped writing and looked up. "I'm sure we can meet again. I understand how you must feel. Let's give it a break, maybe a month or two, okay?"

She shook her head. "No," she said. "I've thought about it. I need to make a clean break. I made the mistake of falling in love with Bernhard. I don't want to have this to remind me of him after he has gone back to his country and his family. We cannot meet again."

He was careful and casual in asking the question: "Anything new on STEEPLECHASE?"

"Yes, I figured it out. The connection with Bernhard had eluded me for quite some time. I had assumed that he knew about the operation because he was an important member of government. But I was wrong. He knows because of his father's business."

"How so?"

"His father is over eighty and is anxious for someone else in the family to get involved in the business so that the family has some other representation on the board before the old man dies. Bernhard's older brother has absolutely refused to be a part of it. Over the past few months his father has been trying to convince Bernhard to come in as an officer of the company and take a seat on the board. The family used to control about thirty percent of the stock, but it's down to one or two percentage points now. Against his father's wishes, the board has lavished stocks and options on the young president of the company."

"What's the connection?"

"Bernhard told me that as part of their discussions, his father let him in on what was going on with STEEPLECHASE. That's also been the source of his information on the arrangements between the Germans and the Japanese. Apparently the company, Deutsche Bayrische Werke, has been running the operation on behalf of the German government. Their own people—the private sector—are doing it so that the government can deny responsibility if anything happens."

"And what about the mole in the United States?"

"An enthusiastic but unwitting soul. Some bureaucrat on the National Security Council staff. A kid. But someone with access to American policy makers."

"Is that all?"

The Comtesse looked deeply into the eyes of the American CIA officer who had been running her as an agent. She knew that *he* knew this was their last meeting and that he would pump her for everything she knew.

"One of your own," she answered. "There is a man at DBW in Munich who used to be a colonel in Stasi. I don't know his name, but he should be easy to locate there. He has been running a CIA officer for years. Bernhard says that the CIA officer has been the cut-out between the Germans and the person on the National Security Council staff."

"Anything else?"

"No," she said. "There is nothing else."

The Comtesse reached under the table and got a shopping bag. She handed it to the American.

"For me?"

"Something for you to remember me by. From Alsace."

He pulled the tissue-wrapped present out of the bag and placed it on the table. He carefully unwrapped it. It was a blue glazed wine pitcher with an inscription.

The Comtesse read as the American turned the pitcher in his hand. *"Le vin dissipe la tristesse."*

"Wine drives away sadness," he translated. "Thank you."

The American nodded and waved the waiter over to pay.

She remained seated as he got up. She closed her eyes. She was holding her delicate Limoges china tea cup so tightly that it was about to shatter.

He bent over and gave her a kiss on both cheeks. For the first time, he gave her shoulder a little squeeze as he left her.

"Au revoir," he said quietly. He whispered into her ear, *"Merci beaucoup, Marie."*

Her eyes were still closed. *"Au revoir,"* she replied. She opened her eyes and looked straight ahead at the point in space he had occupied.

He snaked through the tables out of the room, putting on his topcoat. He took one last look in her direction before he stepped outside to walk back to the crypto room at the American embassy to send his final report on operation REDWING.

She was invisible behind the leather screen.

62 ❑ ❑ ❑ ❑

Greer brought the rented twenty-two-foot sailboat about directly into the wind and uncleated the sheets to the jib and mainsail. There was a light chop on the bay water. He dropped the lines and they went slack. The two sails immediately started luffing noisily in the wind, the sound of the empty canvases flapping powerlessly overhead.

The forward motion of the sailboat eventually slowed to a stop. Greer secured the boom in a neutral position and scooted along the seat to the back of the boat.

He kept the boat turned into the wind by controlling the tiller extension with one hand. With the other hand he lifted the pair of zoom binoculars. He adjusted the focus, bringing the Berkeley shoreline into crisp focus.

There closest to him was the Berkeley marina where he had chartered the boat for the morning and the long pier extending out into the San Francisco Bay. The slips were full of boats put up for the winter. He lowered the binoculars and looked around. It was a Wednesday in winter at ten o'clock in the morning, and he was the only sailboat within sight. Traffic on I-80 and the Oakland Bay Bridge two miles off the port bow was bumper to bumper, carrying many of the boat owners to their jobs in downtown San Francisco.

The Marriott at the marina was an easy test. The binoculars were the most powerful that had been available in the Chinatown electronics store. From his position about a half mile away from the marina he could see into one of the open hotel windows on the top floor. There was a television on. He saw a morning news anchor mouthing words on the set as a man sat on the edge of his bed in his T-shirt and boxers, pulling up his socks.

Behind the marina and the Marriott rose the city of Berkeley. Somewhere in the middle of it all was his shabby little hotel on Shattuck Avenue.

Greer reached into his coat pocket and got a hand full of brochures and stuck them under his leg on the seat to keep the sea breeze from blowing them away. On the way to the bus stop earlier in the morning, he had slipped into the Chamber of Commerce to pick up a map of Berkeley and literature on the city's sights. The bus he had caught downtown dropped him off at the western end of University Avenue where it dead-ended into the marina road.

He got the map out and oriented himself to the landmarks. He easily sighted Sather Tower on the Berkeley campus. Behind the campus rose the Berkeley hills. He readjusted the focus of the glasses for the farther distance and traced the ridge along to the south.

He saw rising above the tree line about two miles from the university campus what he thought he was looking for. He adjusted the binoculars. The building snapped into crisp focus and shone like a dazzling white Mediterranean castle on the high hill overlooking Berkeley and the bay.

Greer sorted through the brochures. He found the one on the Claremont Resort Hotel and studied the color pictures. He looked at the building through the binoculars again. There were ten-story-tall turrets and towers. The photographs matched perfectly. It was definitely the Claremont.

Greer felt a surge of adrenaline upon recognizing the building. In less than twenty-four hours, the leaders of seven of the most powerful countries in the western world would be there signing historic economic agreements.

Erich Reagor had a plan.

On the flight from Munich to New York, the idea had finally come to him: how he could get Greer out into the open in a large American city that he knew nothing about other than what he had read or seen on TV. But now he had a definite plan. On the New York to San Francisco leg of the trip, he had worked out the details and was feeling impatient to get things going.

Reagor sat in the back seat of a taxi taking him from the San Francisco airport to downtown. He was very unhappy with the fact that Greer Whitaker had killed Bob Reed. Good old Robert, he thought. Reagor smiled to himself. How he did hate to be called Robert. Reed had once told him that Reagor was the only person other than his mother who had ever called him that. And he hated his mother. He didn't have a father, so the fact was significant, from a controller's point of view. Reagor had written it down in his notebook after the meeting when he had learned about that little annoyance. It was just one more button of Reed's that Reagor could push.

Robert Reed. Stasi agent. Someone whom he had blackmailed for over twenty years. But, still, it was Robert. How could you spend almost your entire adult lifetime knowing someone that intimately and not have developed at least a small amount of affection?

Reagor thought back to the last time he had seen Reed. It was in the Orangery at the Belvedere Palace in Vienna. They had met there fifty or sixty times over the years. Being assigned to various responsibilities in the Western Europe Division during his CIA career, Reed had found it easy to slip into Vienna. Many times, he just worked out a long layover on his way to or from someplace else. For his part, Reagor loved the art galleries in the Upper Belvedere. It was a natural place to meet. And, with all the queers hanging out in the Orangery, no one thought twice about two grown men strolling casually down the graveled paths.

When he arrived at Kennedy Airport in New York, there had been a voice-mail message for him in the DBW phone system. It was Stettler. In a very short message without explanation, Stettler had called him back to Munich. He had told him to catch the next flight out of New York back to Germany.

Was Stettler jacking him around? Wasn't it okay to take some initiative and go himself to the United States to finish a job that his people had utterly failed to do? He had never consulted with Stettler before on something as straightforward as this. Out of courtesy, Reagor had left a coded phone message for Stettler telling him he was going to America. He had told Stettler about Stephanie Becker's failure. Stettler knew about everything—Greer Whitaker's recruitment, Stephanie Becker's involvement, the old tie with Robert Reed, the involvement of Kate Mallotte. So why would Stettler object? Reagor knew how to take orders, but it was personal now. There was the matter of Robert being dead. And the young Greer Whitaker had tricked him about the diskettes. Stephanie was probably right. She didn't know she was bringing back fake data. But there could be no regrets. Stephanie would have been eliminated anyway; she knew far too much. Whitaker had made him look like a fool. Reagor was in no mood to change his plans, especially now that he had a way to get Whitaker.

Reagor shifted his weight in the taxi as they took the exit ramp which would lead them into the city. Reagor put his hands out low in front of him, below the back of the front seat. He looked at his hands flexing. Reagor had even decided how he would kill Whitaker. He would crush his windpipe and watch him suffer an agonizingly slow death. It would probably only take a minute and a half, two minutes at most. But it would be pain that Greer Whitaker could never have imagined. Reagor had seen it—done it—before. There would be a look of total helplessness on the face as the body tried to cope with what had just happened. Then the eyes would roll back into the head. After that, Whitaker's body would relax and it would all be over. He could feel his hands around Whitaker's throat right then.

Reagor thought back to being in New York six hours earlier. After listening to Stettler's message at the airport, Reagor had punched in the code to get back into the electronic voice-mail administrator. He punched another series of codes, then input Stettler's extension. He heard Stettler's own greeting on the voice-mail system: *"This is Hans Stettler. I'm sorry I'm not able to take your call, but if you will please leave your name and phone number along with a brief message, I will call you back. Have a nice day."*

The message had ended and Reagor waited for a beep.

"This is Erich Reagor. I don't have a phone number. Go fuck yourself."

"A strange place to meet, don't you think, Uncle?"

Jacko and his Uncle Hiro stood on the back of a commercial fishing boat pulling out into the Bay. The sound of the diesel engine was deafening as the boat churned through the choppy water out to sea.

"Safer this way, nephew."

Hiro looked about the Japanese crew as they busied themselves with chores. He motioned to the cockpit and a man with a briefcase joined them.

"He brings instructions from the crypto room at our consulate in the city," Hiro said. The man handed over the briefcase. "Please look away," Hiro said to the man with a smile.

The man turned around, facing the open water. Silently, Hiro reached inside Jacko's coat and tapped the gun in Jacko's shoulder holster. Hiro nodded and looked at the back of the man's head.

Jacko removed the gun and shot the man at the base of his skull. The body slumped to the deck.

Hiro said, "Sometimes it *is* necessary to kill the messenger. He was the one who decoded the message from Tokyo. We cannot risk any more security problems with this operation. Here are your instruc- tions."

Without any other signal, two crew members dragged the man away and began hacking the body to pieces.

Jacko opened the briefcase and read the materials. There was a detailed biography of Greer Whitaker, along with color photographs. There were also photographs of Kate Mallotte.

"The girl?" Jacko asked.

"According to the Germans, a romantic interest. Also CIA. Our moles at Langley indicate that she has been summoned to lunch with her boss, the Director of Central Intelligence, today at the San Francisco Hilton. Greer Whitaker was last seen down the coast in Big Sur, presumably heading north. We feel strongly that he may be coming here to disrupt the Group of Seven meeting. Very simply, follow the girl and you've got an excellent chance of finding Mr. Whitaker."

As Jacko and his uncle spoke, the two crewmen scented the water with buckets of fish blood.

"Why now?" asked Jacko.

"They were keeping us informed all along about the progress of the operation but—as we had suspected—they were losing control. Whitaker was their unwitting agent. We started getting concerned when he disappeared. As soon as we found out that the Germans' own controller had become a renegade, we pressed the Germans and they reluctantly agreed that it was time for us to intervene. Whitaker knows about our agreement with the Germans. The other details don't matter. It's obviously an embarrassment for German intelligence, but they've been cooperative. They realize the value in turning over this part of the operation to us now."

"What are my orders?" Jacko asked.

"Kill Greer Whitaker. Do it before the conference. Tokyo has already made that commitment to the Germans. Your father has assured everyone that you have the resources to put an end to this."

The sharks had arrived. One crewman threw chunks of the messenger to the hungry fish while the other hosed down the deck.

"I'll not disappoint the family," Jacko said.

63 ❑ ❑ ❑ ❑

Kate hated heights. And she was a goner for sure at this height if the Big One hit now.

She waited for Ben Gibbons at one P.M. in the forty-fourth-floor restaurant of the downtown San Francisco Hilton. She looked out the floor-to-ceiling windows on a clear day across San Francisco Bay to Berkeley. She looked directly down at the street and felt queasy. From her table she could see on her left the Bay Bridge, which had collapsed in the last big earthquake, crushing cars and people on the lower level. On her right she could just barely spot Candlestick Park, the scene of much hysteria during the catastrophe.

Ben had come out for the G7 conference. He had left word at Langley for Kate to join him. He had no idea she was already in the city.

Kate heard the elevator door chime ring and the Director of Central Intelligence popped out and strode over to her table.

"You look awful, Kate!" he said by way of a greeting.

"Thanks *a lot.*"

Ben sat and took in the view.

"This is incredible, isn't it?" he said.

"It's nice," she agreed halfheartedly.

Gibbons got serious quickly. "You know, I really appreciate everything you're doing on this investigation. You must be exhausted. You've been working on this for almost three weeks solid."

Kate told her first lie of the day to her boss: "We haven't been able to find him, Ben."

How could she tell him that she had him but he got away? He didn't even know Greer was no longer in Europe. At this point, *she* didn't even know where he was. This was no time to get squeamish about REDWING, she told herself.

"You haven't heard anything? You've still got our European allies pressing hard, don't you?"

"There's been no letup on the pressure we've put on the intelligence services and national police forces." That much, at least, was true. Let them think Greer is still in that part of the world.

Gibbons said, "I think at this point the best thing we can do is just stand by in case he turns up. Keep monitoring the situation. Agree?"

"Agree." She looked nervously out the window again. Looking far off at the other side of the bay wasn't as scary as looking straight down to the street below.

A young man in a heavily starched white jacket came by and poured water for them. There was no one nearby.

"Kate," Gibbons started out, "we need to talk." He avoided looking Kate in the eye. He picked up the menu and started glancing over it.

"Yes?"

Gibbons was still scanning the menu, seemingly oblivious to Kate. He stuck his finger onto the page. "Crab cakes," he said. He looked up at Kate.

"What is it, Ben?"

Gibbons looked directly at Kate. "You're off the case," he said. "I'm sorry. You've done good work, but it hasn't been good enough. I want you to take a few days off out here and get rested up before going back to Washington. Ride the trolley. Go to a museum. Have a nice dinner somewhere. You're more valuable to me back there helping me to run the office."

The waiter came by, stood with pen poised, and asked if they were ready to order.

Kate was curt: "No, we're not, thank you." The waiter left.

Kate pushed down the menu that Gibbons was holding up between them.

"Is this why you asked me to meet you here?"

Gibbons gave her a sour look. "I'm afraid you've let your emotions creep into your work where Greer Whitaker is concerned. I'm getting pressured from the White House to resolve this thing quickly and quietly. At this point there's no indication that Whitaker is going to be found. And I don't want to have to make another trip to the White House to explain another murder of an American citizen by Greer Whitaker. I'm going to turn this over to someone else after the G7 conference."

Kate rolled her eyes up at the ceiling in disgust. "That's unfair," she said. "Have I ever let my personal life interfere with my professional responsibilities?"

Gibbons was silent, looking out the window. Kate saw what he was watching. There was a sailboat tacking away from them that she figured Ben would rather be on at the moment.

"Well? Have I?" Kate struggled to restrain herself. She narrowed her eyes and tightened her lips. "Oh, *I* see. I didn't find Greer before the summit meeting, so it's back to a desk job for me. I suppose this effectively ends my fast track in the Agency, doesn't it? *And*, I suppose *I'll* be the one to take the fall in the Agency for letting Greer have access to the most classified information we have. I develop a relationship outside of the office and it becomes an issue. I'm no fool, Ben. I can see exactly where this is going."

Did 'he buy it? She had almost screwed up REDWING by falling in love with Greer. Now here was a chance to distance herself from him —at least in the eyes of Ben Gibbons. Actually, she could work better without having Ben Gibbons and the White House looking over her shoulder as she tried to track Greer down.

Gibbons was playing it cool. "It's a judgment call on my part, Kate, and that's the way I see it. Let's just leave it at that for now, shall we? We can pick up on this in about a week back in the office . . . *After* the conference is over."

Kate pushed her chair back abruptly, stood up, and threw the linen napkin from her lap down onto the table.

She stuck her finger right into Gibbons' face.

"Screw you, Ben," she said.

Kate made the call to Knowles in Langley from the hotel lobby. "He told me I'm officially off the case."

Knowles snorted, "Well, you may be officially off the case, but that's never stopped our section from pushing on with the Agency's legitimate business, has it?"

"No."

"You need to be aware of something important that's come up, Kate. Are you where you can talk a minute?"

Kate looked around the lobby. "I can listen," she said.

"NSA just sent over a partial intercept from Tokyo they just decoded from the Japanese embassy. It confirms everything we've always thought about their involvement and, more specifically, about Jacko Takiyama. Things are happening fast. I'll cut right to it. Waiting for you at the reception desk should be a videotape. There's a letter you need to see, too. Can't go into it over the phone. Jacko got to one of the analysts at the Agency. You need to watch the tape to understand. And, Kate?"

"Yes?"

"The intercept indicated that the Japanese are also after Greer now. Jacko's in charge."

"Oh, my God . . ."

"NSA only got part of the message. They're still working on it. There was something else about the DCI's schedule. I suspect more leaks here in Langley."

In her hotel room at the Hilton, Kate read a photocopy of a handwritten note with a CIA letterhead.

A suicide in the Agency wasn't all that unusual, she knew. Any population of professionals under stress was going to have a certain statistical probability of suicides. Kevin Hatu was an Agency analyst. After Hatu had died, they had found the note—a draft letter to CIA counterintelligence—in his office. In the note he confessed to spying for the Takiyama family. He had already guessed that they were running him on behalf of the Japanese government. He just couldn't sort out the conflicts—the Agency, his country, his Japanese-American parents, their homeland . . . and his friend Jacko Takiyama. Having pieced it back together, Kate now knew that Jacko used his friendship with Kevin Hatu to gain access to U.S. foreign-policy thinking and intelligence estimates on Japan. She also now knew that Kevin Hatu had been proactively changing the CIA's intelligence estimates to make Japan look like less of an economic threat to the United States than it really was. Hatu had suppressed reports of Japanese intelligence operations that were coming in the daily CIA station cables.

Kate loaded the VCR. There was a note from Knowles inside the tape box. Apparently Kevin had a hidden video camera in his study at home to protect his stereo system. He had been burgled twice in the past year and he was mad as hell about it.

Kate watched the soundless tape. Jacko comes in the front door. They have drinks together. Kate imagines they talk about home, probably reminiscing about the old days at university. No business, just drinks and jokes. They're loose. They play a bar game, the one where someone puts a pack of cigarettes on the floor, puts his hands behind his back, and tries to knock it over with his nose without falling flat on his face. Kevin misses a couple of times. He's still on his knees. He's laughing his head off. Then Jacko says something. Kevin isn't laughing anymore. He starts to get up to hug Jacko, but Jacko yells at him and he's back on his knees. He's crying. Jacko gives him a handgun, then watches as Kevin puts the barrel into his mouth. Kevin is crying, gagging on the barrel. Jacko puts Kevin's finger on the trigger, yells at him some more. Kevin can't do it. Nice guy that he is, Jacko helps him out. Kevin closes his eyes, hands wrapped around the gun, finger shaking on the trigger. Jacko pulls Kevin's finger back himself.

Kate stops the film. It's a creepy tape—black and white, no audio, just a dark spray of blood and brains on the wall. If Jacko did that to his best friend, what was he going to do to Greer?

Where would Greer be at this moment? she asked herself. He had been adamant in Big Sur about doing it "his way." He had vowed to tell the world about the theory or die trying. Wouldn't he want to be at the center of the action? At the Group of Seven conference?

Jacko had disappeared, dropped completely out of sight according to the careful plans he had developed in case the law ever got too close. He had set up headquarters in a nondescript house in Mill Valley on the other side of the Golden Gate Bridge.

He received a visit from an employee of an electronics firm who was also on the Takiyama payroll. Jacko listened to the telephone conversation Kate Mallotte had had with the person named Knowles in Langley.

"You guys do good work," Jacko said at the end of the tape. "How far can you pick up conversations with that dish?"

"Fifty yards—through glass."

"Nice job."

"I'm happy as long as you're happy, Jacko."

"Just keep all that equipment of yours on her. I want to know every word she utters."

Jacko motioned to one of his men. "You've got people posted throughout the hotel, right?"

"And cars waiting on the streets."

"I want a helicopter standing by in the city with its engines running twenty-four hours a day. Day or night, Kate Mallotte is going to be followed by land, air, or sea. Understand?"

"I understand, Jacko."

It was the afternoon on the day before the official start of the economic conference. The leaders of the G7 nations chatted among themselves at the base of the risers set up near the statue of the Buddha. The American organizers of the photo opportunity for the media had selected the Japanese Tea Garden in the Golden Gate Park to help lull the Japanese into complacency before they kicked their teeth in the next day when the real work began at the Claremont in Berkeley.

The atmosphere was energized with the sound of the bay breeze blowing through the trees overhead and the swishing sound of orange and white *koi* in the pools. The boxwoods were neatly trimmed, the ornamental gates and lanterns perfectly positioned. There was a merry babble among the media, most of them happy to be out of the path of a Canadian cold front swooping down upon the East Coast. California was three time zones and an Ice Age away from all that misery back home in Washington, D.C.

Aides to the presidents and prime ministers pointed out on preprepared diagrams where they should stand when it was time.

Dwight Conrad paced nervously among the photographers and cameramen, checking the light coming through the trees and looking at his watch. He rubbed his hands together in anticipation of the first official function of the conference.

Conrad saw the President craning his head over the other leaders. He was over a foot taller than Kyahaka, the Japanese prime minister, who was standing next to him. Conrad weaved through the maze of tripods over to the group.

The President pulled Conrad to the side. "Kyahaka's all smiles."

Conrad looked down on the Japanese prime minister with a frown.

"Let's see if he's still smiling by the end of the day when he's signed the side agreements," said Conrad. "By then, he'll have turned over the keys to the Japanese economy."

The President flashed a cheesy smile of his own at the others. It was the same fake smile Conrad had seen a thousand times during the last campaign.

The President spoke out of the side of his mouth as he smiled and nodded to his counterparts: "Let's get this thing going, Dwight."

Conrad passed through the crowd of leaders, telling each one that it was time to take his place. The President found Gelling, the German chancellor, and escorted him to his position on the front row of the riser beside himself. On his other side was the Japanese prime minister. The four other leaders stood tightly on the second tier behind them.

The TV camera lights turned on and the camera flashes started popping. The President grabbed the hands of the German chancellor and the Japanese prime minister and held them up overhead.

Conrad stood to the side and watched with his chin in his hand, Jack Benny style.

The President squinted through the lights to find Conrad to give him a thumbs up.

Conrad smiled back and returned the gesture.

The cameras kept flashing. Everyone was all smiles. The Japanese were apparently resigned to the new trade agreements. The Germans had done their part in pressuring the Japanese through back channels. The Germans had assured the White House the previous evening that everything was in order.

Order. The German virtue.

Everything was in place, Conrad assured himself. In twenty-four hours, it would be a done deal.

Conrad caught the President's eye again and gave him another thumbs up.

64 ❑ ❑ ❑ ❑

All of the morning network TV shows were broadcasting live from outside the Claremont.

It was the media event they had hoped for. The White House had promised a show complete with fireworks and marching bands. The President's people had been telling reporters in off-the-record briefings that it would be his finest hour. The level of expectation was high—

some people thought perhaps *too* high. The media, the President's opponents, and, of course, the President himself had built the two and a half day conference up as a do-or-die event for his Administration. It would be the defining moment of his presidency.

Greer channel-surfed with the TV remote control. It was the first full official day of meetings at the economics conference. From one channel to the next, the background was the same: a pair of palm trees on the grounds of the Claremont framing the co-hosts' heads against the backdrop of the glinting San Francisco Bay. A tiny, out-of-focus tugboat moved slowly across the water between their heads. The bay breeze rushed up into the Berkeley hills and pushed hard at the co-hosts' hair, but the hair spray kept everything in place in the picture except the swaying palm trees.

The television showed the steel-plated black limousines with bullet-proof glass take their turns driving up to the awning in front of the main door and delivering the heads of state. Greer had already watched France, Canada, and Great Britain arrive to the playing of their national anthems by a Marine Corps band in bright red uniforms and white gloves.

One of the news commentators remarked that the limousines were taking different routes to the conference site as a security precaution. Greer spread his map out on the bed and considered the likely alternatives. There was, of course, no way of knowing from which direction the dignitaries would be originating. Assuming that some of them had stayed in San Francisco the previous night, the Oakland Bay Bridge was the only reasonable alternative to get to the other side of the bay, other than taking a helicopter. Across the bridge, the freeway from San Francisco dumped out onto land in a dozen different directions, any of which eventually could be taken to the Claremont.

One good possibility was taking Ashby due east up into the hills. Greer moved his finger on the map along the road to the point at which it intersected Shattuck Avenue. It was possible that at that very moment a shiny stretch limo carrying the President of the United States was speeding up Ashby toward the intersection less than a mile south from his hotel.

Greer took out the binoculars and stood as far as he could to the left side of the window to get a long view down Shattuck. He dared not lean out the window and put himself at risk of being seen. He pressed the glasses against the wall, but still could see only a few blocks down the street.

Greer could hear a considerable amount of activity coming from the other direction. He moved to the other side of the window and focused the binoculars toward the noise. The television news truck generators had been grinding for two days, keeping the juices flowing to the satellite uplink equipment. Ever since yesterday afternoon's pre-conference photo op at the Japanese Tea Garden, the area around the media compound had been humming with rental cars and people coming and going. The street vendors had set up card tables full of jewelry on the sidewalks and all of the shops along Shattuck Avenue had been spruced up for the onslaught of tourists generated by the conference.

Closer to him was the BART station. A large group of people emerged from underground and spilled out onto the streets of down-town Berkeley. The train from San Francisco had just arrived. There seemed to be an equal mixture of university students and people who were on their way to gawk at the international leaders at the conference. The ones he had pegged as students walked quickly up a street toward the university and out of sight. The gawkers crossed the street to the bus stop and waited for a ride up the hill to the Claremont.

Three of the people who had come out of the BART station kept on walking past the bus stop toward Greer's hotel to the shops and tables along the sidewalk. They were all women. He focused the binoc-ulars again on them as they began ducking in and out of the stores. They all seemed to be young, well-dressed, and very attractive. One of them seemed to have more of an interest in the sidewalk tables of wares than the others, who tended to linger in the shops out of sight of his field glasses. She was a blonde who filled her sweater and jeans nicely, Greer thought.

Greer watched her stop at one of the tables and talk to a Rastafarian with a huge, brightly colored crocheted hat on top of his dreadlocks. They were about a block and a half away. Greer saw the woman picking up things off the table and putting them back. She was talking with the Rastaman now and shaking her head. She pointed to something, held it up to her chest like a necklace, then put it back down again. They talked for a couple of more minutes, then she started to walk off.

He followed her down the sidewalk, talking loudly and waving his hands in the air, but she was still shaking her head. Hard sell, Greer reasoned.

The Rastaman finally gave up and went back to his table. The girl was still walking, having reached a stretch of the block without many stores. She was only a half block away now, and Greer refocused the binoculars to get a good look at her face.

It was Kate. *Unmistakably,* Kate.

Greer felt a cold sweat break in the palms of his hands and on his forehead.

No way, he told himself.

The girl stopped to look in a window of the store almost directly across the street. Greer took another look. It was her from all angles, he decided. He had spent every day for almost three months with that woman. He sure as hell knew what she looked like, even from the back!

Greer instinctively crouched down behind the window sill so he would be less visible. The next thought that crossed his mind was that she had somehow found him and come to take him out. If that were true, the place could be crawling with backup just waiting for him to make a move.

Greer peeked over the window sill and watched her looking at what seemed to be a map, trying to get her bearings. She folded the map and turned east up the hill.

Then Greer saw two Asian men, dressed in business suits, approaching the corner that Kate had just turned. Greer looked at them through the binoculars. One of them was pointing in her direction. They both had pulled out handguns and walked quickly toward the corner. Kate was being followed.

Greer gave it only a moment's thought, then reached for the rifle. He put the barrel out the window, resting it on the window sill, and sighted squarely on the man in front. They were just about to reach the corner. Greer took a deep breath, held it, and started a slow squeeze on the trigger.

Then suddenly he heard shouting closer by and moved his head away from the scope to see what the commotion was. Across the street in front of a dry cleaner was another pair of Japanese men in business suits—along with another Asian standing in the doorway of the shop —all pointing up to his window. Greer quickly withdrew the rifle from the window sill and the curtains fell together, hiding him from the view of the street.

What was that all about? he asked himself. Greer gazed through the slit in the curtains and saw that the two men running toward the corner had turned back, running now toward the men in front of the dry cleaners. The shopkeeper watched impassively as the four men crossed the street in the direction of his hotel.

Greer parted the curtains once more to confirm they were still coming, but they were already out of sight. He heard the front door of the hotel opening and footsteps coming inside. They were coming for him.

Greer heard the feet running up the stairs. He was trapped. The only escape was the window leading to the street three floors below.

Just then he was startled by a hard knock at a door down the hall, followed by more hard knocks at other doors. They were going up and down his side of the hallway banging on doors, trying to find out which room he was in.

They reached his door. Three hard knocks. Greer raised the rifle toward the door and stood terrified waiting for something to happen.

From down the hall, Greer heard the sound of wood breaking and bullets ricocheting in other rooms. Silencers, he thought. Doors burst open. The men were shouting in Japanese.

Suddenly, at his own door, there was a short burst of air and small pieces of wood flying into the room as a crescent of holes splintered through the old wooden door.

Greer scrambled to the other side of the bed onto the floor, leveling his rifle at the door.

There was another—more extended—burst of bullets and then the door flew open, banging against the inside room wall. Two Japanese men in dark business suits stood in the doorway, each with a fold-up Uzi stuck in the crook of his arm.

The one on the right stepped halfway into the room and looked to the right, seeing his reflection in the mirror in the darkened bathroom. He startled himself, crouched, and sprayed the mirror with bullets. The other followed quickly into the room, instinctively pointing his Uzi in the same direction. Greer let out an audible sound as he sucked in his breath. The first gunman heard him and took one step to the side, then turned his head to look back.

"Here he—"

Greer squeezed the trigger once, then quickly shifted his aim and popped off another shot, striking the first gunman in the head and the other in the chest.

Greer's gun had been loud. He froze in his position behind the bed, knowing that there were two more gunmen in the hallway.

Suddenly, a barrel was blazing in Greer's direction. Greer ducked his head down and kept firing blindly toward the door. The bullets flew in both directions for what seemed to Greer an eternity. Then he heard a cry and heard something fall hard into his room. Greer stopped firing. He looked at himself quickly to confirm that he was all right. He poked his ahead around the side of the bed and saw that a third Japanese had fallen in, his throat presumably having caught a ricocheting bullet in the hallway. Then Greer heard a light metallic sound and low cursing. The sound of an ammo clip jamming?

Greer jumped over the bed and rushed the door, throwing himself down hard at the threshold in the direction of the sound he had heard and pulling the trigger on his semiautomatic rifle as fast as he could. He was staring into the face of the fourth man, who was on one knee against the wall trying to reload his Uzi. In his excitement, Greer missed with the first three shots, then blew a hole through the last man's gut.

Greer sat on the floor and looked around the room. Most of his equipment had been in the line of fire and had taken a hit. He turned on the radio transceiver and watched the LEDs light up. He felt a piece of something soft on his upper lip. He wiped at it with his forearm and looked at it. It was part of the first man's brain stuck to his lips. He shuddered.

Someone had certainly heard all the shooting—his at least, he thought. The Uzis had silencers.

Greer hustled up off the floor and went into the bathroom to wipe the mess off himself. Under the jacket of the man lying face down in the room he saw a piece of backup hardware, a handgun stuck into a holster in the back. Greer took the gun. No waiting period for a handgun if you just kill the owner first, Greer thought. He didn't need the rifle anymore.

Something was bugging him. The Asian guy from the dry cleaner across the street talking to the Japanese. Could it be the Japanese were now actively involved in an operation, as well? Yesterday the man at the dry cleaner had watched Greer get out of the taxi and go into the hotel. He had smiled at Greer. Greer had assumed it was a Chinese laundry. Then he remembered the calendar in the window with the picture of Mount Fuji. Japanese. His mistake.

Kate had made a show of taking Ben Gibbons' advice and had had a perfectly uneventful afternoon shopping in Berkeley. Actually, she wanted to be close to where the G7 conference was taking place and had been checking her messages at Langley on the hour. At three o'clock she stopped at the pay phone outside the used book store on Telegraph Avenue to check in at the office again.

"It *can't* be," she said to herself. She hung up, confused. Lev Trifinov was supposed to be dead.

Her liaison at the FBI had left a message for her at Langley saying that the San Francisco FBI office had taken a phone call earlier in the morning from a former Russian agent of hers from Moscow. He had used the code name that she had given him and said that he was trying to get in touch with her; Kate was the only other person in the world who could have known the code name. Kate fondled the scrap of paper with a phone number on it. He had said it was an emergency. He left the phone number along with the message saying that she should call it and have the dispatcher get in touch with him—just ask for Lev. He said that he was now a taxi driver in San Francisco. At the end of the FBI agent's own message, he had forwarded Lev's message, which had come in on his voice-mail. Kate listened to the thick Russian accent. It was definitely Lev. The last time she had heard his voice was when they had met in the safe room on Lermontov Prospect, the night that Lev had been dragged from his bed and taken to Lyubianka prison to be tortured, then shot, because he had been caught working for her.

How could he be alive? she wondered. Her other sources in Moscow had confirmed his death. She had cried for him, sent his wife an anonymous ration of meat, and closed her file on Lev Trifinov. A dead spy reincarnated as a Russian émigré taxi driver?

She looked at the phone number and grabbed the telephone handpiece, holding it down in its cradle. Lev? she asked herself. He had risked his life for her and the CIA. It might be Agency business, she reasoned. Who knows? He might have information that could save

CIA lives. He'd done it before. Those last thoughts convinced her she was doing the right thing. It was at least worth a phone call. *And,* Lev was someone she would trust with her life.

Kate picked up the phone and dialed.

Half a block away, a man sat in a van surrounded by electronic surveillance gear. He pulled the recorder away from the cellular phone, finished playing back the phone conversation Kate Mallotte just had.

"I don't know anything about it," Jacko said over the phone to the man in the van. "Trifinov—sounds Russian. What the fuck. We've got night vision on that helicopter, don't we? Don't let her out of your sight tonight."

Erich Reagor was disgusted with himself over what had just happened in the dark outside the dance club in the Tenderloin district.

He had guessed that the woman who had thrust her tongue into his mouth was in her mid-thirties. She was very tall and the long muscular arms that held his head firmly at an angle to kiss him were what he had expected from a healthy American woman. He had been sexually predisposed ever since getting into town and seeing the youthful, fit women walking through the financial district at lunchtime in their business suits and running shoes. He wanted a California woman to add to his worldwide collection of conquests. He had had American women before—in Washington, D.C.—but they had all been whores, even if he had never paid. The woman he had been with tonight had moved her hand down from his neck to his hip, then slid down to his crotch to touch the bulge. He had decided that she was it, even if she was a little on the slutty side.

Now, though, he was in a taxi heading south on Market Street to another part of the city. The pamphlet in the hotel lobby had indicated that the Castro district was only about a ten-minute ride from the Tenderloin. It was never his intention to go there tonight. He had wanted something quick in the street before his meeting later. Just enough to get him through the next couple of days so that the urge wouldn't interfere with the work he had to do. The bitch, he thought. For once, he thought he'd do it the right way. Find where the women were in a city and go there. Against his instincts, he had gone. And for the first time, he'd been deceived.

He patted his coat pockets to see if everything was still there. She could have taken something as she had groped him. He felt his wallet in the right breast pocket and the cassette-sized box in the other. Normally he would have put the package into a hotel safety deposit box, but he had brought it along on this trip for a special reason. He didn't want to leave it someplace where there was even the slightest chance that it would be lost. Having it so close—directly over his heart—helped to remind him why he was in San Francisco and what he had to do.

Reagor didn't like ambiguity. He wanted to know what he was getting—one way or the other.

After he had responded to the woman and touched her in the same place, it was clear what was going on. He had pushed her head up against the wall, lifting her off the ground, and slowly crushed the fraud's larynx. If it was a man he had wanted, he would have done that. He'd rather kill the bitch than fuck her, and he did. It was almost as good as an orgasm.

Just before eight o'clock at night, Dwight Conrad wrapped the Scotch tape around and around the four fingers of his hand with the sticky side out. The President sat in a chair behind an ornately carved desk in the VIP suite in the Claremont Hotel.

"Two minutes, Mr. President," said one of the assistants from the White House communications office.

Conrad patted down the shoulders and lapels of the President's dark blue suit jacket, picking up pieces of lint with the tape.

The President was euphoric, exuding a confidence Conrad hadn't seen for a long time.

"We're in, Dwight. Another four years. Look what we did after only one afternoon at the negotiating table! The Japanese today . . . What tomorrow!"

"Yes, sir." Conrad motioned to the makeup artist to powder the President's face again. "Got the pen, sir?"

"Right here, Dwight." He patted his coat breast. He shuffled through the typewritten copy of the talk he would give from the TelePrompTer. He found the page he was looking for. He rehearsed the line again: ". . . and so, my fellow Americans, today," he said, while reaching into his jacket and pulling out the pen, "I have signed with this very pen a guarantee for us and—more importantly—for our children and grandchildren—the economic security and prosperity that will come from America being able to compete on a fair, level playing field with Japan. . . ."

The President neatened the pile of papers in front of him.

"Very good, sir. It'll be a killer address."

"Yeah." The President frowned.

"Dwight?"

"Yes, sir."

"Whatever happened to that lunatic on Randall's staff? He's still in Europe, isn't he?"

"The CIA's still looking, sir."

"That's not the answer I wanted to hear."

"The Secret Service is aware of the situation," he answered. "They've put on extra security to make sure there won't be any problems. I doubt he'd try anything. He's had plenty of opportunities to try already."

"Just make sure nothing screws up this conference, Dwight. We've got the full day of meetings, then the big press conference."

"Yes, sir. I know."

The communications assistant stepped forward toward the desk again. "One minute, Mr. President."

"Don't embarrass me, Dwight. Things are going our way now. Corporate America regards me as a hero. None of those SOBs voted for me or gave me money the last election, but they're behind me now. I just pulled off the economic coup of the century."

Conrad gave the President a final look-over. He reached across the desk and straightened the President's tie.

"Thirty seconds."

Conrad stepped backward to the side of the camera.

"Dwight," called the President, motioning him back over.

"Yes, sir."

"Just a thought. Is Ben Gibbons still on top of this thing? He was pretty involved a couple of weeks ago and seemed to be making some headway."

"He's been working with the foreign intelligence people. Apparently there was a CIA employee—a woman—who was romantically involved with Jenkins' assistant. She was trying to lure the guy back in, but she was too close to her work. She's off the case now."

"Fifteen seconds, everyone."

The President frowned again. He lowered his voice. "The CIA's not involved in this thing, is it? I mean, CIA doesn't have anything to do with Randall's death, right? There aren't going to be any surprises, are there, Dwight?"

"Mr. Conrad," reminded the communications assistant. Conrad moved quickly out of the shot.

The President was still looking oddly at Conrad as the communications assistant silently counted down the last five seconds on her fingers and pointed at the President, cueing him to begin talking.

Conrad pointed to the TV camera, but the President couldn't take his eyes off him.

They were live.

"Dwight?" the President asked, oblivious of the camera.

America saw the President of the United States calling the chief of staff's name, looking to the side of the camera with a profoundly troubled look on his face.

65 ❏ ❏ ❏ ❏

At eight-fifteen that night, Erich Reagor stood at the intersection of Columbus and Vines on the edge of Chinatown under the flashing lights of a club featuring "Sexsational Live Nude Girls." It had just stopped raining and the streets were black and wet, reflecting the electric colors of the neon signs and traffic.

It didn't hurt to look, he had told himself. He stood near the door and caught glimpses of the dark interior as men came and went. Loud rock music from inside competed with the sounds of cars idling and honking their horns in the streets. He saw a girl wearing nothing but a long strand of pearls dancing through a fast strobe light on a stage. Reagor felt a hot flash. The door opened and closed again quickly as another patron went in. Reagor could see the girl again, swinging around a pole out toward the men who were sitting at the bar around the stage, her breasts jostling above their heads. She was blond and showed her large white teeth as she smiled sweetly down on them, forever the angel out of reach. The men just sat on their stools with their heads back, stirring their drinks, and following her movements with expressionless faces.

Reagor wiped his sweaty palms on his trousers.

There was no time for this, he reminded himself. Tonight was about finding Greer Whitaker.

The light changed and Reagor stepped into the street. Across the intersection opposite the strip club was the Vesuvio Café and just around the corner to the right City Lights Bookstore.

The brass bell on the back of the door clanged as Reagor stepped through. There were lots of young people dressed in black, looking at paperbacks. There was a green and yellow Greenpeace flag on the wall. It could have been Berlin, he thought. He took directions from the hand-lettered signs on the walls and walked through the fiction section toward the back room. In the corner was a tile mosaic at the base of a staircase—the words Vitalini Fotographia Italiana told him he was almost there. The sign overhead pointing upstairs read Poetry & Beat Literature.

Reagor took the steep wooden steps slowly; they creaked with every footfall. At the top of the steps was another room lined with more books. The room was lit with a single high-wattage bare light bulb hanging from a cord in the ceiling.

There was a man with a scraggly gray beard and a cap on his head who was sitting on a chair near the window, reading silently from a thin paperback. His lips moved as he scanned the page. He looked up from his reading as Reagor took a few steps in his direction, then went back to his book.

Reagor looked around. They were alone.

As Reagor walked over to the man, the silently moving lips began to speak: " '*Like a skein of loose silk blown against a wall/she walks by the railing of a path in Kensington Gardens, and she is dying piece-meal of a sort of emotional anæmia. . . .*' "

"Lev."

"Erich." He nodded a greeting without smiling. "*Privyet.*"

It had been years since Reagor had laid eyes on Lev Trifonov. Reagor had become involved with the case of the former literature professor from Moscow University when it became known that he was being recruited by a CIA officer in Moscow named Kate Mallotte.

Reagor, of course, had already fingered Kate as a CIA officer based on information provided by Reed. Reed had told Reagor that the CIA thought they had recruited the spy of the century. Trifinov had many years earlier given up his university position to devote himself full-time to politics. Through a combination of hard work, shrewdness, and cultivating the right contacts, he had won a place on the Central Committee of the Politburo. The CIA believed that he was the only member of the Central Committee to have ever been recruited by a Western intelligence agency.

Lev closed the book, a collection of Ezra Pound's poems.

"I tried London, Erich. The rain depressed me. They are an island nation—wet and insular and inbred. It makes for a nervous race of people. I needed space."

Reagor nodded. "I know, comrade."

Lev Tifonov was not what he had appeared to be to CIA field officer Kate Mallotte and her American supervisors. He was from the beginning to the very end a loyal and faithful servant of the Soviet people. He was—contrary to the impression given to Kate—actually a double agent cooperating fully with the KGB in providing details of how the CIA went about recruiting and running their Russian agents. He gave Kate volumes of disinformation about the workings of the Politburo. When his KGB controllers had got everything out of the relationship that there was to be had, they bored of the game and faked Trifinov's arrest. They leaked word through known CIA informants that Lev had been executed in Lyubianka prison. The CIA never found out what had happened. They assumed that Lev had got careless one night and had been caught on the way to a dead drop. Lev Trifinov just disappeared. About that same time, several other of Kate's agents disappeared after being hauled out of bed in the middle of the night. Kate accepted an offer from the new CIA Director to return to Washington as an aide in the DCI's office.

Trifinov had been secretly moved to London, given a new identity by the KGB, and worked under deep cover as a bookseller in the antique district of Belgravia. He mainly fed the Soviets information heard on the streets about Russian émigrés living in Britain. Reagor first came into direct contact with him when Reagor was tracking down an East German defector whom British intelligence was hiding in the city. Trifinov's small shop became a trusted drop for messages from Stasi's own network of agents working in London. Reagor's job was to visit Trifinov's place and retrieve the information. Reagor and Trifinov were spending long lunches together two or three times a month before the Wall fell.

Trifinov feared that once the Russians and the new unified German government began exchanging information with the West about operations prior to the collapse of the Communist states, he would be exposed and subject to deportation or arrest. Reagor had received the prearranged signal that Trifinov wanted to meet. Trifinov wanted help at a time when Reagor himself was hurriedly cleaning out his own files and preparing for a new life in Munich. Reagor was, nonetheless, helpful. With Reed's help and through other contacts at the American embassy in London, Reagor at great risk to himself had worked magic for his old friend and arranged for him to leave London and emigrate to the United States. Reagor had suggested that Trifinov move to the quiet Russian community in San Francisco. There would be work for him there as a taxi driver. Not glamorous, but at least it wasn't London and it wasn't Moscow. He could enjoy the California sunshine without having to be looking over his shoulder. For this, Trifinov was eternally grateful.

Trifinov spoke. "Kate was hesitant to meet me tonight, but I told her the lives of some of her other former Russian agents were at stake. I told her the Russian government still had a few in prison and were about to start executing them. She was convinced once I told her that there was the possibility something could be worked out between the two governments—a swap, maybe—but she needed to act immediately before they were dead. I told her I trust no one but her and insisted that we meet alone. Where would you like for me to bring her?"

Reagor unfolded his map of San Francisco and oriented himself, running his finger along major streets.

"Pier Twenty-six," said Reagor. "Under the Bay Bridge." He looked at his watch. "I want you to drop me off there first on your way out. How long until you're back?"

"Give me forty-five minutes."

"Let's ride around," Trifinov said as he pulled away from the front of the San Francisco Hilton.

Kate sat up front with Trifinov in the taxi. He was a bear of a man with oversized hands and feet, his huge proportions almost too big to manipulate the car's controls. Trifinov spoke loudly, excitedly, gesturing with his right hand as he steered them with his left hand down Market Street toward the bay.

"I still have contacts in Moscow, you know. They're telling me if I know anyone who can help, that I should call them right away. I didn't want anyone here to know about my past, but those are my friends, too. I called the FBI in San Francisco and asked them to find you. I didn't know you would come so quickly."

Kate looked suspiciously at her old agent Lev. "I thought you were dead," she said.

He took his eyes off the road to look at her. "It's not true!" he said incredulously.

Kate turned sideways in the seat. "What happened? I had heard the KGB killed you."

"They tortured me," Trifinov said indignantly. "They tried to break me. They wanted to know all about you and what I did for you. When that didn't work, they drugged me. I don't know what I told them. I must have been passed out for days. I woke up in a cell somewhere. Months later I found out I was in East Germany. One day the Russian guard disappears and an East German soldier came. He unlocked the door to my cell, gave me a suit of clothes and a hundred-deutsche-mark bill, and kicked me out. I was standing on a street in Dresden, watching the Soviet Army pulling out."

Kate was quiet.

Trifinov continued. "I had cousins in America. I called them and they sponsored me to come here. I didn't want anything to do with my past life in Moscow. It's not much of a living, but at least I felt safe."

"Tell me who I need to speak to in Moscow," Kate said. "Who are the other agents still alive?"

"Pavlov, Eugeny, Ekaterina . . ."

"Ekaterina?"

"Yes, I heard she was lost in the Gulag, but they found her and now want to put her on trial as a traitor and execute her."

"Lev, you need to take me back to the hotel so I can start making calls immediately."

"I knew you'd want to know." He checked his rearview mirror, then his side mirrors several times. "You told me you'd come alone."

"I am, Lev."

Trifinov shook his head. "You lied. We're being followed."

Trifinov suddenly hit the gas hard and threw the taxi hard into the lane of oncoming traffic. Kate turned to look and saw another car matching the maneuver.

"That's no one I know, Lev. I swear."

Trifinov grunted, then turned the wheel and turned sharply down a side street. He cracked his window, listened, then rolled the window down some more. He looked up through the windshield to the sky.

"Helicopter, too," he said.

"I swear, Lev."

"That's fine. I can take care of that." He floored the pedal again and blew through an alley. "No problem, Kate." Trifinov rushed through the streets and at last succeeded in losing the car behind him. But the helicopter was still above them.

Trifinov got onto a ramp leading to the Oakland Bay Bridge. There were two levels: the traffic leaving the city was on the bottom, shielding them from the eye in the sky. Trifinov drove half way across the bridge, then stopped. Another taxi, surprised by the suddenness of the maneuver, bumped them from behind.

Trifinov quickly opened his door and dragged Kate across the street out the driver-side door.

"Lev!"

"Come on, Kate."

The driver of the taxi behind them was already out of his car looking at the damage. He started to protest, but saw Trifinov's size and backed off. Trifinov hit him with one hard blow to the side of the head and the man collapsed. Trifinov threw Kate into the other taxi, then he got behind the wheel and moved the vehicle around the one stopped in front.

"What are you doing!" said Kate.

"I'm trying to hold a private meeting, Kate."

Trifinov sped through to the other end of the bridge and emerged on the Oakland side. He exited, then caught the ramp back to San Francisco. The helicopter circled overhead, looking for the number on the top of Lev's old taxi, still hidden under the upper deck of the bridge.

"Just take me back," Kate said.

"Sure."

Trifinov drove silently for several more blocks, then circled back in the direction of the bridge. He pulled onto the Embarcadero and drove along the street with the piers jutting out into the bay.

The taxi drove back under the bridge. Kate turned in her seat to look at the cars passing overhead toward the other side of the bay.

"Where are we going?" she asked.

Trifinov stopped the taxi under the bridge at the warehouse that fronted the pier. On the wide door was the number Twenty-six. Trifinov pushed in the emergency brake and got a driver's log book off his dash.

"What are you doing, Lev?" asked Kate.

Trifinov got a pen out of his shirt pocket and clicked it to start writing on the log.

"Lev, let's go!"

Kate looked quickly around the car and saw a figure coming up from behind. She grabbed the door handle and made a motion to open the door, but Trifinov grabbed her wrist and pulled with his powerful grip. He looked at Kate, smiled showing brown teeth and swollen gums, and gave a deep sigh.

Suddenly Kate's door opened. The sound of the cars on the lower level of the Bay Bridge overhead was beating down on them, echoing around the space below the bridge. A man bent down and smiled at her.

"Welcome to San Francisco, Miss Mallotte," he said. "My name's Erich Reagor. I had the pleasure of meeting you once before at a reception in Moscow. Apparently we have a lot more in common now. Let's talk."

66 ❑ ❑ ❑ ❑

The sun pushed up over the back of the Berkeley hills, then got mired in the fog. The light hadn't yet found the deeper recesses of the narrow back alleys of the town. The sound of traffic grew. But it was the sound of a basketball bouncing and a backboard wobbling that woke Greer up.

Greer had spent the night sleeping sitting up in a doorway in the alley, sheltering his precious transceiver under his knees from the light rain that had fallen in the evening. He uncurled himself, stood up, and stretched. He was bruised and sore from throwing himself onto the floor during the shoot-out with the Japanese at his hotel. He was stiff from sleeping in the cool, damp night air. Greer looked around him at the other bums still asleep in the alley. Join the crowd, he told himself.

After the Japanese had come after him, Greer had hid in the utility room of the hotel until well after dark. Around ten o'clock at night, he broke through a window and scurried away from the hotel.

At the end of the alley he could see a small city park overgrown with uncut grass and spectacular, tall tangerine-orange poppies and huge purple thistles growing like weeds. There was a group of sun-burned men sitting on the benches in the weak shade of a stand of cyprus trees on the other side of a childless sandbox. A couple of teenagers were already shooting hoops at six in the morning on a crumbling half court while a girl sat on a fence watching.

Greer caught his reflection in a window before he crossed the street to the park: greasy, uncombed hair and the now ratty goatee. He would fit in well with the bums in the park. His reflection was weak and he couldn't see his eyes. Had he acquired the crazed look yet of many of the street people he had seen? He clutched his transceiver and lugged it across the street like the only worldly possession of a vagrant.

Greer walked past the homeless men and junkies congregating on the benches, some asleep, some awake enough to curse the day and wish they were dead. He hurried to the stand of cypress trees to get out of view of the street. It was dark in the middle of the tight circle of trees. Greer's first clue that he was not alone was the overpowering smell of urine, combined with the stench of dirty bodies and stale alcohol breath. After his eyes adjusted to the darkness beneath the trees, he saw the bodies lying in awkward positions in tattered clothes, looking as if they had been shot and left on the edge of a clearing on some Civil War battlefield. Greer decided it wasn't a safe place for him to be.

The blooms were dried and shriveled to black in the center of the violet plant in the pot on the fountain's edge. The velvety dark green leaves were healthy, however, suggesting the flower could be redeemed.

Some of the water from the fountain splashed randomly onto the plant like large raindrops. The sun had finally burned off the fog and now hovered benignly over the university's student union plaza at noon, soaking the flower in life-giving sunshine. The plant's owner—it seemed to Greer a college student—sat reading a book while stroking the leaves. It was as if he were petting a dog. This was, after all—Greer reminded himself—Berkeley.

Greer passed quickly by and sat on a bench nearby under one of the gnarled, leafless trees set into an island of cement. He hoped to pass more for a college student than a vagrant. From his position Greer could see anyone coming into the wide plaza. There were students scattered about eating lunch, munching on bagels from the deli around the corner, drinking fruit juices. The transceiver was now safely stored in a locker at the student center. The gun he kept cradled under his shirt.

Greer got out the cellular phone that Kate had dropped in the car at Big Sur. It was portable and calls were almost impossible to trace. Greer had tested the phone and found that it was only partially charged. He had kept the phone turned off to avoid draining the battery, rendering the phone useless for his own purposes. Earlier in the morning he had accidentally hit the POWER button and only seconds later the phone started ringing. He had shut the phone off, figuring it was someone trying to get in touch with Kate. Now he pushed the POWER button so he could test the battery again, and seconds later it started to ring. He didn't answer it. He kept the phone on for a while longer. There was a pattern. Four rings, then a minute or so of silence, followed by four more rings.

The phone rang again. On impulse, Greer flipped open the phone to answer the call, but didn't say anything. Immediately he heard Kate's voice.

"Greer! Greer!"

She's okay, was the first thing that went through his mind. She's trying to get in touch with me again. Of course she would have known to call him on the phone he had taken from her.

"Greer!"

He didn't know whether to answer or not.

"Greer!"

She was insistent, calling his name as if she were positive he was listening.

"Kate."

"Greer . . ."

Commotion, then another voice, a man's voice. "Greer . . ."

Oh, God, no, Greer thought. He recognized it immediately as the man with the German accent, the man from the videotape of Stephanie.

"Greer . . ." he said again.

"I'm listening."

"I'm calling regarding Kate Mallotte. There are no theatrics involved this time as with Stephanie Becker."

"What do you want?"

"You know what I want. The diskettes, Greer. The diskettes."

Greer heard a beep on the line.

"What's that?" Greer asked.

"What's what?"

Greer looked at the LCD display on the phone. The word "Lobat" was showing.

"Greer," the man said again. "It is because of your deception of Stephanie Becker about the diskettes that she is now dead. Just as Kate Mallotte is about to be dead if you don't hand over the diskettes. Too beautiful to see her gutted like a tuna, don't you think?"

"Put her back on."

"Sorry. The diskettes, Greer. This is about the diskettes."

As he listened, Greer saw a pair of young Asian men dressed casually coming out of the student union, serious expressions on their faces. Weren't they coming in his direction?

"I don't have the diskettes anymore." He eyed the Asians warily.

"Come, now, Greer. Let us be reasonable about this."

"I don't have them. I can't give them to you because I don't have them. *Listen* to me. They're someplace I can't get to."

He wasn't quibbling with Kate's life on the line. He really *couldn't* get to the diskettes now. The phone beeped rapidly. The battery was about to go.

"Her entrails will be spread like spilled bait on the wharf. Don't be stupid."

"I told you. I don't have them!"

The two Asian men headed straight toward him now, only twenty yards away and approaching at a brisk walk. More Japanese hit men? They were looking directly at him. He had to make a decision fast.

"Scraps for seagulls, Greer."

"Okay, okay. Where is she?"

"Bring the diskettes?"

The phone was beeping again, this time faster.

"Yes, dammit!" he shouted into the phone. "Where is she?"

"Meet me at . . . o'clock tonight . . . at the entr. . . . of . . . ." The transmission was breaking up. " . . . eet you at the . . .tersection."

"What time? Where?"

"Sev . . . clock. Pier Seventy-four. Don't dis . . . me. She won't look as . . . ith her head . . . bloody newspaper like a fillet of fish. You know I will. And don't . . ."

The phone was dead.

Greer got up fast off the bench and stood up, reaching under his shirt for the trigger on the handgun. The two men stopped only six feet away and stood smiling at him. A classic silent face-off. Greer started to bring the gun out from under his shirt. One of the Asians made a slight bowing motion with his head as he started to talk.

"Are you finished with this bench?" he asked politely.

Greer noticed they were both holding wrapped-up sandwiches, chips, and cans of Coke. Greer took his finger off the trigger.

"Sure," Greer said. "I'm finished."

"Thank you very much."

They sat down, squinting up happily at the California sun, and popped their Coke cans. Greer backed away from them halfway across the plaza toward the student union.

It was seven-thirty at night and Greer worried as he watched the lights of Oakland and the Berkeley hills twinkle across the San Francisco Bay. There were no streetlights at Pier Seventy-four, only the flame from the top of the ten-story-tall vent pipe that burned off vapor from the huge holding tanks. Greer stood close to the base of one of the tanks, watching how the wind pushed the huge ball of fire around, moving his shadow in circles around him like a drunk swinging around a lamp-post.

Where was Kate? Where was the German? He had been waiting for forty-five minutes. Had he heard the wrong place or wrong time in the garbled cellular phone transmission?

Greer walked around the circumference of the tank, stepping

through the oily, black compacted sand. Something dinged the metal side of the tank somewhere around the other side and Greer froze. He stopped to listen. An errant seagull? All he heard was the sound of the gases being noisily consumed by the flame over his head.

He walked a little farther, back around to the side facing the street where the taxi had dropped him off.

The sound of feet landing heavily behind him. A hand landed on Greer's shoulder with the force of a mauling bear paw. Greer turned to see and caught a swipe across the face so sudden and hard that he thought the lower half of his face had been knocked off. A package of diskettes spilled out from under his shirt as he hit the ground. Lev Trifinov smiled with ugly teeth from under the shadow of his beret. He steadied himself with one hand on a rung of the ladder running up the side of the tank he had jumped from.

"I've read about you in the paper," Trifinov said with his thick Russian accent. "You don't look like much of a killer to me." Trifinov grabbed Greer by the arm, lifted him off the ground, and pushed him against the metal wall of the tank. "Certainly weasely enough to be a spy, but only a bad spy. Only bad spies get caught, you know." He grunted. "And you've been caught."

Trifinov picked up the diskettes and pocketed them. He pulled Greer in front of him and shoved him forward. Trifinov twisted Greer's arm upward behind his back. "Walk," he ordered.

Trifinov guided him along a chain-link fence to a warehouse a couple of hundred yards away. Around the corner was a wide, unlit pier and on the pier a taxi idling, its windows fogged from the inside so Greer could see nothing. One of the backseat doors opened partially on its own. Trifinov opened it all the way and shoved Greer inside.

"Good evening, Mr. Whitaker—you little shit."

That voice. At last, thought Greer, face to face with the German, the one who had caused all the grief.

Erich Reagor sat in the backseat. Kate was facing forward in the front seat on the passenger's side, her hands seemingly bound behind her. She was strangely still, her eyes glazed and staring off past the end of the pier. Trifinov got behind the wheel on the driver's side and wiggled the diskettes in the air for Reagor to see. He hit the button to lock the doors.

"Kate?"

"Don't worry about Kate, Mr. Whitaker. She's going to be fine. She was a little—how shall I say—overexcited after talking to you and I have given her something to calm her. She will soon be back to her normal self."

The Russian laughed quietly to himself.

"What have you done to her?"

Reagor just smiled back at Greer. "This time, Mr. Whitaker, there will be no mistakes about the diskettes."

Trifinov was flipping up the screen to a laptop computer in the front seat.

"You see, Mr. Whitaker, my friend Lev here came to America not to drive taxis but to work in Silicon Valley. He's traded in his taxi license for a degree in computer science. He's a very successful computer programmer now. He found the taxi clientele . . ."

"Disagreeable," finished Trifinov.

"You see, a modern Renaissance man. A bighearted lion of a man."

Lev chuckled. "A *lion* . . ." He roared softly and shook his head. He laughed.

"Literature professor, Politburo member, taxi driver, computer whiz"—Reagor looked over the seat at the laptop—"and sometime hooligan."

Trifinov grinned and nodded as he tapped in commands on the keyboard.

Greer heard the diskette whirring in the hard drive. How much longer until the Russian would find not the fake data of the other diskettes, but nothing at all? The diskettes he had bought at the student union before he left the campus to come to this meeting. He really *didn't* have access to the diskettes.

Greer turned in his seat to fully face Reagor. Greer made a dramatic, distracting gesture to cover his mouth for a loud sneeze and at the same time reached behind his back with his other hand to insert his finger into the trigger guard of the gun. Reagor saw the move.

"Take the girl!" shouted Reagor. "He's got something on him!"

Trifinov sighed loudly and hit the button to unlock the doors. Greer pulled the gun from behind his back and held it on Reagor as he fumbled with the door handle behind his back. Trifinov moved quickly for such a large man, and was already around the other side of the car pulling Kate out of the front seat. Greer turned for an instant to find the door handle and pulled it up. He fell backward out of the taxi onto the ground. He turned quickly and scrambled to follow Kate, but felt himself being jerked back inside. There was a terribly powerful grip around his throat. He instinctively tried turning to see what was holding him back, but the force behind him was too strong.

"Drop the gun!" shouted Reagor. Greer held on tightly to the gun, but found it almost impossible to concentrate on what he was doing. It had all happened so quickly. He hadn't had a moment to slide the safety switch off. He felt as if he were about to lose consciousness. With one strong push from both of his legs against the inside of the taxi, he shot back toward Reagor, knocking the back of his own head hard against Reagor's chin.

The grip relaxed momentarily and Greer lurched forward out of Reagor's reach. He threw himself out of the backseat, then reached up and slammed the door behind him as hard as he could without looking back. There was a loud cry. Greer's eyes were watering so hard that he couldn't see clearly in the dark. He wiped his eyes and turned around. The taxi door was slightly ajar with two pairs of hands sticking out. He could see the ten badly mangled fingers that had prevented the door from closing all the way when he had shut it. In the back seat Reagor was lying down on his side moaning loudly.

Greer turned his attention to the commotion on the side of the warehouse.

"Kate!" he called out. There was no reply. He slid the safety switch off the gun and ran to the corner of the building.

Trifinov was behind Kate with his fingers interlocked on top of her head, his powerful hands over her skull.

"Drop the gun, my friend, or I'll crush her head."

Greer was about to put the gun down and hesitated just long enough for Kate to reach back with her bound hands and grab Trifinov's genitals, giving them a brutal squeeze and twist, all in one motion. The unexpected pain caused an involuntary lowering of Trifinov's hands to protect his fully torqued gonads, giving Kate the chance to break free.

"Shoot him!" yelled Kate as she fell to the ground.

Trifinov was bent over holding his groin. He looked up quickly toward Greer with his face screwed up in pain. Greer pulled the trigger and shot him in the forehead. Trifinov's cap went sailing upward, still spinning in the air into the dark as he collapsed.

As the shot echoed across the water, Greer heard a sound coming from the taxi. There was a phrase being repeated.

"Are you all right?" he asked Kate.

"Dazed, but not dead," she replied with a slur. "I wasn't as catatonic as they thought." She sounded awful, though.

Greer helped Kate back over to the taxi. Greer held the gun in front of him and cautiously looked through the back windshield. He saw Reagor balled up in the backseat shaking.

"Mein handen. Ich kann tote ihn nicht."

"What's he saying?" asked Kate.

"His hands. He can't kill me."

Greer looked at Kate. Her eyelids were drooping. Greer asked her, "Do you know who that is?"

She started to answer, then slumped toward Greer. He caught her weight and laid her gently onto the ground. Her eyes were still open. "I came because I love you," she said. Then she seemed to pass out.

Greer raised his gun and aimed at one of Reagor's knees. Greer fumed at the thought of the pain and terror this man had caused him. He was the voice he had heard with Reed in the Tower Gallery in Washington, the very same voice of the videotape of Stephanie. Certainly he was the person with whom Reed had been aligned, the two of them using Greer for their own cruel purposes. And he was also the one who had summoned Stephanie back from Heidelberg to torment him after all these years.

Greer pulled the trigger.

The glass shattered and there was another loud moan from inside the taxi.

Kate started, the sound awakening her. "Don't," Kate said weakly.

Greer saw that Reagor had been struck with a jolt of pain and flinched just before the bullet had been fired. He had missed. It still felt good getting off a shot.

Kate was too drugged to make decisions. She must have conserved just enough energy for Greer's arrival so that she could maybe save him and herself, too. Greer looked down on the pitiful man writhing on the seat, clutching his hands between his knees. He was going to kill the son of a bitch.

Greer raised the gun and aimed through the glass at Reagor's head. He started pulling the trigger.

"No, Greer!" Kate said. She was starting to revive. "Not again! Let this one go. He'll get what he deserves, but you're not the one to do it. Don't dirty your own hands by killing him."

"Jenkins' theory. We do it my way?"

Kate nodded. "Yes. We do it your way."

Greer relaxed his trigger finger and lowered the gun.

"Come on—let's get out of here before the police come."

Greer walked around to the side of the car and opened the back door. He grabbed Reagor's hair and yanked on it hard, pulling him from side to side, causing Reagor unbearable pain in his broken hands. Reagor let out loud yelps like a wounded dog and looked up helplessly into Greer's face.

"*Gehe zum Teufel!*" Greer yelled at him. Go to hell! He threw Reagor's head onto the seat.

Greer slammed the door closed and helped Kate up to search for a BART station in the city.

67

At eleven o'clock the next morning, Kate flashed her CIA security pass at the Secret Service agent checking credentials at the Claremont Resort Hotel. He compared the photo on the ID with her face. She was stunning. She noticed that he tried to sneak a long up-and-down look at her in her form-fitting bright red pants suit. She had made sure her hair was perfect, even a little "bigger" than usual. Unlike most times, she wanted a lot of attention today. The Secret Service agent acknowledged the special clearance for U.S. security and intelligence agencies with unrestricted access and waved her through. She turned back just to make sure he was watching her walk away.

Even though the closing press conference with all the G7 conference leaders wasn't starting for another hour, the journalists had already begun gathering in the great hall in the middle of the hotel. At the front was a raised podium where the leaders would sit. Dozens of rows of folding metal chairs were set up in the room. At the back were the television cameras.

Kate wandered down a row of chairs near the front. She recognized the names taped to the back of the chairs as belonging to the reporters from the regular White House beat. She walked a few more rows back and found a chair that wasn't reserved. She almost collapsed with exhaustion.

Out of desperation for a place to stay after escaping from Trifinov and the German, Kate and Greer had gone back to the Berkeley marina. Greer stayed at a distance while Kate found the dockmaster talking with a couple who had just tied up for the night. After much begging, Kate persuaded him to rent her a night's stay aboard one of the cabin cruisers at the marina. She got Greer and sneaked him aboard. She found that not only did heights make her sick, but so did the movement of a boat in the water, even though it was a relatively calm sea. She slept badly in a berth close to the head in case she needed to make a run for it. There would be time for true reconciliation with Greer later. The first priority was the economic conference.

In another hall in the hotel, she knew that the Group of Seven leaders were concluding their meetings. She imagined what the President was doing, how he was circulating among the others, smiling big, working the crowd like a campaign stop. After a technical miscue, his address on television two nights ago had gone exceedingly well. He sounded powerful, in control. He had not so subtly engaged in some Japan-bashing. The overnight polls in the morning's papers showed a significant rise in his approval rating from only just before Christmas. He was a national hero. No one was better at judging the shifting winds of American politics and making a quick correction. He was back at the helm, stronger than ever.

Jacko Takiyama straightened his black waiter's bow tie and smoothed his uniform in the mirror in the men's room in the basement of the Claremont. He ran his fingers lightly back over the side of his head.

The uniform belonged to the brother of a member of the Takiyama organization. The brother had worked as a waiter in the hotel's restaurants for four years and was—as were all the regular employees—scheduled to work the entire week of the conference. All of the employees had gone through security clearance to be able to work the conference. With his hair trimmed slightly shorter and some oil to slick it back on the sides, Jacko had taken over the brother's persona for the afternoon.

Jacko wasn't worried about being recognized as someone other than the brother. He would stay away from the other hotel employees who would know him. He was Japanese. To the Anglo security men, he knew, all Asians looked alike.

Jacko had been at each of the public events for the G7 leaders. At the photo op in the Japanese Tea Garden, he was hiding nearby the Buddha disguised as a gardener. During the agreement-signing ceremonies yesterday at the hotel, he was a limousine driver in a black chauffeur's outfit. He was waiting for Greer Whitaker to make his move.

It was the one job that he no longer trusted anyone else to do. The family honor was at stake. The failures of his own people were unforgivable. Whether or not it had been Whitaker who had killed four of his men at the Shattuck Avenue hotel was still a debatable point. But his men had lost Kate Mallotte two nights earlier as she rode with the Russian taxi driver. The people involved that night had already been disposed of in a very public way so that everyone else in the organization would learn a lesson. The Takiyama soldiers had made the front page of the newspaper—the photo showed six men hanged from street lights on Union Square.

Jacko had found out about Greer Whitaker almost too late in the game, but it wasn't over yet. Where else would Greer Whitaker be if not at the conference? It made sense. Like the hotel full of the glory-hungry politicians, Greer Whitaker would find his way to the center of the action. If the American got through and disrupted the conference, it would be Jacko's fault. He wasn't prepared to allow that to happen, however. He would stop the American or die trying.

He checked the mirror one last time. He had been able to get in an hour's practice the previous morning at the Bay Town Indoor Shoot and Lunch Club. Jacko smoothed the uniform jacket again. The semi-automatic handgun didn't show.

The President strode into the hall confidently, smiling and waving to members of the traveling White House press corps, acknowledging the loud applause and standing ovation. In addition to the usual gang of

White House reporters, there were representatives from media from all over the globe. He stepped up onto the dais and invited the other members of the conference to join him.

He stood smiling from side to side, winking at people he knew in the audience as he waited for the applause to die down. Dwight Conrad and Ben Gibbons stood to the side and gave him the thumbs-up sign. Such enthusiasm from journalists was unusual. Kate knew he was eating it up. Three months ago he and the press hated each other. Oh, what a difference a conference makes, she thought.

The President wanted to regain the intimacy with the American people that he had developed during the last election but that was lost over the first three years of his presidency. He clipped on the wireless mike and sat on the stool in front of the dais.

He opened the floor for questions, calling first on network journalists to ensure coverage on the evening news.

"Mr. President, what impact will the new agreements with Japan have on the economic growth of the country?" "Mr. President, don't you think that your getting these agreements signed will silence your critics in Congress and elsewhere who have been critical of your ability to develop and move an economic agenda forward?" "Mr. President, in light of the fact that your popularity and approval ratings have risen so dramatically in the last week, wouldn't you consider this week's conference to be the turning point in your administration and the real beginning of your reelection campaign?" The usual hostility of the press was totally absent.

After fielding the questions from the TV networks, he moved to the wire services and major newspapers. He called on reporters by their first names. Then he called on several unknown reporters to add some diversity to the questions and make the smaller papers feel that they had a chance.

Kate's bright red suit and blond hair caught his eye.

"Yes, ma'am," he said, pointing to Kate. He smiled. "You in the red suit."

Kate rose with a notepad in hand. All heads turned in her direction.

"Thank you, Mr. President. Kate Mallotte with the CIA. I'm representing Randall Jenkins and Greer Whitaker, who for obvious reasons couldn't be here today."

"Kate," Gibbons warned as he approached her. Cameras flashed. TV cameras swiveled.

"Mr. President," Kate continued, "if you don't mind, the question is short."

The President stood to meet the two Secret Service agents who were walking toward him. They got between him and the rest of the room and started to escort him off.

Two other pairs of Secret Service agents were coming down the side aisles from the back of the room. They walked briskly, reaching the opposite ends of Kate's row at the same time.

Kate spoke into a small radio: "It's not going to work. They're not going to let me talk. Do you read me?"

Greer answered her over the radio: "Just let me know when to take over."

Kate spoke again as the Secret Service men were just about to reach her: "Mr. President, could you tell us please why the CIA was involved in the death of your National Security Adviser, Randall Jenkins?"

The President stopped just before he got off the side of the dais. "What did she say?" His Secret Service protection tried to force him to keep walking, but he resisted.

Just then, the four Secret Service agents converged on Kate and she said quickly into the radio to Greer: "I'm out. They're cutting me. . . ." The radio was knocked out of her hand.

"Kate?" Greer said over the radio as it hit the ground.

Then there was a booming voice over the public address system: "Mr. President, this is Greer Whitaker." The room got quiet. Everyone looked around to find out the source of the voice.

Greer was broadcasting over the frequency of the President's wireless mike with the transceiver from the cabin cruiser docked at the Berkeley marina. It had taken him two days with his scanner to find the frequency of the hotel's audio system while he was still in the Shattuck Avenue hotel. He had found it during sound checks three days earlier as a communications assistant was reciting the Gettysburg Address to check sound levels. When he heard the assistant doing his impression of the President answering questions from the press, he knew he had nailed it. Now Greer had the television in the cabin cruiser's salon tuned to CNN; the yacht was receiving TV signals from its satellite dish.

"Mr. President," Greer continued, "you and everyone else here today need to review the facts surrounding the death of Randall Jenkins. There's a coverup in your Administration. The CIA officer who just addressed you will verify everything I'm saying."

The President stood behind the Secret Service agents listening intensively.

Greer continued, talking fast: "Copies of a briefing paper outlining Randall Jenkins' discovery of an international conspiracy along with the diskettes containing the statistical proof are available here today for the media at the reception desk. There's also a special packet of information with more classified information for your own personal review, Mr. President. Someone on your staff is keeping information from you about why Randall Jenkins was murdered."

Dwight Conrad yelled, "Somebody cut the sound!"

"The agreements you just signed with Japan are a sham, Mr. President. The German government . . ."

Suddenly a deafening blast blew, and the President was thrown down to the floor and covered by his escort. At the same moment, one of the Secret Service men holding onto Kate's arm fell backward. People screamed and pointed to the side of the room from which the shot had come. Heavy white smoke was clouding the view of the side doorway. A hand holding a gun penetrated the haze and fired again with a brilliant flash. Kate spun around and crashed across a row of chairs.

The hand withdrew into the smoke and was gone.

There was screaming and shouting as people scrambled to the floor and rushed for the exits.

Greer saw the chaos on the live feed on his TV. The CNN camera panned the room wildly trying to capture the anarchy.

"Kate? Kate?" Greer said over the sound system. There was fear in his voice. He couldn't see her anymore in the TV's crowd shots. "Kate?"

The audio engineer finally pulled the plug on the wireless mike system.

There was complete pandemonium.

The smell of gunpowder hung heavily over the room as the smoke wafted up to the ceiling of the Claremont.

By the morning of the next day, Kate lay in San Francisco General Hospital under sedation in serious but stable condition from the bullet that tore through her shoulder. She was oblivious to the events happening outside her hospital room.

The final casualty list compiled by the FBI included one Secret Service agent killed by a gunshot wound, two journalists killed in the line of fire and five others wounded, and three people trampled to death.

The entire Group of Seven delegation had already left the United States quickly. Four of the seven made brief statements at the airport, expressing their deep regret and sorrow over the events that had transpired and for the loss of life. They pledged not to let terrorists affect their work. Japan and Germany rushed out of the country without a comment.

Hans Stettler, Erich Reagor's boss, had already received a message that someone from the American embassy in Bonn was trying to get in touch with him to answer some questions. Stettler would deny everything. The small group of collaborators in the German government would deny everything. Reagor was still missing, but Stettler wasn't worried.

The Takiyama family and the Japanese government were fatalistic about what was going on. Same strategy, different plan. After things calmed down, the two countries would get together again.

After Greer had given himself a clean shave, he turned himself in at the San Francisco FBI office. He wouldn't give them the satisfaction of saying that they had captured him. He was officially charged with espionage, murder, and—on the evidence of the rifle found in the Shattuck Avenue hotel with his fingerprints all over it—conspiracy to assassinate the President. He was then flown immediately on a government jet to Washington, D.C. He was driven in a windowless van into the basement of the Federal District Court where he was arraigned. Bail was denied.

The FBI had found no good leads in trying to track down the Claremont Hotel assailant. Jacko Takiyama had slipped quietly back to Japan to visit his family with a prepaid first-class ticket. One way.

The media now had the background documents and computer diskettes Greer had prepared. The day after the shooting, portions of Greer's materials were reprinted in newspapers across the country. The White House as yet had released no information and held no formal briefings. Off-the-record statements by Administration spokesmen assured that the President was doing fine; White House photos were released showing him in meetings in the Oval Office with his staff.

There was an army of reporters and cameramen camped outside the houses of the Director of Central Intelligence and the White House Chief of Staff. Neither, however, had been home since flying back to Washington.

68 ❏ ❏ ❏ ❏

Two days after the shooting, Kate was well enough to sit propped up in her hospital bed. Having just awakened from a twelve-hour sleep, she was still trying to clear her head as the sun was setting outside.

She was under twenty-four-hour guard. Outside her door were two San Francisco policemen and a federal marshal. As soon as she was able to leave the hospital, she expected to be charged as an accessory in Greer's espionage case and for assisting a fugitive. Perhaps even the murder case.

She picked up the remote control and switched on the TV suspended from the ceiling at the end of her bed. She clicked through the channels looking for the evening news. She found a reporter standing in front of the White House and turned up the volume.

"... So, in an announcement only moments ago, White House Chief of Staff Dwight Conrad announced to reporters that the President will be addressing the nation tonight. Although he gave no indication as to the subject of the President's talk, we have to surmise he will be addressing the events that have unfolded at the San Francisco economic conference. We can also assume it has something to do with the release today of Greer Whitaker, who had been previously charged with espionage and murder in the case of the late Randall Jenkins, the President's longtime friend and National Security Adviser." The TV cut to a clip of Greer leaving the Federal District Courthouse, waving weakly to the press, then ducking into the backseat of a car. "It's our understanding that Mr. Whitaker met personally with the President late this afternoon for about two hours after his release from custody. Copies of court papers we have just received indicate that all charges against Mr. Whitaker have been dismissed. Back to you ..."

Out of the corner of her eye, Kate saw the red light flashing on the phone next to her bed. The ringer had been turned off. She was immobilized and couldn't move to reach it, so she rang for the nurse to help.

The nurse came in followed by the marshal.

"Have you heard the news, Miss Mallotte?" the nurse asked excitedly as she picked up the phone and held it to Kate's ear.

Kate looked at her and shook her head as she answered the phone. "Hello?"

"I'm out, Kate." It was Greer. "I just left the White House. They told me you were okay. The Feds wouldn't let me call you while I was in jail. I called as soon as I could. *Are* you okay?"

Kate was overcome with emotion. "I'm doing fine now, Greer." She was alive and on the mend, and Greer was finally safe. She started to cry.

"Hey," said Greer. "Everything's going to be all right. I'm coming back out there to be with you tomorrow. Just hang in there, okay?" he said tenderly.

Kate sniffled back the tears. "I'll be all right. I'm a mess," she said.

"Yeah," Greer said, "but you're my mess. You've got a TV in your room, don't you?"

"Yes."

"Don't miss the President tonight. Keep it together until tomorrow morning, okay? I'll be there before noon."

"Greer . . ."

"I'll be there, I promise. I'll explain everything. Watch the President. Gotta go . . ."

Dwight Conrad moved the framed pictures of the President's family on the credenza behind his desk so that the television would be sure to pick them up, even if slightly out of focus. Conrad knew that the perception was the reality and anything that could be done to convey the perception of stability and normalcy in the White House was important. Especially now.

It was thirty minutes before the televised address was to begin, but the President hadn't yet arrived. For moral support, Conrad had gathered a few key people in the Oval Office to be in the room while the President addressed the nation. Also, he figured that if the ship of state was going down, he wanted all responsible hands on deck with him. He wasn't going down alone.

The supporters talked quietly among themselves as the technicians rechecked the lighting and audio. The President's wife eyed Ben Gibbons suspiciously as Conrad consulted with the people from the White House Communications Office. Conrad reviewed the script he had written himself and made a few minor changes on the TelePrompTer.

The director of the FBI stood to the side, watching all the preparations. Ultimately, he'd be the one who would have to conclude the investigation. There was tremendous pressure from the media and the administration to ferret out all the moles at CIA and explain how things could have gone so wrong. Congress had insisted that the FBI handle the investigation into the CIA, since no one in Langley was now free of suspicion.

The FBI reported to the White House that Greer's story had checked out. He had passed two polygraphs. Gibbons had already confirmed the substance of his information about Randall Jenkins and the theory. The CIA had confirmed to the President the day before that Jenkins' theory appeared valid, based on the evidence Greer had collected and the statistical work Jenkins had performed. The case of the Claremont shootings, however, looked as if it would probably never be solved. The FBI Director sensed that if his crack FBI investigators hadn't found any clues over the course of the past few days, he'd never be able to locate the triggerman who had caused so many deaths. The trail was getting colder by the minute.

"Where the hell's the President?" asked Conrad.

It had been the question on everyone's mind. Conrad caught the eye of the President's wife and she went up to the First Family's quarters to check on her husband.

A few minutes later the President arrived with his wife, who guided him to his chair behind the desk. He avoided looking into anyone's eyes. The makeup artist quickly powdered him, taking away the clammy look. He shuffled the script in front of him and spoke softly to Conrad about a few of the changes that had been made.

Conrad gave the President a gentle pat on the back and assumed his usual position right next to the camera.

"Okay, everybody," he said. "Let's get focused. This is going to be one hell of an address. We're about to witness history being made tonight."

The President looked up at Conrad and nodded. "Thanks, Dwight," he said.

"Show time!" said Conrad.

The President took a deep breath as the communications assistant gave the President the final countdown. . . .

"Good evening." His voice was strong. "Tonight I address you from the Oval Office. During the days that have passed since the tragedy at the economic summit in San Francisco, the FBI—in full cooperation with the Central Intelligence Agency and other departments of the federal government—has been investigating the events and allegations made public. Tonight, I want to reassure you that everything possible has been—and will be—done to maintain our national security. I also want to share with you the facts—as we know them today—concerning the actions of certain individuals who were employed by the U.S. government and the actions of certain foreign nationals and their sponsoring governments.

"A thorough analysis of the situation by the U.S. intelligence agencies indicates with an extremely high degree of certainty that the government of the Federal Republic of Germany was operating an intelligence operation inside the United States against our nation. I have been also informed by the CIA that there is a high probability that the German government was ultimately responsible for the death of Randall Jenkins. Although for reasons of national security I cannot reveal certain specifics, I can say that the German government has conceded the substance of the facts relating to this matter. Earlier this evening I personally telephoned German Chancellor Gelling and explained the position of the United States, which I will explain to you in a moment, as well.

"Our intelligence also indicates the involvement of the government of Japan. There is evidence that strongly suggests an individual or individuals at the direction of the Japanese government is responsible for the massacre in San Francisco of innocent United States citizens. After speaking with Chancellor Gelling, I also spoke with Japanese Prime Minister Hayakawa to explain the position of the United States.

"The objectives and motivations of the Japanese and German governments were *clearly* hostile. Evidence suggests that these governments negotiated a secret treaty between themselves, the purpose of which was heinous and repugnant to those nations who cherish liberty and despise totalitarianism. The late Randall Jenkins had characterized this new relationship as a new alliance between Japan and Germany formed for the purpose of dominating the world by using the sophisticated and subtle weapons of the latter half of this century—economics. Their aim was to control and manipulate the economic well-being of free nations by working in concert.

"And so, effective immediately, we are taking the following steps. First, we are abrogating all agreements signed last week concerning trade with the German and Japanese governments. Second, we are revoking Most Favored Nation trade status for those governments. Third, we have identified certain foreign nationals from Japan and Germany who we suspect have been operating under diplomatic cover in the United States as intelligence officers in their embassies and consulates; these individuals have been declared persona non grata and have until noon tomorrow to leave the United States.

"We will, of course, continue with a thorough review of our intelligence operations to ensure that they have not and are not being compromised. Tomorrow, I will be announcing the appointment of a special investigator from outside the intelligence community who will conduct the review of intelligence operations. I am confident that we will be able to effectively address any flaws in our current security arrangements and develop new systems that will safeguard our country from this or any other threat to our national security in the future.

"Before I close, I must mention the courageous actions of two individuals who risked everything—including their careers and their lives—in pursuit of the truth and preservation of the Republic. I am happy to report that Kate Mallotte, the CIA officer who was shot in San Francisco, is making a good recovery.

"The other individual has demonstrated uncommon dedication and perseverance under the most trying circumstances. Greer Whitaker is someone you have undoubtedly heard about in connection with the Randall Jenkins case—the assistant to Randall Jenkins, who mysteriously disappeared after Jenkins' death in Germany. Since last week, certain facts have come to light that prove that not only was Greer *not* responsible for Jenkins' death, but against extraordinary odds was able to bring word of Randall Jenkins' work to light. And for this, every American owes him an enormous debt of gratitude. His contribution to the future welfare of our country is immeasurable. Tonight, I ask you to join me in saluting Greer Whitaker, a true national hero.

"Finally, I ask you to pray for our nation. Pray for the families and friends of those who were killed or injured in the San Francisco massacre.

"God bless you, and God bless America. Good night. . . ."

The White House had timed the President's address for maximum effect.

Wall Street heard the crash of Tokyo's stock market before the Presidential Seal had faded from the television screen. The Nikkei trading floor opened just as the President was signing off. Within fifteen minutes of the opening bell, the Nikkei was down over forty percent, wiping out billions of dollars of Japan's national wealth. Before the Japanese government could intervene and close the stock market, the Nikkei fell another twenty percent. By noon, the Japanese prime minister had resigned. The news also reported a suicide—a young executive home from America, dead from a self-inflicted handgun wound. Kiro Takiyama and the organization mourned the death of his son.

The German stock exchange in Frankfurt never opened, having several extra hours to contemplate the Japanese experience. The entire German financial system was beginning to collapse. The Americans could have intervened, but instead they stood by and watched the German economy slip into the abyss. Chancellor Gelling and his cabinet ministers submitted their resignations to the German president so that a new government could be formed.

The Fascists marched in the streets, shouting obscenities and looking for scapegoats.

69 ❑ ❑ ❑ ❑

At four in the afternoon—five hours after the normal checkout time —Pablo, the seventy-two-year-old security guard, broke through the flimsy door on the fifth floor in the seedy hotel near Sixth and Mission Avenues on the edge of the Tenderloin district. The maid had told him that the key turned in the lock and the bolt moved, but the door wouldn't budge.

The hotel rented rooms by the hour, and Pablo had seen a lot of unusual stuff before in the fifteen years he had worked there, but nothing like the sight he saw inside Room 512. The door had been jammed shut with a straight-back wooden chair. Pablo waved the maid away.

"Don't look," he said. "Call the police."

Pablo looked at the scene as if he were on a movie set. It couldn't be real, he said to himself.

On his left was a single bed. There were two men—naked—locked in an obscene position—both quite dead, he was sure. On the bedside table was a syringe, a sooted spoon, and a cigarette lighter.

Pablo moved closer to the bed. The man on top was still sitting up, leaning forward a little over the torso of the man on the bottom. Around the top man's neck was a dog choker chain threaded through itself by the ring on either end, attached to a leash which was tied to the foot of the bed. The chain and leash were what kept the body from falling forward. Pablo took a close look at the man's neck. The individual links of chain had got caught on each other, preventing the chain from sliding freely. The man on top had died of asphyxiation, apparently an accident.

The face of the man on the bottom was buried in the pillow. He was dead, too. Pablo saw the tracks in his left arm. Too much excitement for one night, Pablo told himself. Probable heart attack.

Pablo's daughter, a nurse at San Francisco General Hospital, had told him stories that he hadn't wanted to hear. He had begged her to find another job, to get away from the tainted blood and open sores on the bodies of the patients she cared for. But she had been trained as a nurse and she had compassion for the unknowing, the abandoned, and the unloved. What she had no tolerance for were the excesses— the sickos who pushed themselves and those around them with drugs and unimaginable perversions. Pablo took a look at the man on top with the choker around his neck. His daughter had seen that kind, too. Getting their kicks out of being asphyxiated just up to the point of dying, just to push the physical sensation as far as it could go. This one had pushed for the last time.

On the right side of the room was a small television on the dresser. The television had been left on, but the screen was white and the speaker was hissing loudly. There was a cord running from the TV to a small camcorder lying on its side. There was also an empty cassette-sized box. Pablo peered down at the camcorder through the little window that showed that there was a tape in it.

Pablo saw that the tape had played out. He took his handkerchief out and pressed the REWIND button. As the tape rewound, Pablo heard the sirens down the street. They would be there in three minutes, and up the stairs in another two. There wasn't enough time to rewind the whole tape and he was curious as to what the two men could have been watching. He pushed the STOP button, then PLAY.

The film was black and white, even though the television was color. The picture looked like the tapes he had seen on TV of the hidden cameras used in police sting operations. There was something in the upper-right-hand corner that looked like a date, but maybe in a foreign language. He could make out the year—1973.

At first Pablo couldn't tell what was going on in the picture. The film was dark. There was movement, but the grainy black and white failed to pick up the subtleties of the shadows.

"Robert," a man's voice suddenly said.

It startled Pablo until he realized that it had come from the tape.

There were awful animal-like noises in the background. The picture in the video became suddenly clearer, or maybe Pablo had just figured out what was going on. There were two men, locked in the same position as the two men on the bed in the room in which he was standing. Pablo couldn't take his eyes off the screen, even though he wanted desperately to. He studied the picture more closely. The man on top in the video was the same dead man who was on top only six feet away. Now that he knew what he was looking at, the face of the man on the bottom on the tape came into clear focus. He was in pain, but saying nothing.

"Robert," he heard the voice say again, this time more urgently. The voice seemed to have an accent of some sort.

"Ro-bert." The voice was insistent.

Pablo saw the lips of the man on top move.

"Robert!"

There was definitely an accent.

"Robert—Robert—Robert!"

It was a German accent, Pablo concluded.

70 ❑ ❑ ❑ ❑

Kate stood at Greer's side in the East Ballroom of the White House with her arm in a sling. Two weeks had passed since Greer had flown out to California to be with her. He had spent almost every moment in her hospital room until she had recovered sufficiently to make the trip back to Washington, D.C. Kate and Greer stood at the front of the room on display for the media, blinking in the bright flashes of the cameras.

Dwight Conrad opened the medal box for the President. The President placed the Presidential Freedom Medal around Greer's neck. The group of Administration department heads and well-wishers broke into thunderous applause. The President shook Greer's hand vigorously for almost half a minute. Kate looked up at Greer admiringly. He reached down and squeezed her hand.

The President turned to address the gathering.

"It is my great privilege to be able to recognize the heroic accomplishments of Greer Whitaker today. The story of his heroic struggle to bring the truth to me and the American people is one that will be read by generations in history books. We all owe a huge debt of gratitude to Greer.

"As you all know by now, Greer is something of a superpatriot. When he answered a call placed to him by the Central Intelligence Agency to interview for a position as a field officer, Greer responded with a genuine desire to join the intelligence agency as a way to serve his country. Unfortunately, at the time, for reasons still not quite clear, his qualifications were not given the appropriate level of review and he therefore was not asked to join the CIA. Also, a mole in the CIA perverted Greer's dedication to his country and deceived him into unwittingly assisting a foreign intelligence service.

The President turned to Gibbons. "Ben, would you like to say a few words?"

The Director adjusted the microphone on the lectern. He avoided looking at Kate.

He was subdued. "Mr. President, I am happy to announce that

Greer Whitaker has accepted a job with the Central Intelligence Agency. Greer will head a special investigative office within the Directorate of Counterintelligence. Beyond that, the specific conditions of his employment and his assignments are classified."

Gibbons turned and extended his hand to Greer. "Greer, it's my pleasure to welcome you to the Central Intelligence Agency."

The room erupted again as they shook hands.

"Thank you, Ben," said the President. "Some of you may be wondering about Kate Mallotte. Ben has just informed me that she will be retiring early from the Agency, but will continue to work as a consultant." The President looked at Greer and Kate. "I hope you don't mind my announcing this," he said, "but it's also my understanding that the two of you will be getting married next week. I wish you all the best in the world."

Again, the room broke out in applause. The cameras captured Greer giving Kate a quick kiss. The cover for a dozen weekly news magazines and a half dozen tabloids had just been made.

On the other side of town, Covey and Knowles kept a small black and white television on as they worked through lunch at their cramped conference table. No medal ceremonies, no public recognition, no performance bonus. Not even a congratulatory phone call from their peers. Just another day at the office, cross-checking files and reading internal memos. There was even more work to do now.

"I've already got eight large withdrawals," said Covey. He was looking at a computer monitor which displayed the past two weeks' bank account activities for all of the Agency's employees. The CIA people had no idea the Agency had reached this far, this fast into their lives. It was all part of the new security program that Kate Mallotte had instituted during her tenure as head of the secret counterintelligence group. "Three in Western Europe section and five out of the Far East. These people are scared. We'd better pull their passports this afternoon. How's yours coming?"

"Seven in the Administration. Damn. This is too easy."

Covey turned the television off. First the bank accounts, then the phone taps. There was so much to do, so few who could be trusted to do it.

"Think she'll ever be back?" asked Knowles.

Covey's dark, bulging lenses reflected the CIA field officer names and bank account numbers. He looked up at the dried flower arrangement on the empty desk. A nice woman's touch, he thought. Framed photos of laughing dead Russians, Mexican beads, a piece of tattered sail, a compote of redwood pine straw, a paper napkin from a restaurant, scraps of people and places, souvenirs—remembrances—important pieces of someone's life, waiting to be picked up and fondled again.

"She never left," he answered.

Close to midnight, Dwight Conrad stared into the bottom of a cognac snifter in the lounge of the Hay-Adams Hotel across the street from the White House. On the other side of the lounge, a piano player was improvising something jazzy for an empty room.

"I should just go ahead and declare bankruptcy now," said Conrad. "The legal bills will wipe me out," he said.

Ben Gibbons sat across from him. "You really think we'll be indicted?" he asked. His own cognac sat untouched in front of him.

"*Hell* yes. What's the difference, anyway? We'll get hauled in front of a grand jury by the Special Prosecutor the President's going to appoint next week. It doesn't matter if you're innocent or guilty. You still have to pay a lawyer to handle the thing. A decent one will run you four hundred bucks an hour in this town. Then there's the congressional hearings. Again, you gotta have a lawyer. I figure the tab could easily run a couple of hundred thousand."

"But the President *needs* you," said Gibbons. "After all, you're the one who got him out of this mess. The President would have never thought of giving Whitaker the medal and a job."

Conrad just shrugged.

"What about me?" asked Gibbons.

"You're as dead as I am. You don't think the President's going to allow you to get off scot free, do you?" He looked Gibbons directly in the eye. "The mole recruited Whitaker on your watch. You'll have to take the fall for this. I've already had the leadership from both sides of the aisle in Congress asking me for your head on a platter. It's just a matter of time. We're liabilities. *I'm* out. *You're* out. It just depends on how long you can take the heat. Do yourself a favor. Turn your resignation in now and avoid a lot of grief. I'm turning mine in first thing tomorrow."

Gibbons shook his head. "I can't believe this."

"Believe it. It's happening."

"Look," said Gibbons, leaning across the table, "what if we cooper-ated with each other? We take a couple of days and get our story straight. It's not too late to go through our notes and take out anything that might be . . . *problematic*."

"I didn't take any notes on any of this and I hope to God you didn't either."

"It's worth a try, isn't it? They can't pin anything on us."

"Get a lawyer, Ben."

71 ❏   ❏   ❏   ❏

Kate stayed in the rental car while Greer walked across the grassy lawn at Inspiration Point in the National Military Cemetery at the Presidio. On the way to their honeymoon in Hawaii, Greer insisted that they spend a day in San Francisco.

The groundskeeper had given him a photocopied map of the plots. Greer wandered among the markers, looking at the inscriptions.

Greer saw a freshly covered grave and headed toward it.

He was in no hurry. He needed a few minutes to himself. He couldn't shake the news he had been given yesterday before leaving Washington. A group of amateur explorers had come across an oddity in an abandoned salt mine in the Watzmann mountain in Berchtes-gaden. They thought at first they had come across the carcass of some animal that had been dragged in from the forest and mauled. The Germans informed the CIA of the finding. It was the desiccated re-mains of Stephanie Becker. Greer opted not to read the full report or look at the pictures. Stephanie had been buried quietly earlier in the day in Heidelberg.

Greer stood over the flat bronze marker. RANDALL JENKINS. The only sounds were the wind snapping the American flag overhead and the clanging of the rope and hardware against the metal pole.

He hadn't brought any flowers. Randall wouldn't have liked that. Not his style.

Greer got his Presidential Freedom medal from the pocket in his windbreaker and placed it over the marker. He unfurled a small American flag and pushed it into the soft dirt over the grave.

Greer stood back and gave a snappy salute.

"Rest in peace, Randall Jenkins."

THE END